The Complete Classical Wisdom Collection (Vol. 3)

Discourses & Enchiridion with Nicomachean Ethics
— Practical Philosophy for Virtuous Living

A Modern Translation

Adapted for the Contemporary Reader

Epictetus | Aristotle

Translated by Tim Zengerink

Table of Contents

Preface - Message to the Reader

What If You Could Help Rebuild the Greatest Library in Human History?

Thousands of years ago, the Library of Alexandria stood as the crown jewel of human achievement — a sanctuary where the collected wisdom of every known civilization was gathered, preserved, and shared freely.

And then, it was lost.

Through fire, conquest, and the slow erosion of time, humanity lost not just books — but ideas, dreams, discoveries, and stories that could have changed the world forever.

Today, the Library of Alexandria lives again — and you are invited to be a part of its restoration.

Our mission is simple yet profound:

To rebuild the greatest library the world has ever known, and to translate all timeless works into every language and dialect, so that no seeker of knowledge is ever left behind again.

By joining our movement to rebuild the modern Library of Alexandria, you become part of an unprecedented mission:

- **Unlimited Access to the Greatest Audiobooks & eBooks Ever Written:**

  Instantly explore thousands of legendary works—Plato, Shakespeare, Jane Austen, Leo Tolstoy, and countless more. All instantly available to read or listen, placing a complete literary universe at your fingertips.

- **Beautiful Paperback & Deluxe Editions at Printing Cost**

  Own any title as an elegant paperback, deluxe hardcover, or stunning collectible boxset—offered to you at true printing cost, delivered straight to your door. Build your personal Library of Alexandria, crafted for beauty, built for durability, and worthy of proud display.

- **Fresh Translations for Modern Readers—in Every Language & Dialect**

  Enjoy timeless masterpieces reimagined in clear, contemporary language—no more outdated phrases or obscure references. Alongside the original versions, we're tirelessly translating these classics into every language and dialect imaginable, ensuring accessibility and understanding across cultures and generations.

- **Join a Global Renaissance of Literature & Knowledge**

  You directly support expanding our library, publishing deluxe editions at true cost, translating works into all global languages, and bringing humanity's greatest stories to people everywhere. By joining today, you're not just preserving a legacy of masterpieces; you set in motion a powerful wave of literary accessibility.

Become a Torchbearer of Knowledge.

Join us for free now at **LibraryofAlexandria.com**

Together, we will ensure that the light of human wisdom never fades again.

With gratitude and a shared love of knowledge,
The Modern Library of Alexandria Team

Visit:

www.libraryofalexandria.com

Or scan the code below:

Introduction

The Art of Ethical Living:
Wisdom from the Stoa and the Lyceum

What does it mean to live well—not merely to survive or to succeed, but to live a life of integrity, meaning, and inner peace? That question has guided the minds of philosophers for millennia, and in this volume of The Complete Classical Wisdom Collection, we bring together two of antiquity's most enduring answers: the Stoic teachings of Epictetus and the ethical framework of Aristotle.

This volume includes the Discourses and Enchiridion (or "Handbook") of Epictetus, alongside selections from Aristotle's Nicomachean Ethics and the brief but insightful work On Sense and the Sensible. Together, these texts form a guide not only to personal virtue but to practical living—a synthesis of clear thinking, moral courage, and an abiding commitment to the examined life.

Though Epictetus and Aristotle differ in background, tone, and metaphysics, they share a conviction that happiness (eudaimonia) is not the product of luck or external conditions but the result of cultivating virtue and wisdom. They argue that true freedom is inner freedom: the ability to master oneself, to act according to reason, and to align with the nature of things. In an age of distraction, instability, and noise, their message is as necessary as ever.

This introduction will guide the reader through the central teachings of both philosophers, explore the connections and contrasts between their visions of the good life, and highlight how their insights can illuminate our daily experience. More than historical documents, these works are living invitations—to think more clearly, act more justly, and become the kind of person whose life reflects order, purpose, and peace.

Epictetus:
Stoic Freedom and the Power of Inner Discipline

Born into slavery in the Roman Empire around 50 CE, Epictetus eventually gained his freedom and became one of the most influential Stoic teachers of his time. He did not write books himself—his teachings were recorded by his student Arrian, who compiled them into the Discourses and the concise Enchiridion. What emerges from these texts is a philosophy of resilience, clarity, and inner sovereignty.

The core principle of Epictetus's Stoicism is a simple but radical idea: we must distinguish between what is in our power and what is not. Our thoughts, judgments, desires, and actions are within our control. External events—fate, fortune, other people's opinions, health, wealth—are not. To base our happiness on the latter is to live in bondage. To focus on the former is to become free.

Epictetus does not deny that life is difficult. Instead, he argues that adversity is an opportunity for growth. Illness, poverty, exile, and even death can be met with calm and courage if we train ourselves to respond with reason rather than emotion. "It's not what happens to you, but how you react to it that matters."

The Discourses are wide-ranging in scope, offering practical advice on topics such as friendship, discipline, grief, criticism, and self-respect. The tone is direct and sometimes stern, but always infused with a deep respect for the dignity of the human soul. Epictetus believes that philosophy is not a theoretical pursuit—it is a daily practice, a way of life, a kind of spiritual training.

The Enchiridion distills the essential teachings into a portable manual of self-mastery. It is designed to be memorized, internalized, and used. It reminds the reader to accept events as they come, to cultivate gratitude, and to live in harmony with the rational order of nature. Above all, it calls for integrity—to act in alignment with one's values, regardless of circumstance.

Epictetus is a philosopher of personal power, not in the modern sense of ambition, but in the classical sense of moral autonomy. He teaches that no one can take from us the most important thing: the ability to choose how we think and act. In an uncertain world, this is the truest form of stability.

Aristotle:
Reason, Virtue, and the Fulfillment of Human Potential

Several centuries earlier, in the golden age of Greek philosophy, Aristotle laid the foundations for a comprehensive philosophy of life. A student of Plato and tutor to Alexander the Great, Aristotle combined rigorous analysis with practical insight. His Nicomachean Ethics is a profound exploration of what it means to live a good life— a life that is not merely pleasant or successful, but fully human.

Aristotle begins with the idea that all human beings seek happiness, or eudaimonia, but that true happiness is not a fleeting feeling—it is the flourishing of our nature through the consistent practice of virtue. Virtue, for Aristotle, is a state of character formed by habits and guided by reason. It is not innate, but developed through deliberate action.

The ethical life is one of balance. Each virtue is a mean between extremes: courage lies between cowardice and rashness; generosity lies between stinginess and wastefulness. Virtue is not about rigid rules, but about discernment—knowing what is appropriate in each situation. This requires not only theoretical understanding, but practical wisdom (phronesis), which is cultivated over time.

Unlike the Stoics, who often advocate emotional detachment, Aristotle sees emotion as part of a healthy moral life—provided it is rightly ordered. Anger, desire, and fear are not to be eliminated but disciplined. The virtuous person feels the right thing, at the right time, for the right reason.

Aristotle also emphasizes the social nature of the good life. Friendship, community, education, and civic engagement are essential to human flourishing. The highest form of life, however, is contemplative: the life of the mind seeking truth, and the soul aligned with reason.

In On Sense and the Sensible, Aristotle turns to a different but related domain: the workings of perception. Here, he analyzes how the senses operate, how they relate to the mind, and how perception connects us to the world. Though more technical, this short treatise complements the Ethics by grounding human awareness in physical and psychological processes.

Together, these texts present a unified vision: that the human being is a rational animal meant to live in accordance with virtue, reason, and natural order. Happiness is not a matter of chance or indulgence—it is the result of a life well-lived.

Philosophy as Practice: Integrating the Stoic and the Aristotelian

While Epictetus and Aristotle differ in many respects—tone, method, and metaphysics—they both offer a vision of philosophy as a practical art. For them, the goal is not knowledge for its own sake, but transformation: to become wise, courageous, just, and free.

- Epictetus teaches us to let go of what we cannot control and focus on governing our minds and actions.
- Aristotle teaches us to develop virtues through habit, to think clearly, and to live in harmony with our nature.

Both call for introspection, discipline, and a deep sense of responsibility. They agree that happiness does not depend on luck or pleasure, but on character. They show us that freedom is not the absence of rules, but the presence of inner order.

In a time when many are searching for meaning, stability, and moral clarity, these classical voices remain vital. They remind us that philosophy is not a luxury—it is a necessity. It is not something we learn once, but something we practice daily.

Welcome to The Complete Classical Wisdom Collection (Vol. 3). May its teachings serve not only to inform your thinking but to shape your life. May they guide you toward the peace that comes from principle, the strength that comes from discipline, and the joy that comes from a life lived with purpose.

Discourses, Enchiridion
& Selected Writings

Epictetus

Book 1

Chapter 1
On the Things That are in Our Power and Not in Our Power

Out of all the abilities we have, none of them can truly look at itself. Because of that, they also can't approve or disapprove of themselves. For example, how much can grammar think about itself? It can only judge what is written and spoken. And how about music? It can judge melodies. But can either grammar or music think about themselves? Not at all. When you need to write something to a friend, grammar can tell you which words to use, but it won't tell you whether you should write or not. The same goes for music: it can guide you on musical sounds, but it won't tell you if now is the right time to sing or play the flute, or if you should do neither. So, which ability will tell you these things? The one that can think about both itself and everything else. And what is this ability? It's our ability to reason. This is the only ability we have that can examine itself, figure out what it is, what power it has, and how valuable it is. It also looks at all our other abilities. For what else tells us that gold is beautiful? The gold doesn't say it itself. It's the ability that judges appearances. What else judges music, grammar, and other abilities, shows their uses, and points out when to use them? Nothing else does.

So, as it should be, the best and highest ability we have is the only thing the gods put in our control—using appearances correctly. But all other things are not under our control. Why is that? I think that if the gods could have, they would have put these other things in our control too, but they couldn't. Since we live on earth and are tied to our bodies and companions, how could we not be limited by these external things?

But what does Zeus say? "Epictetus, if it were possible, I would have made your small body and your little property free and not subject to any obstacles. But now, understand this: your body isn't yours, it's like finely molded clay. And since I couldn't give you what I wanted, I gave you a small part of us—the ability to pursue or avoid things, to desire or dislike things, and to use the appearances of things. If you take care of this ability and see it as your only possession, you'll never be stopped, never face obstacles, you won't complain, blame, or flatter anyone."

"Do these seem like small things to you?" I hope not. "Be satisfied with them, then, and pray to the gods." But now, when we can focus on one thing and attach ourselves to it, we prefer to focus on many things—our body, property, brother, friend, child, and even our slave. Since we're tied to so many things, they weigh us down and pull us down. This is why, when the weather isn't right for sailing, we worry and keep checking which way the wind is blowing. "It's blowing from the north." What does that matter to us? "When will the west wind blow?" It will blow when it wants to or when Aeolus, the god of the winds, decides. We don't control the winds, Aeolus does. What should we do then? Make the best use of what's in our control and accept the rest as they are. What is their nature? Whatever God wishes.

"Must I be the only one to lose my head?" Would you want everyone to lose their heads just to comfort you? Will you not stretch out your neck like Lateranus did when Nero ordered his beheading? After he stretched out his neck and received a weak blow that made him pull back for a moment, he stretched it out again. And earlier, when Nero's freedman Epaphroditus visited him and asked why he offended the emperor, he said, "If I want to explain, I'll tell your master."

What should a man be ready to say in such circumstances? Nothing but, "What's mine and what's not mine? What's allowed to me and what's not?" I must die. Must I die in sorrow? I must be put in chains. Must I also feel sad? I must go into exile. Does anyone stop me from going with a smile, cheerfulness, and peace? "Tell me the secret you hold." I won't, because that's my choice. "But I'll put you in chains." My leg, you mean. "I'll throw you into prison." You mean my body.

"I'll cut off your head." Did I ever tell you my head couldn't be cut off? These are the things philosophers should think about, write about daily, and practice.

Thrasea used to say, "I'd rather be killed today than exiled tomorrow." What did Rufus reply? "If you think death is worse, how foolish is your choice? But if you think it's easier, who gave you the choice? Will you not learn to be content with what is given to you?"

What did Agrippinus say? He said, "I am not an obstacle to myself." When he heard his trial was happening in the Senate, he said, "I hope it turns out well. But it's the fifth hour,"—this was his exercise time before his cold bath—"let's go exercise." Afterward, someone told him, "You've been condemned." He asked, "To exile or death?" "To exile," the man replied. "What about my property?" "It's not taken from you." "Then let's go to Aricia and have dinner," Agrippinus said.

This is what it means to study what one ought to study: to make desire and aversion free from obstacles and from everything a person would avoid. I must die. If now, I'm ready. If later, then I'll eat dinner because it's time, and after that, I'll die. How? Like someone giving up something that belongs to someone else.

Chapter 2
How a Man on Every Occasion Can Maintain His Proper Character

Being rational is tolerable for us; what's irrational is not. Blows aren't naturally unbearable. How so? See how Spartans endure whipping when they've learned it's reasonable. Hanging yourself isn't unbearable. When you believe it's rational, you go and hang yourself. In short, we'll find that nothing pains humans as much as what's irrational, and nothing attracts them as much as what's rational.

But what's rational or irrational appears differently to different people, just like what's good or bad, profitable or not. That's why we need discipline, to learn how to adapt our ideas of rationality and irrationality to different situations in line with nature. To judge what's rational and irrational, we not only consider external things but also what suits each person. For one person, it's rational to hold a chamber pot for another, thinking that if he doesn't, he'll be punished and won't get food. But if he does, he won't suffer anything bad. But for another person, it's intolerable to hold a chamber pot, even more so to let someone else do it for him. So if you ask me whether you should hold the chamber pot or not, I'd say that getting food is better than not, and being whipped is worse than not being whipped. So if you judge by these things, go and hold the chamber pot. But you might say, "That's not worthy of me." Then it's you who must bring that into the decision, not me. You know yourself, how much you're worth to yourself, and at what price you sell yourself because people sell themselves at different prices.

That's why when Florus wondered if he should perform in Nero's spectacles, Agrippinus told him to go ahead. When Florus asked why Agrippinus wasn't going, Agrippinus replied, "Because I don't even consider such things." Those who begin to deliberate about such matters and weigh the value of external things are close to forgetting their own character. Why do you ask me if life is better than death? I say life. Pain or pleasure? I say pleasure. But if not acting in a tragedy will get me beheaded, then act in it. But I won't. Why? Because you see yourself as just one thread in the tunic, so you need to fit in with the others, just as a thread doesn't aim to stand out. But I want to be the purple thread, the small part that's bright and makes the rest look graceful and beautiful. Why do you tell me to be like everyone else? If I do, how can I still be purple?

Priscus Helvidius understood this and acted accordingly. When Vespasian commanded him not to go into the Senate, he replied, "You can stop me from being a senator, but as long as I am, I must go in." "Well, go in, but say nothing," said the emperor. "Don't ask my opinion, and I'll be silent," Priscus replied. "But I have to ask your opinion," said Vespasian. "And I must say what I think is right," said

Priscus. "But if you do, I'll put you to death." "When did I ever tell you I was immortal? You'll do your part, and I'll do mine. It's your part to kill, and mine to die, but not in fear. Your part is to banish me, and mine is to leave without sorrow."

What good did Priscus do, being just one person? What good does the purple thread do in the toga? It stands out as purple and serves as a fine example to everything else. But in such cases, another person would have thanked Caesar for sparing him. But such a man Vespasian wouldn't have even stopped from entering the Senate because he knew he'd either sit there quietly like an empty vessel or say what Caesar wanted, and perhaps even more.

There was also an athlete who faced death unless he allowed a part of his body to be cut off. His philosopher brother came to him and asked, "What are you going to do, brother? Shall we have it cut off and then return to the gym?" But the athlete chose to keep his dignity and died. When someone asked Epictetus how he did it, whether as an athlete or philosopher, Epictetus replied, "He acted as a man, a man who had been proclaimed a champion in the Olympic Games and had trained hard for it, not just someone practicing in a small gym." Another person might let his head be cut off if it meant he could keep living. But some people have such a strong sense of character that they incorporate it into everything they do and every decision they make.

"Come on, Epictetus, shave your head." If I'm a philosopher, I would say, "I won't shave my head." "But I'll cut your head off if you don't." If it helps you, go ahead.

Someone once asked, "How can each of us know what suits our character?" Epictetus replied, "How does a bull know when a lion attacks? It knows its own strength and steps forward to defend the herd. It's clear that with power comes the understanding of it, and those who have power won't be unaware of it. A bull isn't made in a day, and neither is a brave person. We must train ourselves in the winter to be ready for the summer campaign, and not rush into things that don't concern us.

Think carefully about the price at which you sell your will. If nothing else, at least don't sell it for too little. But what is great and superior might belong to Socrates and those like him. "Why then, if we are naturally like that, aren't more of us like him?" Is it true that all horses become fast or all dogs become skilled at tracking? "Then, since I'm naturally slow, should I not try at all?" Of course not. I'm not better than Socrates, but if I'm not worse, that's enough for me. I'll never be as strong as Milo, but I still take care of my body. I'll never be as rich as Croesus, but I don't neglect my property. In short, we don't ignore taking care of anything just because we might not reach the highest level.

This is the approach we must take in life, understanding our limitations, but always striving to be the best we can within them. Even if we can't reach the level of greatness that others have, we should still aim to be the best version of ourselves.

Chapter 3
How a Man Should Act Based on the Belief that God is the Father of Everyone

If someone truly believes that we are all children of God, and that God is the father of both humans and gods, then he would never think poorly of himself. Imagine if Caesar adopted you; you would likely become very proud. So, if you know that you are the child of Zeus, wouldn't you feel proud too? However, we don't always think this way. Since humans are made of both a body, like animals, and reason and intelligence, like the gods, many people focus more on their body, which is mortal, rather than on their mind, which is divine and eternal.

Those who think that they are meant for honesty, humility, and proper use of their mind will not think lowly of themselves. But many people do the opposite. They might say, "What am I? A poor, miserable person with a weak body." It's true that your body is weak, but you have something much better than that—your mind. So why do you focus on your weak body and neglect your mind, which is stronger?

Because some of us focus more on our bodies, we start to act like animals—some become like wolves, untrustworthy and harmful; some become like lions, wild and untamed; and most of us become like foxes, or even worse animals. What else is a person who spreads lies or acts with malice but a fox, or something even worse? So, be careful not to become one of these unfortunate creatures.

Chapter 4
On Progress or Improvement

When someone is making progress, they learn from philosophers that "desire" means wanting good things, and "aversion" means staying away from bad things. They also learn that happiness and calmness can only be reached if they get what they desire and avoid what they don't want. So, such a person removes desire from themselves completely and puts it off for later. But they only avoid things that are within their control. If they try to avoid something that's outside of their control, they know that sometimes they'll end up facing what they wanted to avoid, and this will make them unhappy. Now, if virtue brings good fortune, calmness, and happiness, then moving towards virtue is the same as moving towards these things. It's always true that wherever perfecting something takes us, progress is getting closer to that point.

So why do we admit that virtue is what I've described but still seek progress in other things and show off about it? What does virtue produce? It produces calmness. So, who is really improving? Is it the person who has read many books by Chrysippus? But does virtue mean understanding Chrysippus? If it does, then progress is nothing more than knowing a lot about Chrysippus. But now we say that virtue produces one thing, and getting closer to it is something else—namely, progress or improvement. Someone might say, "This person can already read Chrysippus by themselves." Indeed, you are making great progress. But what kind of progress? Why do you make fun of the person? Why do you distract them from realizing their own misfortunes? Won't you show them what virtue does so they can see where to look for improvement? Look for it there, wretched person, where your work lies. And where is your work? It's in desire and aversion—so you won't be disappointed in your desires, and you won't fall into what you want to avoid. It's in your pursuit and avoidance— so you don't make mistakes. It's in agreeing or not agreeing with things—so you won't be deceived. The first and most important things are those I've mentioned. But if you're trembling and crying to avoid what you fear, tell me how you're improving.

Do you then show me your improvement in these things? If I were talking to an athlete, I'd say, "Show me your shoulders"; and they might say, "Here are my weights." You and your weights deal with that. I'd reply, "I want to see the result of using those weights." So, when you say: "Take this book on active powers and see how I've studied it." I reply, "Slave, I'm not asking about that, but how you practice pursuit and avoidance, desire and aversion, how you plan and prepare yourself—whether it's in line with nature or not. If it is in line, give me proof, and I'll say you're making progress. But if it's not, go away, and not only explain your books but write such books yourself. And what will you gain by it? Don't you know that the whole book costs only five denarii? Is the person explaining it worth more than five denarii? Never look for the actual thing in one place and progress toward it in another."

So, where is progress? If any of you, turning away from external things, focuses on their own will to work on it and improve it through effort, so it becomes in line with nature—strong, free, unrestricted, unhindered, trustworthy, modest; and if they've learned that anyone who desires or avoids things they can't control can neither be trustworthy nor free, but must change with those things and be tossed around by them like a ship in a storm, and must submit to others who have the power to give or prevent what they desire or want to avoid—

finally, when they get up in the morning, if they observe and follow these rules, bathe like a trustworthy person, eat like a modest person; in the same way, if in every situation that arises, they work out their main principles like a runner does with running, and a singer does with their voice—this is the person who is truly making progress, and this is the person who hasn't traveled in vain. But if they've put all their effort into reading books and work only on that, and have traveled for that, I tell them to go back home immediately and not to neglect their responsibilities there; because the reason they've traveled is meaningless. But the other thing is something—to study how a person can remove complaining and groaning from their life, and saying, "Woe is me," and "Poor me," and to remove bad luck and disappointment, and to learn what death is, and exile, and prison, and poison, so they can say when they're in chains, "Dear Crito, if it is the will of the gods, let it be so," and not say, "Poor me, an old man; have I lived to see this?" Who says this? Do you think I'll name some unknown person of low status? Doesn't Priam say this? Doesn't Oedipus say this? No, all kings say it! What else is a tragedy but the troubles of people who value external things, shown in this kind of drama? But if someone must learn through fiction that no external things, which are beyond our control, affect us, I would like this fiction, through which I could live happily and peacefully. But you must decide for yourselves what you want.

What, then, does Chrysippus teach us? The answer is, "to know that these things are true, from which happiness comes and peace arises. Take my books, and you'll learn how true and natural these things are that make me free from troubles." Oh, great good fortune! Oh, the great benefactor who shows us the way! Everyone has built temples and altars for Triptolemus because he gave us food through farming. But to the person who discovered the truth and brought it to light and shared it with everyone, not just the truth about how to live, but how to live well, who of you has built an altar, or a temple, or dedicated a statue, or who thanks God for this? Because the gods gave us the vine or wheat, we sacrifice to them: but because they produced in the human mind the wisdom to show us the truth about happiness, shall we not thank God for this?

Chapter 5
Against the Academics

Epictetus said that if someone argues against obvious truths, it's not easy to convince them to change their mind. But this isn't because the person is strong or because the teacher is weak; it's because when someone remains stubborn like a rock, even after being proven wrong, how can we reason with them?

There are two types of stubbornness: one affects understanding, and the other affects a person's sense of shame. When a person decides not to agree with what is clearly true or refuses to stop arguing against it, they become stubborn in their understanding. Most of us are afraid of physical pain and would do anything to avoid it, but we don't care as much about hurting our souls. And when it comes to the soul, if someone is in such a state that they can't understand anything or grasp any ideas, we think they're in a bad condition. But if someone's sense of shame and modesty is gone, we sometimes mistakenly call that strength.

Do you understand that you're awake? "I don't," the person replies, "because I don't even understand when I'm dreaming that I'm awake." Is there no difference between these two states? "None at all," he replies. Should I keep arguing with this person? What can I do to make him realize he's become numb to the truth? He does understand, but he pretends that he doesn't. He's worse off than a dead person because he doesn't see the contradiction: he's in a bad condition. Another person might see the contradiction but doesn't care and doesn't try to improve: he's in an even worse condition. His modesty and sense of shame are gone, and while his ability to reason hasn't been completely lost, it has become like an animal's. Should I call this strength of mind?

Certainly not, unless we also consider it strength when people do or say anything that comes into their head without self-control.

Chapter 6
On Providence

Epictetus said that from everything that exists or happens in the world, it is easy to praise Providence if a person has these two qualities: the ability to see how everything fits together and a thankful attitude. If a person doesn't have these two qualities, one person won't see the purpose of the things that exist and happen, and another won't be thankful for them, even if they do understand them. For instance, if God had created colors but hadn't given us the ability to see them, what would their use be? None at all. On the other hand, if He had given us the ability to see but hadn't created objects to be seen, what use would that be? None at all. Now, if He had made both vision and objects, but hadn't created light, what use would they be? Again, none at all. So, who made these things fit together so perfectly? And who made the knife to fit into its case and the case to fit the knife? Was it no one? And indeed, from the very structure of things that have reached their completion, we can tell that the work is certainly the act of some creator, and it hasn't been made without a purpose. So, if each of these things shows evidence of a creator, don't visible things, the ability to see, and light also show evidence of Him? And the existence of male and female, and the desire each has for union, and the ability to use the parts of the body that were made for this—don't these also reveal the work of a creator? If they don't, let's think about how our understanding works: when we encounter physical objects, we simply receive impressions from them, but we also choose certain things from them, ignore others, add, combine, and move from some things to others that are similar. Isn't this enough to make some people realize there's a creator and not forget about Him? If it isn't, let them explain to us what makes each thing, or how it's possible that things so wonderful and purposeful could exist by chance and by their own movement.

Are these things found only in humans? Many things are indeed found only in us, things that the rational animal particularly needed. But you'll find many things we share with irrational animals. Do these animals understand what happens? No, they don't. For using things is one thing, and understanding them is another. God needed irrational animals to use the appearances of things, but He needed us to understand how to use them. So it's enough for them to eat, drink, sleep, reproduce, and do all the other things that they do. But for us, to whom He has also given the ability to understand, these things are not enough. If we don't act in a proper and orderly way, in line with the nature and purpose of each thing, we'll never achieve our true purpose. Where the natures of living beings are different, their actions and purposes are also different. So for those animals whose nature is only to use things, just using them is enough. But for an animal that also has the power to understand how to use things, unless there is the proper exercise of understanding, it will never achieve its true purpose. So God made each animal with a purpose: one to be eaten, another to help with farming, another to provide milk, and another for some similar use. For these purposes, what need is there to understand appearances and be able to distinguish them? But God created humans to be spectators of God and His works, and not just spectators, but also interpreters. For this reason, it is shameful for humans to start and end where irrational animals do. Instead, we should start where they do and end where nature intended us to end: in contemplation and understanding, living in harmony with nature. So be careful not to die without having been spectators of these things.

But you would take a journey to Olympia to see the work of Phidias, and you would think it a misfortune to die without having seen such things. But when you don't need to take a journey, and the works of God are right in front of you wherever you are, won't you want to see and understand them? Won't you realize what you are, what you were born for, and what purpose your ability to see serves? But you might say, "There are some unpleasant and troublesome things in life." Aren't there unpleasant things at Olympia? Don't you get sunburned? Don't you get pushed around by crowds? Don't you have uncomfortable places to bathe? Don't you get wet when it rains? Don't you deal with a lot of noise, clamor, and other unpleasant things? But I suppose that balancing all these things with the magnificence of the spectacle makes you bear and endure them. Well, then, haven't you received abilities that will help you bear everything that happens? Haven't you received greatness of soul? Haven't you received courage? Haven't you received endurance? So why should I worry about anything that might happen if I have greatness of soul? What can disturb me, upset me, or seem painful? Shouldn't I use the abilities I've been given for their intended purpose, instead of complaining about what happens?

"Yes, but my nose runs," you say. So why do you have hands? Isn't it so you can wipe your nose? "But is it reasonable that there should be runny noses in the world?" Isn't it better to wipe your nose than to complain about it? What do you think Hercules would have been if there hadn't been a lion, a hydra, a stag, a boar, or certain unjust and evil people that he had to drive away and defeat? What would he have done if those challenges didn't exist? It's obvious that he would have wrapped himself in a blanket and slept. In that case, he wouldn't have been Hercules, because he would have spent his life in luxury and ease. Even if he had been strong, what good would that have been if he didn't face challenges? What use would his strength, his arms, his endurance, and his noble spirit have been if he hadn't been tested and exercised by those challenges?

"So, should a person create challenges for themselves, like bringing a lion or a boar or a hydra into their country?" That would be foolish and crazy. But since challenges do exist, they are useful for showing what kind of person we are and for exercising our strengths. So when you recognize these things, look at the abilities you have, and when you've looked at them, say: "Bring now, Zeus, any challenge you want, for I have been given the means and powers by You to honor myself through whatever happens." But instead of doing this, you sit around, trembling with fear that something bad will happen, and you weep, lament, and groan about what does happen, and then you blame the gods. What else can come from such weakness but impiety?

And yet, God has not only given us the abilities to handle everything that happens without being crushed or broken by it, but like a good king and a true father, He has given us these abilities freely, without any hindrance, completely under our control, and without reserving any power for Himself to stop or obstruct us. You, who have received these powers freely and as your own, don't use them. You don't even recognize what you've been given or who gave it to you. Some of you are blind to the giver and don't acknowledge your benefactor, while others, out of weakness, blame God. But I will show you that you have the abilities for greatness of soul and courage. But what abilities do you have for blaming and accusing others? Show those to me.

Chapter 7
On the Use of Sophistical Arguments, Hypotheticals, and Similar Things

Epictetus said that dealing with tricky and hypothetical arguments, as well as those based on questions and answers, is important for understanding our duties in life, even though most people don't realize this. In every situation, we try to find out how a wise and good person should handle things properly. So, let people either say that a serious person won't get involved in debates, or that if he does, he won't care about avoiding rash or careless behavior when questioning and answering. But if they don't agree with either of these points, then they must admit that we need to look into the topics that involve questioning and answering.

What is the goal of reasoning? It is to establish true statements, remove false ones, and avoid agreeing with unclear ideas. Is it enough, then, to have just learned this? "Yes, it's enough," someone might say. But is it also enough for someone who doesn't want to make a mistake with money to only know that they should accept real coins and reject fake ones? "No, it's not enough." What else is needed? The ability to test and tell the difference between real and fake coins. Similarly, in reasoning, just knowing the goal isn't enough; you also need the ability to examine and tell the difference between what's true, what's false, and what's unclear. "Yes, that's necessary."

What else is important in reasoning? "You need to accept what follows logically from what you've agreed to." Is it enough just to know this? No, it's not. You need to learn how one thing leads to another, and when one thing follows from one thing or several things together. Think about whether it's necessary for someone who wants to be good at reasoning to develop the ability to prove the points he's discussing and understand the arguments of others. He should also avoid being tricked by people who use false reasoning as if they were proving something. This is why practicing and exercising with logical arguments has become important and necessary.

But sometimes we agree on the starting points, or assumptions, of an argument, and something follows from them that isn't true, but it still logically follows. What should I do in that case? Should I accept the false conclusion? How can I do that? Should I say that I didn't really agree to the assumption? "But you can't do that either." Should I say that the conclusion doesn't follow from what we agreed on? "But you can't do that either." So what should be done in this situation? Think of it this way: borrowing money doesn't make someone a debtor forever; they remain in debt only if they don't repay the money. Similarly, you're not forced to accept the conclusion just because you agreed to the assumptions—you have to stick with what you agreed to. If the assumptions stay the same as when you agreed to them, then you must accept the conclusion. But if the assumptions change in any way, you must withdraw your agreement and reject the conclusion that doesn't follow from the original agreement.

So, we should carefully examine these kinds of assumptions and pay attention to how they change during questioning, answering, or drawing conclusions. This is important to avoid being confused or tricked by false reasoning, especially when we don't see what the real conclusion should be. Why should we examine this? So that we don't get involved in discussions in a careless or confusing way.

The same applies to hypotheses and hypothetical arguments. Sometimes it's necessary to accept a hypothesis as a starting point for the argument that follows. Should we allow every hypothesis that's proposed, or not? If not, which ones should we allow? And if someone has accepted a hypothesis, must they always stick to it? Or can they sometimes withdraw from it while still accepting the logical consequences and avoiding contradictions? Yes, but what if someone says, "If you accept this hypothesis, I'll lead you to an impossible conclusion"? Should a wise person avoid engaging with such a person and refuse to discuss it with them? But who else but a wise person can use reasoning, is skilled in questioning and answering, and can't be tricked or deceived by false reasoning? Shouldn't he take care when he enters into an argument, making sure he doesn't do so rashly or carelessly? And if he doesn't take care, how can he be the kind of person we think he is? Without some practice and preparation, how can he maintain a consistent and logical argument? If this isn't the case, then all these discussions are unnecessary and go against our idea of what it means to be a good and serious person.

So, why are we still lazy, negligent, and slow to take action, and why do we look for excuses not to work hard or be careful in developing our reasoning? "If I make a mistake in these matters, it's not like I've killed my father!" someone might say. But where was there a father involved in this situation that you could kill? What, then, have you done? The only mistake possible here is the one you've already made. This is what I told Rufus when he blamed me for not finding the one thing missing in a certain argument: "I suppose," I said, "that I've burned down the Capitol." "Fool," he replied, "was the thing missing here the Capitol?" Are the only crimes burning down the Capitol or killing your father? But to use the appearances presented to you recklessly, foolishly, and carelessly, to not understand arguments, demonstrations, or sophisms, or, in short, to not see in questioning and answering what is consistent with what you've agreed to or not—is there no error in that?

Chapter 8
The Abilities of the Untrained Are Not Reliable

Epictetus said that just as we can change things that are equal to one another in many ways, we can also change the forms of arguments and reasoning. Here's an example: "If you borrowed money and didn't repay it, you owe me the money. You didn't borrow money and didn't repay it; so, you don't owe me the money." To be able to do this skillfully is especially important for a philosopher because if an enthymeme is an incomplete form of reasoning, it's clear that someone who is trained in complete reasoning must also be good at the incomplete kind.

"Then why don't we practice this more often?" someone might ask. I would reply that right now, even though we don't practice these things and aren't distracted from studying morality, we still don't make much progress in becoming better people. So, what should we expect if we add this practice? Especially since it would not only distract us from more important things but could also make us conceited and arrogant. The power of arguing and persuasion is great, and if someone practices it a lot and adds some flair with language, it can easily lead to arrogance, especially if the person isn't well-trained. Any skill gained by someone who is untrained and weak can bring the danger of making them proud and boastful. How could you convince a young person who is good at these things that they shouldn't let the skill control them, but instead, they should control the skill? Doesn't he just dismiss all advice and show off, refusing to listen to anyone who tries to correct him or remind him of what he's neglecting?

"But wasn't Plato a philosopher?" someone might ask. "And wasn't Hippocrates a doctor? But look at how Hippocrates speaks."

Does Hippocrates speak like that because he's a doctor? Why are you mixing up things that just happened to be part of the same person? If Plato was handsome and strong, should I also try to become handsome and strong, as if that were necessary for philosophy, just because a certain philosopher was both handsome and a philosopher? Shouldn't you choose to see and understand what makes a person a philosopher and what other qualities they might have? If I were a philosopher, should you also become lame just because I am?

What then? Am I taking away the abilities you have? Not at all; just as I wouldn't take away your ability to see. But if you ask me what the true good of a person is, I can only tell you that it's a certain state of the will in response to what we perceive.

Chapter 9
How Understanding Our Connection to God Leads to Important Outcomes

Epictetus said that if what philosophers say about our connection to God is true, then what should we do other than what Socrates did? When someone asks you where you're from, don't say that you're from Athens or Corinth, but instead say that you're a citizen of the world. Why do you say you're an Athenian? Why not just say you're from the small corner of the earth where your body was born? Isn't it obvious that you call yourself an Athenian or Corinthian because those cities are larger and include not only your small birthplace and family but also the entire country your ancestors came from?

So, if someone understands how the world is run and learns that the greatest and most important community is the one made up of both humans and God, and that from God come not only our father and grandfather but all living beings—especially rational beings, who are naturally connected to God through reason—why shouldn't that person call themselves a citizen of the world and a child of God? And why should they be afraid of anything that happens among humans? If being related to Caesar or some other powerful person in Rome is enough to make us feel safe, respected, and free from fear, then wouldn't having God as your creator, father, and protector free us from sorrow and fear?

But someone might ask, "How will I get food if I have nothing?"

Think about slaves and runaways—what do they rely on when they leave their masters? Do they rely on land, slaves, or silver? No, they rely on nothing but themselves, and yet they still find food. So, should a philosopher who travels to foreign places rely on others instead of taking care of themselves? Should they be less capable than animals, which are self-sufficient, always finding the food and way of life that suits them and is in harmony with nature?

I believe that an elder should be here, not just to stop you from having low thoughts or talking poorly about yourselves, but to make sure that none of us young people, after realizing our connection to God and seeing that we are tied to our bodies and the things we own, decide to throw off these burdens as if they were too painful to bear and leave to return to our divine family. This should be the task of a true teacher, if they are doing their job. You should go to them and say, "Epictetus, we can no longer stand being tied to this weak body, feeding it, giving it drink, resting it, and cleaning it, and doing what others want because of it. Aren't these things unimportant to us? Isn't death nothing to fear? Aren't we, in a way, children of God? Didn't we come from Him? Let us go back to where we came from. Let us finally be free from these chains that bind us and weigh us down. Here, there are robbers, thieves, courts, and tyrants who think they have power over us through our bodies and possessions. Let us show them that they have no power over us." And I would say, "Friends, wait for God. When He gives the signal and releases you from this duty, then go to Him. But for now, endure living in the place where He has put you. Your time here is short and easy to bear if you think about it the right way. What tyrant, thief, or court can scare those who don't care about their bodies or possessions? So wait, and don't leave without a good reason."

This is the kind of thing a teacher should say to serious students. But what happens now? The teacher is like a lifeless body, and you are lifeless too. After eating well today, you sit down and worry about tomorrow, wondering how you'll find something to eat. Poor soul, if you have food, you'll have it; if you don't, you'll leave this life. The door is open. Why do you grieve? Where is there room for tears? Why should you flatter anyone? Why should one person envy another? Why admire the rich or powerful, even if they are strong and bad-tempered? What can they do to us? We won't care about what they can do, and what we do care about, they can't touch. How did Socrates behave in situations like this? He acted like a person who knew he was related to the gods. When he was on trial, he said to his judges, "If you tell me that you'll let me go if I stop speaking as I do, and stop bothering the young and the old with my words, I'll tell you that you're being ridiculous. You think that if one of our military leaders assigns me a post, it's my duty to stay there and be ready to die a thousand times before I leave it. But if God assigns me a place and a way of life, you think I should leave it?" Socrates spoke like a man who truly believed he was connected to the gods. But we think of ourselves as nothing more than stomachs, intestines, and shameful parts. We are afraid, we desire, we flatter those who can help us with these things, and we fear them too.

One time, a man asked me to write to Rome for him. He was someone who, according to most people, had fallen on hard times. He used to be wealthy and important, but he had lost everything and was living here. I wrote on his behalf in a humble way, but when he read the letter, he gave it back to me and said, "I asked for your help, not your pity. Nothing bad has happened to me."

Similarly, Musonius Rufus used to test me by saying, "This or that will happen to you because of your master." And I would reply that these are just normal events in life. He would ask, "Why should I ask someone else for something when I can get it from you?" Because, in truth, what a person has within themselves, it's unnecessary and foolish to seek from others. Should I, who can find greatness of soul and a noble spirit within myself, seek land, money, or a government position from you? I hope not; I wouldn't be so ignorant of my own abilities. But when someone is cowardly and weak, what else can be done for them except to write letters on their behalf, as you would for a dead body: "Please allow us to take care of the body of so-and-so and give us a little bit of blood to work with." For such a person is, in fact, just a body and some blood, nothing more. But if they were anything more, they would know that no person can make another person miserable.

Chapter 10
Against Those Who Eagerly Seek Power and Status in Rome

Epictetus said that if we put as much effort into our own work as the old men in Rome do in their duties, we might actually achieve something. I know a man who is older than me, who is now in charge of the corn supply in Rome. I remember when he passed through here on his way back from exile, talking about his past and saying that after his return, he would focus only on spending the rest of his life in peace and quiet. "After all," he said, "how little of life do I have left?" I replied, "You won't do that. As soon as you catch the scent of Rome, you'll forget everything you've said. And if you get a chance to enter the imperial palace, you'll eagerly go in and thank God for it." He responded, "If you ever see me setting even one foot in the palace, think what you will of me." So what happened? Before he even entered the city, he received letters from Caesar, and as soon as he got them, he forgot everything he had said and continued to add one responsibility after another. I wish I were by his side now to remind him of what he said when he passed through here and to show him that I'm better at predicting human behavior than he is.

So, am I saying that humans are meant to do nothing? Of course not. But why aren't we active in the right ways? For instance, when my day starts, I remind myself of what I need to teach my students. But then I think, "Why should I care how someone else learns? The first thing I should do is get some sleep." And really, how does what others do compare to what we do? If you observe what they do, you'll see. What do they spend their day doing? They keep accounts, discuss among themselves, and give and take advice about small things like a bit of grain, a piece of land, and minor profits. Is it the same thing to receive a request like, "I beg you to allow me to export a small amount of corn," as it is to receive one like, "I beg you to learn from Chrysippus what the order of the world is, what role the rational being plays in it, and to consider who you are and what the nature of good and bad is"? Are these things the same? Do they require the same level of care? Is it equally shameful to neglect one as it is the other?

So, are we the only ones who are lazy and love sleep? No, in fact, you young men are even more so. We older folks, when we see young people having fun, want to join in and play with them. And if I saw you being active and serious, I would be even more eager to join you in your pursuits.

Chapter 11
On Family Affection

When a magistrate visited Epictetus, he asked him several questions and inquired if he had children and a wife. The man replied that he did. Epictetus then asked how he felt about his situation. The man said, "Miserable." Epictetus asked, "In what way?" because people don't marry and have children to be miserable but to be happy. The man replied, "I'm so miserable about my children that when my little daughter was sick and in danger, I couldn't bear to stay with her. I left home until someone told me she had recovered."

Epictetus asked, "Do you think you acted rightly?" The man responded, "I acted naturally." Epictetus said, "Convince me that what you did was natural, and I'll convince you that everything natural is also right." The man replied, "This is how most fathers act." Epictetus didn't deny that, but he pointed out that just because something is common doesn't mean it's right. For example, just because tumors are common doesn't mean they're good for the body. Similarly, just because most people do wrong doesn't mean doing wrong is natural. Epictetus asked the man to show him how his behavior was natural. The man said, "I can't, but can you show me how it wasn't natural and wasn't right?"

Epictetus then said, "If we were discussing colors, what would we use to tell the difference between white and black?" The man answered, "Our sight." "And if we were talking about hot and cold, or hard and soft, what would we use?" The man replied, "Our touch." Epictetus continued, "So, since we're discussing what is natural and what is done rightly or wrongly, what should we use to judge this?" The man said, "I don't know." Epictetus responded, "Not knowing how to judge colors or smells isn't a big problem, but if someone doesn't know how to judge what is good and bad, and what is natural and what is against nature, isn't that a serious problem?" The man agreed that it was.

Epictetus then asked, "Do all things that seem good to some people seem good to everyone? For example, when it comes to food, do Jews, Syrians, Egyptians, and Romans all have the same opinions?" The man replied, "No, it's not possible." Epictetus pointed out that if the Egyptians' opinions are correct, then the others must be wrong, and if the Jews are correct, then the others must be wrong. The man agreed. Epictetus then explained that ignorance leads to a lack of learning and training in what is necessary. The man agreed again.

So Epictetus said, "Now that you know this, will you focus on nothing else but learning the standard for what is natural and using it to judge everything?" The man agreed. Epictetus then asked, "Does loving your family seem natural and good to you?" The man said, "Yes, certainly." "Is this love natural and good, and is it not also good to act reasonably?" The man agreed that it was. "Is reason ever in conflict with love?" Epictetus asked. The man said, "I don't think so." Epictetus pointed out that if one thing is natural, the opposite must be unnatural. The man agreed.

Epictetus continued, "So, if we find something that is both loving and reasonable, we can say it's right and good." The man agreed. "So, was it reasonable to leave your sick child?" Epictetus asked. The man admitted that it wasn't reasonable. Epictetus then asked if it was loving. The man said, "Let's think about it." Epictetus then asked if the mother loved the child and whether she should have left too. The man replied, "No, she shouldn't have." "What about the nurse? Does she love the child?" The man said, "Yes, she does." "Should the nurse have left?" Epictetus asked. The man replied, "No, by no means." "What about the child's teacher? Should he have left?" The man agreed that he shouldn't have.

Epictetus concluded, "So, should the child have been left alone, without help, because of the great love of her parents and caregivers? Should she have died in the hands of those who didn't care for her?" The man admitted that this would be wrong. Epictetus pointed out that it's unfair and unreasonable to think that just because you have affection, you can do something that you wouldn't allow others with the same affection to do. It's absurd.

Epictetus then asked, "If you were sick, would you want your family and friends to love you so much that they'd leave you alone and deserted?" The man replied, "No, by no means." "Would you want to be so loved that through their excessive affection, you'd always be left alone in sickness? Or would you rather pray to be loved by your enemies so they'd leave you?" The man agreed that this would be ridiculous. Epictetus concluded, "So, your behavior wasn't really loving at all."

Epictetus then asked if nothing moved the man to leave his child. The man admitted that something must have, but he wasn't sure what it was. Epictetus explained that it's important to understand that the cause of all our actions—whether we do something or not, say something or not, feel happy or sad, avoid something or pursue something—is our own will. It's not the event itself but our will to do or not do something. The man agreed.

Epictetus explained that it wasn't the death of Patroclus that caused Achilles to mourn, but his own will to do so. Another person might not have reacted the same way. In the same way, it was the man's will that made him run away from his sick child. If he had willed to stay, he would have stayed. And now, if he chooses to go to Rome, it's because he wills to do so, and if he changes his mind, he won't go.

Epictetus then asked if he had convinced the man. The man replied that he was convinced. Epictetus continued, "So, from now on, when we do something wrong, we'll blame nothing else but our own will. We'll work to fix our will just as we would work to remove tumors or abscesses from the body. And we'll understand that when we do something right, it's also because of our will. We won't blame others for our problems—neither slaves, neighbors, spouses, nor children—because if we don't think something is a problem, we won't act as if it is. And whether we think something is a problem or not is up to us, not external events." The man agreed.

Epictetus concluded, "So from now on, we'll focus on examining our opinions and nothing else—not land, not slaves, not horses or dogs—just our opinions." The man agreed. Epictetus then pointed out that the man would need to become a dedicated student of philosophy, someone whom others might ridicule if he truly intended to examine his own opinions. And he would know that this work isn't something that can be done in an hour or a day.

Chapter 12
On Contentment

When it comes to the gods, people have different beliefs. Some say that gods don't exist. Others say they exist but are inactive and don't care about anything. A third group says gods exist and care, but only about big, heavenly things, not about anything on earth. A fourth group says gods care about both earthly and heavenly things, but only in a general way, not about individual things. Finally, there's a fifth group, which includes people like Ulysses and Socrates, who say, "I do nothing without your knowledge."

The first thing we need to do is to figure out which of these beliefs is true. If there are no gods, why should we follow them? If gods exist but don't care about anything, then why should we follow them? But if gods do exist and care about things, and if they communicate with us, then we should consider how to follow them. A wise and good person, after thinking about all this, will submit their mind to the one who rules everything, just like good citizens follow the laws of their country. Someone learning should approach their teacher with this intention: "How can I follow the gods in everything, be content with how they manage things, and become truly free?" For a person is free if everything happens according to their will and no one can stop them.

But what is freedom? Is it madness? Certainly not. Freedom and madness don't go together. "But," you might say, "I want everything to happen just as I like, in whatever way I like." That's madness. Don't you know that freedom is something noble and valuable? But wanting things to happen without thinking isn't noble; it's foolish. Think about writing. Do I wish to write someone's name however I want? No, I learn to write it correctly. The same goes for music and every other skill. If we didn't learn to do things properly, knowledge would be worthless. So, when it comes to the greatest and most important thing—freedom—should I be allowed to want whatever I want without thinking? Of course not. Learning means learning to wish for things to happen as they do happen. And how do things happen? They happen according to the plan set by the one who rules everything. This ruler has created summer and winter, plenty and scarcity, virtue and vice, and all opposites for the harmony of the whole. To each of us, this ruler has given a body, body parts, possessions, and companions.

Remembering this plan, we should approach learning, not to change the way things are—because we can't, and it wouldn't be better if we could—but so that we can keep our minds in harmony with the way things happen. Can we avoid interacting with others? How could we? And if we live with others, can we change them? Who has the power to do that? So, what's left? How can we interact with others in a way that lets them do what they think is right, while we still stay true to nature? You may not want to endure it and might be discontent. When you're alone, you call it solitude. When you're with others, you call them cheats and thieves. You complain about your parents, children, siblings, and neighbors. But when you're alone, you should call it peace and freedom, and see yourself as like the gods. When you're with others, you shouldn't see it as a crowd or trouble, but as a festival and gathering, and accept everything with contentment.

What happens to those who don't accept things? They remain as they are. If someone is unhappy being alone, let them be alone. If someone is unhappy with their parents, let them be a bad child and grieve. If someone is unhappy with their children, let them be a bad parent. "Throw him in prison," you might say. But what is prison? It's just being somewhere against your will. If you're somewhere against your will, you're already in prison. But Socrates wasn't in prison because he was there willingly.

"Must my leg then be injured?" you might ask. Are you really going to complain about the world because of one injured leg? Won't you willingly give it up for the good of the whole? Will you be upset with what Zeus has planned, which he and the Fates decided when you were born? Don't you realize how small a part of the whole you are? I mean physically. In terms of intelligence, you're not less than the gods, because intelligence isn't measured by size but by thought.

Won't you choose to place your value in what makes you equal to the gods? "But I'm unhappy because of my parents." Did you get to choose your parents? Did you get to say, "Let this man and this woman come together so I can be born"? No, it was necessary for your parents to exist first and then for you to be born. What kind of parents? The ones you got. Now that they're your parents, is there no solution for you? If you didn't know how to use your eyes, you'd be miserable if you closed them when there were colors to see. But you have greatness of soul and nobility of spirit to handle everything that happens, and you don't know it. Doesn't that make you more unfortunate? You have the power to deal with whatever happens, but you turn away from that power right when you need it most. Shouldn't you thank the gods that they've made you above the things that aren't in your control and responsible only for what is in your control? As for your parents, the gods have freed you from responsibility, just like with your siblings, body, possessions, death, and life. What are you responsible for? Only for how you use your perceptions. So why do you burden yourself with things you're not responsible for? You're just making trouble for yourself.

Chapter 13
How to Live in a Way That Pleases the Gods

When someone asked how a person could eat in a way that pleases the gods, Epictetus replied, "If you can eat justly, contentedly, calmly, temperately, and with order, won't that be pleasing to the gods?" But if you ask for warm water and the servant doesn't hear you, or if he hears you but brings only lukewarm water, or if he's not even around, and you don't get upset or angry, isn't that pleasing to the gods?

"How then should a person deal with such a servant?" you might ask. Epictetus replied, "You, who are also a servant, won't you bear with your own brother, who shares the same father, Zeus, and comes from the same divine origin? But if you've been placed in a higher position, will you immediately act like a tyrant? Won't you remember who you are and whom you rule? They are your family, your brothers by nature, the children of Zeus."

"But I bought them, and they didn't buy me," you might say. Epictetus responded, "Look at where your thoughts are focused—on earthly things, on these worthless human laws. But you're not looking toward the laws of the gods."

Chapter 14
That God Watches Over Everyone

When someone asked Epictetus how a person could believe that all their actions are watched by God, he replied, "Do you believe that everything is connected in one big whole?" The person said, "Yes, I do." Epictetus continued, "Do you also believe that things on earth are connected to things in heaven?" The person agreed. "Then how do things like plants follow God's command so precisely? When He tells them to flower, they flower. When He tells them to grow, they grow. When He tells them to produce fruit, they do so. When He tells the fruit to ripen, it ripens. And when He commands the fruit to fall, it falls. When He tells the leaves to drop, they drop. And when He tells the plants to rest, they rest. How else could there be such big changes on earth, like the phases of the moon or the changing of the seasons?"

"But if plants and our bodies are so closely connected with everything in the universe, isn't it even more true of our souls? Our souls are connected to God as parts of Him, and doesn't God notice every movement of these parts as if they were His own? Now, can you think about divine things and human affairs at the same time? Can you sense and understand many things at once, agree with some, disagree with others, and sometimes wait to decide? Can you keep so many thoughts in your mind and, being moved by them, remember similar thoughts? Can you hold on to many skills and memories of countless things? If you can do all this, can't God oversee everything, be present with everything, and get a sense of everything? The sun can light up such a large part of the world, leaving only the part that is in the earth's shadow. The sun is just a small part of the universe compared to the whole. So can't the one who made the sun and controls its movement also see everything?"

"But I can't understand all these things at once," the person might reply. Epictetus responded, "Who said you have the same power as Zeus? But even so, He has placed a guardian spirit with each of us, a personal guide who never sleeps and is never fooled. Who could take better care of us? So, when you close your doors and sit in darkness, never say you are alone because you are not. God is within you, and your guardian spirit is within you. They don't need light to see what you are doing. To this God, you should swear an oath, just as soldiers swear an oath to Caesar. But while soldiers are paid to swear that they will put Caesar's safety above all things, you, who have received so many great blessings, won't you swear? Or if you do, won't you keep your oath? And what should you swear? Never to disobey, never to complain, never to blame anything God has given you, and never to do or suffer anything unwillingly. Is this oath like the soldier's oath? Soldiers swear not to put anyone above Caesar; in this oath, you swear to honor yourself above all."

Chapter 15
What Philosophy Teaches

When someone asked Epictetus how he could persuade his brother to stop being angry with him, Epictetus replied, "Philosophy doesn't promise to get you things from outside. If it did, it would be overstepping its bounds. Just as a carpenter's material is wood and a sculptor's material is copper, the material for the art of living is each person's life. 'What about my brother's life?' you might ask. That's his own business, not yours. But in your case, your brother's anger is one of those outside things, like a piece of land, like health, or like reputation. Philosophy doesn't promise you any of these things. Philosophy says, 'In every situation, I will keep the part of you that governs your actions in harmony with nature.' Whose governing part? 'The one in whom I live,' philosophy says.

"How can I stop my brother from being angry with me?" Bring him to me, and I will talk to him. But I have nothing to say to you about his anger.

When the person asking for advice said, 'I want to know how, even if my brother isn't reconciled with me, I can keep myself in a state that is in harmony with nature,' Epictetus replied, 'Nothing great is produced quickly, not even a grape or a fig. If you tell me now that you want a fig, I will tell you that it needs time: it must first flower, then grow fruit, and then ripen. So, if the fruit of a fig tree doesn't mature quickly, would you expect the fruit of a person's mind to mature so quickly and easily? Don't expect it, even if I tell you so.'"

Chapter 16
On Providence

Don't be surprised if other animals, unlike humans, have everything they need for their bodies—like food, drink, and even a place to sleep—without needing shoes, bedding, or clothes. But we, as humans, need all these extra things. Animals weren't made for their own sake but to serve others, so it wouldn't make sense for them to need more. Imagine how difficult it would be if we had to take care of ourselves and also worry about clothing and feeding cattle and donkeys. Think about how soldiers are always ready for their commander—fully equipped with shoes, clothes, and weapons. But it would be really hard for the commander to go around putting shoes and clothes on each of his thousand soldiers. In the same way, nature has made animals that serve us ready and prepared, needing no extra care. That's why even a small child with just a stick can easily lead a herd of cattle.

But instead of being thankful that we don't have to worry about animals as we do ourselves, we often complain about God not giving us everything we want. Yet, in the name of Zeus and the gods, any one of the things that exist would be enough to make a person realize the care and wisdom of God—at least a person who is modest and grateful. Don't just think about the big things, but consider this: grass produces milk, milk produces cheese, and skins produce wool. Who created or designed these things? No one, you might say. That's an incredible amount of shamelessness and foolishness!

Let's put aside the great works of nature and look at the smaller, less important things she does. Is there anything less useful than a beard? But even here, nature has used it in the best possible way. Hasn't she used it to distinguish males from females? Doesn't every man's nature immediately declare from a distance, "I am a man. Treat me as a man, speak to me as a man. Expect nothing else—see the signs?" In the case of women, just as nature made their voices softer, she also removed the beard from their faces. You might argue that the human race would have been better off without these marks of distinction, forcing each of us to announce, "I am a man." But isn't the beard a beautiful, dignified, and respectable sign? How much more attractive is it than a rooster's comb or a lion's mane? For this reason, we should respect the signs that God has given us. We shouldn't try to get rid of them or blur the differences between the sexes as much as we can.

Are these the only signs of God's care in us? What words could ever be enough to praise them and give them the recognition they deserve? If we truly understood, wouldn't we spend our time, both together and alone, singing hymns and praising the deity, and talking about His blessings? Shouldn't we, while digging, plowing, and eating, be singing this hymn to God? "Great is God, who has given us such tools to work the earth: great is God who has given us hands, the ability to swallow, a stomach, invisible growth, and the power to breathe even while we sleep." This is what we should sing on every occasion, and we should sing the greatest and most divine hymn of all for giving us the ability to understand these things and use them properly.

Well then, since most of you have become blind to this, shouldn't there be someone to fill this role and, on behalf of everyone, sing this hymn to God? What else can I do, a lame old man, but sing hymns to God? If I were a nightingale, I would do the work of a nightingale; if I were a swan, I would do the work of a swan. But now I am a rational being, so I must praise God. This is my job, and I will do it. I won't leave this duty as long as I'm allowed to keep it, and I encourage you to join in this same song with me.

Chapter 17
Why Logical Thinking Is Necessary

Since it is reason that helps us understand and improve everything else, it is important that we understand and improve reason itself. But how should we understand reason? Should we use reason itself, or something else? If we use something else, it must either be reason or something greater than reason, which is impossible. If we use reason to understand reason, who will understand that reasoning? If reason can understand itself, then the reasoning we started with can do the same. But if we keep needing something else to understand each step, the process will go on forever.

Someone might say, "Fixing our decisions is more important than studying logic." If you want to talk about that, I'm ready to listen. But if you tell me, "I don't know if your argument is true or false," and if I use a word you don't understand and you ask me to explain it, I won't continue without addressing that. That's why the Stoic philosophers put logic first, just like when we measure grain, we first define what the measurement is. If we don't first define what a measuring tool is, how can we measure or weigh anything accurately? In the same way, if we don't fully understand the standard of judgment for everything else, how can we ever truly understand anything else?

Someone might argue, "But a measuring tool is just a piece of wood and doesn't produce anything." That's true, but it helps us measure grain. They might also say, "Logic doesn't produce anything." We'll discuss that later, but even if we agree with that, we can still say that logic helps us examine and understand everything else, just like a scale helps us weigh things. And who says this? Not just Chrysippus, Zeno, and Cleanthes, but even Antisthenes, who said, "The beginning of education is examining words." Socrates said the same, and Xenophon wrote that Socrates began by asking, "What does this word mean?"

Is your great achievement understanding and interpreting Chrysippus? Who says that? What, then, is your achievement? It's understanding the will of nature. Do you understand it all by yourself? If so, what more do you need? If "all people make mistakes without meaning to," and you've learned the truth, then you must already be doing the right thing. But, by Zeus, I don't fully understand the will of nature. Who, then, interprets it? People say Chrysippus does. So, I try to understand what this interpreter of nature says. But if I don't understand him, I look for someone who can explain it to me, like reading something in a foreign language.

But should the interpreter be proud of his skill? There's no reason for pride, not even for Chrysippus if he only interprets the will of nature but doesn't follow it himself. How much less should his interpreter be proud? We don't need Chrysippus for his own sake, but to help us follow nature. Just like we don't need someone who reads omens for their own sake, but because we believe they can help us understand the signs from the gods. We don't admire the crow or raven, but the god who sends us signs through them.

So, I go to this interpreter, this philosopher, and ask him to explain the signs for me. He interprets them, saying, "You have a mind that is naturally free from obstacles and constraints. Let me show you how, starting with your ability to agree with the truth. Can anyone stop you from agreeing with what is true? No. Can anyone force you to accept something false? No. So, in this area, your mind is free from obstacles. Now, what about your desires and choices? Can one impulse overpower another? Can one desire or fear overpower another?"

Someone might say, "If someone threatens me with death, they force me to act." But it's not the threat itself that forces you; it's your decision that it's better to do what they want than to die. So, it's your own mind that compels you, not the external threat. If God had created that part of us, which is part of Himself, to be forced or constrained by anything, He wouldn't be God, nor would He be caring for us as He should. This is what I find in the signs: If you will it, you are free; if you will it, you won't blame anyone or complain. Everything will be according to your will and the will of God. This is why I go to this interpreter, not admiring him for his interpretation, but for the wisdom it reveals.

Chapter 18
Why We Should Not Get Angry at People's Mistakes

If what philosophers say is true, that in all people, thought and action come from a single source—our feelings—then it makes sense that when we agree with something, it's because we feel that it's true, and when we disagree, it's because we feel that it's not true. And, by Zeus, when we're unsure, it's because we feel uncertain. The same goes for when we're drawn toward something; it's because we feel it's good for us. It's impossible to think one thing is good and yet desire something else. And again, it's impossible to think one thing is fitting and yet be driven to do something else. If all this is true, why are we still angry with people who make mistakes? "They are thieves," someone might say, "and robbers." What do you mean by "thieves and robbers"? They've simply gone astray when it comes to understanding what is good and what is bad. Should we be angry with them or rather feel sorry for them? Just show them their mistake, and you'll see how quickly they'll stop making it. But if they don't realize their error, they have nothing better than their own opinion.

Should this thief or adulterer be put to death, you ask? Not at all. Instead, you should ask, "Should someone be put to death who is in a state of error and confusion about the greatest matters and is blind, not in seeing black and white, but in distinguishing between what is good and what is bad?" And if you put it this way, you'll realize how inhuman a thought it is that you're expressing. It's as if you're saying, "Shouldn't this blind person or this deaf person be put to death?" If losing the greatest thing—a good moral purpose—is the greatest harm that can happen to someone, and if a person is deprived of this very thing, then what reason do you have to be angry with them? If you must feel something that goes against nature because of another person's misfortune, feel pity for them instead of hating them. Drop this readiness to take offense and this spirit of hatred. Don't use the same words that angry people use, like "These cursed and awful fools!" Fine, but how did you suddenly become so wise that you're angry at fools? Why, then, do we get angry? Because we admire the things that these people take from us. If you stop admiring your clothes, you won't be angry at the person who steals them. If you stop admiring your wife's beauty, you won't be angry at her adulterer. Remember, a thief or an adulterer doesn't have any power over the things that are truly yours, only over things that belong to others and aren't under your control. If you give these things up and count them as nothing, who will you still have a reason to be angry with? But as long as you admire these things, be angry with yourself, not with the people I've mentioned. Think about it: you have fine clothes, and your neighbor doesn't. You have a window and want to show them off. He doesn't know where the true good of a person lies, but he believes it's in having fine clothes—the same belief you have. Shouldn't he come and take them? When you show a cake to hungry people and then eat it all by yourself, aren't you asking for them to try to snatch it from you? Stop tempting them, stop having a window, and stop showing off your clothes.

Something similar happened to me recently. I keep an iron lamp by my household gods, and when I heard a noise at the window, I ran downstairs. I found that the lamp had been stolen. I thought to myself that the person who stole it wasn't acting unreasonably. So, I said to myself, tomorrow you'll find a lamp made of clay. A person can only lose what they already have. "I lost my cloak." Yes, because you had a cloak. "I have a headache." You don't have pain in your horns, do you? So, why are you upset? Our losses and pains only relate to things we possess.

"But the tyrant will chain—" What? Your leg. "But he will cut off—" What? Your head. What, then, will he neither chain nor cut off? Your moral purpose. This is why the ancients advised us to "Know yourself." So, what comes next? By the gods, we should practice with small things and then move on to greater ones. "I have a headache."

Well, don't say "Oh no!" "I have an earache." Don't say "Oh no!" I'm not saying you can't groan, just don't groan deep inside yourself. And if your servant is slow in bringing your bandage, don't shout and make a face and say, "Everybody hates me." Why wouldn't they hate someone like that? From now on, trust in these teachings and walk around with your head held high, free, not relying on the size of your body like an athlete, because you shouldn't aim to be invincible like a donkey.

Who, then, is the invincible person? The one who isn't shaken by anything outside their control. Then, I start thinking about each situation, just like I would with an athlete. "This person won the first round. What will he do in the second? What if it's scorching hot? What will he do at the Olympics?" It's the same with this situation. If you put a silver coin in front of someone, he might ignore it. Yes, but if you put a pretty girl in front of him, what then? Or if it's dark, what then? Or if you tempt him with a bit of fame, what then? Or insults, what then? Or praise, what then? Or death, what then? He can overcome all these things. But what if it's scorching hot—meaning, what if he's drunk? What if he's mad with sadness? What if he's asleep? The person who passes all these tests is what I call the invincible athlete.

Chapter 19
How to Conduct Oneself Around Tyrants

If a man has some kind of superiority, or even just thinks he does, even if he doesn't, it's unavoidable that this man, if he's uneducated, will become arrogant because of it. For example, the tyrant declares, "I am the mightiest in the world." Very well, but what can you actually do for me? Can you give me a desire that is free from any obstacles? How could you do that? Do you even have that yourself? Can you protect me from things I want to avoid? Do you have that ability yourself? Or can you make choices that are always correct? How can you claim to have that power? Come on, when you're on a ship, do you trust yourself, or do you trust the skilled navigator? And when you're in a chariot, do you trust anyone other than the skilled driver? How is it with other skills? It's the same. So, what does your power really amount to? "Everyone pays attention to me." Yes, and I pay attention to my little plate, wash it, and wipe it clean, and I hang up my oil flask on the wall. What does that mean? Are these things better than me? No, but they are useful to me, so I take care of them. Also, don't I pay attention to my donkey? Don't I wash its feet? Don't I brush it? Don't you know that everyone pays attention to themselves, and to you, just like they do to their donkey? Who pays attention to you as a person? Show them to me. Who wants to be like you? Who follows you with enthusiasm, like people followed Socrates? "But I can cut off your head." Well said! I forgot that I should treat you like I treat a fever or cholera and set up an altar to you, just like they have an altar to the God Fever in Rome.

So, what is it that really upsets and confuses people? Is it the tyrant and his guards? How can that be? No, far from it! It's not possible for something naturally free to be disturbed or blocked by anything but itself. It's a person's own judgments that upset them. For example, when the tyrant says, "I will chain your leg," the person who values their leg highly replies, "Please, have mercy on me," but the person who values their moral purpose says, "If it seems better to you, then chain it." "Don't you care?" "No, I don't care." "I will show you that I am your master." "How can you be my master? Zeus has set me free. Do you really think he would let his own son be made a slave? You are, however, master of my dead body. Take it." "So you mean that when you come near me, you won't pay attention to me?" "No, I pay attention only to myself. But if you want me to say that I pay attention to you too, I do, but only in the same way I pay attention to my pot."

This isn't just selfishness; it's the nature of human beings. Everything a person does is for themselves. Why, even the sun does everything for its own sake, and, for that matter, so does Zeus himself. But when Zeus wants to be the "Rain-bringer," "Fruit-giver," and "Father of men and gods," you can see that he can't achieve these things or earn these titles unless he's useful to everyone. And in general, he has made human nature so that we can't get any of our own true goods unless we contribute something to the common interest. So, it follows that it's no longer considered unsocial for a person to do everything for their own sake. What else would you expect? That a person should neglect themselves and their own interests? And in that case, how can there be room for one and the same principle of action for all, namely, that of appropriating things to their own needs?

What then? When people have ridiculous opinions about what lies outside the scope of their moral purpose, thinking it's good or bad, it's completely unavoidable for them to pay attention to the tyrant. I wish it were only tyrants and not their servants too! And yet how can a man suddenly become wise when Caesar puts him in charge of his chamber pot? How can we suddenly say, "Felicio has spoken wisely to me"? I wish he would lose his job as chamber pot manager so that you may think he's a fool again! Epaphroditus had a cobbler who was useless, so he sold him. Then, by some chance, the man was bought by someone in Caesar's household and became Caesar's cobbler. You should have seen how much Epaphroditus respected him then! "How is my good Felicio doing?" he used to ask. And if someone asked us, "What is your master doing?" we'd answer, "He's consulting Felicio about something." But didn't he sell him because he was useless? So, who suddenly made him wise? This is what it means to honor something outside the scope of moral purpose.

"He's been given a tribuneship," someone says. Everyone who meets him congratulates him; one person kisses his eyes, another kisses his neck, and his slaves kiss his hands. He goes home, and he finds lamps being lit. He climbs up to the Capitol and offers a sacrifice. But who ever offered a sacrifice to give thanks for having had the right desires or for making choices according to nature? Because we give thanks to the gods for the things we consider good.

Today, a man was talking to me about becoming a priest of Augustus. I said to him, "Man, drop it; you'll be spending a lot of money for nothing." "But," he says, "those who draw up deeds of sale will inscribe my name." "Do you really plan to be there when the deeds are read and say, 'That's my name they wrote'? And even if you could be there whenever someone reads them, what will you do if you die?" "My name will stay after me." "Inscribe it on a stone, and it will stay after you. But come on, who will remember you outside of Nicopolis?" "But I will wear a crown of gold." "If you desire a crown at all, take a crown of roses and put it on; you will look much more elegant in that."

Chapter 20
How Reason Reflects on Itself

Every art or skill focuses on certain things. Now, when the art or skill is similar to what it deals with, it naturally reflects on itself; but when it's different, it can't. For example, the skill of leather-working is about working with hides, but the skill itself is completely different from the hides, so it doesn't reflect on itself. Similarly, the skill of grammar deals with written language, but it isn't itself written language, right? Not at all. For this reason, it can't reflect on itself.

So, what purpose did nature give us reason for? For the proper use of the impressions we get from the outside world. But what is reason itself? It's something made up of certain kinds of impressions from the outside world. So, it naturally can reflect on itself. Now, what are the things that wisdom helps us to understand? Things that are good, bad, and neither good nor bad. So, what is wisdom itself? It's a good thing. And what is foolishness? It's a bad thing. Do you see, then, that wisdom naturally reflects on both itself and its opposite? Therefore, the first and most important task of a philosopher is to test the impressions they receive and figure out which ones to trust, and to apply none that hasn't been tested.

You all know how careful we are with money, where we feel we have something at stake. We've even invented a whole art for testing coins, and the tester uses many methods—sight, touch, smell, and finally hearing. He drops the coin and listens to the sound it makes, and he's not satisfied with just one test but listens to the sound repeatedly, like a musician catching a tune.

So, when it comes to things where we feel it's important not to make a mistake, we put a lot of effort into telling the difference between things that could lead us astray. But when it comes to our reasoning ability, we yawn and sleep, accepting any and every impression without questioning it, because the loss we suffer doesn't seem important to us.

Therefore, if you want to realize how careless you are about what's truly good and bad, and how much more you care about things that don't really matter, think about how you feel about physical blindness versus being mentally deceived. You'll see that your feelings about good and bad are far from where they should be. "Yes, but this requires a lot of preparation, hard work, and learning many things." Well, what did you expect? Do you think you can master the greatest skill with little effort? And yet the most important teaching of philosophers is very brief. If you want to know, read what Zeno says and you'll see.

What's so long about his statement: "To follow the gods is the purpose of life, and the essence of good is using impressions properly"? If you ask, "What, then, is God, what is an impression, and what is the nature of the individual and the universe?" you already have a long explanation. If Epicurus comes and says that the good lies in the body, again the explanation gets lengthy, and you have to learn what the main faculty within us is and what our true nature is. Just as it's unlikely that the good of a snail lies in its shell, is it likely that the good of a human lies in their flesh? But think about yourself, Epicurus; what higher faculty do you have? What is it within you that thinks things over, that examines everything, and that, after examining the body itself, decides that it's the most important thing? And why do you light a lamp, work so hard for us, and write so many books? Is it so we won't fail to know the truth? Who are we? And what are we to you? And so the explanation gets longer.

Chapter 21
To Those Who Wish to Be Admired

When a person knows their proper place in life, they don't chase after things that are beyond that place. Man, what exactly do you want to happen to you? As for me, I'm content if I can desire and avoid things in a way that follows nature, if I can make choices and refusals that align with how I'm meant to, and if I can use my purpose, plans, and decisions according to my nature. So, why do you walk around in front of us like you've swallowed a stick and can't bend? "It has always been my wish that people who meet me would admire me and say as they follow me, 'Oh, what a great philosopher!'" But who are these people you want to be admired by? Aren't they the same people you usually say are crazy? What then? Do you really want to be admired by people you think are mad?

Chapter 22
On Understanding What We Already Know

Preconceptions are ideas that all people have in common, and one person's preconception doesn't contradict another's. For example, who among us doesn't think that what is good is also something useful and worth choosing, and that in every situation, we should seek and strive for what's good? And who doesn't believe that doing what's right is admirable and proper? So, when do contradictions happen? They happen when we apply our preconceptions to specific situations. For instance, one person might say, "He acted bravely and did the right thing," while another might say, "No, he's just acting crazy." This is where conflicts between people begin. The conflict isn't about whether we should prioritize doing what's right and holy, but about whether a particular action, like eating pork, is holy or unholy.

This was also the reason for the conflict between Agamemnon and Achilles. Let's imagine bringing them here to ask them what they think. Agamemnon, don't you think we should do what is proper and noble? "Yes, we should." And you, Achilles, do you agree that we should do what's noble? "I completely agree with that." Well, then, apply your preconceptions to this specific situation. That's where the conflict starts. One says, "I shouldn't have to give Chryseis back to her father," while the other says, "Yes, you should." Clearly, one of them is applying the preconception of "what one ought to do" incorrectly. Then, the first one says, "Fine, if I have to give Chryseis back, then I should take something from one of you as compensation," and the other replies, "Are you going to take the woman I love?" "Yes, the woman you love," the first one answers. "So, should I be the only one who loses something?" "But should I be the only one who gets nothing?" And so, a conflict arises.

So, what does it mean to get an education? It means learning how to apply these natural preconceptions correctly to each situation, in a way that aligns with nature, and also to understand that some things are within our control, while others are not. What's within our control are our moral choices and all the actions that come from those choices. But things like our bodies, body parts, possessions, parents, siblings, children, and our country—basically everything we interact with—are not under our control. So, where should we place the idea of "good"? To which group of things should we apply it? Should we apply it to things that are within our control? But isn't health a good thing, and a healthy body, and life itself? And what about children, parents, or our country? And who would tolerate you if you denied that these are good things? So, let's say these things are good. But then, can a person be truly happy if they suffer injury or don't get what is good? It's not possible. And can they maintain good relationships with others? How could they? Because it's in my nature to look out for my own interest. If it's in my interest to have a farm, then it's in my interest to take it from my neighbor. If it's in my interest to have a cloak, then it's also in my interest to steal it from a bathhouse. This thinking is what causes wars, rebellions, tyrannies, and conspiracies.

And again, how will I be able to fulfill my duty toward Zeus? If I suffer injury and am unlucky, then he isn't paying attention to me. And then we hear people say, "Why should I care about him if he can't help us?" Or, "Why should I care about him if he wants me to be in this miserable state?" The next step is that I begin to hate him. So, why do we build temples for the gods and make statues of them, as if they were evil spirits—as if Zeus were a god of fever? And how can he still be called "Savior," "Rain-bringer," and "Fruit-giver"? In truth, if we think that what is good lies in these external things, all these problems follow.

What, then, should we do?—This is a question for someone who truly wants to understand life and is deeply thinking about it. Such a person might say to themselves, "I don't really know what is good and what is bad right now; am I not being irrational?" Yes, but if I decide that the good is within the things I can control, people will laugh at me. Some old man with many gold rings on his fingers will come along, shake his head, and say, "Listen to me, my child; of course, you should study philosophy, but you also need to be sensible. All this stuff is nonsense. You can learn a syllogism from the philosophers, but you know better than they do what you ought to do."

Why, then, do you criticize me if I know? What should I say to this person? If I stay quiet, he'll be furious with me. So, I must say, "Forgive me, just as you would forgive someone who is in love; I'm not in control of myself; I'm crazy."

Chapter 23
Against Epicurus

Even Epicurus understands that we are naturally social beings, but since he believes that our good lies in our physical bodies, he cannot say anything that contradicts this belief. So, he strongly insists that we should neither admire nor accept anything that isn't connected to the nature of what's truly good; and in this, he is correct. But how, then, can we still be social beings if love for our own children isn't a natural feeling? Why do you advise the wise person not to raise children? Why are you worried that they will suffer sorrow because of their children? Does sorrow come to them because of a household slave named

Mouse? What difference does it make if little Mouse in their house starts to cry?

No, Epicurus knows that once a child is born, it is no longer within our power not to love and care for it. For the same reason, Epicurus says that a wise person shouldn't get involved in politics, because he understands what is required of someone who engages in politics. Of course, if you are going to live among people as if you were just another fly among flies, then what is stopping you? But even though Epicurus knows this, he still dares to say, "Let's not raise children." Yet, a sheep doesn't abandon its own lamb, nor does a wolf abandon its cub; so, should a human abandon their child? What do you want us to do? Should we be as foolish as sheep? But even they do not desert their offspring. Should we be as fierce as wolves? But even they do not desert their offspring. Come on, who would follow your advice when they see their child fallen on the ground and crying?

In my opinion, if your mother and father had known that you were going to say such things, they would not have abandoned you!

Chapter 24
How We Should Deal with Life's Challenges

It's in tough situations that people show who they really are. So, when a difficulty comes your way, remember that God, like a coach, has paired you with a strong opponent. Why? someone might ask. So that you can become a champion, like an Olympic victor; but that can't happen without some hard work and sweat. In my opinion, no one has a better challenge than the one you have, if only you're willing to use it the way an athlete uses a sparring partner to get better.

And now we're sending you to Rome as a scout, to check things out. But no one sends a coward as a scout, someone who, at the first noise or shadow, comes running back in fear, saying, "The enemy is already upon us." So now, if you come back and tell us, "The situation in Rome is terrifying; death is terrible, exile is terrible, insults are terrible, poverty is terrible; run away, everyone, the enemy is here!" we'll say to you, "Go away and keep your warnings to yourself! Our mistake was sending someone like you as a scout."

Diogenes, who was sent as a scout before you, brought back a different report. He says, "Death is not a bad thing, since it's not dishonorable"; he says, "Bad reputation is just noise made by madmen." And what a report he gave us about hard work, pleasure, and poverty! He says, "Being naked is better than wearing a fancy red robe; and sleeping on the bare ground," he says, "is the softest bed." And he proves these points with his own courage, his calmness, his freedom, and even his body, which is healthy and strong. "There's no enemy nearby," he says; "everything is peaceful." How do you know, Diogenes? "Look!" he says, "I haven't been hit by any missile, have I? I haven't been wounded, have I? I haven't run away from anyone, have I?"

This is what it means to be a true scout, but you come back and report one fear after another. Won't you go back out and observe more carefully, without this cowardice?

What should I do, then?—What do you do when you get off a ship? You don't pick up the rudder or the oars, do you? What do you pick up, then? Your own luggage, your oil flask, your bag. So now, if you remember what belongs to you, you'll never claim what belongs to someone else. He says to you, "Give up your fancy red robe." Here, take the plain one. "Give that up too." Here's the simple toga. "Give up your toga." Here, I'm naked. "But you make me jealous." Fine, then, take my whole body. Am I still afraid of the man to whom I can throw my body? But he won't leave me as his heir. So what? Did I forget that none of these things belong to me? How, then, do we call them "mine"? Just like we call the bed in the inn "mine." If the innkeeper dies and leaves you the beds, you'll have them; but if he leaves them to someone else, they'll have them, and you'll look for another bed.

If you don't find one, you'll have to sleep on the ground; just do so with courage, snoring and remembering that tragedies happen among the rich and powerful, but no poor man plays a tragic role except as part of the chorus. Now the kings start off in a state of prosperity:

"Hang the palace with garlands";
then, about the third or fourth act, comes—
"Alas, Cithaeron, why did you receive me?"

Slave, where are your crowns, where's your diadem? Do your guards help you at all? So, when you approach one of these powerful people, remember that you're approaching a tragic character, not the actor, but Oedipus himself. "But so-and-so is blessed; he has many companions to walk with." So do I; I fall in line with the crowd and have many companions to walk with.

But, to sum it all up: remember that the door has been left open. Don't be more of a coward than children, who say, "I won't play anymore," when the game doesn't please them. So, when things seem unbearable to you, just say, "I won't play anymore," and leave; but if you stay, stop complaining.

Chapter 25
On The Same Theme

If all this is true, and we're not just being foolish or pretending when we say, "What's good or bad for a person lies in their moral choices, and everything else doesn't really matter to us," then why are we still worried and afraid? No one has control over the things we truly care about, and the things other people do have control over don't concern us. So, what else is there to talk about?—"But give me some instructions."—What instructions can I give you? Hasn't Zeus already given you directions? Hasn't he given you something that is truly yours, something that can't be hindered or restrained, while everything else that isn't yours can be controlled by others? What instructions did you bring with you when you came into this world from him? What orders?

Protect what's truly yours by all means, but don't go after what belongs to someone else. Your faithfulness is yours, your self-respect is yours; so who can take these things from you? Who but you can stop you from using them? But how do you act? When you chase after things that aren't yours, you lose what is truly yours.

Since you have these directions from Zeus, what more do you want from me? Am I greater than Zeus or more trustworthy? But if you follow his commands, do you need any others? Hasn't he already given you these instructions? Bring out your preconceptions, bring out the proofs of the philosophers, bring out what you've often heard, bring out what you've said yourself, bring out what you've practiced.

So, how long should we follow these teachings and not give up? As long as the game is enjoyable. During the Saturnalia festival, a king is chosen by lot because it's part of the game. The king gives orders: "You drink, you mix wine, you sing, you go, you come." I obey, so as not to spoil the game. "Come, suppose you're in a bad situation." I don't suppose that; and who can force me to think that? Again, we've agreed to play the story of Agamemnon and Achilles. The one who plays Agamemnon says to me, "Go to Achilles and take away Briseis." I go. He says, "Come," and I come. Just as we behave in these hypothetical scenarios, we should behave the same way in real life. "Let it be night." So be it. "What then? Is it day?" No, because I've agreed that it's night. "Let's suppose you think it's night." So be it. "But go on and think it's night." That doesn't fit the situation.

In the same way, let's suppose you're unhappy. So be it. "Are you, then, unfortunate?" Yes. "What then? Are you troubled by bad luck?" Yes. "But go on and assume you're in a terrible state." That doesn't fit the situation; plus, there's another force that stops me from thinking that.

So, how long should we follow such commands? As long as it's useful, and that means as long as I keep my dignity and stay consistent.

Furthermore, some people are too grumpy and sharp-tongued and say, "I can't stand dining at this person's house where I have to listen to him every day talk about how he fought in Moesia: 'I told you, brother, how I climbed to the top of the hill; well, now I'm under siege again.'" But another person might say, "I'd rather dine there and let him babble all he wants." It's up to you to weigh these options, but don't do anything feeling burdened, troubled, or thinking you're in a terrible situation; no one is forcing you into this. Has someone made smoke in the house? If it's a little smoke, I'll stay; if it's too much, I'll go outside. You should remember this: the door is always open. But someone says, "Don't live in Nicopolis." I agree not to live there. "Nor in Athens." I agree not to live in Athens, either. "Nor in Rome." I agree not to live in Rome, either.

"Live in Gyara." I agree to live there. But living in Gyara seems like there's too much smoke in the house. I'll leave for a place where no one will stop me from living; that place is open to everyone. And as for the last inner garment, that is, my own body, beyond that, no one has any control over me. That's why Demetrius said to Nero, "You threaten me with death, but nature threatens you." If I care too much about my body, I've made myself a slave; if I care too much about my possessions, I've made myself a slave; because at that moment, I show what I can be caught with, and it will hurt me. Just like when a snake pulls its head back, and someone says, "Strike that part of him that he's protecting," you can be sure that your master will attack you at the point you especially want to protect.

If you remember all this, who will you flatter or fear anymore?

But I want to sit where the senators do.—Do you realize that you're making things cramped for yourself, that you're crowding yourself?—How else can I get a good view in the amphitheater?—Don't become a spectator, and you won't be crowded. Why are you making trouble for yourself? Or wait a little while, and when the show is over, sit down in the senators' seats and relax. In general, remember this: we crowd ourselves, we make things cramped for ourselves, and by that, I mean that the decisions of our will crowd us and make things cramped.

Why, what is the matter of being insulted? Stand by a stone and insult it; what will happen? If a person listens like a stone, what good does it do to insult them? But if the person insulting has found a weak spot, then they accomplish something. "Strip him." Why do you say "him"? Take his cloak and strip that off. "I've offended you." Good for you! This is what Socrates practiced, and that's why he always had the same expression on his face. But we prefer to practice and rehearse anything rather than how to be free and untroubled. "The philosophers talk in riddles," you say. But aren't there riddles in other arts? And what's more puzzling than to cut a man's eye so that he can see? If someone said this to a person who didn't understand surgery, wouldn't they laugh? What's surprising, then, if in philosophy, too, many things that are true seem puzzling to those who don't understand?

Chapter 26
Understanding the Law of Life

As someone was reading the hypothetical arguments, Epictetus said, "There is a rule in dealing with hypotheses: we must accept whatever the hypothesis or premise demands. But much more important is the rule for life: we must do what nature demands. If we want to act according to nature in every situation, it's clear that we should aim to neither avoid what nature requires nor accept what goes against it. That's why philosophers first train us in theory, where things are easier, and then move on to more difficult matters. In theory, nothing stops us from following what we're taught, but in real life, many things pull us away. So, it's ridiculous for someone to say they want to start with the harder things because it's not easy to begin with what's most difficult.

And this is the defense we should use with parents who get angry because their children study philosophy. 'Okay, Father, I'm making mistakes because I don't know what my duties are or what I'm supposed to do. Now, if this is something that can't be taught or learned, why do you blame me? But if it can be taught, then teach me; and if you can't, let me learn from those who claim they know. What do you think? That I choose to do wrong on purpose and avoid what's good? Of course not! So, what's causing my mistakes? It's my ignorance. Don't you want me to get rid of that? Has anger ever taught anyone how to steer a ship or play music? Do you think your anger will help me learn how to live?'

Only someone who truly dedicates themselves to philosophy can talk like this. But if someone just reads these subjects and goes to philosophers only to show off at a dinner party with their knowledge of hypothetical arguments, what are they really doing? Just trying to impress some senator sitting next to them? In Rome, the opportunities to show off are great, and the wealth in Nicopolis looks like child's play compared to Rome. That's why it's hard for someone to control their desires in Rome because there are so many distractions. I knew a man who clung to the knees of Epaphroditus, crying, because he was miserable—he had nothing left but a million and a half sesterces. What did Epaphroditus do? Did he laugh at him like you're laughing now? No, he just said in amazement, 'Poor man, how did you manage to keep silent? How did you endure it?'

Once, when Epictetus had confused a student who was reading the hypothetical arguments, and the person who had set the passage for him to read laughed at him, Epictetus said to the latter, 'You are laughing at yourself. You didn't give the young man any preparation or check if he could follow these arguments, but you treat him like a reader. Why then,' he added, 'do we trust someone who can't even follow a judgment on a complex argument to give praise or blame, or to judge what is done well or poorly? If this person speaks badly of someone, does that person pay attention to him? If he praises someone, does that person feel proud? When the person giving praise or blame can't even figure out basic logic?'

This is where philosophy starts—with an understanding of the state of one's own mind. Once a person realizes their mind is weak, they won't want to use it on big matters. But as it is now, some people who can't even handle small tasks buy a whole treatise and try to understand everything at once. So they get overwhelmed, suffer from indigestion, and then deal with colics, fluxes, and fevers. They should have first considered whether they were capable of handling it. However, in theory, it's easy to prove someone wrong, but in real life, people don't accept it when they're proven wrong, and we end up hating the person who corrected us. But Socrates used to tell us not to live an unexamined life."

Chapter 27
The Different Types of Appearances and How to Handle Them

External impressions come to us in four different ways: sometimes things really are what they seem to be; sometimes they aren't, and they don't seem to be; sometimes they are, but don't seem to be; and sometimes they aren't, but they seem to be. So, in all these situations, it's the job of an educated person to get things right. Whatever is bothering us, we should bring in the right tools to deal with it. If what's bothering us are tricky arguments from philosophers like Pyrrho and the Academics, we should bring in the right tools to deal with those. If it's the convincing appearances of things that make us think something is good when it isn't, we should bring in tools to handle that. If it's a habit that's troubling us, we should find tools that help us develop a better habit. So, what tools can we find to deal with bad habits? The answer is: build the opposite habit.

You might hear people saying, "That poor person! They died; their father died, and their mother too. They died too young and far from home." When you hear that, think about the arguments on the other side. Pull yourself away from those expressions of pity and build a habit of seeing things differently. To deal with tricky arguments, we need to practice logic and get used to thinking clearly. To deal with convincing appearances, we need to have our preconceptions ready, polished like weapons, and always on hand.

When death seems like a bad thing, we need to be ready with the argument that it's our duty to avoid evil, but death is something that can't be avoided. What can I do? Where can I go to escape it? Imagine I'm Sarpedon, the son of Zeus, so I can nobly say, as he did: "Since I've left home for war, I want to either win the prize for bravery myself or let someone else win it if I can't. If I can't achieve something great, I won't be jealous if someone else does." Even if acting like Sarpedon is too much for us, isn't the other option within our reach? Where can I go to escape death? Show me the place, show me the people who don't die; show me a magic spell against it. If I don't have one, what do you want me to do? I can't avoid death.

Instead of avoiding the fear of it, should I die crying and shaking? The root of sorrow is wanting something that doesn't happen. So, if I can change things to be the way I want, I change them; but if I can't, I might get so frustrated that I want to hurt the person standing in my way. It's human nature not to tolerate losing something good or falling into something bad. Finally, when I can't change things, and I can't harm the person in my way, I sit down and complain, blaming Zeus and the other gods—because if they don't care about me, what good are they to me? "But," you might say, "that's impious." What could be worse than what I'm going through now? In short, we need to remember this: unless piety and self-interest are combined, no one can stay pious. Don't these ideas seem important?

Let the follower of Pyrrho or the Academics come and argue against us. I, for one, don't have time for such debates, nor can I defend commonly accepted opinions. If I had a minor legal case about a piece of land, I would call in someone else to be my lawyer. So, what evidence do I trust? The evidence that fits the situation. When it comes to the question of how perception works—whether it happens through the whole body or just one part—maybe I don't know the answer, and both ideas confuse me. But I'm absolutely sure that you and I aren't the same person. How do I know this? When I want to eat something, I don't bring the food to your mouth but to mine; when I want bread, I don't grab dirt, but I go for the bread as if it's my target. And you, who doubt the evidence of the senses, do you do anything different? When you want to take a bath, do you go to a mill instead?

So, should we do our best to stick to common sense and be on guard against arguments that try to overturn it? Who disagrees with that? But only the person who has the ability and time should focus on these studies, while the person who is trembling, confused, and heartbroken should spend their time on something else.

Chapter 28
Why We Shouldn't Be Angry with Others: And What Is Truly Important and Unimportant in Life

Why do we agree with something? It's because it seems true to us. It's impossible to agree with something that doesn't seem true. Why? Because our mind naturally agrees with what's true, disagrees with what's false, and holds back when it's unsure. How do we know this? Try to feel that it's night right now—it's impossible. Try to stop feeling that it's daytime—you can't do it. Try to believe that the stars are an even number—that's also impossible. So, when someone agrees with something false, remember that they didn't do it because they wanted to. As Plato said, "Every soul is unwillingly deprived of the truth." It only seemed to them that the false thing was true.

Now, when it comes to actions, we have things that are similar to true and false perceptions: what's right and wrong, what's useful and harmful, what's appropriate for me and what's not. "Can someone think something is good for them but still not choose it?" No, they can't. Take the person who says:

"Now, now, I see the terrible things I'm about to do, But my passion is stronger than my better judgment."

This happens because she thinks that following her passion and getting revenge on her husband is better than protecting her children. "But she's mistaken." If you show her clearly that she's wrong, she won't do it. But until you do, what else can she follow besides what seems true to her? Nothing. So why are you angry with her for making such a huge mistake and becoming more like a snake than a person? Why not feel sorry for her instead? Just like we feel sorry for people who are blind or crippled, why don't we feel sorry for those who have become blind or crippled in their ability to reason?

Anyone who remembers that a person's actions are based on what seems true to them—whether it's right or wrong—will understand that if they're right, they're blameless, and if they're wrong, they suffer for it themselves. It's impossible for someone else to suffer the consequences of my mistakes. Whoever keeps this in mind won't get mad at anyone, won't be angry with anyone, won't insult or blame or hate anyone.

So, you think such big and terrible things come from something so small—a wrong impression? Yes, and nothing else. The entire story of the Iliad is just about a sense impression and how a poet used it. Alexander had the impression that he should take Menelaus' wife, and Helen had the impression that she should go with him. Now, if Menelaus had thought it was a good thing to lose such a wife, what would have happened? We wouldn't have the Iliad or the Odyssey.

But do such important things really depend on something so small? What do you mean by "important things"? Wars, conflicts, deaths of many people, and the destruction of cities? What's so important about all that? What, nothing important in that? Why, what's so important about the deaths of many cows and sheep, or the burning of many nests of swallows or storks? How can you compare this to that? It's very similar. People's bodies died in one case, and cows' and sheep's bodies died in the other. People's small houses were burned, and so were the nests of storks. What's so important or scary about that? Or show me how a person's house and a stork's nest are different as places to live.

Does a person really not differ from a stork?—Of course, he does; but not in these things.—In what ways, then, does he differ? Look and you'll find that the difference is in something else. See if it's not in his ability to understand what he's doing, in his ability to live socially, in his faithfulness, self-respect, and intelligence. So where is the great good or evil in people? It's exactly where the difference lies. If that part of us is kept safe and strong, and our self-respect, faithfulness, and intelligence aren't destroyed, then we're safe. But if any of these qualities are destroyed or taken away, then we're destroyed too. And that's where the important things are.

Did Alexander's downfall come when the Greeks attacked Troy with their ships, when they were destroying the land, and when his brothers were dying? Not at all. No one falls because of someone else's actions; what happened then was just like destroying storks' nests. No, Alexander fell when he lost his self-respect, his faithfulness, his respect for the laws of hospitality, and his decency. When did Achilles fall? When Patroclus died? Not at all. Achilles fell when he got angry, when he cried over a captured girl, when he forgot that he was there to fight a war, not to win over a sweetheart.

These are the downfalls that happen to people; this is the siege of their city, the destruction of it—when their correct judgments are torn down, when these are destroyed. So when women are taken into captivity, and children are enslaved, and men are killed, aren't all these things evils? Why do you think that? Let me know where you got that idea. No, instead, let me show you why they aren't evils. Let's look at the evidence, bring out your preconceptions.

This is why I can't understand what people do. When we want to judge weights, we don't just guess; when we want to judge what's straight and what's crooked, we don't just guess; in short, whenever it matters to us to know the truth, we don't just do things at random. Yet when it comes to the most important things—the only causes of doing right or wrong, of success or failure—this is the only time we act randomly and without thought. We don't have anything like a scale or a standard to go by, but some impression comes along, and we immediately act on it. What, am I any better than Agamemnon or Achilles—are they to do and suffer such terrible things because they followed their impressions, while I should be satisfied with mine? And what tragedy comes from anything other than this? What is the Atreus of Euripides? His impression. The Oedipus of Sophocles? His impression. The Phoenix? His impression. The Hippolytus? His impression. What kind of person do you think ignores this? What do we call people who follow every impression they have?—Madmen.—So, are we acting any differently?

Chapter 29
On Steadiness and Determination

The core of what is good comes from a certain kind of decision-making, and the same goes for what is bad. So, what about things outside of us, like events or objects? These are just tools we can use, and how we use them determines whether our decisions are good or bad. How do we make good decisions? By not being overly impressed by these outside things. If our judgments about these things are correct, then our decisions will be good; but if our judgments are wrong, then our decisions will be bad. This is the rule that God has given us, and He says, "If you want something good, get it from yourself." But you might say, "No, I want it from someone else." Don't do that—get it from yourself.

So, when a tyrant threatens me and orders me to come, I ask, "Who are you threatening?" If he says, "I will put you in chains," I reply, "You are threatening my hands and feet." If he says, "I will cut off your head," I reply, "You are threatening my neck." If he says, "I will throw you into prison," I say, "You are threatening my whole body." And if he threatens to send me into exile, I give the same answer. Does this mean he's not threatening me at all? If I believe that none of these things really matter to me, then no, he's not threatening me at all. But if I'm scared of any of these things, then yes, he is threatening me. So, who should I fear? The person who controls things that are under my control? But no one controls those. The person who controls things that aren't under my control? Then why should I care about them?

Do you philosophers teach us to look down on our rulers? Not at all. Who among us tells you to challenge what they have control over? Take my body, take my property, take my reputation, take the people around me. If I encourage anyone to try to control these things, let them accuse me. "Yes, but I want to control your thoughts too." And who gave you that power? How can you control someone else's thoughts? "By scaring them," he says, "I can control them." You don't understand that the thoughts control themselves—they aren't controlled by anything else. Nothing can overpower our decisions, except our decisions themselves. That's why God's rule is fair and just: "Let the better always win over the worse." "Ten are stronger than one," you might say. Stronger for what? For putting someone in chains, for killing them, for dragging them away, for taking their property. Yes, ten can overpower one in that way. But in what way are they worse? If the one has better judgments, and the ten do not. So, can they overpower the one in that way? How could they? But if we weigh them, won't the heavier side go down?

So, could someone like Socrates go through what he did with the Athenians? Don't call it "Socrates' suffering." Let's describe it as it is: The body of Socrates was taken and dragged to prison by stronger people, someone gave poison to Socrates' body, and the body grew cold and died. Does this seem amazing to you? Does it seem unfair? Do you blame God for this? Did Socrates get nothing in return for this? What was truly good for him? Should we listen to you or to Socrates himself? What does Socrates say? "Anytus and Meletus can kill me, but they can't hurt me." And again, "If this is what God wants, then so be it." But can you prove that someone with worse judgments can win over someone with better ones? You can't. You won't even come close. This is a law of nature and of God: "Let the better always win over the worse." Win in what? In what they are better at. One body can be stronger than another; several people can be stronger than one; the thief can be better at staying awake than I am. That's why I lost my lamp—because the thief was better at staying awake. But he paid a high price for the lamp; for a lamp, he became a thief, for a lamp, he became untrustworthy, for a lamp, he became like an animal. This seemed profitable to him!

But now someone grabs me by my cloak and pulls me into the marketplace, and others shout, "Philosopher, what good are your judgments if you're being dragged off to prison or about to be executed?" What kind of philosophy lesson could I have taken that would prevent me from being dragged off if a stronger person grabs my cloak? Or would stop me from being thrown into prison if ten people push me in? Have I learned nothing else? I've learned that everything that happens outside my control doesn't really matter to me. So, have you gained nothing from this understanding? Why are you looking for your benefit in something other than what you've learned is important?

As I sit in prison, I think to myself, "This person who's shouting at me doesn't understand what's really happening, doesn't follow what's being said, and hasn't taken the time to learn what philosophers teach. Don't let it bother you." "But get out of prison." If you don't need me in prison anymore, I'll leave; if you need me here again, I'll come back. For how long? As long as reason decides I should stay with this body; but when reason says it's time to go, then take the body and go. Just make sure I don't give up my life irrationally, out of cowardice, or for a trivial reason. Because God doesn't want that either—He needs this universe, and He needs people who live in it. But if He signals that it's time to retreat, like He did with Socrates, I must obey Him, just like a soldier obeys his general.

What then? Should I tell everyone this? Why? Isn't it enough for me to believe it myself? For example, when children come to us and clap their hands and say, "Today is the festival of Saturnalia," do we tell them, "This is not really a good thing"? No, we clap our hands with them. So, when you can't change someone's mind, remember that they're like a child, and clap your hands with them. But if you don't want to do that, just stay silent.

A person should remember all this and, when faced with a challenge, realize that this is the time to show whether we've learned anything. A young person leaving school and facing a challenge is like someone who has practiced solving puzzles, and if they're given an easy one, they say, "No, give me a harder one so I can really test myself." Athletes don't want to face opponents who are too easy: "He can't lift me," one might say. "That person over there is stronger." But when the real test comes, do they cry and say, "I wanted to keep practicing"? Practice what? If you don't learn to apply these lessons in real life, what's the point of learning them? I imagine someone sitting here thinking, "I wish I had a challenge like the one this person is facing! I'm tired of sitting around—I want to be like an Olympic champion! When will someone bring me a real test?" That's how you should all be thinking. Even the gladiators in Caesar's arena complain if they don't get a chance to fight, and they beg their trainers to let them fight one-on-one. Will none of you have the same spirit? I wanted to go to Rome just to see what my athlete is doing, how he's practicing for his challenge. "I don't want this kind of challenge," he says. Is it up to you to choose your challenge? You've been given a body, parents, siblings, a country, and a role in it. And now you come to me and say, "Change my challenge"? Don't you have the ability to use what you've been given? You should say, "It's your job to set the challenge, and mine to face it well." No, instead you say, "Don't give me this kind of puzzle, give me another one; don't challenge me in this way, challenge me another way." Soon, the actors in tragedies will start thinking their costumes and masks are who they really are. Everything we have is just a tool for the task. Show me what you've got, so we can see if you're a true actor or just playing a role. If someone took away your costume and mask, and put you on stage without them, would you still be an actor? If you have a voice, you are.

And so it is in life. "Take on a leadership role." I take it, and I show how an educated person behaves. "Give up your status and wear simple clothes." What then? Haven't I learned to use my voice well? "What role are you playing now?" I'm a witness summoned by God. God says, "Go and testify for Me; you are worthy of being My witness. Is there anything outside of your control that is truly good or bad? Do I harm anyone? Have I put anyone's well-being under the control of anyone but themselves?" What kind of witness will you be for God? "I'm struggling, Lord, and suffering; no one cares about me, no one helps me, everyone blames and criticizes me." Is this the testimony you're going to give? Is this how you'll disgrace the honor God gave you, deeming you worthy to be brought forward as a witness for such an important matter?

But the person in power over you declares, "I judge you to be impious and wicked." What has happened to you? "I've been judged impious and wicked." Nothing else? "Nothing." But if he had judged a logical argument and declared, "I judge that the statement, 'If it is day, there is light,' is false," what would happen to the logical argument? Who is being judged here, who has been condemned? The logical argument, or the person who made a mistake in judgment? Who is this person who has the authority to judge you? Does he know what piety or wickedness is? Has he studied it? Has he learned it? Where? Under whom? Yet a musician doesn't care if someone says that a low note is high, nor does a mathematician care if someone says that the lines from the center to the edge of a circle are not equal; but should an educated person care when an ignorant person judges what is holy and unholy, or what is just and unjust?

How unfair it is for educated people to act like this! Is this what you've learned here? Will you leave the petty arguments to those who can't think deeply, so they can sit in a corner and collect their small fees, or complain because no one gives them anything? Won't you instead step forward and use what you've learned? What's missing now is not arguments; the books of the Stoics are full of them. What's missing now? A person who will use them, who will bear witness to these teachings through their actions. This is the role I want you to take, so that we no longer need to use old examples in school but can have an example from our own time. Whose job is it to think about these things? The person who is dedicated to learning; because humans are naturally curious. But it's shameful to think about these things like runaway slaves; instead, sit free from distractions and listen, now to a tragic actor and now to a musician, not like runaway slaves do. For at the very moment when one of them is listening and praising the actor, he glances around, and if someone mentions the word "master," they all panic. It's shameful for philosophers to contemplate the works of nature in this way. What is a "master"? One person is not the master of another person, but life and death, pleasure and pain are their masters. Bring Caesar to me without these things, and you'll see how steadfast I am. But when he comes with them, thundering and lightning, and I'm afraid, what have I done but recognized my master, like the runaway slave? But as long as I have, in a way, a break from these threats, I'm acting like a runaway slave watching a play; I bathe, I drink, I sing, but I do it all in fear and misery. But if I free myself from these masters, those things that make masters terrifying, what trouble do I have left, what master do I still have?

What then? Should I announce this to everyone? No, but I should treat those who are not philosophers with consideration and say, "This person advises me as he thinks best for himself; so I excuse him." Socrates excused the jailer who cried for him when he was about to drink the poison, and said, "How kindly he cried for us!" Did he then say to the jailer, "This is why we sent the women away"? No, he said that to his close friends, those who were ready to hear it; but he treated the jailer with kindness, like a child.

Chapter 30
What We Should Keep in Mind During Tough Times

When you come into the presence of some important person, remember that Another, by Zeus, watches from above what is happening, and you must strive to please Him rather than this person. The One above might ask you, "In your teachings, what did you call exile, imprisonment, chains, death, and dishonor?" You would reply, "I called them 'things that don't really matter.'" "What, then, do you call them now? Have they changed in any way?" "No, they haven't changed." "Have you, then, changed?" "No, I haven't changed." "Tell me then, what are 'things that don't really matter'?" "Those that are independent of our moral choices." "Tell me also what follows." "Things independent of our moral choices are nothing to me." "Tell me also what you thought were 'the good things'?" "A proper moral purpose and a correct use of external impressions." "And what was your goal?" "To follow You."

"Do you say all that even now?" "I say the same things even now." Then enter in, full of confidence and mindful of all this, and you will see what it means to be a young man who has studied what he ought, even when he is in the presence of men who have not studied. As for me, by Zeus, I imagine that you will feel somewhat like this: "Why did we make such great and elaborate preparations for something that amounts to nothing? Was this what authority really is? Was this what all the grand entrances, the chamberlains, the armed guards amounted to? Did I really spend so much time listening to those long discourses for something so insignificant? All this never amounted to anything, but I was preparing for it as though it were something of great importance."

Book II

Chapter 1
That There Is No Conflict Between Confidence and Caution

Some people might find what the philosophers say to be strange, but let's do our best to understand if it's true that "we should do everything with both caution and confidence at the same time." Caution might seem like it's the opposite of confidence, and opposites don't usually go together. But what seems confusing to most people is actually about something different: If we said a person should be both cautious and confident about the same thing, then it would make sense to say that we're mixing things that don't go together. But that's not what's happening here.

Think about it this way: If we've often heard and learned that "the nature of what's good or bad depends on how we use our thoughts and feelings, and that things outside our control are neither good nor bad," then there's nothing strange about what the philosophers say. If they say, "When it comes to things outside our control, we should be confident, but when it comes to things within our control, we should be cautious," it makes sense. If the bad things come from using our moral choices poorly, then we should be cautious about these things. But if things outside our control aren't really good or bad, then we can be confident about them.

So, we can be cautious and confident at the same time, and by Zeus, we can be confident because we're cautious. Because we're careful about the things that are truly bad, we can be confident about the things that aren't.

But sometimes we act like deer that run away from feathers and into a net. They mix up what they should be afraid of and what they should be confident about, and this gets them into trouble. We do the same thing; we're afraid of things that are outside our control, but we're confident about things that actually matter. To be fooled, or to act rashly, or to do something shameful, or to desire something wrong doesn't matter to us as long as we get what we want in things that lie outside our control. But when we face death, exile, hardship, or dishonor, that's when we panic and run away.

As a result, we mix up what's really important and what isn't. We turn our natural confidence into boldness, desperation, recklessness, and shamelessness, while we turn our natural caution and self-respect into fear, cowardice, and anxiety. If a person directed their caution toward moral choices and actions, then they would also gain control over their will to avoid bad things. But if they use their caution on things outside their control, which depend on other people, they'll end up full of fear, instability, and anxiety. It's not death or hardship that's really scary, but the fear of death or hardship. That's why we praise the person who said, "Not death is dreadful, but a shameful death."

So, our confidence should be about death, and our caution should be about the fear of death. But we do the opposite—we run away from death, but we don't care much about how we judge death. Socrates was right when he called these things "bugbears." Just like how masks seem scary to children because they don't understand them, we're also afraid of events because we don't understand them. And it's for the same reason that children are scared of "boogeymen." What is a child? Someone who doesn't know much. What is a child? Someone who needs to learn. When a child knows something, they're no worse than we are. What is death? It's a bugbear. Look at it closely, and you'll see it doesn't bite. The body will be separated from the spirit, either now or later, just as it was separate before. Why are you upset if this happens now? If it doesn't happen now, it will happen later. Why? Because the universe needs it to keep moving forward. It needs things that are happening now, things that will happen, and things that have already happened.

What is hardship? It's a bugbear. Look at it closely, and you'll see what it really is. The body is treated roughly, and then it's treated kindly again. If you can't handle it, the door is open; if you can, then endure it. The door should always be open, and then we won't have any trouble.

So, what's the result of learning these ideas? It's the best and most fitting thing for someone who's truly educated—peace of mind, fearlessness, and freedom. We shouldn't listen to the crowd, who say, "Only the free can be educated," but instead listen to the philosophers, who say, "Only the educated are free." What does that mean? It means that at this time, freedom is nothing but the right to live as we want. "Nothing else." Tell me, then, do you want to live in error? "We do not." Well, no one who lives in error is free. Do you want to live in fear, sorrow, or turmoil? "Of course not." Then, no one who lives in fear, sorrow, or turmoil is free. But whoever gets rid of these things is also free from slavery.

So, how can we still trust those lawmakers who say that only the free should be educated? The philosophers say, "We don't let anyone but the educated be free"; that is, God doesn't allow it. So, when a man turns his slave around before the praetor, has he really done anything? He has done something—he turned his slave around. What else? He has to pay a tax of five percent of the slave's value. But does this make the slave free? Not really. Just like a person who has power over others might not be free if they're still a slave to money, a lover, a child, a tyrant, or even a friend of a tyrant. If they're afraid of any of these things, then they're still a slave.

That's why I keep saying, "Practice these things and be ready—know what you should face with confidence and what you should face with caution." Face with confidence what's outside your control, and with caution what's within your control.

"But haven't I read to you, and don't you know what I'm doing?" What have you been working on? Fancy words! Keep your fancy words! Show me instead how you handle desire and aversion—whether you don't fail to get what you want, or don't fall into what you don't want.

As for your fancy phrases, if you're wise, you'll take them somewhere else and erase them. "But didn't Socrates write?" Yes, and who wrote more than he did? But how did he write? He couldn't always have someone around to test his ideas, so he tested himself and practiced what he preached. That's what a philosopher writes about, not fancy phrases and "said he, said I."

When the time comes, are you going to show off your fancy writing and boast, "Look how I write dialogues"? Don't do that. Instead, boast like this: "Look how I handle my desires and aversions. Bring on death, bring on hardship, bring on imprisonment, bring on dishonor, bring on condemnation, and see how I face them." That's the right way for a young person to show what they've learned. Leave the other things to others—don't talk about them, and if someone praises you for them, don't accept it. Let yourself be known as someone who knows how to handle their desires and aversions. Let others practice lawsuits, problems, and logic puzzles. You practice how to die, how to be chained, how to be tortured, how to be exiled. Do all these things with confidence, trusting in the One who called you to face them and deemed you worthy of this position. When you do, you'll show what a rational mind can do when it faces challenges beyond its control.

And so, the paradox we talked about won't seem impossible or strange anymore—because you'll see that you can be both cautious and confident at the same time: confident in what's outside your control, and cautious in what's within your control.

Chapter 2
On Peace of Mind

Think about what you want to achieve when you go to court and what you want to protect. If you want to maintain your freedom to make moral choices and keep your inner peace, then you have nothing to worry about. If you focus on controlling what is within your power and are satisfied with that, then what else matters? Who can take that away from you? If you want to be self-respecting and honorable, who can stop you? If you don't want to be forced to do something, who can make you desire what you don't want or avoid what you think is right?

But what if the judge does something that seems terrifying? Even then, how can he make you fear what you are facing? If your desires and fears are under your own control, what more do you need? This is your defense, your proof, and your victory.

This is why Socrates, when told to prepare for his trial, said, "Haven't I been preparing for this all my life?" When asked how, he replied, "By focusing on what is within my control." "How did you do that?" he was asked. "I have never done anything wrong, whether in private or public life," Socrates answered.

But if you want to protect external things like your body, money, or reputation, then start preparing right now. Study your judge and opponent carefully. If you need to beg, beg. If you need to cry, cry. If you need to groan, groan. Once you hand over control of your own things to external forces, you become their slave. Don't let yourself be pulled in different directions—decide now whether you want to be free or a slave, educated or uneducated, brave or cowardly. Either endure to the end or give up right away. But don't take many blows only to give up in the end. If that seems shameful, then start thinking right now about where true good and evil lie. Where truth is, that's where caution and confidence should be.

Do you think that if Socrates had cared about protecting external things, he would have said, "Anytus and Meletus can kill me, but they cannot harm me"? Was he so foolish that he didn't see this approach wouldn't lead to that goal, but to something else? Why wouldn't he add something provocative, like my friend Heracleitus, who had a small lawsuit over a piece of land in Rhodes? After he made his case, he added, "But I'm not going to beg you, and I don't care what your decision is. It's you who are on trial, not me." And he ruined his case because of that. What was the point of saying that? Just don't beg, but don't add, "I'm not going to beg," unless it's the right time, like when

Socrates deliberately provoked his judges. If you plan to say something like that, why even bother showing up? Why answer the summons at all? If you want to be crucified, just wait—the cross will come. But if reason tells you to answer the summons and do your best to persuade, then do that, but always keep true to your character.

Looking at it this way, it's silly to say, "Give me advice." What advice can I give you? Instead, you should say, "Help my mind to adapt to whatever happens." Asking for advice is like an uneducated person saying, "Tell me what to write when someone tells me what to write." If I say, "Write Dio," and then the teacher says, "No, write Theo," what will he write? But if you've practiced writing, you'll be able to write whatever is dictated to you. If you haven't practiced, what advice can I give you now? If circumstances change, what will you say or do?

So remember this general rule, and you won't be at a loss for advice. But if you're obsessed with external things, you'll be tossed around by the will of your master. And who is your master? The person who has power over anything you care about or wish to avoid.

Chapter 3
For Those Who Refer Others to Philosophers

Diogenes gave an excellent answer to a man who asked him for a letter of recommendation. He said, "That you are a man, he will know at a glance. But whether you are a good man or a bad one, he will only discover if he has the skill to tell the difference between good and bad. And if he doesn't have that skill, he won't discover the truth, even if I write him a thousand letters."

It's like if a silver coin asked to be recommended to someone to be tested. If the person is an expert at testing silver, the coin will prove itself. We should have something similar in our daily lives so that I can say, just like the silver tester does, "Bring me any coin, and I will tell you if it's real."

Now, when it comes to logical arguments, I say, "Bring me any argument, and I will tell you whether it can be analyzed correctly or not." How so? Because I know how to analyze arguments myself. I have the skill needed to evaluate whether someone is handling arguments properly.

But what do I do in everyday life? Sometimes I call something good, and sometimes I call it bad. What is the reason? The opposite of what happens with arguments—in this case, it's because of ignorance and inexperience.

Chapter 4
To the Man Who Committed Adultery

Epictetus was talking about how humans are naturally meant to be loyal and trustworthy. He said that if someone destroys this trust, they are destroying what makes them truly human. At that moment, a man walked in who was known as a scholar, but who had also once been caught committing adultery in the city. Epictetus continued, saying that if we give up on being loyal, which is something we're naturally meant to be, and start making plans to be with someone else's wife, what are we really doing? We are ruining and destroying not just ourselves, but the very idea of trust, self-respect, and respect for the gods. Is that all? No, we are also destroying friendships, our communities, and the state itself.

So, what kind of person does this make us? How am I supposed to treat you now? As a neighbor, a friend? What kind of friend? As a fellow citizen? How can I trust you? If you were a broken pot that couldn't be used for anything, we would throw you out on the trash heap, and even there, no one would pick you up. But if, as a person, you can't act like a decent human being, what are we supposed to do with you? If you can't even be a friend, can you at least be a good servant? And who is going to trust you to do that? Should we just throw you out on the trash heap like a useless piece of garbage? And yet, you still say, "But I'm a scholar!" No, you are a bad person, and you are useless. It's like if wasps complained that no one cares about them, when everyone actually runs away from them and, if they can, they swat them down. You sting everyone you touch, causing trouble and pain. What do you want us to do with you? There is no place for you.

You might say, "But aren't women naturally meant to be shared?" I agree. And a little pig at a feast is also meant to be shared by the guests. But after the portions have been handed out, if you really want to, go ahead and grab someone else's portion, steal it secretly, or slip your hand in and take some for yourself. If you can't tear off a piece of the meat, at least get your fingers greasy and lick them. You would be a great companion at a feast, right? A dinner guest worthy of Socrates! Come on now, isn't the theater also shared by all the citizens? So, if people are sitting there, go ahead and throw one of them out of their seat if you want.

In the same way, women are also shared by nature. But when the law, like a host at a banquet, has given them out, aren't you willing to look for your own share instead of stealing from someone else? "But I'm a scholar and I understand what Archedemus said." Fine, then, understand what Archedemus said and go ahead and be an adulterer, a liar, a wolf, or a monkey instead of a decent person. What is stopping you?

Chapter 5
How Living Carefully Aligns with Having a Noble Spirit

Things themselves are neutral, but how we use them is not neutral. So how can someone stay strong and peaceful while also being careful and neither reckless nor negligent? It's like playing a game with dice. The dice themselves are neutral, and we can't control how they land. But using what happens wisely and carefully, that's our job. In the same way, the main job in life is this: to look at situations and compare them, and say to yourself, "What happens outside of me isn't under my control; my choices are under my control. So where do I look for good and bad? Inside myself, in what is truly mine." But when it comes to what belongs to someone else, never call it "good" or "bad" or "a benefit" or "a harm."

Does that mean we should be careless with things outside our control? Not at all. Because being careless with them would harm our moral character, which is unnatural. We should use these things carefully because how we use them is important, but we should do so with steadiness and peace of mind, knowing that the things themselves are neutral. In what really matters—our choices—no one can stop or force us. The things that can be stopped or forced are not truly good or bad, but how we use them can be good or bad, and that is under our control. It is hard to balance carefulness with material things and calmness in the face of them, but it's not impossible. Otherwise, happiness would be impossible.

We should act like we are on a voyage. What can I control? I can choose the captain, the crew, the day, and the moment to sail. Then, a storm comes. What can I do then? My job is done. Now it's the captain's job. But what if the ship sinks? Then what do I do? What I can do—I drown without fear, without screaming or blaming the gods, but knowing that everything born must die. I'm not eternal; I'm a human, just a part of the whole, like an hour in a day. I must come like the hour and pass like the hour. So what difference does it make if I pass by drowning or by illness? I must pass away somehow.

This is like how skilled ball players play. They don't care whether the ball is good or bad; they care about how they throw and catch it. Skill and grace are what matter, not the ball itself. But if we catch or throw the ball with fear or panic, where's the fun? How can we stay calm or see what's coming next in the game? But one player might say, "Throw!" Another might say, "Don't throw!" And another, "Don't throw it up!" That would be a fight, not a game.

Socrates knew how to play ball in life. How? He knew how to handle himself in court. He said, "Tell me, Anytus, what do you mean when you say I don't believe in God? Who do you think the daemons are? Aren't they either the offspring of gods or a mix of gods and humans?" When Anytus agreed, Socrates said, "Who would believe in mules but not believe in horses?" In speaking like this, he was playing the game well. At that moment, his "ball" was imprisonment, exile, drinking poison, leaving his wife and making his children orphans. These were the things he was dealing with, but he played the game well.

We should also act like this, focusing on playing the game well, but being indifferent to the actual "ball" because it's just a ball. We should try to do well with whatever material we're given, but not let it define us. Like a weaver works with whatever wool he's given, another might give you food, money, and even your body, and can take them away too. You should take what you're given and do your best with it. Then, if you come through it without harm, others might congratulate you, but the one who truly understands will praise you for how you handled yourself, not just that you got out unharmed. But if you escaped by doing something dishonorable, they will feel the opposite.

So, how can we say that some external things are natural and others are not? It's like thinking that the foot is separate from the body. If you think of the foot alone, it's natural for it to stay clean. But if you think of it as part of the body, it's natural for it to step in mud, get scratched, and even sometimes be cut off to save the whole body. Otherwise, it's not really a foot.

We should think the same about ourselves. What are you? A person. If you think of yourself as separate, it's natural to want to live a long life, be rich, and stay healthy. But if you think of yourself as part of a whole, it's natural to sometimes be sick, take risks, be in need, and even die before your time. Why are you upset? Don't you know that if the foot were separate, it wouldn't be a foot anymore? And if you are separate, you're not really a person anymore. What is a person? A part of society; first, of the society of gods and people, and then of the smaller societies that are like copies of the whole universe.

"Do I have to go on trial now?" Well, would you have someone else get sick now, or someone else take a risk, or someone else die, or someone else be judged? In a world like ours, with these bodies and these fellow humans, these things are bound to happen, some to one person, some to another. It's your job to step up and do your part, to handle things as they should be handled. Then if the judge says, "You're guilty," you can say, "I hope things go well for you. I've done my part; now you should see if you've done yours." Remember, the judge takes a risk too.

Chapter 6
Understanding What 'Indifferent' Things Are

A hypothetical statement is neutral: the judgment you make about it is not neutral; it is either knowledge, an opinion, or a mistake. In the same way, life itself is neutral, but how you live it is not. So when someone tells you that certain things in life are neutral, don't become careless. And when someone urges you to be cautious, don't become obsessed with material things. It's important to know your own abilities and limits so that in areas where you're not prepared, you can stay calm and not get upset if others do better than you. For example, in logical arguments, you might be better than others, and if they feel bad about it, you can remind them, "I've learned this, and you haven't." Similarly, in areas where practice is needed, don't seek things that require experience you don't have; let those with practice take the lead, and stay strong-minded.

When you go to greet someone, how should you do it? Not in a lowly way. If you're shut out because you didn't know how to push your way in through a window, and you find the door closed, you'll either leave or climb through the window. But still, speak to him. How? Not in a lowly way. But what if you don't get what you want? Was that your responsibility or his? Why do you claim something that belongs to someone else? Always remember what belongs to you and what belongs to others, and you won't be disturbed. Chrysippus wisely said,

"As long as the future is uncertain, I always stick to what is most likely to preserve what is natural." For God has given me the ability to make choices. But if I knew it was my fate to get sick, I would move toward it; for if a foot had a mind, it would willingly step into the mud. Why are ears of corn grown? Is it not so they can dry out? And don't they dry out so they can be harvested? They are not separate from the cycle of nature. If they had awareness, should they wish never to be harvested? But it would be a curse for ears of corn to never be harvested. So we should understand that it is also a curse for people to never die, just like it would be to never ripen or be harvested. But since we must be harvested, and we know we will be, we get upset about it. This happens because we don't know what we are or haven't studied what it means to be human, the way horse experts know what it means to be a horse. But Chrysantas, when he was about to strike an enemy, stopped when he heard the trumpet signal to retreat. He thought it was better to follow the general's orders than his own desires. But we don't choose to obey when necessity calls, and instead, we cry and complain about our situation, calling them "circumstances." What kind of circumstances? If you call everything around you circumstances, then all things are circumstances. But if you only call hardships by this name, what hardship is there in the natural process of dying? What kills you might be a sword, a wheel, the sea, a tile, or a tyrant. Why do you care how you go to the underworld? All ways are equal. But if you want the truth, the way the tyrant sends you is quicker. A tyrant never took six months to kill a man, but a fever often takes a year. These things are just sounds and the noise of meaningless words.

"I'm in danger of losing my life because of Caesar." And am I not in danger living in Nicopolis, where there are so many earthquakes? And when you cross the Adriatic Sea, aren't you risking your life? "But I'm also in danger of my reputation." Your own? How? Who can force you to hold an opinion you don't want? But are you worried about someone else's opinion? And what danger do you face if others have false opinions? "But I'm in danger of being exiled." What does it mean to be exiled? To be somewhere other than Rome? "Yes, but what if I'm sent to Gyara?" If you like it, you'll go; if not, you can go somewhere else, just like the one who sent you there will also go, whether he wants to or not. Why then do you make such a big deal out of going to Rome? It's not worth all this trouble for a young person to say, "It wasn't worth it to have listened so much, written so much, and spent so much time with an old man who isn't worth much." Just remember to distinguish between what belongs to you and what doesn't, and never claim what belongs to others. A court and a prison are both places, one high and the other low, but you can keep your will steady if you choose to, no matter where you are. We will be like Socrates when we can write hymns in prison. But as we are now, could we endure someone in prison asking, "Would you like me to read hymns to you?" "Why are you bothering me? Don't you know the suffering I'm going through? How can I listen to hymns in such a situation?" What situation? "I'm going to die." And will other people live forever?

Chapter 7
How We Should Approach and Use Divination

Because of an unreasonable belief in divination, many of us neglect our duties. What more can a fortune teller predict than death, danger, or illness, or things like that? If I must face danger for a friend or if it is my duty to die for him, why do I need a fortune teller? Don't I already have within me a sense that tells me what is good and what is bad, and what the signs of both are? So why do I need to look at animal guts or the flight of birds? And why do I listen when someone says, "This is for your own good"? Does he know what is good for me? Does he know what is truly good? And just because he knows how to read animal organs, does that mean he understands the difference between good and evil? If he knows that, then he must also know what is beautiful and ugly, what is just and unjust. Tell me, what exactly is this sign you're seeing for me? Is it life or death, poverty or wealth? But whether these things are good for me or not, I won't ask you. Why don't you give advice on grammar instead? Why do you give advice on matters we all argue about and don't fully understand? The woman who planned to send a month's worth of supplies to Gratilla while she was in exile gave a good answer when someone said that Domitian would take what she sent. She replied, "I'd rather have Domitian take everything than not send it at all."

So what makes us keep going to fortune tellers? It's fear, the fear of what will happen. This is why we flatter them. "Will I inherit my father's property?" "Let's see; let's sacrifice to find out." Yes, whatever the gods decide. When the fortune teller says, "You will inherit it," we thank him as if he gave it to us. This is why they take advantage of us.

So what should we do? We should approach divination without desire or fear, just like a traveler asks a local which of two roads leads to his destination. He doesn't prefer one road over the other; he just wants the road that will get him where he needs to go. In the same way, we should look to God as our guide, like we use our eyes—not asking them to show us what we want to see, but accepting whatever they show us. But now, we nervously grab the hand of the fortune teller, ask God for help, and beg the fortune teller, saying, "Please, master, let me get through this safely." Fool, would you want anything other than what's best? Is there anything better than what God wants? Why are you trying to corrupt your own judge and mislead your advisor?

Chapter 8
Understanding the Nature of Goodness

God is good. But good is also beneficial. It makes sense then that where God's nature is, there also is the nature of good. So what is the nature of God? Is it flesh? No. Is it land or wealth? No. Fame? No. Is it intelligence, knowledge, and reason? Yes. So that is where the nature of good is—right here in reason. You wouldn't look for it in a plant, would you? No. Would you look for it in an animal? No. If you're looking for it in a rational being, then why are you still looking anywhere other than in what makes rational beings better than irrational ones? Plants don't even have the ability to understand what they see, and that's why you wouldn't call them good. So the good must involve understanding what we see. But is that all it takes? If you say that's enough, then you would have to say that animals can be good or bad too. But you don't, and you're right not to. Even if animals can understand what they see, they don't know how to use that understanding. And this makes sense because they exist to serve others and have no authority over anything. The donkey doesn't exist to be better than others. No, but we needed an animal strong enough to carry loads, so it needed to be able to walk. For that, it needed to understand what it saw. But that's where it stopped. If the donkey could also understand how to use what it saw, then it wouldn't be serving us anymore. It would be equal to us.

So won't you look for the nature of good in rational beings? Because if it's not there, you won't find it anywhere else, not in a plant or an animal. "But aren't plants and animals also made by God?" Yes, they are, but they aren't greater things or parts of the gods. But you are a greater thing; you are a piece of God himself. Why don't you know your noble origin? Why don't you remember where you came from? When you eat, do you not remember who you are and what you are feeding? When you are with a woman, do you not remember who you are? When you are talking, exercising, or just being social, do you not realize that you are nourishing a god within you? Fool, you carry a god with you, and you don't even know it. Do you think I'm talking about a god made of silver or gold, something outside of you? No, you carry him within you. But you pollute him with your dirty thoughts and actions. If you had a statue of God, you would never dare to do the things you do. But when God himself is present within you, watching and listening to everything you do, you're not ashamed of your actions or thoughts. You don't even know your own nature, and you provoke God's anger.

So why do we worry when we send a young man out into the world, afraid that he will act improperly, eat improperly, or behave badly with women? Are we worried that his ragged clothes will humiliate him, or that fancy clothes will make him proud? If he acts this way, he doesn't know his own god. He doesn't know with whom he is going out into the world. Can we stand it when he says, "I wish I had God with me"? Don't you already have God with you? Why are you looking for another when he's already with you? Or do you think God would tell you anything different? If you were a statue made by a famous artist, like Athena or Zeus, you would think about both yourself and the artist. And if you had any sense, you would try to do nothing that would shame the artist or yourself, and you'd try to appear in a way that honors the artist's work. But now, since Zeus made you, do you not care how you appear? Is the artist who made a statue the same as the one who made you? Is the statue's craftsmanship like your own? A statue is just marble, bronze, gold, or ivory, and once it's made, it stays the same forever. But God's works, like you, can move, breathe, and think. You can use your senses and understand what you see. Being made by such a creator, how could you dishonor him?

Not only did God make you, but he also trusted you to take care of yourself. He said, "There is no one else more suitable to watch over you than you." So he entrusted you to yourself, to keep yourself modest, faithful, brave, and free from fear or distress. And yet, you fail to do this. Some may ask, "Where did this person get such arrogance and pride?" I am not yet as serious as a philosopher should be because I'm still not fully confident in what I've learned. I'm still afraid of my own weaknesses. But once I gain confidence, you will see in me the face and the posture of a true philosopher. Then I will show you the perfected and polished statue. What do you expect? A proud and arrogant face? Does the Zeus in Olympia lift his eyebrows in pride? No, his expression is calm, like one ready to say, "My word is final and will not change." This is how I will show myself to you—faithful, modest, noble, and calm. What, do you expect me to be immortal too, never to grow old or get sick? No, but I will face death and illness in a way that befits a god. This is the power I have. This I can do. The rest I do not possess, nor can I do. But I will show you the strength of a philosopher. What strength is that? It is having desires that are never frustrated, avoiding things that are within your control, having the right goals, working hard, and being wise in what you agree to. These are what you will see.

Chapter 9
When We Fail to Live as We Should, We Turn to Philosophy

It is not an easy thing to do just one thing: to live up to what it means to be a man. So, what is a man? A man is a rational being who is also mortal. What separates us from wild animals? It's our ability to reason. And what separates us from other creatures, like sheep? It's the same thing. So, make sure you don't act like a wild animal, because if you do, you lose what it means to be a man. Make sure you don't act like a sheep, because if you do, you also lose what it means to be a man. What do we do when we act like sheep? When we eat too much, act lewdly, or do things without thinking, we lower ourselves to the level of sheep. What do we lose? Our ability to reason. When we act violently, argue all the time, or behave with anger, we lower ourselves to the level of wild animals. So, some of us become like big wild animals, and others like small, bad-tempered ones. This is why some people say, "I'd rather be eaten by a lion." But in all these ways, we destroy what it means to act like a man. When is a complex statement correct? When it fulfills the promise of its nature. The same goes for a flute, a lyre, a horse, or a dog—they are preserved when they do what they are meant to do. So, is it any wonder that a person is also preserved or lost in the same way? Each person is improved and preserved by doing what they are meant to do: a carpenter by doing carpentry, a grammarian by doing grammar. But if a man gets used to writing badly, his skill will naturally be corrupted and destroyed. In the same way, modest actions keep a person modest, and immodest actions destroy that modesty. Honest actions keep a person honest, and dishonest actions destroy honesty. On the other hand, bad actions strengthen bad habits: shamelessness makes a person more shameless, dishonesty makes a person more dishonest, abusive words make a person more abusive, and greed makes a person more greedy.

This is why philosophers tell us not to be satisfied with just learning but also to add practice and study. We've spent a long time doing the wrong things, and we've practiced opinions that are contrary to the truth. If we don't also practice the right opinions, we will be nothing more than people who repeat the ideas of others. Who among us can't talk about good and bad things according to the rules of philosophy? We can say that some things are good, some are bad, and some are neutral. Good things are virtues and the things that come from virtues. Bad things are the opposite, and neutral things are wealth, health, and reputation. But what happens if, in the middle of this discussion, there's a loud noise or someone laughs at us? We get disturbed. Philosopher, where are those ideas you were just talking about? Where did they come from? Only from your lips. Why do you misuse the wisdom others have provided? Why do you treat serious matters like a game of dice? It's one thing to store up bread and wine in a pantry, and another thing to eat them. What you eat gets digested, turns into muscle, flesh, bones, blood, healthy skin, and healthy breath. Whatever is stored up can be taken out and shown whenever you want, but it doesn't benefit you unless it's used. What's the difference between explaining these doctrines and explaining the ideas of others with different views? Sit down and explain Epicurus's ideas according to the rules of philosophy, and maybe you'll explain them better than Epicurus himself. Why then do you call yourself a Stoic? Why do you deceive people? Why do you act like a Jew when you're a Greek? Don't you see why someone is called a Jew, a Syrian, or an Egyptian? And when we see a person who tries to act in two different ways, we say, "This person isn't a Jew, but he's acting like one." But when someone fully embraces Jewish teachings and lives by them, then he is both in name and in fact a Jew. In the same way, we too, when we are not true to ourselves, are Jews in name but not in fact. Our actions don't match our words; we're far from practicing what we say and what we claim to know. So, when we can't even live up to what it means to be a man, we add the burden of claiming to be a philosopher. This is like a man who can't lift ten pounds trying to lift the stone that Ajax lifted.

Chapter 10
How to Discover a Man's Duties Based on the Titles He Holds

First, think about who you are. You are a human being, and as a human, nothing is more important than your ability to make choices. Everything else is under your control, and your ability to choose is free and not controlled by anyone else. Now, think about how your ability to reason separates you from other beings. It separates you from wild animals and from domesticated animals like sheep. Additionally, you are a citizen of the world, a part of it—not a servant, but one of the leading parts because you have the ability to understand how the world works and see the connections between things. So, what does it mean to be a good citizen? It means that you don't just think about what is good for you personally, but you consider the whole community, acting as a hand or foot would if they had the ability to reason. They would never move or desire anything without thinking about how it affects the whole body. Philosophers say that if a good person knew what the future held, they would even accept their own sickness, death, or injury because they understand that these things happen according to the larger plan of the universe, and that the whole is more important than the part, and the community is more important than the individual. But since we don't know the future, our duty is to stick to the things that are naturally better choices, because we were made for this purpose.

Next, remember that you are a son. What does it mean to be a son? It means understanding that everything a son has belongs to the father. It means obeying him in all things, never blaming him to others, never saying or doing anything that would harm him, and always yielding to him and helping him as much as you can. After this, know that you are also a brother, and as a brother, you should make concessions, be easily persuaded, speak well of your brother, never argue over things that are outside of your control, and readily give them up so you can gain more of the things that are within your control. Think about how much better it is to gain a good attitude rather than a piece of lettuce or a seat. How much greater is that advantage!

Then, if you are a senator, remember that you are a senator. If you are a young person, remember that you are young. If you are old, remember that you are old. Each of these roles comes with specific duties. But if you go and blame your brother, I would say to you: You have forgotten who you are and what your role is. If you were a blacksmith and misused a hammer, you would have forgotten what it means to be a blacksmith. And if you forget what it means to be a brother and instead become an enemy, would that not mean you've changed into something else? And if instead of being a human, who is a social and tame animal, you become a harmful wild animal, treacherous and biting, have you not lost something important? But do you think the only loss that matters is losing money? Do you think no other loss harms a person? If you lost the ability to read or play music, would you consider that a loss? And if you lose modesty, self-control, and gentleness, do you think that's nothing? The first losses I mentioned are caused by things outside of your control, but the second set of losses happen because of our own choices. And while it's not shameful to lose the first set, it is shameful and unfortunate to lose the second set.

What does someone lose if they become immoral? They lose their humanity. What does someone lose if they cause someone else to become immoral? They lose many other things, and they also lose their humanity. What does someone lose if they commit adultery? They lose their modesty, self-control, decency, and their sense of being a good citizen and neighbor. What does someone lose if they become angry? They lose something else. What does a coward lose? Something different. No one becomes bad without suffering some loss or damage.

If you only look for damage in the loss of money, then you would say that none of these people have been harmed. In fact, they might even gain something if they acquire some money by their actions. But if you think this way, then even someone who loses their nose wouldn't be harmed in your eyes. "But," you say, "they are physically mutilated." Well, what about someone who only loses their sense of smell? Don't they lose anything? Is there no part of the soul that benefits the one who has it and harms the one who loses it? "Tell me what you mean by that." Don't we have a natural sense of modesty? "Yes, we do." So, if someone loses this, don't they suffer damage? Don't they lose something that belongs to them? Don't we also have a natural sense of loyalty, affection, and a desire to help others? The person who allows themselves to be harmed in these ways, can they really be free from harm and injury?

"What then? Should I not hurt the person who has hurt me?" First, think about what harm really is, and remember what you've learned from philosophers. If good comes from your choices and actions, and evil also comes from your choices and actions, then think about what you're really saying: "Since this person has hurt themselves by doing something unjust to me, should I hurt myself by doing something unjust to them?" Why don't we think this way? But when there is some harm to our body or possessions, we consider it harm; and when the same thing happens to our ability to choose and act, we think it's no big deal. Someone who has been deceived or who has done something unjust doesn't suffer in their head, their eye, or their hip, and they don't lose their property, so we think it doesn't matter. But whether we have a will that is modest and loyal or shameless and disloyal, we don't care much about it, except when we're in school and talking about philosophy. That's why our progress is limited to just a few words, and beyond that, it doesn't exist at all.

Chapter 11
What The Beginning of Philosophy Is

The beginning of philosophy, for someone who starts it the right way, is realizing how weak and unprepared we are in understanding important things. When we are born, we don't naturally know what a right-angled triangle is, or what a quarter tone or a half tone in music is. We learn these things through teaching and practice. Because of this, people who don't know these things are aware that they don't know them. But when it comes to concepts like good and bad, beautiful and ugly, right and wrong, happiness and misfortune, proper and improper behavior, and what we should or shouldn't do, who ever came into the world without some idea of them? That's why we all use these words and try to match them to different situations, saying things like: "He did well," "He didn't do well," "He did what he should," "He didn't do what he should," "He was lucky," "He was unlucky," "He is just," "He is unjust." Who doesn't use these terms? Who among us waits to learn them like we wait to learn about shapes or sounds? The reason for this is that we come into the world already knowing some things naturally, and we add our own confidence to them. A person might say, "Why shouldn't I know what is beautiful and what is ugly? Don't I already have a sense of it?" Yes, you do. "Don't I apply it to specific things?" Yes, you do. "Don't I apply it correctly?" That's the big question, and that's where confidence comes in. People start with what everyone agrees on, but then they move to what is debated by applying their ideas incorrectly. If they had the power to apply these ideas correctly, what would stop them from being perfect? But now, since you think you're applying these ideas correctly, tell me why you think that. "Because I believe it's right." But another person doesn't see it the same way, and they believe they're right too. Or don't they? "They do believe so." Is it possible for both of you to be right when you have opposite views? "No, it's not possible." So, can you show us anything better than just thinking you're right? Does a madman do anything other than what seems right to him? Is his feeling that something is right enough for him? "No, it's not enough." Then, look for something beyond just what seems right. "What is that?"

This is the beginning of philosophy: realizing that people disagree with each other, wondering why they disagree, rejecting and doubting what only seems to be true, investigating whether what seems true really is true, and finding some standard, like how we use a scale to weigh things or a ruler to check if something is straight. This is the beginning of philosophy. Should we say that everything that seems right to everyone really is right? How can that be when people's opinions contradict each other? So, not everything that seems right is right, but only what seems right to us? Why should our views be better than those of the Syrians or the Egyptians, or better than mine or any other person's? They aren't better. So, what seems right to everyone isn't enough to decide what really is right. In the case of weights or measurements, we don't trust just what we see; we use a standard. In this case, is there no standard higher than what seems right? How could it be that the most important things in life have no clear sign or standard to guide us? There must be a standard. So why don't we look for that standard, find it, and then use it consistently, not even moving a finger without it? I believe this is what cures the madness of those who rely only on what seems right and misuse it. When we find that standard, we can then use it to judge things accurately based on principles that are clear and well-understood.

What are we trying to understand? For example, pleasure. Subject it to the standard, weigh it on the scale. Should the good be something we can trust and rely on? Yes. Should it be something secure? Yes, it should. Is pleasure something secure? No. Then take it off the scale and throw it far away from the category of good things. But if you can't see this clearly, and one scale isn't enough for you, use another. Is it right to be proud of what is good? Yes. Is it right to be proud of present pleasure? Be careful not to say it is. But if you do, then I won't even consider you worthy of using the scale. This is how things are tested and weighed when we have the right standards. And to philosophize is to examine and confirm these standards. Then, using them once we know them is the mark of a wise and good person.

Chapter 12
On the Art of Discussion

What a person needs to learn in order to be able to engage in the art of disputation has been clearly explained by our philosophers (the Stoics); but when it comes to actually using these skills, we lack practice. If you give any one of us an uneducated person to discuss with, we often don't know how to handle the situation. When the uneducated person starts to say things that don't make sense, we don't know how to guide the conversation. Instead, we either insult or make fun of the person, saying, "He's uneducated; it's impossible to do anything with him." But a good guide, when he finds someone lost, helps him find the right path. He doesn't mock or scold him and then leave him behind. You should also try to show the uneducated person the truth, and you will see that he follows it. But if you can't show him the truth, don't mock him—recognize your own shortcomings instead.

How did Socrates handle this? He would make his opponent in a debate agree with him and didn't need any other witnesses. That's why he could say, "I don't care for other witnesses; I'm always satisfied with the evidence from my opponent, and I don't need the opinions of others—just the opinion of the person I'm debating with." Socrates made the conclusions from natural ideas so clear that everyone could see the contradiction if there was one, and they would back away from it. For example, he would ask, "Does an envious person feel joy?" "No, he feels pain," they would answer. Then he would ask, "Is envy pain over bad things?" The person would respond, "What envy is there of bad things?" So, Socrates made the person admit that envy is pain over good things. Then, he would ask, "Would anyone envy people who mean nothing to them?" "No, they wouldn't." Once the person clearly understood what envy was, Socrates would move on without asking for a definition of envy. If the person had defined envy, Socrates wouldn't have said, "You've defined it badly," or, "The words of your definition don't match what envy is." These are technical terms that are hard for uneducated people to understand, and philosophers can't just abandon these terms. But we should be able to make an uneducated person, who follows their natural instincts, either agree with or reject something without needing to use these difficult terms. Knowing our own limitations, we often avoid these kinds of discussions; at least those of us who are careful do. But most people, especially the rash ones, jump into these debates, confusing themselves and others. In the end, they walk away after insulting their opponents and getting insulted themselves.

Socrates, however, had a special ability: he never got angry in a debate, never said anything insulting, and never used abusive language. Instead, he would patiently deal with abusive people and find a way to end the argument. If you want to understand the great power he had in this way, read Xenophon's Symposium, and you'll see how many arguments he was able to resolve. This is why poets often praise this ability:

"Quickly with skill he settles great disputes." – Hesiod

However, in our current time, especially in Rome, it's not safe to do this. If you try, you can't do it secretly; you'll have to approach someone of high rank or wealth and ask him questions like, "Can you tell me to whom you've entrusted your horses?" "Of course, I can." "Have you entrusted them to just anyone, or to someone who knows about horses?" "Certainly not to just anyone." "What about your gold or silver, or your clothes?" "I'm careful about those too." "And what about your body? Have you entrusted its care to anyone?" "Yes, I have." "To someone with experience, like a doctor or a trainer?" "Without a doubt." "Are these the best things you own, or do you have something even more valuable?" "What do you mean?" "I mean the thing that uses these other things and judges each of them." "You mean the soul?" "Yes, that's exactly what I mean." "I agree; the soul is much more valuable than anything else I have." "Then can you show us how you've taken care of your soul? It's not likely that someone as wise and respected as you would allow the most valuable thing you possess to be neglected or ruined." "Certainly not." "But have you taken care of your soul yourself, or have you learned from someone else how to do it, or have you figured it out on your own?"

This is where it gets risky, because the person might say, "What business is this of yours? Who are you?" And if you keep pressing, he might even raise his hands and hit you. I used to admire this way of teaching until I found myself in similar dangerous situations.

☐

Chapter 13
On Anxiety (Solicitude)

When I see someone anxious, I ask: What does this person want? If he didn't want something that's not in his control, how could he be anxious? For example, when a musician is playing alone, he doesn't feel anxious. But when he performs in front of an audience, he becomes anxious, even if he has a good voice and plays the instrument well. Why? Because he doesn't just want to play well; he also wants to get applause, which is something not in his control. So, where he has skill, he is confident. If you bring in someone who knows nothing about music, the musician doesn't worry about him. But in situations where a person lacks knowledge or practice, that's where anxiety appears. What kind of situation is this? It's when someone doesn't understand what a crowd is or what it means to receive their praise. The musician may know how to play the highest and lowest notes, but he doesn't know what public praise means or what power it has in life. Because of this, he's bound to tremble and turn pale. So, when I see someone afraid, I don't say he's not a musician, but I do say other things, and not just one thing, but many. First of all, I say he's a stranger who doesn't know where he is. Even though he's been here a long time, he doesn't know the laws of the place, the customs, or what is allowed and what isn't. He hasn't even hired a lawyer to explain the rules to him.

A person wouldn't write a will without knowing how it should be written, or without hiring someone who knows. Nor would he carelessly sign a contract or write a security note. But he uses his desires without getting advice, and he acts, moves, and makes decisions without any guidance. "What do you mean without advice?" He doesn't realize that he's wanting things he's not allowed to have, and he doesn't want what he's forced to have. He doesn't know what's truly his and what belongs to someone else. But if he did know, he would never be stopped or hindered, and he wouldn't be anxious. "How is that possible?" Is anyone afraid of things that aren't bad? No. Is anyone afraid of bad things that are still within his control so that they might not happen? No, certainly not. If the things that are beyond our control are neither good nor bad, and all the things that are within our control are up to us, and no one can take them from us or give them to us unless we allow it, then where is the room for anxiety?

But we are anxious about our bodies, our little bit of property, and what Caesar might decide, but we're not anxious about our internal thoughts. Are we worried about not forming false opinions? No, because that's in our control. Are we worried about not acting against nature? No, not even that. So, when you see someone turn pale, just like a doctor would say by looking at the complexion, "This person's spleen is not right, or this person's liver is off," you should say, "This person's desires and fears are not in order. He's not on the right path; he's feverish." Nothing else makes a person change color, tremble, chatter his teeth, or make his knees weak and shift from foot to foot.

That's why when Zeno was going to meet Antigonus, he wasn't anxious. Antigonus had no power over the things that Zeno cared about, and Zeno didn't care about the things that were in Antigonus's power. But Antigonus was anxious when he was going to meet Zeno because he wanted to please Zeno. But this was something outside his control. Zeno didn't want to please Antigonus, because no one who is skilled in any art cares about pleasing someone who has no skill in that area.

Should I try to please you? Why? Do you know the standard by which one person judges another? Have you made an effort to understand what makes a person good or bad, and how a person becomes one or the other? Then why aren't you good yourself? "How," he asks, "am I not good?" Because no good person laments, groans, or cries. No good person turns pale and trembles or worries about how someone will receive him or listen to him. Slave, it will be however it pleases the other person. Why do you worry about what belongs to others? Is it the other person's fault if he receives what you say poorly? "Certainly." And can one person's fault be in someone else? "No." Then why are you anxious about something that belongs to someone else? "Your question makes sense, but I'm worried about how I'll talk to him." Can't you talk to him however you choose? "But I'm afraid I might get flustered." If you were going to write the name "Dion," would you be afraid of getting flustered? "Of course not." Why? Is it because you've practiced writing the name? "Yes, that's why." Well, if you were going to read the name, wouldn't you feel the same way? Why? Because every skill brings with it a certain level of confidence in what belongs to that skill.

Have you not practiced speaking? What else did you learn in school? Syllogisms and tricky arguments? For what purpose? Wasn't it to learn how to speak well? And isn't speaking well the same as speaking at the right time, carefully, intelligently, without making mistakes, and with confidence? "Yes." So, when you're riding a horse and go out into an open field, do you worry about being matched against someone on foot? Do you worry about something you've practiced and the other person hasn't? "Yes, but that person I'm going to talk to has the power to kill me." Then tell the truth, unfortunate man, and don't brag or claim to be a philosopher. Don't refuse to acknowledge those who have power over you. As long as you are focused on your body, follow anyone who is stronger than you. Socrates practiced speaking, and he spoke the way he did to tyrants, to judges, and even in prison. Diogenes practiced speaking, and he spoke the way he did to Alexander, to pirates, and to the person who bought him. These men were confident in the things they practiced. But you should go back to your own affairs and stay out of things. Go sit in a corner, work on your arguments, and propose them to someone else. You don't have what it takes to lead a state.

Chapter 14
On Naso

When a certain Roman entered with his son and listened to someone reading, Epictetus said: "This is the method of instruction," and then he stopped. When the Roman asked him to continue, Epictetus said: "Every art, when it is being taught, causes effort for those who are not familiar with it and who are unskilled. The things that come from the arts immediately show their use for the purpose they were made, and most of them contain something attractive and pleasing. For example, watching a shoemaker learn is not a pleasant thing, but the shoes he makes are useful and also nice to look at. The process of a blacksmith learning is very unpleasant to someone who doesn't understand the art, but the work shows the use of the skill. You see this even more in music; if you watch someone learning, the process seems very unpleasant, yet the results of music are pleasing and enjoyable even to those who know nothing about it."

In the same way, we think the work of a philosopher is something similar: he must align his desires with what is happening so that nothing that happens goes against what he wants, and nothing that doesn't happen is something he wishes for. From this alignment comes the ability to pass through life without failing in desires, without encountering things we would avoid, and without uneasiness, fear, or distress. The philosopher lives in harmony with himself and with others, maintaining both natural and acquired relationships, like being a son, a father, a brother, a citizen, a husband, a neighbor, a fellow traveler, a ruler, or one who is ruled. This is how we see the work of a philosopher. The next question is how this should be done.

We see that when a carpenter learns certain things, he becomes a carpenter. When a pilot learns certain things, he becomes a pilot. Isn't it the same with philosophy? Is it enough to just want to be wise and good, or is there also a need to learn certain things? We then ask what these things are. Philosophers say that first, we must learn that there is a God and that he provides for everything. Also, that it is impossible to hide our actions, intentions, or thoughts from him. The next thing to learn is the nature of the gods, because once we know what they are like, anyone who wants to please and obey them must try to be like them. If God is faithful, then man must also be faithful. If God is free, man must also be free. If God is kind, man must also be kind. If God is great, man must also be great. By being an imitator of God, man must do and say everything in a way that is consistent with this fact.

Where should we begin? If you want to enter into this discussion, I'll tell you that the first thing you must understand is the meaning of words. "So, you're saying that I don't understand words now?" You don't understand them. "Then how do I use them?" You use them just like an illiterate person uses written language, or like cattle use their senses: using is one thing, understanding is another. But if you think you understand them, pick any word you like, and let's see if we both understand it the same way. "But it's unpleasant to be corrected, especially when I'm old and have maybe served in the military three times." I know that too: you come to me as if you're not lacking anything, and what could you even imagine you're missing? You're rich, you have children and a wife, and probably many slaves. Caesar knows you, and in Rome, you have many friends. You fulfill your obligations to everyone; you know how to repay someone who does you a favor and how to return the same kind of treatment to someone who wrongs you. So, what do you lack? If I show you that you lack the most necessary and important things for happiness, and that until now you've focused on everything except what you should, and to top it off, that you don't know what God is, what man is, what is good, or what is bad, and if I say that you know nothing about yourself, how could you stand me and stay here? It's impossible; you'd leave in anger. But what harm have I done to you? Is it like a mirror offending an ugly man because it shows him his true reflection? Is it like a doctor insulting a sick man when he says, "You're not well. You have a fever; don't eat today and just drink water"? No one says, "What an insult!" But if you tell a man, "Your desires are out of control, your fears are too low, your intentions are inconsistent, your actions don't align with nature, your opinions are rash and false," he immediately leaves, saying, "I've been insulted."

Our way of dealing with life is like being at a crowded market. Beasts are brought to be sold, along with oxen, and most people come to buy and sell. But there are a few who come just to watch the market, to see how it's run, why it's happening, who set it up, and for what purpose. The same is true in life: some people, like cattle, are only concerned with things like possessions, lands, slaves, and government positions. These are just like fodder to them. But there are a few who attend life's market to observe, to think about what the world is, who governs it, and whether it has a purpose or if it all happens by chance. If it has an administrator, what kind of administrator is he, and how does he govern? Who are we, who were created by him, and for what purpose? Do we have some connection or relationship with him, or not? This is how these few people think, and then they focus on understanding this one thing, and then they leave. What happens then? They are ridiculed by the majority, just like spectators at a fair are mocked by traders. And if the animals had any understanding, they would mock those who admired anything other than fodder.

Chapter 15
On Those Who Stubbornly Hold on to Their Beliefs

When some people hear that a person should be firm in their decisions, and that our will is naturally free and cannot be forced, while everything else can be hindered and is under the control of others, they think they should stick to everything they've decided without changing. But first of all, what they have decided must be reasonable. I want strength in the body, but the kind of strength that exists in a healthy, well-trained body. If I see that you have the strength of someone who is frantic and boast about it, I would tell you to see a doctor because that is not true strength, but a lack of proper strength. In a similar way, those who hear these teachings the wrong way may experience the same problem. This happened to one of my companions who, for no good reason, decided to starve himself to death. I heard about it on the third day of his fasting and went to see what was going on. He said, "I have decided." But tell me, what made you decide this? If you have decided wisely, we will sit with you and help you on your way. But if your decision was unreasonable, then change your mind. "We must stick to our decisions," he said. What are you saying? We should stick to our decisions only if they are right. If you are now convinced that it's night when it's actually day, do not change your mind if you wish, but stay firm and say, "We must stick to our decisions." Shouldn't you first check whether your decision is sound and reasonable, and only then build firmness and security on it? But if you lay a rotten and weak foundation, won't your little building fall even faster, the more and stronger the materials you put on it? Would you leave us and life behind without any good reason, even though you are a friend, a companion, and a fellow citizen of both the large and small community? And while you are committing this act of destroying a person who has done no wrong, do you say that you must stick to your decision? And if one day you decide to kill me, should you stick to that decision too?

This man was eventually persuaded to change his mind, but it's impossible to convince some people nowadays. So now I understand what I didn't before: the saying that you can't persuade or break a fool. May I never have the misfortune of having a foolish wise man as my friend—nothing is more stubborn. "I'm determined," the man says. Madmen are also determined, but the more firmly they hold to things that don't exist, the more medicine they need. Shouldn't you act like a sick person and call for a doctor? "I'm sick, master, help me; tell me what I should do. It's my duty to obey you." The same applies here: "I don't know what I should do, but I've come to learn." "No, talk to me about something else. I've already made up my mind about this." What else should we talk about that's more important and useful than convincing you that it's not enough to just make a decision and never change it? That's the attitude of madness, not of health. "I'll die if you force me to change this." Why? What's happened? "I've decided." I'm lucky that you haven't decided to kill me. "I don't take money." Why not? "I've decided." Be careful, because the same determination that makes you refuse money now might later make you take it for no reason and say, "I've decided." Just like in a sick body where fluids move from one part to another, a troubled soul doesn't know which way to go. But if stubbornness is added to that confusion, then the problem becomes impossible to cure.

Where is the good? In the will. Where is the bad? In the will. Where is neither good nor bad? In things that are beyond our control. But do any of us really think about these lessons outside of the classroom? Does anyone practice answering these questions on their own? Is it day? Yes. Is it night? No. Is the number of stars even? I can't say. When someone offers you money, have you practiced saying that money is not a good thing? Have you trained yourself in these answers, or only in arguing about tricky questions? Why then are you surprised that in the areas you've studied, you improve, but in the areas you haven't, you remain the same? When a public speaker knows that he's written a good speech, memorized it, and has a good voice, why is he still anxious? Because he's not satisfied with just practicing. What does he want? He wants praise from the audience. He's trained in giving speeches, but not in handling praise and criticism. When did he learn what praise is, what blame is, what their nature is, what kind of praise to seek, or what kind of blame to avoid? And when did he practice the discipline that comes with these things? So why are you still surprised that in the things a person has learned, they excel, but in those they haven't, they're just like everyone else?

The musician knows how to play, sings well, and has a fine appearance, but he trembles when he steps on stage. He understands music, but he doesn't understand what a crowd is, what applause is, or what ridicule is. He doesn't know what anxiety is, whether it's something we control or something outside of us, whether it can be stopped or not. That's why, if he's praised, he leaves the stage feeling proud, but if he's ridiculed, his pride is punctured, and he deflates.

This is how we are too. What do we admire? External things. What are we focused on? External things. So, is it any wonder that we fear and feel anxious? What happens when we think the things happening to us are bad? It's not in our power not to be afraid or anxious. Then we say, "Oh God, how can I not be anxious?" Fool, don't you have hands? Didn't God give them to you? Sit down and pray that your nose won't run. Wipe it instead and don't blame him. What has God given you in this situation? Hasn't he given you endurance? Hasn't he given you strength of mind? Hasn't he given you courage? When you have these things, do you still need someone else to wipe your nose? But we neither study these things nor care about them. Show me someone who cares about how they do something, not just about getting the thing done. Who, when they're walking, cares about how they're walking, not just about getting somewhere? Who, when they're planning something, cares about how they're planning, not just about achieving their goal? If he succeeds, he's elated and says, "Didn't I tell you that when we plan something, it's bound to happen?" But if things turn out differently, the poor man is crushed and doesn't even know what to say. Who among us has consulted an oracle about how to act, not just about the outcome? Who among us hasn't gone through life asleep, indifferent? Who? Show me someone, and I'll finally see the person I've been searching for, someone who is truly noble and sincere, whether young or old.

So why are we still surprised when we're well-practiced in thinking about things, but in our actions, we're low, indecent, worthless, cowardly, and impatient? We don't care about these things, nor do we study them. But if we had feared not death or exile, but fear itself, we would have studied to avoid what we consider to be evils. Now, in the classroom, we're argumentative and full of talk, but drag us into real-life practice, and we fall apart miserably. Let some challenging situation arise, and you'll see what we've really been studying. Because we lack discipline, we exaggerate situations and make them worse than they are. For example, when I'm on a ship and look at the deep sea, or when I see no land, I lose my mind and imagine that I'll have to drink all this water if I'm shipwrecked, even though only a small amount would be enough. What really disturbs me? The sea? No, it's my opinion. When an earthquake happens, I imagine the whole city will collapse on me, but isn't just one small stone enough to crush my skull?

So what really weighs on us and disturbs us? What else but our opinions? What else but our opinions burdens someone who leaves behind friends, family, familiar places, and routines? Children, for example, cry when the nurse leaves them for a short time, but they forget their sorrow if they get a small treat. Do you want us to compare you to little children? No, by Zeus, because I don't want to be comforted by a small treat, but by right opinions. And what are these? They're the things a person should study all day, so they're not affected by anything that's not theirs, whether it's a person, a place, a gymnasium, or even their own body. They should always remember the law and keep it in mind. And what is the divine law? It's to keep what is truly ours and not to desire what belongs to others. It's to use what is given to us, and when it's taken away, to give it up readily and with gratitude for the time we had it, without crying for our "nurse and mother." Because what difference does it make what we're attached to? What makes you better than someone who cries for a lost love if you grieve over a gymnasium, a portico, young men, or places of entertainment? Someone else might lament that they can no longer drink the water from a certain stream. Is the water from another source worse? But I was used to the first water. And you'll get used to the other one too. Then, if you become attached to that as well, you'll cry for that too and write a sad poem about it.

When then shall I see Athens again and the Acropolis? Wretch, are you not content with what you see daily? Is there anything better or greater to see than the sun, the moon, the stars, the whole earth, and the sea? But if you understand the one who governs the Whole and carry him within yourself, do you still desire small stones and a beautiful rock? When you're about to leave behind even the sun and moon, will you sit and cry like children? What have you been doing in the school? What did you hear, what did you learn? Why did you write yourself down as a philosopher, when you could have written the truth: "I attended some introductory lectures, and I read some Chrysippus, but I didn't even approach the door of a philosopher." How could I possess anything like what Socrates had, who died the way he did, who lived the way he did, or anything like what Diogenes had? Do you think any of those men wept or grieved because they wouldn't see a certain person, or be in Athens or Corinth, or because they would be in Susa or Ecbatana instead? If a person can leave a banquet when they choose, and no longer be entertained, do they stay and complain? Do they not stay only as long as they enjoy it? Such a person, I suppose, would endure perpetual exile or even be condemned to death. Will you not grow up now, like children, and take on more solid responsibilities, and stop crying for "mothers and nurses," which are the lamentations of old women? "But if I leave, I'll make them sad." Will you make them sad? No, it's not you causing them sorrow, but the same thing that causes you sorrow: their opinion. What should you do then? Change your own opinion, and if these women are wise, they will change theirs too. If they don't, they will mourn by their own fault.

My friend, as the saying goes, make a desperate effort for peace of mind, freedom, and greatness of soul. Lift up your head at last as if released from slavery. Dare to look up to God and say, "Deal with me however you will; I am of the same mind as you; I am yours. I refuse nothing that pleases you: lead me where you will: clothe me in whatever way you choose. Do you want me to hold office, to be a private citizen, to stay here or be exiled, to be poor or rich? I will defend your decisions to others, showing them what each situation truly is." But you won't do this; instead, you'll sit in a corner and wait for your "mother" to feed you. Who would Hercules have been if he had stayed at home? He would have been Eurystheus, not Hercules. Well, and in his travels, how many close friends did he have? But nothing was dearer to him than God. That's why it was believed he was the son of God, and he was. In obedience to God, he went about purging the world of injustice and lawlessness. But you're not Hercules, and you can't cleanse the wickedness of others; nor are you Theseus, able to purge Attica of its evils. Clear away your own. From yourself, from your thoughts, cast out sadness, fear, desire, envy, malice, greed, weakness, and excess. But you can't get rid of these things unless you focus only on God, fix your thoughts on him, and dedicate yourself to his commands. If you choose anything else, you'll be forced to follow what's stronger than you, always seeking peace and never finding it because you're looking for it where it isn't, and ignoring it where it is.

Chapter 16
How to Apply General Ideas to Specific Situations

Where does good come from? It comes from our choices. Where does evil come from? It also comes from our choices. Where can we find neither good nor evil? In things that are beyond our control. But do any of us really think about these lessons outside of school? Do we practice by ourselves to give the right answers to questions, like we do in class? Is it day? Yes. Is it night? No. Is the number of stars even? I can't say. When money is offered to you, have you practiced responding correctly, saying that money isn't really good? Have you trained yourself in giving these answers, or just against tricky arguments? Why are you surprised, then, if you've improved in things you've studied but stayed the same in things you haven't?

When a speaker knows they've written well, memorized their speech, and has a pleasant voice, why are they still anxious? Because they aren't satisfied with just studying. What else do they want? They want to be praised by the audience. So, they've practiced speaking well, but they haven't practiced how to handle praise and criticism. When did they learn what praise is, what blame is, or what kind of praise to seek and what kind of blame to avoid? When did they practice the discipline that comes with understanding these things? So why are you still surprised that a person excels in what they've learned but is just like everyone else in areas they haven't studied?

A musician knows how to play the lute, sings well, and wears fine clothes, but they still tremble when they step on stage. They understand the music, but they don't understand what a crowd is, what the shouts of a crowd mean, or what ridicule is. They don't know what anxiety is, whether it comes from us or from others, or whether it can be stopped. That's why if they're praised, they leave the stage feeling puffed up, but if they're ridiculed, their confidence deflates like a punctured balloon.

The same goes for us. What do we admire? External things. What do we focus on? External things. So is it any wonder that we fear and worry? What happens when we think something bad is coming our way? It's not in our power not to be afraid; it's not in our power not to worry. Then we ask, "Oh God, how can I stop worrying?" Fool, don't you have hands? Didn't God give them to you? Sit down and pray that your nose doesn't run. Or instead, just wipe it and don't blame God. What, has God given you nothing to deal with your problems? Hasn't he given you endurance? Hasn't he given you courage? Hasn't he given you strength? When you have these tools, do you still look for someone else to wipe your nose? But we don't study these things or care about them.

Show me a person who cares about how they do something, not just about getting something. Who cares about their own effort, not just the result? When someone is making a decision, do they care about the decision itself, or just about getting what they want? And if they succeed, they're proud and say, "Didn't I tell you it would work out?" But if it doesn't, they're crushed, not even knowing what to say about what happened. Who among us has ever consulted a seer about our actions? Who hasn't just drifted through life without paying attention?

So why are we still surprised that we're good at thinking about things, but in our actions, we're weak, indecent, lazy, and cowardly? We don't care about these things or study them. But if we feared fear itself, not death or exile, we would have studied how not to fall into what we see as evil. Now, in the classroom, we're quick to argue and full of words. But when it comes to real-life practice, we're a mess. Let something troubling happen, and you'll see what we've really been studying and practicing. Without discipline, we always make things seem worse than they are.

For example, when I'm on a ship and look out at the deep sea, or see that there's no land in sight, I panic and imagine that if we're shipwrecked, I'll have to drink all that water. I forget that only a few pints would be enough to drown me. What really disturbs me? The sea? No, it's my opinion. Again, when there's an earthquake, I imagine the whole city is going to collapse on me, but isn't one small stone enough to kill me?

So what really weighs us down and disturbs us? What else but our opinions? What else but opinions makes someone sad when they leave their friends, home, and routines? Little children cry when their nurse leaves, but they forget their sadness if they get a small treat. Do you want us to compare you to little children? No, because I don't want to be comforted by a small treat, but by the right opinions.

And what are these right opinions? They're the ones we should study all day, so we're not affected by anything that isn't ours—not by a friend, a place, a gym, not even by our own body. Instead, we should remember the law and keep it in mind. And what is the divine law? To keep what's ours, not to claim what belongs to others, but to use what's given and not desire what isn't. And when something is taken away, to give it up willingly and be thankful for the time we had it. If you do that, you won't cry for your nurse or your mom. What does it matter what controls a person, whether it's something big or small? How are you any better than someone who cries for a girl, if you're upset over a gym or a group of young people or places of amusement? Another person might complain that they'll no longer drink from the Dirce spring. Is the water from the Marcian aqueduct any worse than the water from Dirce? But I was used to the water from Dirce. And you'll get used to the other water too. Then if you get attached to that, you'll cry over it too, just like Euripides wrote about the hot baths of Nero and the Marcian water. That's how tragedy is made when ordinary things happen to silly people.

When will I see Athens again and the Acropolis? You fool, aren't you content with what you see every day? Is there anything better or greater to see than the sun, the moon, the stars, the whole earth, and the sea? But if you understand the one who controls everything, and carry that understanding within you, do you still desire small stones and a pretty rock? What will you do when you have to leave even the sun and the moon? Will you sit and cry like a child? What have you been doing in school? What did you hear and learn? Why did you call yourself a philosopher when you should have just said, "I learned a few things, read Chrysippus, but I never really became a philosopher"? How could I possess anything like what Socrates had, who lived and died as he did, or anything like what Diogenes had? Do you think any of these men wept or grieved because they wouldn't see a certain person, or a certain place, or be in Athens or Corinth, but instead in Susa or Ecbatana if that's what happened?

If a person can leave a party whenever they want, and stop having fun, do they still stay and complain? Or do they only stay as long as they're enjoying themselves? I suppose such a person would handle exile or a death sentence just fine. Will you not grow up now, like children, and eat more solid food instead of crying for your mom and nurse? "But if I leave, I'll make them sad." You make them sad? No, what makes them sad is the same thing that makes you sad: opinions. What should you do, then? Change your opinion, and if these women are wise, they'll change theirs too. If not, they'll keep crying because of their own foolishness.

My friend, as the saying goes, make a desperate effort for peace of mind, freedom, and greatness of spirit. Lift your head as if you're finally free. Dare to look up to God and say, "From now on, deal with me as you will. I'm on your side. I'm yours. I refuse nothing that pleases you. Lead me where you want. Dress me how you want. Is it your will that I should hold a public office, or live as a private person, stay here, or be exiled, be poor, or be rich? I'll defend all these choices to others. I'll show them the true nature of each situation." But you won't do this. Instead, you'll sit in comfort and wait for your mom to feed you.

Who would Hercules have been if he'd stayed home? He would have been Eurystheus, not Hercules. And how many close friends did he have on his journeys? But nothing was dearer to him than God. That's why people believed he was the son of God, and he was. In obedience to God, he went about ridding the world of injustice and lawlessness. But you're not Hercules, and you can't rid the world of other people's wickedness, just as you're not Theseus, able to clean up Attica. Clean up your own life instead. Get rid of sadness, fear, desire, envy, hatred, greed, laziness, and lack of self-control. But you can't get rid of these things unless you focus only on God, love him above all, and follow his commands. If you choose anything else, you'll always be sighing and groaning, forced to follow what's stronger than you. You'll keep searching for peace of mind but never find it, because you're looking for it where it doesn't exist, and ignoring where it really is.

Chapter 17
How We Should Struggle Against Appearances

What is the first thing someone who wants to be a philosopher should do? They need to let go of pride, which means thinking they already know everything. It's impossible for a person to start learning something if they believe they already know it. When it comes to deciding what should be done or not done, what is good or bad, beautiful or ugly, we all talk about these things randomly and then go to philosophers. We praise, criticize, accuse, blame, judge, and decide on matters of what is honorable and dishonorable. But why do we go to philosophers? Because we want to learn what we don't think we know. And what is it that we want to learn? Theorems, which are ideas or principles. We want to learn what philosophers say because we find their ideas elegant and sharp, and some of us want to learn because we hope to benefit from it.

It's ridiculous to think that a person wants to learn one thing but will end up learning something else, or that someone will make progress in something they don't learn. But many people are deceived by this idea, just like the rhetorician Theopompus was when he criticized Plato for wanting to define everything. Theopompus said, "Did none of us use the words Good or Just before you, or were we just saying these words without understanding what they really mean?" But who told you, Theopompus, that we didn't have natural ideas of these things, like preconceptions? We can't apply preconceptions to real situations if we haven't broken them down and figured out what specific thing should be connected to each preconception.

You could make the same argument against doctors. Before Hippocrates, who didn't use the words healthy and unhealthy, or were we just saying these words without meaning? We also have a basic idea of what health is, but we struggle to apply it correctly. That's why one doctor might say, "Don't eat," another says, "Eat more," another says, "Let out blood," and another says, "Use cupping." What's the reason for this? Isn't it because people can't properly apply the idea of health to specific situations?

The same thing happens in life. Who among us doesn't talk about what is good and bad, or what is useful and not useful? We all have some idea of these things, but is our understanding clear and complete?

Prove it. How do you prove it? By correctly applying the idea to specific situations. For example, Plato applies definitions to the idea of what is useful, but you apply them to the idea of what is useless. Can both of you be right? How is that possible? Doesn't one person apply the idea of good to wealth, while another applies it to pleasure or health? If we all know what these words mean, why do we argue, fight, and blame each other?

And why am I bringing this up? If you know how to properly apply your ideas, why are you unhappy, why are you frustrated? Let's not even talk about the second topic, which is about how we pursue things and our duties related to them. Let's also skip the third topic, which is about how we agree to things. I'll give up on those two topics for now. Let's focus on the first topic, which clearly shows that we don't properly apply our preconceptions. Do you now desire what is possible and what is within your power? Then why are you frustrated? Why are you unhappy? Do you try to avoid things that are unavoidable? Then why do you encounter what you want to avoid? Why are you unlucky? Why, when you want something, does it not happen, and when you don't want something, it does happen? This is the greatest proof of unhappiness and misery: I wish for something, and it doesn't happen. And what could be more miserable than that?

Medea couldn't stand this, and that's why she ended up killing her children. It was an act of a strong spirit, at least in this way: she knew how painful it is when something you wish for doesn't happen. She thought, "This is how I'll get back at him (her husband) for wronging and insulting me. But what will I gain if I punish him this way? How should I do it? I'll kill my children, but I'll also punish myself. But what do I care?" This is what happens when a person's soul is filled with strong but misguided energy. She didn't know where the power to make things happen lies. It's not something you can get from the outside, or by changing and adapting things. Don't desire the man (Jason, Medea's husband), and nothing you desire will fail to happen. Don't stubbornly wish that he will live with you, don't desire to stay in

Corinth, and in general, don't desire anything other than what God wills. And who can stop you? Who can force you? No one can force you any more than they can force Zeus.

When you have such a guide and your wishes and desires match his, why do you still fear disappointment? Give up your desire for wealth and your fear of poverty, and you won't be disappointed. Give up your desire for health, and you won't be unlucky. Give up your desire for political positions, honors, your country, friends, children—basically, for anything that's not in your control—and you won't be unlucky. But give your desires to Zeus and the other gods; surrender them to the gods. Let the gods lead, let your desire and aversion align with the gods, and how can you be unhappy anymore? But if you, lazy person, still envy, complain, are jealous, and afraid, and you never stop complaining about yourself and the gods, why do you still talk about being educated? What kind of education do you mean? Do you think you've been learning sophistical arguments? Wouldn't it be better if you could unlearn all these things and start from the beginning, realizing that you haven't even touched the heart of the matter yet? Then, starting from this foundation, you should build everything else so that nothing happens that you don't want, and nothing you want fails to happen.

Show me one young person who has come to a philosophy school with this intention, who has become a champion for this cause and says, "I'll give up everything else, and it's enough for me if I can live my life free from obstacles and troubles, to hold my head high like a free person, and to look up to heaven as a friend of God, fearing nothing that might happen." Point out such a person to me so I can say, "Come, young person, and take possession of what is rightfully yours, for it is your destiny to excel in philosophy: these books are yours, these teachings are yours." Then, after they've worked hard and practiced in this area, let them come back to me and say, "I want to be free from passions and worries; I want to know, as a pious person and philosopher, what my duties are to the gods, to my parents, to my brothers, to my country, and to strangers." I would say, "Come to the second area of study; this too is yours."

"But I've now studied the second area enough, and I would love to be steady and unshaken, not only when I'm awake, but also when I'm asleep, when I'm drunk, and when I'm feeling down." You are aiming high, like a god, with these ambitions.

No, instead, "I want to understand what Chrysippus says in his treatise on the Pseudomenos (the Liar)." Won't you hang yourself, wretched person, with such a goal? And what good will it do you? You'll read the whole thing with sadness, and you'll speak about it to others with trembling. That's what you do. "Brother, do you want me to read to you, and you read to me?" You write excellently, my friend, just like Xenophon, and you, just like Plato, and you, just like Antisthenes. Then, after sharing your dreams with each other, you go back to the same things: your desires are the same, your aversions are the same, your pursuits are the same, your goals are the same, you wish for the same things, and work for the same things.

Then, you don't even seek out someone to give you advice, but you get upset when you hear things like what I'm saying now. You say, "That old man was so mean: when I was leaving, he didn't cry or say, 'You're going into danger. If you come back safely, my child, I'll light candles.'" This is what a kind person would do, right? It would be a great thing if you did come back safely, and maybe it would be worth lighting candles for such a person because you should be immortal and free from illness.

As I said, we need to throw away this conceit of thinking we know something useful. We need to approach philosophy like we approach geometry or music. If we don't, we won't make any progress, even if we read all the works of Chrysippus, Antipater, and Archedemus.

Chapter 18
How We Must Struggle Against Impressions

Every habit and skill grows stronger and increases by practicing the related actions: the habit of walking grows by walking, and the habit of running grows by running. If you want to be a good reader, then read; if you want to be a writer, then write. But if you haven't read for thirty days straight and have done something else instead, you will notice the effect. Similarly, if you have been lying down for ten days, try to get up and take a long walk, and you will see how weak your legs have become. In general, if you want to develop any habit, practice it regularly; if you don't want to develop a habit, avoid doing it and do something else instead.

The same is true for the emotions and feelings in your mind: when you get angry, you need to understand that not only has this negative thing happened to you, but you have also strengthened the habit of anger, like adding fuel to a fire. When you have given in to sexual desire with someone, don't just think of this one defeat; realize that you have also increased your lack of self-control. It is impossible for habits and skills to not be created when they didn't exist before, and for them not to be increased and strengthened by repeated actions.

This is also how, as philosophers say, diseases of the mind develop. For example, when you first desire money, if you apply reason to see the harm in this desire, you can stop it, and your mind's ability to control itself is restored. But if you don't take steps to cure this, your mind will no longer return to its original state, and the desire will become stronger the next time it appears. When this happens repeatedly, your mind becomes hardened, and the obsession with money becomes a mental illness. Just like someone who has had a fever and hasn't fully recovered, the same thing happens with diseases of the mind. Certain traces and marks are left behind, and unless you completely get rid of them, when the problem arises again, it will cause even more damage. If you don't want to be someone with a bad temper, don't feed the habit: don't do anything that will make it stronger. At first, stay calm, and count the days you haven't been angry. Maybe you used to get mad every day; then it was every other day; then every third day, then every fourth. But if you manage to go thirty days without getting angry, make a sacrifice to God. The habit first starts to weaken, and then it is completely destroyed. "I haven't gotten upset today, or yesterday, or any day for two or three months. But I was careful when something frustrating happened." If you can say that, you're on the right track.

Today, when I saw an attractive person, I didn't think, "I wish I could be with her," and I didn't feel jealous of her husband. For anyone who thinks that way is also wishing to be an adulterer. I didn't let myself imagine anything more. I patted myself on the back and thought, "Well done, Epictetus, you've solved a tricky problem, even better than those famous puzzles." And if the person showed interest in me, sent signals, or even came close, and I still resisted and won over my desire, that would be a victory greater than solving any riddle. Such a victory is something to be proud of, not just solving logical puzzles.

How can this be done? Be willing to approve of yourself, be willing to appear beautiful to God, and desire to be pure in your mind and in your relationship with God. Then, when any temptation comes to you, as Plato says, seek purification, go to the temples of the gods who protect people from harm. Or just surround yourself with good and just people, whether they're alive or dead. Go to Socrates and think of him lying next to Alcibiades, ignoring his beauty: consider what a victory he gained over himself, like an Olympic champion, even greater than Hercules. One might rightly greet him, "Hail, wondrous man, who has conquered more than just boxers or wrestlers." By keeping these examples in mind, you'll be able to resist temptation. But first, don't let yourself be swept away by the first impression. Pause and say, "Wait a moment, let me see what you really are." Don't let the first impression paint a vivid picture that draws you in; instead, bring up a better, noble thought to push away the bad one. If you practice this regularly, you'll see how strong you become.

This is the true athlete, the person who trains against temptations. Stop, don't get carried away. The struggle is great; it's for kingship, freedom, happiness, and peace of mind. Remember God: call on Him for help and protection, just as sailors call on the gods during a storm. For what is a greater storm than the one caused by overwhelming desires that take away reason? The storm itself is just an appearance. If you remove the fear of death, no matter how much thunder and lightning there is, you'll see calmness and peace in your mind. But if you lose the battle and think you'll win next time, and then say the same thing again, you'll eventually be in such a bad state that you won't even know you're doing wrong. You'll even start making excuses for your actions, proving the old saying true: "The one who delays suffers more."

Chapter 19
To Those Who Embrace Philosophical Ideas Only for Debate

There's a famous argument called "the ruling argument," which comes from a contradiction between three ideas. The ideas are: that everything in the past must be true; that an impossible thing cannot come from a possible thing; and that something is possible even if it's not true and never will be. Diodorus noticed this contradiction and used the first two ideas to prove that nothing is possible unless it's true or will be true. Another person might believe that something can be possible even if it's not true and never will be, and that an impossible thing cannot follow a possible thing. But this person won't agree that everything in the past must be true, as some followers of Cleanthes believed, and which Antipater strongly defended. Others believe that something can be possible even if it's not true and never will be, and that everything in the past is necessarily true. However, they would say that an impossible thing can follow a possible thing. But it's impossible to believe all three ideas at the same time because they contradict each other.

So, if someone were to ask me, "Which of these ideas do you believe?" I would say that I don't know, but I've heard the story. Diodorus believed one thing, the followers of Panthoides and Cleanthes believed another, and Chrysippus believed a third. "What's your opinion, then?" I wasn't made to examine these ideas, compare what others have said, and form my own opinion on the matter. So, I'm not much different from a person who just memorizes facts. Who was Hector's father? Priam. Who were his brothers? Alexander and Deiphobus. Who was their mother? Hecuba. I've heard this story. From whom? From Homer. And Hellanicus also wrote about the same things, and maybe others like him too. And what do I know about the ruling argument? Nothing. But, if I want to show off, especially at a party, I might impress the guests by listing those who have written on these topics. Chrysippus wrote brilliantly about possibilities, Cleanthes wrote specifically on the subject, and Archedemus also wrote about it. Antipater not only wrote about possibilities but also separately about the ruling argument. "Haven't you read their works?" I haven't read them. "Read them." And what will you gain from reading them? You'll just become more foolish and annoying than you are now; because what else have you gained from reading them? What's your opinion on the matter? None; but you'll talk about Helen and Priam, and the island of Calypso, which never was and never will be. And in this case, it's not so important if you only remember the story and don't form your own opinion. But in matters of ethics and morality, this happens to us much more than in the things we're discussing now.

"Tell me about good and evil." Listen:
The wind from Ilium to Ciconian shores brought me. —Odyssey

Some things are good, some are bad, and others are indifferent. The good things are virtues and things that relate to virtues; the bad things are vices and things that relate to vices; and the indifferent things are those that lie between virtues and vices, like wealth, health, life, death, pleasure, and pain. "How do you know this?" Hellanicus says it in his Egyptian history; what difference does it make if he says it, or if

Diogenes says it in his ethics, or if Chrysippus or Cleanthes says it? Have you examined any of these things and formed your own opinion? Show me how you behave during a storm at sea. Do you remember this distinction between things when the sail is flapping and someone who knows nothing about navigation stands by you while you're panicking and says, "Tell me, by the Gods, what you were just saying: Is it a vice to suffer shipwreck? Does it have anything to do with vice?" Won't you pick up a stick and hit him on the head? "What does that matter now? We're drowning, and you come to mock us?" But if Caesar calls you to court, do you remember the distinction then? If you're walking in pale and trembling, and someone comes up to you and says, "Why are you trembling, man? What are you so worried about? Does Caesar, who's inside, have the power to give virtue and vice to those who come before him?" You would reply, "Why do you mock me and add to my troubles?" "Still, tell me, philosopher, why are you trembling? Are you afraid of death, prison, physical pain, banishment, or disgrace? What else is there? Is there any vice or anything that partakes of vice? What did you use to say about these things?" "What business do you have with me, man? My own troubles are enough for me." And you're right. Your own troubles are enough, your lack of courage, your boasting when you sat in the lecture hall. Why did you show off with ideas that weren't yours? Why did you call yourself a Stoic?

Observe your actions, and you'll see which philosophy you truly follow. You'll find that most of you are Epicureans, a few are Peripatetics, and they're weak ones at that. How will you show that you truly value virtue above all else or even consider it superior? But show me a real Stoic, if you can. Where or how? But you can show me plenty of people who can repeat the arguments of the Stoics. Do these same people recite the Epicurean ideas any worse? And the Peripatetic ideas, don't they handle them just as well? So who is a Stoic? Just as we call a statue a work of Phidias if it's made according to his art, show me a person who lives according to the teachings they speak about. Show me a person who is sick and happy, in danger and happy, dying and happy, in exile and happy, in disgrace and happy. Show me such a person: I truly want to see a Stoic. You can't show me someone who's fully formed, but at least show me someone who's on the path, who's making progress toward becoming a Stoic. Do me this favor: let an old man see something he's never seen before. Do you think you need to show me the Zeus of Phidias or the Athena, a statue made of ivory and gold? No, show me a human soul ready to think as God does, ready not to blame either God or man, ready not to be disappointed by anything, not to feel harmed by anything, not to be angry, not to be envious, not to be jealous; and why not say it directly? A person who is aiming to go from being a human to being like God, and who, while still in this mortal body, thinks of themselves as united with Zeus. Show me such a person. But you can't. So why do you deceive yourselves and others? Why do you put on a disguise that doesn't belong to you and walk around as thieves, stealing names and ideas that aren't yours?

Now, I am your teacher, and you are my students. My goal is to make you free from restraint, compulsion, and hindrance; to make you free, prosperous, happy, and to look to God in all things, big and small. You are here to learn and practice these things. So why don't you finish the work if you have the purpose you ought to have, and if I have the qualities I ought to have? What's missing? When I see a craftsman with the materials he needs, I expect to see the finished work. Here is the craftsman, here are the materials; what is lacking? Isn't this something that can be taught? It is. Isn't it within our power? Yes, it's the only thing that's fully within our power. Neither wealth, nor health, nor reputation, nor anything else is in our power except the right use of our thoughts and perceptions. This right use is naturally free from restraint and impediment. So why don't you finish the work? Tell me why. Is it because of me, or because of you, or because of the nature of the thing itself? The thing itself is possible and is the only thing fully within our power. So it must be either my fault or your fault, or, more likely, both of ours. So, are you willing that we finally begin to work toward this goal in this school, and to forget about the past? Let's make a start. Trust me, and you will see.

Chapter 20
Against Followers of Epicurus and of the Academy

Ideas that are true and clear are so important that even those who argue against them end up using them. You might think that the best proof something is true is when even the person who denies it still needs to rely on it. For example, if someone says that nothing is universally true, they still must agree that the statement "nothing is universally true" is true in every case. What else could this be but admitting that everything universally affirmed is false? Similarly, if someone says, "You can't know anything for sure," or "You shouldn't believe anything," or "It's not possible to learn anything," they are contradicting themselves because they are trying to teach you that nothing can be taught.

How is this different from those who say, "No one agrees with anyone," but still want you to agree with them? Epicurus, for example, tried to destroy the idea that people are naturally connected, but he had to use the very thing he was trying to deny. He would say, "Don't be fooled, people; there's no natural connection between rational beings; believe me. Those who say otherwise are deceiving you." But if he didn't believe in natural connections, why did he care if we were deceived? Why did he put so much effort into convincing us? If what he said was true, he should have just lived quietly, eating, drinking, and enjoying himself without worrying about what others believed.

Why should he lose sleep, write so many books, and argue so much if it didn't matter? It's like he's saying to his fellow Epicureans, "Let's tell everyone that natural connections don't exist, but let's keep the benefits of them for ourselves." So, what woke Epicurus from his peaceful life and made him write all those things? It was nature itself, which is stronger than any human reasoning. Nature pulled him to do what she wanted, even though he resisted. Just as a vine grows like a vine and an olive tree grows like an olive tree, a human cannot completely lose the qualities of being human. Even someone who tries to deny natural desires cannot fully remove them.

Epicurus tried to deny all the responsibilities of being a person, a family member, a citizen, or a friend, but he couldn't get rid of basic human desires because that's impossible. What a shame it is when a person, who has been given the ability to understand truth by nature, doesn't try to improve and build on that understanding but instead tries to destroy the very tools that allow us to know the truth. What do you say, philosopher? Do you think piety and holiness are good things? "Yes, I can prove they are good." Then prove it so that people can learn to respect the divine and not be careless about the most important things. "Do you have the proof?" Yes, I do, and I'm glad.

"Then listen to the opposite view: There are no gods, and if there are, they don't care about us. There's no connection between us and them, and this talk about piety and holiness is just lies made up by boastful people or lawmakers trying to scare wrongdoers." Congratulations, philosopher, you've managed to convince young people to dismiss divine things. "Doesn't that make you happy?" Not at all. You've also taught that justice doesn't exist, modesty is foolish, and that relationships like father and son don't matter. Congratulations again, philosopher, keep persuading young people so that more will share your views.

These ideas are definitely not what helped build strong cities or the values that held Spartan society together. Do you think the Spartans died at Thermopylae because they believed that everything was meaningless? Then these same people get married, have children, and take part in public life, even becoming priests and interpreters of the gods they claim don't exist. What hypocrisy and deception! What are you doing, man? Are you contradicting yourself every day and still not giving up these cold arguments? When you eat, where do you put your hand? To your mouth or your eye? When you wash, do you call a pot a dish or a ladle a spit?

If I were a slave to one of these people, even if I had to suffer daily, I would trick them. If they asked for olive oil, I'd bring them vinegar and pour it on their heads. "What is this?" they would ask. "It looked like oil to me," I'd say. Or if they asked for a barley drink, I'd bring them a bowl of something sour. "Didn't I ask for barley drink?" they would say. "Yes, master," I'd reply. "This is it; smell and taste it. How do you know if your senses are deceiving you?" If I had a few like-minded friends, we could drive them mad or make them change their ways. But instead, they mock us while using all the things that nature provides and then try to deny their reality.

How ungrateful and shameless can people be when they eat bread every day and still claim they don't know if there is a Demeter, Persephone, or Pluto? They enjoy the night, day, seasons, stars, sea, and land, along with the cooperation of humanity, and yet they don't consider any of these things. They just want to spout their little arguments, and after filling their bellies, they head off to the bath without a care about what they've said or who they've influenced. They don't care if a young person who hears them loses their moral values, or if an adulterer uses their words to justify their actions, or if someone neglecting their parents finds excuses in these teachings. What is good or bad to you? This or that?

Why should anyone bother responding to such people or trying to convince them? It's more likely to change the mind of a stubborn person than to make these people see their own mistakes.

Chapter 21
On the Inconsistency of the Mind

Some things people easily admit, while others they don't. No one will admit that they are foolish or lack understanding; instead, you'll hear everyone say, "I wish my luck matched my intelligence." But people do admit they are timid, saying, "I'm a bit timid, I admit, but in other ways, you won't find me foolish." A person won't easily admit to being reckless, and they definitely won't admit to being unjust. They will never confess to being envious or a busybody. However, most people will admit to being compassionate. Why is this? The main reason is inconsistency and confusion about what is good and bad. But different people have different reasons. Generally, they won't admit to things they believe are disgraceful. They think timidity is a sign of a good nature and that compassion is also good, while foolishness is seen as the mark of a slave. They won't admit to things that are harmful to society. But in the case of most mistakes, they confess them because they believe there is something involuntary about them, like with timidity and compassion. If someone admits they are reckless, they usually blame love or passion as an excuse for their lack of control. But people don't think injustice is involuntary at all. They also believe jealousy has something involuntary about it, which is why they admit to being jealous too.

Living among people who are so confused, so unaware of what they say, of the problems they have or don't have, why they have them, or how they can be fixed, it's worth asking yourself constantly, "Am I like them? What do I think of myself? How do I behave? Do I act wisely? Do I act with self-control? Do I ever say, 'I've been taught to be ready for anything that might happen'?" Do I have the humility to admit when I don't know something? Do I go to my teacher like someone seeking answers from an oracle, ready to obey? Or do I, like a whining child, go to school just to learn facts and understand books that I didn't understand before, so I can explain them to others? Man, you've had an argument with a poor servant at home, you've turned your household upside down, you've scared the neighbors, and now you come to me pretending to be a wise man, judging how I explain a word, and how I babble whatever comes to mind. You come full of envy and feeling low because you bring nothing valuable from home, and you sit through the discussion thinking of nothing but how your father and brother feel about you. "What are they saying about me? Do they think I'm improving? Are they saying, 'He'll return with all knowledge'? I wish I could learn everything before I return, but it takes so much effort, and no one sends me anything. The baths at Nicopolis are dirty, everything is bad at home, and everything is bad here."

Then they say, no one benefits from going to school. Why? Who goes to school to improve themselves? Who goes to have their opinions purified? Who goes to learn what they need? Why are you surprised if you leave school with the same things you brought in? You didn't come to change your beliefs or correct them or to receive new ones. Not at all. You're more interested in whether you already have what you came for. You want to talk about theories? What then? Don't you just become a bigger fool? Don't your little theories give you a chance to show off? You solve tricky logical problems. Don't you examine the tricky question called the "Liar"? Don't you look into hypothetical problems? Why, then, are you upset if you get exactly what you came for in school? "Yes, but if my child dies or my brother, or if I have to face death or torture, what good will these things do me?" Well, did you come here for that? Did you sit by my side for that? Did you ever stay up late or get up early with this in mind? Or when you went out for a walk, did you ever bring up a real-life situation instead of a theoretical problem, and discuss it with your friends? Where and when did you do this? Then you say, "Theories are useless." To whom? To those who misuse them. Eye drops aren't useless to those who use them correctly. Bandages aren't useless. Weights aren't useless; they're useful to some and useless to others. If you ask me now if logical problems are useful, I'll tell you they are, and if you want, I'll prove it. "How, then, will they be useful to me?" Did you ask if they're useful to you, or if they're useful in general? Let someone with a serious illness ask me if vinegar is useful; I'll say it is. "Will it be useful to me?" I'll say no. First, get your illness under control and heal your sores. And you, O people, first heal your mind and stop your distractions; bring it calm and clear to school, and you'll see what power reason has.

Chapter 22
On Friendship

When someone works hard at something, they naturally begin to love it. Do people work hard on things that are bad? Not at all. Do they put effort into things that don't matter to them? No, they don't. So, they must be focusing on things that are good, and if they focus on them, they love them too. This means that anyone who understands what is good also knows how to love. But if someone can't tell the difference between what's good and what's bad, or between things that are neither good nor bad, how can they truly love? Only those who are wise have the power to really love.

But someone might say, "I'm not wise, but I still love my child." I'm surprised you admit that you're not wise. What are you missing? Can't you see and hear? Don't you notice things around you? Don't you eat food that's good for you and wear clothes that fit you? So why do you say you're not wise? It's because you often get confused and tricked by what you see. Sometimes you think something is good, then later think it's bad, or sometimes you think it's neither good nor bad. You get upset, scared, jealous, and you change your mind a lot. That's why you say you're not wise. And aren't you also inconsistent in your love? Do you sometimes think wealth and pleasure are good and other times bad? Do you sometimes think certain people are good, then later think they're bad? Do you sometimes like them and other times dislike them? Do you sometimes praise them and other times criticize them? "Yes, I do that too." So, do you think someone who has been tricked by another person is really their friend? "No, I don't." And if someone chooses a friend but keeps changing their mind, do they really care about that person? "They don't." And if someone criticizes a person one moment and admires them the next, do they have true affection for them? "No, they don't."

Think about little dogs playing together, and you might say there's nothing more friendly than that. But to see what friendship really is, throw a piece of meat between them, and you'll see what happens.

Now imagine putting a small piece of property between you and your child; you'll quickly find out how much your child might want you gone, and how much you might want your child gone. Then you'll say, "What kind of child did I raise? They've been wanting to get rid of me for a long time." Or imagine an old man and a young man both liking the same woman; they'll both want her, and you'll see how quickly their feelings change. The same goes for fame or danger—it will be just like that. You'll end up like Admetus's father, saying:

"Life gives you pleasure: and why not your father?"

Do you think Admetus didn't love his own child when the child was little? That he wasn't deeply worried when the child was sick? That he didn't often wish he could take the child's place when the child had a fever? But when a real test came, look at what he said. Weren't Eteocles and Polynices from the same mother and father? Didn't they grow up together, live together, eat together, sleep together, and even kiss each other often? If anyone had seen them, they would have laughed at philosophers who say friendship is tricky. But when they fought over the throne, like dogs fighting over a piece of meat, look at what they said:

Polynices: "Where will you stand in front of the towers?" Eteocles: "Why do you ask me?" Polynices: "I'll stand across from you and try to kill you." Eteocles: "I want to do the same."

These were their true feelings.

Don't be fooled: every living thing cares about its own interests more than anything else. So, when something gets in the way of those interests, whether it's a brother, father, child, or someone they love, they'll hate, reject, and curse it. They love their own interests more than anything else. That's their true family, their country, and even their god. So, when they think the gods are getting in the way, they curse them, tear down their statues, and burn their temples, just like Alexander burned the temples of Aesculapius when his dear friend died.

Because of this, if a person puts their interests, their sense of what's right, their goodness, and their love for their country and family all in the same place, they'll be secure in all those things. But if they separate their interests from these other things, putting them in different places, their interests will always win. Wherever someone's "self" and "mine" are, that's where they'll lean. If their self is in their body, they'll be controlled by their physical desires. If it's in their will, they'll be controlled by their choices. If it's in external things, they'll be controlled by those things. If I place myself where my will is, then I can be a good friend, a good son, and a good father because my interest will be in being trustworthy, modest, patient, self-controlled, helpful, and respectful. But if I put myself in one place and honesty in another, then I'll follow Epicurus's idea that honesty is either meaningless or just what people think it is.

This kind of ignorance is why the Athenians fought with the Spartans, why the Thebans fought with both, why the great king fought with the Greeks, why the Macedonians fought with everyone, and why the Romans fought with the Getae. And even before that, the Trojan War happened for these reasons. Alexander was a guest of Menelaus, and if anyone had seen their friendly relationship, they wouldn't have believed anyone who said they weren't friends. But then a beautiful woman came between them, and they went to war over her. So, when you see brothers who seem like close friends, don't assume their friendship is real, not even if they swear it and say they'll never be apart. The ruling principle of a bad person can't be trusted. It's unstable, has no solid direction, and gets overwhelmed by different thoughts at different times. Don't just look at whether they were born to the same parents, grew up together, or had the same teacher. Look at where they place their interests—are they in external things or in their will? If they're in external things, don't call them friends, just like you wouldn't call them trustworthy, brave, or free. Don't even call them human, if you have any sense. For it's not human nature to bite, abuse, and take over empty places or public spaces like wild animals, or to act like robbers in court, or to be indulgent, adulterous, or corrupt. These behaviors come from placing oneself and one's interests in things outside of one's control. But if you hear that someone truly thinks the good lies in their will and in how they see things, don't worry whether they're father and son, brothers, or longtime companions. Once you've figured that out, you can confidently say they're friends, just as you can say they're faithful and just. For where else can friendship exist but where there is faithfulness, modesty, and a shared sense of what's right?

But you might say, "This person treated me well for so long; didn't they love me?" How do you know they didn't see you the same way they see a sponge to clean their shoes or as they care for their pet? How do you know that when you're no longer useful, they won't discard you like a broken dish? "But this woman is my wife, and we've been together for so long." And how long did Eriphyle live with Amphiaraus and have children with him? But then a necklace came between them. And what was the necklace? It was the idea that these things matter. That was what broke the friendship between husband and wife and stopped the woman from being a wife or mother. So, anyone who really wants to be a true friend or have a true friend should remove these ideas, hate them, and drive them out of their soul. Then, first of all, they won't blame themselves, won't be at odds with themselves, won't change their mind, and won't torment themselves. Next, they'll be a true friend to someone who is like them, completely and totally. They'll be patient with someone who is different, kind to them, gentle, and ready to forgive them because they know the person is mistaken about what really matters. They won't be harsh to anyone because they'll understand, as Plato said, that every mind loses the truth against its will. If you can't do this, you can still do what friends do—drink together, live together, travel together, and be born to the same parents—like snakes do. But neither they nor you will be friends as long as you hold onto these wild and cursed beliefs.

Chapter 23
On the Power of Speaking

Everyone finds it easier and more enjoyable to read a book when the words are clear and well-written. Similarly, people are more likely to listen and understand when words are used in a proper and fitting way. Therefore, we cannot say that the ability to express ourselves doesn't matter because that would be both disrespectful to the gifts given by God and a sign of fear. It would be disrespectful because it would mean we are undervaluing the talents given by God, just as if we ignored the gift of sight or hearing. Did God give us eyes for no reason? Did He give them the amazing ability to see far and to understand the things we see for nothing? What is faster or more accurate than sight? Did He create the air, which allows us to see, or the light, without which nothing would be visible, for no reason?

We should not be ungrateful for these gifts, nor should we forget the things that are even more important. We should thank God for our ability to see and hear, for life itself, and for the things that keep us alive, like food, wine, and oil. But we must also remember that God has given us something even better: the ability to use these gifts, to understand them, and to judge their value. What tells us the value of each of these abilities? Is it the ability itself? Have you ever heard your eyesight say anything about itself? Or your hearing? Or any other object? No, they are here to serve the ability that can make use of what we perceive. When you ask what the value of something is, who answers? How can any ability be stronger than the one that uses the others and judges them? Which of these abilities knows what it is and what it's worth? Which one knows when it should be used and when it shouldn't? What ability opens and closes your eyes, decides what you should look at, and what you should avoid? Is it your eyesight? No, it's your will. What ability opens and closes your ears, making you curious or uninterested in what you hear? Is it your hearing? No, it's your will.

So, if the will is the one that controls all these other abilities that are blind and silent, only able to do what they're meant to do, and if the will alone can see clearly and understand the value of everything else, will it ever say that something else is more important than itself? What does your eye do when it's open other than see? But who tells you whether you should look at a certain person's wife and how to do so? The will. And who tells you whether you should believe something you hear or not, and whether you should be affected by it? Isn't it the will? The ability to speak and make words sound good, if it exists as a separate ability, only arranges words like a hairdresser styles hair. But who tells us whether it's better to speak or stay silent, whether to speak in one way or another, and what is appropriate or not? Isn't it the will? Should the will then come forward and say that something else is more important than itself?

What does this mean? Can the thing that serves be greater than the thing it serves? Can a horse be greater than its rider, a dog greater than its hunter, a tool greater than the one who uses it, or a servant greater than the king? What controls everything else? The will. What takes care of everything? The will. What can destroy a person by making them starve, hang themselves, or jump off a cliff? The will. Is there anything stronger in a person than this? And how can things that are controlled by other forces be stronger than the thing that controls itself? What things naturally get in the way of your ability to see? Both your will and things outside of your control. It's the same with hearing and speaking. But what can naturally hinder the will? Nothing outside of the will; only the will itself, when it's twisted. Therefore, the will is either the source of all good or the source of all evil.

Being such a powerful ability, the will should tell us that the most important thing of all is the flesh. But even if the flesh itself claimed to be the best, no one would accept that. But what is it, Epicurus, that tells us what the purpose of life is, what the nature of things is, what the rule of truth is, that leads you to grow a beard, that writes when you're dying that you're spending your last day happily? Is it the flesh or the will? So, do you admit that you possess something greater than the will? Aren't you mad? Are you really so blind and deaf?

Does anyone despise the other abilities? I hope not. Does anyone say that the ability to speak is useless? I hope not. That would be foolish, disrespectful, and ungrateful to God. But a person should give each thing its proper value. For example, even a donkey has some use, but not as much as an ox. A dog has some use, but not as much as a slave. A slave has some use, but not as much as a citizen. A citizen has some use, but not as much as a leader. Just because some things are better than others doesn't mean we should undervalue the usefulness of other things. The ability to speak has value, but it's not as great as the will. When I say this, don't think I'm asking you to neglect the ability to speak, just like I wouldn't ask you to neglect your eyes, ears, hands, feet, clothes, or shoes. But if you ask me what the most important thing is, what should I say? I can't say the ability to speak, but the will, when it's right. Because the will uses the ability to speak, along with all the other small and great abilities. When the will is correct, a bad person becomes good; when it fails, a person becomes bad. It's through the will that we are happy or unhappy, that we blame or praise each other. In short, it's the will that, if we neglect it, causes unhappiness, and if we take care of it, brings happiness.

To deny the importance of the ability to speak and to say that it doesn't exist is not only ungrateful to those who gave it but also cowardly. Such a person seems to fear that if this ability exists, we won't be able to ignore it. This is similar to those who say there's no difference between beauty and ugliness. But if that were true, it would mean that a person would react the same way to seeing an ugly person as they would to seeing a beautiful one, or to seeing something beautiful as they would to seeing something plain. But these are foolish ideas from people who don't understand the nature of things and are afraid that if someone sees the difference, they will be overwhelmed by it. The important thing is to recognize the value of each ability, to understand what is truly the most important, and to always pursue that, considering everything else of lesser value but still taking care of those other things as much as we can. We must take care of our eyes, not because they are the most important thing, but because they help us take care of the most important thing. Our will won't be in its best condition if it doesn't use the other abilities correctly and prioritize some things over others.

What usually happens? People often act like a traveler on their way home who stops at a nice inn and decides to stay there. They forget their purpose: they weren't traveling to the inn, they were just passing through. "But this inn is nice," they might say. And how many other inns are nice? And how many meadows are beautiful? But they're all just places to pass through. Your real purpose is to return home, to relieve your family's worries, to fulfill your duties as a citizen, to marry, to have children, and to take on the responsibilities of a leader. You weren't born to choose the most pleasant places to live, but to live in the place where you were born and where you were made a citizen. This is similar to what we're talking about. Since you must use speech and communication to reach perfection, to purify your will, and to correct how you perceive things, and since teaching often requires a certain way of speaking with variety and sharpness, some people get so captivated by these things that they stay there, one drawn in by the way words are expressed, another by logical puzzles, another by tricky arguments, and still another by something else like these, and they waste away as if they were enchanted by Sirens.

Your purpose was to make yourself able to use your perceptions in a way that's in harmony with nature, to not be frustrated in your desires, to avoid what you should avoid, to never be unlucky or unhappy, to be free, not hindered, not forced, to align yourself with the order of the universe, to obey it, to be content with it, blaming no one, accusing no one, and being able to say with all your heart:

"Lead me, O Zeus, and Destiny."

But if, instead, you get caught up in some clever way of speaking, in some logical puzzle, do you stay there, forgetting your real purpose and saying, "These things are great"? Who says they're not great? But they're only great as a way to reach your real purpose, like inns are along the way. What stops you from being an unhappy person, even if you speak like Demosthenes? And what stops you from being miserable, from feeling sorrow, envy, or disturbance, from being unhappy, even if you solve logical puzzles like Chrysippus? Nothing. You see, these things are just tools, and your real purpose is something else. When I speak like this to some people, they think I'm saying that we should ignore the ability to speak or ignore logical puzzles. But I'm not saying that. I'm saying that we shouldn't get stuck on these things and think they are the most important. If my teaching causes harm to those who listen, then count me among those who do harm. For I cannot see one thing that is truly excellent and supreme and say that something else is, just to please you.

Chapter 24
To Someone Who Was Not Valued by Him

Someone once said to Epictetus, "I've often wanted to hear from you and came to you many times, but you never responded to me. Now, if possible, I beg you to say something to me." Epictetus replied, "Do you think that, just as there is skill in anything else, there is also skill in speaking, and that those who have the skill speak well, while those who don't have it speak poorly?" The person answered, "Yes, I do think so."

Epictetus continued, "So, someone who benefits from speaking and can help others by speaking will do so skillfully. But someone who harms themselves and others by speaking, will they be unskilled in this art of speaking? You may find that some people are harmed and others are helped by what they say. Do you think that everyone who hears something is helped by it, or do you believe that some are helped and some are harmed?" The person replied, "Both types exist."

"In that case," Epictetus said, "those who listen skillfully are helped, and those who listen poorly are harmed. Would you agree that there is a skill in listening just as there is in speaking?" The person agreed. "If you like, consider it this way too. Who practices music? A musician.

Who makes statues? A sculptor. Do you think looking at a statue well requires no skill?" The person replied, "It does require skill."

"Then if speaking properly is the work of a skilled person, do you see that listening properly, to gain benefit, is also the work of a skilled person? But let's put aside for now the idea of speaking and listening perfectly, because we are both far from that level. Still, I believe everyone would agree that anyone who wants to listen to philosophers needs some practice in listening. Don't you agree?"

"Tell me, then, what I should talk to you about. What subject can you listen to?" The person said, "About good and evil." Epictetus asked, "Good and evil in what? In a horse?" The person replied, "No." Epictetus continued, "In an ox?" Again, the person said, "No." "Then in what?" asked Epictetus. The person answered, "In a human being."

Epictetus asked, "Do we know what a human being is? Do we understand what the idea of a human being is? Or have we practiced listening to this kind of topic? Do you understand what nature is? Can you even begin to understand me if I say I'm going to explain it to you? Do you understand what explaining something is, how something is explained, or by what methods? Do you know what is true or false? What follows from a certain point, what contradicts it, or what is consistent or inconsistent?"

Epictetus went on, "But should I push you to study philosophy? And how should I do that? Should I show you how people's opinions clash because they don't agree on what is good or bad, or what is useful or harmful, when you don't even know what a contradiction is? Tell me what I will achieve by talking to you. Make me want to do this. Just as grass that is good for a sheep makes the sheep want to eat, but a stone or bread does not, we also have natural desires to speak when the listener seems to be someone worthwhile, when they make us want to speak. But if the listener is like a stone or a blade of grass, how can they make anyone want to speak? Does a vine ask the farmer to take care of it? No, but by showing that it will benefit the farmer if he does, the vine invites him to care for it. When children are lively and cheerful, who doesn't want to play with them, crawl with them, or mimic their baby talk? But who wants to play with a donkey or bray like it? Even if it's a small donkey, it's still a donkey."

"Why do you say nothing to me?" you might ask. I can only say this: A person who doesn't know who they are, why they exist, what this world is, who they live with, what is good or bad, what is beautiful or ugly, who doesn't understand logic or reasoning, who doesn't know what is true or false, and who can't tell the difference between them, will neither desire according to nature nor avoid things correctly. They won't move toward or away from things in the right way, won't make good decisions, won't agree or disagree properly, and won't hold back judgment when needed. In short, they will go around blind and silent, thinking they are someone important when they are really nobody. Is this a new problem? No, ever since people existed, all errors and misfortunes have come from this kind of ignorance. Why did Agamemnon and Achilles fight? Wasn't it because they didn't know what was useful and what wasn't? Didn't one say it was useful to return Chryseis to her father, while the other said it wasn't? Didn't one believe it was right to take someone else's prize, while the other said it wasn't? Didn't they forget who they were and why they had come to Troy?"

"Tell me, why did you come? To win mistresses or to fight?" The answer would be, "To fight." "With whom? The Trojans or the Greeks?" The answer would be, "With the Trojans." "Then why do you leave Hector alone and draw your sword against your own king? And you, my good man, why do you neglect your duties as king, you who are supposed to protect the people and take care of important matters, and instead argue about a girl with your strongest ally, whom you should be protecting and supporting? Are you now worse than a well-behaved priest who treats these fierce warriors with respect? Do you see what ignorance about what is useful can lead to?"

"But I am also rich," someone might say. Are you richer than Agamemnon? "But I am also handsome." Are you more handsome than Achilles? "But I have beautiful hair." Didn't Achilles have more beautiful, golden hair, yet he didn't spend time styling it? "But I am also strong." Can you lift as much as Hector or Ajax? "But I am of noble birth." Are you the child of a goddess? Is your father descended from Zeus? What good are these things to you if you end up sitting and crying over a girl? "But I am a skilled speaker." Wasn't Achilles also skilled? Didn't he handle the best Greek speakers, like Odysseus and Phoenix, and silence them?

This is all I have to say to you, and I say it unwillingly. Why? Because you haven't inspired me. What do I need to be inspired, like a skilled rider is inspired by a spirited horse? Should I look at your body? You don't take care of it. Should I look at your clothes? They are extravagant. Should I look at your behavior or your expression? They mean nothing. When you come to listen to a philosopher, don't say, "You tell me nothing." Instead, show yourself as someone worth talking to, and you will see how you inspire the speaker.

Chapter 25
How The Art of Reasoning is Necessary

When someone who was present said, "Convince me that logic is necessary," Epictetus replied, "Do you want me to prove this to you?" The person answered, "Yes." Then Epictetus said, "To prove it, I must use a logical form of speech." The person agreed. Epictetus then asked, "How will you know if I am tricking you with my argument?" The person was silent. Epictetus then said, "Do you see that you are admitting logic is necessary, since without it, you wouldn't even know whether logic is necessary or not?"

Chapter 26
Understanding the Nature of Mistakes

Every mistake involves a contradiction, because when someone makes a mistake, they don't want to be wrong—they want to be right. It's clear that they don't do what they wish to do. For example, what does a thief want to do? They want to do what benefits them. But if stealing doesn't actually benefit them, they are not doing what they really want.

Every rational mind naturally dislikes contradictions. As long as someone doesn't understand that they are contradicting themselves, they will continue to do contradictory things. But when they do understand the contradiction, they will avoid it as much as a person avoids something false when they recognize it as false. But as long as something false doesn't appear false to them, they will accept it as true.

The person who is strong in argument and has the ability to encourage and correct others can show each person the contradiction that leads them into error, and can clearly prove how they are not doing what they wish to do, and instead are doing what they don't wish to do. If someone shows this to a person, that person will stop doing what they're doing. But as long as this isn't shown to them, don't be surprised if they keep doing it, because it seems to them that they are doing the right thing.

For this reason, Socrates, trusting in this power, used to say, "I don't need any other witness to what I say; I am always satisfied with the person I am discussing with, and I ask them to give their opinion and to be my witness. Even if they are the only one, they are enough in place of everyone." Socrates knew how the rational mind works, just like a pair of scales that must tip when it sees a contradiction, whether it wants to or not. Show the rational mind a contradiction, and it will move away from it. But if you don't show it, you should blame yourself, not the person who isn't persuaded.

Book III

Chapter 1
On Adornment

A young man, who was studying to be a public speaker, came to see Epictetus. His hair was styled more carefully than usual, and he was dressed in fancy clothes. Epictetus asked him, "Tell me, do you not think that some dogs are beautiful and some horses are beautiful, just like all other animals?" The young man replied, "Yes, I do think so." Epictetus then asked, "Are not some men also beautiful and others ugly?" The young man answered, "Certainly."

Epictetus continued, "Do we call each of these animals beautiful for the same reason, or is each one beautiful for something specific? Think about it this way: A dog is made for one thing, a horse for another, and a nightingale for yet another. We can generally say that each of these animals is beautiful when it is excellent according to its nature. But since the nature of each is different, they each seem beautiful in a different way. Is it not so?" The young man admitted that it was true. Epictetus then said, "So, what makes a dog beautiful might make a horse ugly, and what makes a horse beautiful might make a dog ugly, if their natures are different." The young man agreed, "It seems to be so."

Epictetus then added, "For example, what makes a Pancratiast beautiful might make a wrestler not good, and what makes a runner beautiful might make him look ridiculous. Someone who is beautiful for the Pentathlon might be very ugly for wrestling." The young man agreed again, saying, "It is so." Epictetus asked, "What then makes a man beautiful? Is it the same thing that makes both a dog and a horse beautiful?" The young man responded, "It is." Epictetus then asked, "What makes a dog beautiful?" The young man answered, "The possession of the excellence of a dog." Epictetus continued, "And what makes a horse beautiful?" The young man replied, "The possession of the excellence of a horse." Then Epictetus asked, "What then makes a man beautiful? Is it not the possession of the excellence of a man?"

Epictetus then advised the young man, "If you want to be beautiful, young man, work on acquiring human excellence. But what is human excellence? Think about whom you yourself praise when you praise many people without partiality. Do you praise the just or the unjust?

You praise the just. Do you praise the moderate or the immoderate? You praise the moderate. Do you praise the temperate or the intemperate? You praise the temperate. If you make yourself such a person, you will know that you will make yourself beautiful. But if you neglect these things, you must be ugly, even though you do all you can to appear beautiful."

Epictetus then reflected, "I do not know what more to say to you. For if I say what I think, I may offend you, and you might leave and never come back. But if I do not say what I think, see how I would be acting. If you come to me to be improved, and I do not improve you at all, if you come to me as to a philosopher, and I say nothing to you as a philosopher, how cruel it would be to leave you uncorrected. If at any time later you gain some sense, you might blame me, and say, 'What did Epictetus see in me that when he saw me in such a bad condition, he neglected me and never said a word? Did he so much despair of me? Was I not young? Was I not able to listen to reason? And how many other young men at my age make similar mistakes? I heard that a certain Polemon, who was a very dissolute youth, went through a great change. Well, even if Epictetus did not think I would become like Polemon, he might have at least told me to fix my hair, take off my decorations, and stop plucking the hair out of my body. But when he saw me dressed like this, he kept silent.' I do not say like what; but you will understand when you come to your senses, and know what it is, and what kind of people wear such clothing."

Epictetus then questioned, "If you bring this charge against me later, what defense will I have? Should I say that you would not have been persuaded by me? Was Laius persuaded by Apollo? Did he not ignore the oracle and get drunk instead? Well then, for this reason, did Apollo refuse to tell him the truth? I do not know whether you will be persuaded by me or not; but Apollo knew for sure that Laius would not be persuaded, and yet he still spoke. But why did he speak? I would say in reply: Why is he Apollo, and why does he deliver oracles? Why has he fixed himself in this place as a prophet and a source of truth for the inhabitants of the world to come to him? And why are the words 'Know yourself' written in front of the temple, though no one pays attention to them?"

Epictetus continued, "Did Socrates persuade all his listeners to take care of themselves? Not even one in a thousand. But still, after he had been placed in this position by the deity, as he himself said, he never left it. And what did he say even to his judges? 'If you acquit me on the condition that I stop doing what I do now, I will not agree, and I will not stop. I will go to young and old alike, and speak plainly to every person I meet. I will ask the questions that I ask now, and most especially to you, my fellow citizens, because you are more closely related to me.' Are you so curious, Socrates, and such a busybody? And how does it concern you how we act? And what is it that you say? Being of the same community and of the same kin, you neglect yourself and show yourself to be a bad citizen to the state, a bad kinsman to your kin, and a bad neighbor to your neighbors. Who then are you? Here it is a great thing to say, 'I am the one whose duty it is to take care of men. For it is not every little heifer that dares to resist a lion; but if the bull comes up and resists him, say to the bull, if you like, "Who are you, and what business do you have here?"' In every kind, there is something produced that excels; in oxen, in dogs, in bees, in horses. So do not say to that which excels, 'Who then are you?' If you do, it will find a way to speak and say, 'I am like the purple in a garment; do not expect me to be like the others, or blame my nature for making me different from the rest of men.'"

Epictetus then questioned himself, "What then? Am I such a man? Certainly not. And are you such a man who can listen to the truth? I wish you were. But since I am in a way condemned to wear a white beard and a cloak, and you come to me as to a philosopher, I will not treat you cruelly, nor act as if I despair of you. But I will say: Young man, whom do you wish to make beautiful? First, know who you are, and then adorn yourself accordingly. You are a human being, and this is a mortal animal that has the power to use appearances rationally. But what does it mean to use appearances rationally? It means acting in conformity with nature and doing so completely. So what do you possess that is unique? Is it the animal part? No. Is it the condition of mortality? No. Is it the power to use appearances? No. You possess the rational faculty as something unique. Adorn and beautify this, but leave your hair to the one who made it as he chose."

Epictetus asked, "Come, what other labels do you have? Are you a man or a woman? A man. Then adorn yourself as a man, not as a woman. A woman is naturally smooth and delicate, and if she has much hair on her body, she is seen as a monster and is exhibited in Rome among other monsters. And in a man, it is monstrous not to have hair. If he has no hair, he is a monster; but if he cuts off his hair and plucks it out, what should we do with him? Where should we exhibit him, and under what name should we show him? I will exhibit to you a man who chooses to be a woman rather than a man. What a terrible sight! There is no man who will not wonder at such a notice. Indeed, I think that the men who pluck out their hair do so without understanding what they are doing."

Epictetus then asked, "Man, what fault do you find with your nature? That it made you a man? Should nature have made all human creatures women? And what advantage would you have had in being adorned? For whom would you have adorned yourself if all human creatures were women? But you are not pleased with this. So set to work on the whole business. Take away—what is its name?—that which causes the hair to grow. Make yourself a woman in all respects, so that we may not be mistaken. Do not make one half man and the other half woman. Whom do you wish to please? The women? Please them as a man. But they like smooth men. Will you not hang yourself? And if women took delight in catamites, would you become one? Is this your purpose? Were you born for this, that dissolute women should delight in you? Should we make someone like you a citizen of Corinth, perhaps a leader of the city, or the head of the youth, or a general or supervisor of the games? Well, when you have taken a wife, do you intend to have your hair plucked out? To please whom and for what purpose? And when you have children, will you raise them with the habit of plucking their hair? A beautiful citizen, a senator, a rhetorician. We ought to pray that such young men are born among us and raised well."

Epictetus then pleaded, "Do not do this, I beg you by the Gods, young man. But when you have heard these words, go away and say to yourself, 'Epictetus did not say this to me; for how could he? But some kind God spoke through him. For it would never have occurred to him to say this, since he is not accustomed to talking like this with anyone. Come, let us obey God, so that we may not be subject to his anger.' You say, 'No.' But I say, if a crow's croaking means something to you, it is not the crow that means something, but God speaking through the crow. And if God signifies something through a human voice, will he not cause the man to say this to you, so that you may know the power of the divine? That he signifies to some in this way and to others in that way? And concerning the greatest things and the chief, he signifies through the noblest messenger."

Epictetus ended with, "What else does the poet say? 'For we ourselves have warned him, and have sent Hermes, the careful watcher, the slayer of Argus, to warn the husband not to kill nor wed the wife.' Was Hermes going to come down from heaven to say this to him? And now the Gods say this to you and send the messenger, the slayer of Argus, to warn you not to distort what is well arranged, nor to meddle with it, but to allow a man to be a man, and a woman to be a woman, a beautiful man to be a beautiful man, and an ugly man to be an ugly man. For you are not just flesh and hair, but you are will (proairesis); and if your will is beautiful, then you will be beautiful. But up to now, I dare not tell you that you are ugly, for I think you are more willing to hear anything than this. But see what Socrates says to the most beautiful and blooming of men, Alcibiades: 'Try then to be beautiful.' What does he say to him? Dress your hair and pluck the hairs from your legs? Nothing of that kind. But adorn your will, take away bad opinions. What about the body? Leave it as it is by nature. Another has looked after these things. Trust them to him. What then, must a man be unclean? Certainly not. But what you are and what you are made by nature, cleanse this. A man should be clean as a man, a woman as a woman, a child as a child. You say no, but let us also pluck out the lion's mane so that he may not be unclean, and the cock's comb because he too ought to be clean. Granted, but as a cock, and the lion as a lion, and the hunting dog as a hunting dog."

With this, Epictetus ended his lesson, leaving the young man to reflect on what truly makes someone beautiful.

Chapter 2
What to Focus on for Real Progress: And How We Often Ignore What's Most Important

There are three main areas where a person should practice if they want to be wise and good. The first area is about our likes and dislikes. This means that a person should work on getting what they really want and avoiding what they don't want. The second area is about our actions, like moving toward something or away from something. It also means doing what's right, according to reason, and not being careless. The third area is about not being fooled or making quick decisions. This means being careful when we agree with something, making sure we are thinking wisely.

Out of these three areas, the most important one is about our feelings. Feelings get stirred up when we don't get what we want or when we end up in situations we want to avoid. This makes us feel upset, unlucky, sad, or jealous. These feelings can make it hard for us to listen to reason. The second area is about what duties we have. This means that while we shouldn't be emotionless like a statue, we should still be a good person, a respectful child, a responsible parent, or a good citizen.

The third area is especially important for those who are making progress. It helps secure the other two areas so that even when we are asleep, drunk, or feeling down, we don't make bad choices. Some people might say this is too hard, but many modern philosophers often ignore the first and second areas (feelings and duties) and focus only on the third. They use tricky arguments, draw conclusions from questions, use ideas that aren't real, and sometimes lie. They say a person must be careful not to be fooled. But who needs to do this? A wise and good person. Is this the only thing left for you to work on? Have you already mastered everything else? Are you free from being fooled by money? If you see a beautiful girl, can you resist being swayed by her looks? If your neighbor inherits land, do you not feel jealous? If you still struggle with these things, do you really think you only need to work on being completely steady?

Poor soul, you hear these things with fear and worry, afraid that someone might look down on you or wonder what others might say about you. If someone tells you that during a conversation about who is the best philosopher, a person said that someone else was the best, your small and anxious heart suddenly swells with pride. But if another person says, "You are mistaken; that person is not worth listening to; they only know the basics and nothing more," you become confused, pale, and immediately want to prove that you are a great philosopher. But it's already clear from how you react to these words. Why do you need to prove it further? Don't you know that Diogenes pointed out one of the sophists by simply sticking out his middle finger? When the man got angry, Diogenes said, "This is the person I was talking about; I have pointed him out to you." A person is not shown by pointing, like a rock or a piece of wood, but by showing what they believe in.

Let's also look at what you believe in. Isn't it clear that you don't value your own choices at all? Instead, you focus on things outside your control, like what others will say about you, whether people will think you are smart, or whether you have read the works of famous philosophers like Chrysippus or Antipater. If you have even read

Archedemus, you feel like you have achieved everything. But why are you still uneasy, feeling the need to prove who you are? Do you want me to tell you what kind of person you have shown yourself to be? You have shown yourself to be mean, always complaining, easily angered, fearful, critical of everything, blaming everyone, never at peace, and vain. This is what you have shown us. Now, go away and read Archedemus. But know that if a mouse jumps down and makes a noise, you will be scared to death, just like that man—what was his name?—Crinis, who was also proud because he understood Archedemus.

Poor soul, will you not let go of these things that don't concern you at all? These things are meant for those who can learn them without being upset, for those who can say, "I am not controlled by anger, sadness, or envy. I am not held back or stopped. What is left for me? I have free time, I am calm. Let me now study how to deal with tricky arguments, and how, when a person accepts an idea, they should not be led to something silly." Such things belong to them. For those who are happy, it is appropriate to light a fire, have a meal, and, if they choose, sing and dance. But when the ship is sinking, you come to me and try to raise the sails.

Chapter 3
What a Good Person Should Focus On and Practice Most

The thing that a wise and good person should focus on is their own mind and how they think. Just like a doctor works with the body and a farmer works with the land, a good person's job is to use their mind in a way that matches what is natural and true. It is natural for every mind to agree with what is true, to reject what is false, and to be unsure about what we don't know. It is also natural to want good things and avoid bad things, and to feel neutral about things that are neither good nor bad. Just like a banker can't refuse to accept the emperor's coin, our minds naturally accept what seems good and reject what seems bad.

This is why good is more important than anything else, even our closest relationships. There is no closer connection to me than the good itself. You might think I am hard-hearted for saying this, but that's how I am made; it's like a coin that God has given me. So, if something is good but not beautiful or just, I would still choose the good over my father, my brother, or even my country. Should I give up my own good so that someone else can have it? Why should I? Just because you're my father? But you are not my good. Just because you're my brother? But you are not my good either. But if we believe that good is found in making the right choices, then being a good son, father, or citizen is also good. And if we give up some external things, we can still hold on to what is truly good. If your father takes away your property, he hasn't really harmed you. If your brother gets more of the inheritance, that doesn't take away your sense of right and wrong, your honesty, or your love for your family. No one can take these things from you, not even Zeus, because he has made these things yours alone, free from anyone's control.

So, when you deal with people who value different things, like money or power, they will respond to those things. If a corrupt official comes to your town, he might want silver. If you show him silver, he will give you what you want. If someone loves pleasure, they might want young girls or boys. If someone is a hunter, they might want a good horse or dog. Everyone has their own "coin" that they value, and they will trade what they have for it.

This is why it's important to practice understanding what things really are. When you wake up in the morning, look at everyone you meet or hear about, and ask yourself: What have I seen? Is it something that depends on me or not? If it's not, let it go. Did you see someone who looks good? That's something outside of your control. Did you see someone grieving? Death is outside of your control. Did you meet a powerful official? His position is outside of your control. Let these things go; they are not yours to worry about.

If we practiced this every day, from morning to night, we would really make progress. But instead, we often get caught up in things while we're not fully awake, and only occasionally wake up a little when we are in school. Then, when we see someone grieving, we think, "This person is ruined." When we see someone with power, we think, "This person is happy." When we see someone who has been exiled, we think, "This person is miserable." When we see someone who is poor, we think, "This person is wretched because they have nothing to eat."

We need to get rid of these wrong ideas, and that's where we should focus our efforts. What is crying and grieving? It's an opinion. What is bad luck? It's an opinion. What is political conflict, disagreement, blame, accusation, or disrespect? These are all just opinions, and nothing more. These are opinions about things outside our control, as if they were good or bad. But if we change these opinions to focus on things we can control, I promise that you will become strong and steady, no matter what happens around you. The mind is like a dish of water, and appearances are like light shining on it. When the water is disturbed, the light seems to move, but it really doesn't. When a person feels confused, it's not their knowledge or skills that are shaken, but the part of the mind that holds these things. If the mind is calmed, everything else returns to normal.

With this, Epictetus leaves us to think about what truly matters and what we should focus on in our lives.

Chapter 4
Speaking Out Against Someone Who Acted Inappropriately in a Theatre

The governor of Epirus showed his support for an actor in a way that was not appropriate, and people criticized him for it. Later, the governor told Epictetus that he was upset by the criticism and that he was angry at those who blamed him. Epictetus responded, "What harm did they do? They were just showing support, just like you were." The governor replied, "But does anyone show their support like that?"

Epictetus then said, "When people see you, their governor, a friend of Caesar and his representative, showing support in that way, wouldn't you expect them to do the same? If it's not right to show support like that, then don't do it yourself. But if it is right, why are you angry when they follow your example? Who do the people look up to except you, their leader? Whose example should they follow when they go to the theatre, if not yours?

Look at how Caesar's representative acts: he shouts out, so I will shout out too. He jumps up from his seat, so I will jump up too. His servants sit in different parts of the theatre and shout. I don't have servants, but I will shout as loud as I can, just like them. You should realize that when you enter the theatre, you are setting a rule and example for everyone else on how they should watch the play."

Epictetus continued, "So why did they blame you? Because everyone hates being stopped from getting what they want. They wanted one person to win, and you wanted another. They got in your way, and you got in theirs. You were stronger, so they did the only thing they could: they blamed what blocked them. What do you expect? That you can do whatever you want, but they can't even say what they want? Why are you surprised? Don't farmers curse Zeus when their crops are ruined? Don't sailors curse him during storms? Don't people always complain about Caesar? What then? Doesn't Zeus know this? Isn't Caesar told about it? What do they do? They know that if they punished everyone who complained, they wouldn't have anyone left to rule over.

So, when you go to the theatre, don't just say, 'I want Sophron (an actor) to win.' Instead, say this: 'Let me keep my mind in control and act according to nature. No one is more important to me than myself. It would be silly for me to get upset just because an actor wins or loses. Who do I want to win? The actor who actually wins. That way, whoever wins is the one I wanted to win.' But if you really want Sophron to win, then hold your own games at home—Nemean, Pythian, Isthmian, Olympian—and declare him the winner. But in public, don't try to take more than your share or act like you own the place. If you don't agree with this, then be prepared to be criticized. When you act like everyone else, you put yourself on their level."

With this, Epictetus reminds us that our actions set an example for others, and we must be mindful of the influence we have, especially in public settings.

Chapter 5
Speaking Out Against Those Who Want to Go Home Because of Sickness

"I am sick here," one of the students said, "and I want to go back home." Do you think that at home you will be free from sickness? Have you considered whether you're doing anything here that could help you strengthen your willpower, so you can improve yourself? Because if you're not working on that, there was no point in coming here. Go ahead, go home. Take care of your own matters. If you can't keep your mind in a state that follows nature, maybe you can manage your land better, make more money, take care of your father in his old age, spend time in public places, or hold an official position. But if you are a bad person, you will do all these things badly too.

But if you understand yourself and know that you are replacing bad thoughts with better ones, and if you have changed your life from focusing on things outside your control to things within your control, then if you ever say, "Oh no!" it won't be because of your father or your brother but because of yourself. So, do you still blame your sickness? Don't you know that both sickness and death will come while we're doing something? The farmer is busy in the field, the sailor is busy at sea, so what would you be doing when death catches you? It must catch you while you're doing something. If you can be doing something better than this when you're caught, then do it. I want to be caught by sickness or death while I am focused on taking care of my own will, so I can be free from worry, free from obstacles, free from force, and truly free.

I want to be found practicing these things so that I can say to God, "Have I disobeyed any of your commands? Have I misused the powers you gave me? Did I see things the wrong way or have wrong ideas? Have I ever blamed you? Have I ever criticized how you run things? I was sick because that was your will, and so were others, but I accepted being sick. I was poor because that was your will, but I accepted that too. I didn't hold a public office because you didn't want me to, and I never desired it. Have you ever seen me unhappy because of this? Haven't I always approached you with a happy face, ready to follow your commands and do what you signal? Is it now your will that I leave the company of people? I will leave. I thank you for allowing me to be part of this group of people, to see your works, and to understand how you manage everything." May death come while I am thinking about these things, while I am writing and reading like this.

"But my mother won't hold my head when I am sick." Then go to your mother; you are the kind of person who needs someone to hold your head when you're sick. "But at home, I used to lie down on a comfortable bed." Then go to your bed: you are indeed someone who should lie on such a bed, even when you're healthy. So don't miss out on what you can do there at home.

But what does Socrates say? He says that just as one man enjoys improving his land and another enjoys improving his horse, I enjoy seeing myself get better every day. "Better at what? At using fancy words?" Don't say that. "At little bits of knowledge?" What are you talking about? "I don't see what else philosophers spend their time on." Does it seem like nothing to you to have never blamed anyone, neither God nor man? To have never criticized anyone? To always have the same calm face whether you're going out or coming in? This is what Socrates knew, yet he never said he knew anything or taught anything. But if someone wanted fancy words or little bits of knowledge, he would send them to Protagoras or Hippias, and if someone wanted vegetables, he would send them to the gardener. So who among you has this goal in mind? Because if you did, you would be content in sickness, in hunger, and even in death. If any of you have been in love with a charming girl, you know that what I am saying is true.

Chapter 6
Various Sayings

Someone once asked him how it happened that even though people today have developed reason more, the progress made in the past was greater. He replied, "In what way has reason been developed more today, and in what way was the progress greater in the past? Because in whatever way reason has been developed more now, progress will be found in that same area. Today, reason has been developed for solving logical puzzles, and so progress has been made there. But in the past, reason was developed for keeping the mind in a state that follows nature, and that's where progress was made. So don't mix different things together, and don't expect to make progress in one area while working on another. But look and see if any of us who focus on keeping our minds in line with nature and living that way always does not make progress. You won't find such a person."

A good man is unbeatable because he doesn't get into fights where he isn't stronger. If you, his opponent, want to take his land and everything on it, go ahead—take the land, take his slaves, take his job, take his poor body. But you won't make his desires fail or force him into something he wants to avoid. The only fight he enters is about things that are under his control, so how can he not be unbeatable?

Someone else asked him, "What is common sense?" Epictetus replied, "Just like how there's a basic sense of hearing that lets us tell the difference between sounds, and a more trained ear that can distinguish musical notes, there are basic things that people who aren't completely messed up can see with the common understanding that everyone has. This basic understanding is called common sense."

It's not easy to motivate young men who are weak, just like it's not easy to hold soft cheese with a hook. But those who have a good natural character, even if you try to turn them away, will stick to reason even more. That's why Rufus often tried to discourage his students. He used this method to test who had a good natural character and who didn't. He would often say, "Just as a stone, if you throw it up, will fall back to the earth by its own nature, a man whose mind is naturally good will turn even more toward what he is naturally inclined to, no matter how much you push him away."

Chapter 7
Conversation With the Governor of the Free Cities, Who Was an Epicurean

When the administrator, who was an Epicurean, came to visit him, Epictetus said, "It is right for those of us who are not philosophers to ask you who are philosophers, just like people who visit a new city ask the locals, 'What is the best thing in the world?' so that we too can look for what is best and appreciate it, just like visitors do with the sights in a city. Almost everyone agrees that there are three things related to people—soul, body, and external things. Now, it's up to you philosophers to answer what is the best. What should we tell people? Is the flesh the best? Did Maximus sail as far as Cassiope in winter with his son just to satisfy his flesh? When the administrator replied that it was not, and added, 'Far be it from him,' Epictetus asked, 'Isn't it proper, then, to focus on what is truly the best?' The administrator replied, 'It is certainly the most proper thing.'

'What do we have that is better than the flesh?' Epictetus asked. 'The soul,' the administrator replied. 'And are the good things of the soul better, or are the good things of the body better?' 'The good things of the soul,' said the administrator. 'And are the good things of the soul within the power of our will or not?' 'They are within the power of our will,' replied the administrator. 'Is the pleasure of the soul something within our control?' 'It is,' the administrator answered.

'And what does this pleasure depend on?' Epictetus continued. 'Does it depend on itself? That can't be, because first, there must be a certain substance or nature of good, by obtaining which we get pleasure in the soul.' The administrator agreed. 'So, what do we depend on for this pleasure of the soul? Because if it depends on the things of the soul, then the nature of the good is discovered. For the good cannot be one thing, and what gives us rational pleasure something else. Nor can something that is not good lead to something good. If what comes after is good, then what comes before must also be good. But you wouldn't say this if you are thinking clearly, for that would contradict both Epicurus and the rest of your teachings. So it must be that the pleasure of the soul comes from the pleasure of the body, and therefore, bodily things must be the foundation and the essence of the good.'

'For this reason, Maximus acted foolishly if he made that voyage for any reason other than the sake of the flesh, that is, for the sake of what is best. And a person acts foolishly if he refrains from taking what belongs to others when he is a judge and has the power to take it. But if you like, let's consider only how this can be done secretly and safely, so that no one finds out. For even Epicurus doesn't say stealing is bad, but he does say getting caught is bad. And because it's impossible to be completely safe from getting caught, he says, "Don't steal." But I say that if stealing is done cleverly and cautiously, we won't get caught. Besides, we have powerful friends in Rome, both men and women, and the Greeks are weak, and no one would dare go to Rome to complain. Why do you hold back from your own good? This is foolish. And even if you tell me you do hold back, I won't believe you. Just as it is impossible to believe something that appears false or to reject something that appears true, it is also impossible to hold back from what seems good. But wealth is a good thing, and it is certainly effective in producing pleasure. Why don't you go after wealth? And why shouldn't we take our neighbor's wife if we can do it without being caught? And if the husband foolishly complains, why not throw him out of the house? If you want to be a philosopher as you should be, a perfect philosopher consistent with your teachings, you must act this way. If you don't, then you are no different from us who are called

Stoics, for we also say one thing and do another. We talk about what is good, but we do what is bad. But you will be contradictory in the opposite way, teaching what is bad and practicing what is good.'

'In the name of God, are you thinking of a city of Epicureans? Someone says, "I won't marry." Another says, "Neither will I, because a man shouldn't marry, and we shouldn't have children or get involved in public matters." What will happen then? Where will the citizens come from? Who will raise them? Who will govern the youth, or oversee their physical training? And what will the teacher instruct them in? Will he teach them what the Spartans learned or what the Athenians learned? Bring up a young man according to your doctrines. The doctrines are bad, destructive to a state, harmful to families, and not suitable for women. Get rid of them, man. You live in a leading city; it is your duty to be a magistrate, to judge fairly, to refrain from taking what belongs to others. No woman should seem beautiful to you except your own wife, and no youth, no silver vessel, no gold vessel, except your own. Seek doctrines that are consistent with what I say, and by following them, you will happily abstain from things that have such persuasive power to lead and overpower us. But if, in addition to the persuasive power of these things, we also create a philosophy that helps push us toward them and strengthens us in this direction, what will be the result? In a piece of art, which is the best part—the silver or the workmanship? The substance of the hand is the flesh, but the work of the hand is the most important part, leading the rest. The duties, then, are also threefold: those directed toward the existence of a thing, those directed toward its existence in a particular kind, and third, the most important things themselves. So, in people, we should not value the material, the poor flesh, but the leading things, the most important aspects. What are these? Engaging in public service, marrying, having children, worshipping God, taking care of parents, and generally, having desires, aversions, and pursuits in the way we ought to and according to our nature. And how are we naturally made? Free, noble, modest. What other animal blushes? What other animal can feel shame?

We are made by nature to put pleasure in its place as a servant, to encourage us to act in ways that are in line with nature.'

'But I am rich and want for nothing,' you might say. Why then do you pretend to be a philosopher? Your gold and silver vessels are enough for you. What need do you have for principles? 'But I am also a judge of the Greeks.' Do you know how to judge? Who taught you? 'Caesar wrote me a letter of appointment.' Let him write you an appointment to judge music, and what good will it do you? How did you become a judge? Whose hand did you kiss? The hand of Symphorus or Numenius? In front of whose bedroom did you wait? To whom did you send gifts? Don't you see that being a judge is worth just as much as being Numenius? 'But I can throw anyone I want into prison.' So can you do with a stone. 'But I can beat anyone I want with sticks.' So you can do to a donkey. This is not governing people. Govern us as rational beings: show us what is good for us, and we will follow it; show us what is bad, and we will turn away from it. Make us imitators of you, as Socrates made people imitators of himself. For he was like a governor of people, guiding their desires, aversions, actions, and decisions. He would say, 'Do this; don't do that.' If you don't obey, I will throw you in prison. This is not governing people as rational beings. But I say, 'As Zeus has ordained, so act; if you do not act so, you will feel the consequences, you will be punished.' What will be the punishment? Nothing more than not having done your duty; you will lose the qualities of faithfulness, modesty, and propriety. Don't look for greater penalties than these."

Chapter 8
How We Should Train Ourselves to Deal with Impressions

Just as we practice dealing with tricky questions, we should also practice daily against appearances, because appearances also challenge us with questions. For example, someone's son has died. How should we respond? The event is not within our control, so it's not evil. A father has disinherited his son. What do you think of it? It's something beyond our control, so it's not evil. Caesar has condemned a person. Again, it's beyond our control, so it's not evil. The man is upset by this. Feeling upset is something that depends on our will, so it is evil. But if he has accepted the condemnation bravely, that's within his control, so it's good.

If we train ourselves in this way, we will make progress, because we will never agree to anything unless there's an appearance that we can fully understand. Your son is dead. What has happened? Your son is dead. Anything more? No, that's it. Your ship is lost. What has happened? Your ship is lost. A man has been taken to prison. What has happened? He's been taken to prison. But when people say he has fared badly, they are adding their own opinion.

You might say that Zeus is not doing the right thing in these matters. Why? Because he made you capable of enduring them? Because he made you strong? Because he took away the power of these events to be true evils? Because it's possible for you to be happy even while suffering? Because he has given you an escape when things don't please you? If you don't like what's happening, then leave and don't complain.

If you want to know how the Romans feel about philosophers, listen to this. Italicus, who was the most respected of the philosophers, once got upset with his own friends, and as if he was suffering something unbearable, he said, "I can't stand this; you're killing me! You'll make me just like that man over there," pointing to me.

Chapter 9
To a Rhetorician Who Was Going to Rome for a Trial

When a man came to Epictetus because he was going to Rome for a legal case that concerned his status, Epictetus asked him why he was going to Rome. The man then asked Epictetus what he thought about it. Epictetus replied, "If you ask me what you will do in Rome, whether you will succeed or fail, I can't tell you because I have no rule for this. But if you ask me how you will fare, I can tell you: if you have the right opinions, you will do well; if your opinions are wrong, you will do poorly. For every person acts based on their opinions. Why did you want to be elected governor of the Cnossians? It was your opinion. Why are you now going to Rome? It's your opinion. And you're going in winter, with all its danger and cost. 'I must go,' you say. What tells you this? Your opinion. So, if opinions cause all actions, and a person has bad opinions, the result will match the cause. Do we all have sound opinions, both you and your opponent? How do you differ then? Do you have better opinions than your opponent? Why do you think so? He also believes his opinions are better, just like a madman does. This is not a good way to measure truth. But show me that you have examined your opinions and worked on them.

Just as you are now sailing to Rome to become governor of the Cnossians, and you're not content to stay at home with the honors you already have but desire something greater and more noticeable, when did you ever take a journey to examine your own opinions and get rid of any bad ones? Who have you consulted for this purpose? When have you set aside time for this? At what stage of your life? Look back at the times of your life by yourself if you are ashamed to tell me. When you were a boy, did you examine your own opinions, or did you just do what you did without thinking? When you were a youth and attended the rhetoricians, and practiced rhetoric yourself, did you ever think you were lacking in anything? When you became a young man, involved in public matters, arguing cases, and gaining reputation, who then seemed your equal? And when would you have allowed anyone to examine and show you that your opinions were wrong?

So, what do you want me to say to you now? 'Help me with this matter.' I have no rule for this. And if you came to me for this purpose, you didn't come to me as a philosopher but as you would go to a vegetable seller or a shoemaker. What, then, are philosophers' rules for? They are for this purpose: that whatever may happen, our ruling mind may be and continue to be in line with nature. Does this seem like a small thing to you? 'No; it is the greatest.' What then? Does it require only a short time? Can it be grasped just by passing by? If you can, grasp it.

Then you will say, 'I met with Epictetus just like I would meet with a stone or a statue,' because you saw me and nothing more. But a person truly meets with another as a person when they learn his opinions and, in turn, show their own. Learn my opinions, show me yours, and then say that you have visited me. Let us examine each other: if I have any bad opinions, take them away; if you have any, show them. This is the purpose of meeting with a philosopher. 'Not so,' you might say, 'but this is just a passing visit. While we're hiring the ship, we can also see Epictetus. Let's see what he says.' Then you go away and say, 'Epictetus was nothing; he used bad grammar and spoke in a strange way.' But what else did you come as judges of?

A man might say to me, 'If I pay attention to matters like you do, I will have no land, like you have none; I will have no silver cups, like you have none; nor fine animals, like you have none.' To this, it's enough to say, 'I have no need for such things; but if you possess many things, you have a need for even more. Whether you like it or not, you are poorer than I am.' 'What do I need, then?' 'You need what you do not have: firmness, a mind that is in line with nature, freedom from anxiety. Whether I have a patron or not, what does that matter to me? But it matters to you. I am richer than you: I am not anxious about what Caesar will think of me. That is why I flatter no one. This is what I have instead of silver and gold vessels. You have gold utensils, but your words, your opinions, your decisions, your desires are made of clay. But when I have these things in line with nature, why shouldn't I also focus on reason? I have leisure; my mind is not distracted. What should I do, since I have no distractions? What is more suitable for a person than this? When you have nothing to do, you get bored, you go to the theater, or you wander around without purpose. Why shouldn't the philosopher work to improve his reason? You work on crystal vessels; I work on the problem called 'the liar.' You focus on fancy vessels; I work on the problem called 'the denier.' To you, everything you have seems small; to me, everything I have seems great. Your desire is insatiable; mine is satisfied. This is like when children put their hand into a narrow-necked jar and try to pull out figs and nuts. If they fill their hand, they can't take it out, and then they cry. Let go of a few of them, and you will be able to pull your hand out. In the same way, let go of some of your desires. Don't desire too many things, and you will have what you want."

Chapter 10
How We Should Endure Sickness

When the time comes for each opinion, we should have it ready: at breakfast, the opinions that relate to breakfast; in the bath, those that concern the bath; in bed, those that concern bed.

"Let sleep not come upon your tired eyes
Before you have reviewed each day's actions:
What's been done wrong,
what's been done right, what's been left undone;
From start to finish, examine all, and then
Blame what is wrong, and rejoice in what is right."

We should remember these verses so that we can use them, not just say them out loud, like when people exclaim "Paean Apollo." In the same way, when we have a fever, we should be ready with the opinions that relate to fever; we shouldn't, as soon as the fever starts, lose and forget everything. A man with a fever might say, "If I keep philosophizing, may I be hanged! Wherever I go, I must take care of this poor body so that the fever doesn't come back." But what is philosophizing? Isn't it preparing yourself for things that might happen? Do you realize that you're basically saying, "If I keep preparing myself to handle things patiently, may I be hanged"? That's like someone giving up the Pancratium (a type of athletic competition) after getting hit. In the Pancratium, you can stop and avoid getting hit. But if you give up philosophy, what will you gain?

So, what should a person say when something painful happens? "This is why I trained myself, this is why I disciplined myself." God is asking you to show that you have trained properly, that you've eaten what you should, that you've exercised, that you've followed the coach's instructions. Will you show weakness now that it's time to act? Now is the time for the fever—bear it well. Now is the time for thirst— bear it well. Now is the time for hunger—bear it well. Is it not within your power? Who can stop you? The doctor might stop you from drinking, but he can't stop you from bearing thirst well; he might stop you from eating, but he can't stop you from bearing hunger well.

"But I can't continue my philosophical studies." And what are your studies for? Aren't they so that you may be happy, steady, and in line with nature? What stops you, when you have a fever, from keeping your mind in line with nature? Here is the test of a philosopher. This is part of life, just like walking, sailing, or traveling by land. Fever is part of life too. Do you read while walking? No. Nor do you read when you have a fever. But if you walk well, you have everything that belongs to a person walking. If you bear a fever well, you have everything that belongs to a person with a fever.

What does it mean to bear a fever well? It means not blaming God or people, not being upset about what happens, expecting death calmly and nobly, and doing what must be done. When the doctor comes, don't be afraid of what he says. If he says, "You're doing well," don't be overly happy. What good news has he really given you? And when you were healthy, what good did that bring you? Even if he says, "You're in bad shape," don't lose hope. What does it mean to be sick? Does it mean you're close to the separation of soul and body? What harm is there in that? If you're not close now, won't you be close later? Will the world turn upside down when you die? So why flatter the doctor? Why say, "Please, doctor, I'll be well if you want me to be"? Why give him the chance to act proud? You should treat the doctor like you treat a shoemaker who is measuring your foot or a carpenter who is building your house. The doctor is only dealing with your body, which isn't really yours, but something naturally destined to die.

When you have a fever, you have the chance to act this way. If you do these things, you have done what is within your control. A philosopher doesn't worry about external things, like wine, oil, or even his body, but only about his own ruling mind. So how should he act toward external things? He should not be careless about them. Where, then, is the reason for fear? Where is the reason for anger or fear about things that belong to others or things that have no value? We should have these two principles ready: nothing is good or bad except what depends on the will, and we should not try to control events but follow them.

"My brother shouldn't have treated me this way." No, but he will take care of that. However he behaves, I will act as I should toward him. This is my business; that is someone else's. No one can stop me from doing this, but the other thing can be hindered.

Chapter 11
Miscellaneous Matters

There are certain penalties, almost like laws, for those who disobey the divine order. If someone thinks anything other than what depends on their own will is good, let them feel envy, desire, flattery, and be disturbed. If someone considers anything else to be evil, let them grieve, lament, weep, and be unhappy. And yet, even though we are punished so harshly, we still can't stop.

Remember what the poet says about the stranger:

"Stranger, I must not, even if a worse man comes."

This can even apply to a father: I must not, even if someone worse than you comes, treat my father badly because we are all from Zeus, the father of all. The same applies to a brother, because we are all from

Zeus, who watches over families. And in all other relationships in life, we will find that Zeus is watching.

Chapter 12
On Exercise

We should not make our exercises consist of things that are unnatural and meant to impress others. If we do, we, who call ourselves philosophers, won't be any different from jugglers. It's difficult to walk on a tightrope, and not only difficult but also dangerous. Should we practice tightrope walking for this reason? Or should we practice climbing palm trees or hugging statues? Definitely not. Not everything that is difficult and dangerous is good for practice. What is good for practice is what helps us achieve our goals. And what is our goal? To live with desires and aversions that are free from restraint. What does this mean? It means not being disappointed in what you desire and not falling into anything you would avoid. Our practice should be directed toward this goal. Since it's not possible to avoid disappointment and unwanted outcomes without great and constant practice, you must understand that if you let your desires and aversions focus on things outside your control, you will neither achieve what you want nor avoid what you don't want. And since strong habits tend to prevail, and we are used to focusing our desires and aversions on things outside our control, we need to counter this habit with a new one, practicing where we are most likely to slip up.

If I am inclined to seek pleasure, I will purposely incline in the opposite direction for the sake of practice. If I dislike pain, I will train myself against the appearances that try to make me avoid it. Who is truly practicing? The one who practices not using his desires and only applies his aversion to things within his control, and who practices most in the areas that are hardest to conquer. This is why one person must practice more against one thing and another against something else. So what's the point of climbing palm trees or carrying around tents, mortars, and pestles? Instead, practice enduring insults if you're irritable, or not getting upset if you're dishonored. Then you will make so much progress that, even if someone hits you, you will say to yourself, "Imagine that you have hugged a statue." Also, practice using wine properly so you don't drink too much. Some people foolishly practice this too. But first, you should abstain from wine, and from young girls and fancy cakes. Then, if the occasion arises, test yourself at the right time to see if appearances overpower you as they used to. But at first, stay far away from what is stronger than you. The contest is unequal between a charming young girl and a beginner in philosophy. As the saying goes, an earthen pitcher and a rock do not agree.

After desire and aversion, the second topic is about actions and the decisions to act or not. You must be obedient to reason, doing nothing out of place or time or in a way that is improper. The third topic concerns judgments, which relate to things that are persuasive and attractive. As Socrates said, we ought not to live an unexamined life, so we shouldn't accept an appearance without examining it. We should say, "Wait, let me see what you are and where you come from," like the night watchman who says, "Show me your pass." Do you have the signal from nature that says you can be trusted? Finally, whatever exercises are applied to the body, if they help in any way with desires and aversions, they can be good exercises. But if they are just for show, they indicate someone who is focused on external things and is looking for others to say, "What a great person." That's why Apollonius wisely said: When you exercise for your own good and you're thirsty from the heat, take a mouthful of cold water, spit it out, and tell no one.

Chapter 13
What Solitude Is and the Nature of a Solitary Person

Solitude is a condition of someone who feels helpless. Just because a person is alone doesn't mean they are lonely; and just because someone is among a crowd doesn't mean they aren't lonely. When we lose a brother, a son, or a friend we relied on, we say we are left lonely, even if we are in a busy city like Rome, surrounded by crowds, and have many people living nearby, even slaves. A person who is considered lonely is seen as helpless and vulnerable to harm. This is why we often say we feel lonely when we travel and encounter robbers. It's not the presence of other people that removes loneliness, but the presence of someone who is trustworthy, modest, and helpful.

If being alone was enough to make someone lonely, you could say that even Zeus is lonely during the great conflagration (when everything burns) and that he might complain, "Poor me, I have no Hera, no Athena, no Apollo, no brother, no son, no kin." Some people say that this is what he does when he is alone during the conflagration. But they don't understand how a person lives when they are truly alone because they base their ideas on the natural desire for companionship, mutual love, and the joy of conversation. Still, a person should be prepared for solitude, able to be self-sufficient and content with their own company.

Just as Zeus lives with himself, calm and thinking about his own nature and his role in the universe, we too should be able to talk to ourselves, not feel the need for others, and not be without ways to spend our time. We should observe the divine order and how we relate to everything else, consider how we used to feel about the things that happen and how we feel now, think about what still causes us pain, and figure out how to cure and remove those pains. If anything needs improvement, we should work on it with reason.

Caesar seems to provide us with great peace: there are no more enemies, no battles, no large groups of robbers or pirates, and we can travel freely from east to west. But can Caesar protect us from fever, shipwreck, fire, earthquake, or lightning? Can he protect us from love? He cannot. From sorrow? He cannot. From envy? He cannot. In short, he cannot protect us from any of these things. But the teachings of philosophers promise to give us security even from these troubles. And what do they say? "People, if you listen to me, wherever you are, whatever you are doing, you won't feel sorrow, anger, compulsion, or obstacles, but you will live peacefully and free from worry." When a person has this kind of peace—not given by Caesar, for how could he give it, but by God through reason—wouldn't they be content even when alone? When they reflect, "Now nothing bad can happen to me; no robber, no earthquake; everything is full of peace and calm: every road, every city, every neighbor, every companion is harmless." One person provides me with food; another with clothing; another with thoughts and understanding. And if someone doesn't provide what's needed, God gives the signal to leave, opens the door, and says, "Go." Go where? To nothing terrible, but to the place you came from, to your friends and family, to the elements: what was in you of fire returns to fire, what was of earth returns to earth, what was of air returns to air, and what was of water returns to water. There is no Hades, no Acheron, no Cocytus, no Pyriphlegethon, but everything is full of gods and spirits. When a person thinks about these things and sees the sun, the moon, and the stars, and enjoys the earth and sea, they are neither lonely nor helpless.

"Well, what if someone comes upon me when I'm alone and murders me?" Fool, they don't murder you, just your poor body.

What kind of solitude, then, is left? What need is there? Why do we make ourselves worse than children? What do children do when they're left alone? They play with shells and ashes, build something, then knock it down and build something else. They never lack ways to pass the time. Should I, if you sail away, sit down and cry because I've been left alone and lonely? Do I have no shells, no ashes? But children do what they do out of ignorance, and we are unhappy because of our knowledge.

Every great power is dangerous to beginners. You should bear only what you are able, but according to nature. Sometimes practice living like a sick person so that you can someday live like a healthy person. Abstain from food, drink only water, and sometimes abstain entirely from desire, so that someday you can desire according to reason; and if it is according to reason, when you have something good in you, you will desire it well.

But we don't want to wait; we want to live like wise men right away and be useful to others. Useful how? What are you doing? Have you been useful to yourself? But I suppose you want to teach others? Teach them! You want to be useful to them. Show them through your own example what kind of person philosophy makes, and don't waste time. When you are eating, do good to those who eat with you; when you are drinking, do good to those who drink with you; by yielding to others, being patient, and bearing with them, you do them good, and don't spit your bad moods on them.

Chapter 14
Certain Miscellaneous Matters

Just as bad actors in a tragedy can't perform well on their own but need to be part of a group, some people can't walk alone. If you are truly something, then walk alone and talk to yourself. Don't hide in the crowd. Take a moment to look around, examine yourself, and wake up so you can understand who you are.

When a person drinks water or does anything for practice or discipline, they always tell everyone whenever they get the chance: "I drink water." Is that why you drink water, just to say you do it? If drinking water is good for you, then drink it. But if it's not, then you're being foolish. If it's good for you and you do drink it, then say nothing about it to those who don't like water-drinkers. What, do you want to please those very people?

Some things we do have a final purpose, some are done because of the situation, some are done to follow certain rules, and others are done to fit in with others. Some things are done according to a set way of life.

You need to get rid of two things in people: arrogance and distrust. Arrogance is the belief that you don't need anything. Distrust is the belief that you can't be happy when so many things surround you. Arrogance is removed by proving it wrong, and Socrates was the first to practice this. To see that something is not impossible, investigate and search for answers. This search won't hurt you, and in a way, this is what philosophy is: figuring out how to use desire and avoidance without being hindered.

"I am better than you because my father was a consul." Another says, "I was a tribune, but you weren't." If we were horses, would you say, "My father was faster, I have more oats and a fancier bridle"? If you said this to me, I would say, "Fine, then let's race." Isn't there something in a person, like running in a horse, that shows who is better or worse? Isn't there modesty, loyalty, and justice? Show that you are better in these things, and then you can say you are better as a person. If you brag about being able to kick hard, I'll say you are proud of something that is the behavior of a donkey.

Chapter 15
That We Ought to Proceed with Caution in Everything

Before you do anything, consider what comes before and what follows, and then decide. If you don't think about it first, you might start with enthusiasm but later give up when the consequences show up. "I want to win at the Olympic games." [So do I, by the gods, for it's a fine thing]. But think about what comes before and after; and if it's good for you, go ahead. You'll have to follow a strict diet, avoid rich foods, exercise at set times, in heat and cold, drink no cold water, and no wine even when you want it. In short, you must surrender yourself to the trainer like you do to a doctor. Then in the contest, you might get covered in sand, dislocate a hand, sprain an ankle, swallow dust, get whipped; and after all this, you might still lose. After thinking about all these things, if you still want it, go to the training. If you don't think about them, you'll act like children who play as wrestlers, then gladiators, then blow a trumpet, then act in a play, just because they've seen and admired these things. You do the same: one day you're a wrestler, then a gladiator, then a philosopher, then a public speaker; but with your whole soul, you are nothing. Like a monkey, you imitate everything you see; and you always want something new, but once you get used to it, you don't like it anymore. You've never done anything with careful thought or deep examination; you've just jumped into things with shallow desires. Some people hear a philosopher speak like Euphrates and want to be philosophers themselves.

Man, first think about what it is you want to do, and then consider your own nature and what it can handle. If you are a wrestler, look at your shoulders, your legs, your body: different people are naturally made for different things. Do you think that, by living as you do now, you can become a philosopher? Do you think you can eat, drink, and behave as you do now and still be a philosopher? You will need to stay up late, work hard, overcome certain desires, leave your family, be looked down on by your servant, and be laughed at by others. In everything, you will be in a lower position—in honors, in court, in public life. When you've considered all these things, then, if you still want to, pursue philosophy, if you want to trade these things for peace, freedom, and tranquility. If you haven't thought about these things, don't approach philosophy. Don't act like children, being a philosopher one day, a tax collector the next, then a public speaker, then a government official. These things don't go together. You must choose to be either a good person or a bad one: you must either work on your inner self or on external things; you must either be a philosopher or live like the rest of the crowd.

Someone said to Rufus when Galba was murdered, "Is the world still governed by Providence?" But Rufus replied, "Did I ever base my belief in Providence on Galba's life?"

Chapter 16
Why We Must Be Careful in Our Social Relationships

If a person often interacts with others, whether it's through talking, drinking together, or just being social, they will either start to become like those people or try to change them to be more like themselves. It's like putting a piece of cold charcoal next to a piece that is burning: the cold charcoal will either cool down the hot one, or the hot charcoal will make the cold one start burning. Since the risk is so high, we need to be careful about getting too close to ordinary people, and remember that it's impossible to be around someone who is dirty without getting some dirt on yourself. For example, what if someone talks about gladiators, horses, athletes, or even worse, about people in general? They might say someone is bad or good, or comment on what was done well or badly. And if they laugh at or make fun of others, or show a mean attitude? Are any of us like a musician who, when they pick up their instrument, can instantly tell which strings are out of tune and fix them? Do we have the ability that Socrates had, to guide those around him to become better? How can we have this ability? So, if you spend time with ordinary people, you'll end up being influenced by them.

Why are they more powerful than you? Because they speak from their true feelings, but you only speak from your lips. That's why your words lack strength and sound empty, and it's unpleasant to hear your advice and your so-called virtue that everyone talks about. In this way, ordinary people have an advantage over you: their opinions are strong and unshakable. Until you have strong, well-formed opinions and have developed a real sense of security, be careful about associating with ordinary people. If you don't, you'll lose the good things you've learned in your studies, just like wax melts in the sun. Keep away from the sun until you have strong opinions. This is also why philosophers suggest that people leave their home country because old habits distract them and make it hard to start new ones. We can't stand it when people say, "Look, that person is now a philosopher, even though they used to be different." Similarly, doctors send people with long-term illnesses to different places with different climates, and they are right to do so. You should also adopt new habits instead of sticking to old ones. Focus on your opinions and practice them. But you don't do this: you go to a show, a gladiator match, a gym, or a circus, and then return to the same places and people. There's no good habit, no attention to self-improvement, or careful consideration of how to handle different situations. You should ask yourself: "How should I respond to these situations? In a natural way or against nature? Am I responding correctly or incorrectly? Am I ignoring things that are beyond my control?" If you are not in this state yet, you should distance yourself from old habits and ordinary people if you ever want to start becoming better.

Chapter 17
On Providence

When you find yourself complaining about Providence, take a moment to think carefully, and you will see that things have happened for a reason. For example, you might say, "But the unfair person seems to have the advantage." In what way? "In money." Yes, he might have more money because he flatters others, lacks shame, and stays alert. But is that surprising? Look to see if he has the advantage over you in being trustworthy and modest. You will see that he does not. In the areas where you are better, you will find that you actually have the advantage. I once spoke to a man who was upset because Philostorgus was successful. I asked him, "Would you want to be like Sura?" He replied, "I hope that day never comes." So why are you upset if Philostorgus gets something for what he sells? Why do you think he is lucky if he gains things in ways you dislike? Providence is not wrong for giving better things to better people. Isn't it better to be modest than to be rich? He agreed. So why are you upset when you have the better quality? Always remember that it is a natural law that the superior has an advantage in what they are superior at, and you will not be upset.

"But my wife treats me badly." If someone asks you about this, just say, "My wife treats me badly." Is there anything else to it? No, nothing more. "My father gives me nothing." Is that all? Yes, that's all. To call this an evil is something extra and false that we add ourselves. Instead of trying to get rid of poverty, we should get rid of our negative opinions about poverty, and then we will be happy.

Chapter 18
Why We Must Not Let News Upset Us

When you hear any news that might upset you, remember this: the news is about something that is not within your control. Can anyone tell you that you have a bad opinion or a bad desire? No. But they might tell you that someone has died. What does that have to do with you? They might say that someone is talking badly about you. What does that have to do with you? Or that your father is planning something. Who is he planning it against? Against your will? How can he? Is he planning against your body or your possessions? You are safe; it's not against you. But what if a judge says you've done something wrong? Didn't the judges also say the same about Socrates? Does it matter to you that the judge said this? No. So why are you still upset? Your father has a duty, and if he doesn't do it, he loses the role of being a father and a caring person. Don't wish for him to lose anything else because of this. A person never does wrong in one area and then suffers in another. On the other hand, it is your duty to defend yourself clearly, calmly, and without anger. If you don't, you will also lose the role of being a respectful and generous person. So, is the judge without danger? No; he is in danger too. So why are you still afraid of his decision? What does someone else's wrongdoing have to do with you? Your own problem is giving a poor defense: focus only on this. Whether you are condemned or not is up to someone else and is their problem. If someone threatens you, it's not your problem. If someone blames you, let them handle their own problems. If they are going to condemn you unfairly, that is their fault.

Chapter 19
The Difference Between a Philosopher and an
Uneducated Person

The first difference between a regular person and a philosopher is this: a regular person says, "Oh, how miserable I am because of my little child, my brother, my father." A philosopher, if he ever says, "I'm so miserable," stops and says, "But only for myself." Nothing that is outside of your own control can harm or upset your will; only your own will can do that. So, if we start blaming ourselves when things go wrong and remember that our own opinions are the only things that cause us trouble or make us lose our peace, I swear by all the gods that we have made progress. But right now, we are doing the opposite. For example, when we were children, if we stumbled because of carelessness, the nurse would not scold us but would hit the stone we tripped over. But what did the stone do? Should the stone have moved because of your child's mistake? Also, if we came out of the bath and found nothing to eat, the teacher would not check our hunger but would punish the cook. Man, did we make you the teacher of the cook instead of the child? Correct the child; make him better. Even as adults, we act like children. Someone who cannot play music is like a child in music; someone who cannot read is like a child in learning; someone who has not learned life lessons is like a child in life.

Chapter 20
How We Can Benefit From All External Things

When you hear something that could disturb you, remember this principle: that news is about things that are not within your control. Can anyone report to you that you have formed a bad opinion or had a bad desire? Of course not. But maybe they will report that someone has died. What does that have to do with you? They might say that someone is speaking poorly of you. What does that have to do with you? Or that your father is planning something. Planning against whom? Against your will? How can he do that? But is he planning against your body or your possessions? You are safe; it is not against you. But what if a judge says that you have done something wrong? Didn't the judges say the same thing about Socrates? Does it matter that the judge has said this? No. So why worry about it? Your father has a certain duty, and if he doesn't fulfill it, he loses his role as a father and as someone who cares and is gentle. Don't wish for him to lose anything else because of this. Because a person does not do wrong in one area and then suffer in another. On the other hand, it is your duty to defend yourself firmly and politely, without getting angry. But if you do not, you will lose your role as a son and as someone who behaves modestly and generously. Well, is the judge safe from danger? No; he is also in danger. So why are you still afraid of his decision? What does it matter if it is someone else's fault? It is your own fault if you make a bad defense. Be careful of that. But whether you are condemned or not, since it is the action of another person, it is the evil of another person. If someone threatens you, what about it? He is just a person who is blaming you. Let him deal with his own problems. He is going to condemn you unfairly. He is a miserable person.

Chapter 21
To Those Who Take on the Role of Teacher Too Lightly

People who quickly pick up new philosophical ideas often want to share them right away, just like someone with an upset stomach who vomits their food. First, you need to properly understand and digest these ideas. If you don't, they become like poorly prepared food that's not good to eat. After you've digested them, show us how these ideas have changed you, just like athletes show the results of their training in their muscles or artists show their skills through their work. A carpenter doesn't just talk about carpentry; he builds something to prove his skills. You should do something similar: live like a wise person, handle everyday tasks like a responsible adult, and deal with family and neighbors well. Show us that you've truly learned something valuable from philosophy. Instead of just reading philosophical texts out loud, you should be able to handle life's challenges and show real improvement.

Is it really worth leaving your home and family just to listen to someone explain words? Shouldn't you come back with the ability to endure difficulties, interact well with others, and handle life's ups and downs honorably? How can you offer these things if you don't have them yourself? Have you done anything besides solve logic problems and argue? Just because someone else has a school doesn't mean you should have one too. You can't just start a school casually; you need to have the right experience, guidance from the gods, and personal preparation.

No one sets sail without making sacrifices to the gods or sows seeds without asking for Demeter's help. How can you undertake such a big task without divine guidance? What are you really doing? Are you just copying rituals from sacred places without understanding their purpose? You're not following the proper procedures or showing the right respect, and you lack the preparation needed. You only memorize the words and claim they are sacred by themselves.

You need to approach these matters differently: they are important and not meant for everyone. Wisdom alone might not be enough; you also need the right readiness, qualities, and divine guidance, just like Socrates, Diogenes, and other great teachers had. But you're treating this as if it were a simple business. Just because you have some knowledge doesn't mean you know how or when to use it. Don't handle important things carelessly. Leave it to those who are truly qualified. Don't damage the reputation of philosophy through your actions. If you enjoy studying ideas, do so quietly on your own. Never claim to be a philosopher if you haven't changed in your desires, actions, or understanding. If you're not ready to do this properly, then stop pretending and let those who are capable handle it.

Chapter 22
On Cynicism

When one of his students, who seemed inclined towards Cynicism, asked Epictetus what kind of person a Cynic ought to be and what Cynicism really means, Epictetus replied that they would discuss it in more detail later, but he wanted to say this much: anyone who attempts such a serious task without God's guidance is displeasing to God and is likely to end up behaving improperly in public. Epictetus explained that in a well-managed household, no one steps forward and declares,

"I ought to be the head of the household." If someone did that, the master of the house would turn around, see this person giving orders arrogantly, drag him out, and punish him. The same is true in the great city of the world, where there is also a master who governs everything.

The master of the world might say to the sun, "You are the sun; your role is to circle the earth, creating the year and the seasons, making plants grow and flourish, stirring the winds, calming them, and properly warming people's bodies. Go, travel around, and take care of things from the greatest to the smallest." He might say to a calf, "You are a calf; when a lion appears, do what's natural for you—run away! If you don't, you will suffer." Or he might say to a bull, "You are a bull; step forward and fight, for this is what suits you, and you are capable of it. You can lead the army against Troy; be like Agamemnon. You can fight Hector in single combat; be like Achilles." But if Thersites tried to take command, he would either fail to get it, or if he did, he would disgrace himself in front of many witnesses.

So, consider the matter carefully: it's not as easy as it seems to you. If you think, "I'll just wear a cloak like I do now, sleep on the ground like I do now, carry a small bag and a staff, go around begging, and scold people I meet who pluck their hair or dress their hair nicely or wear fine clothes," then Cynicism is not for you. Stay far away from it; don't even think about it. But if you understand what it really is and don't see yourself as unfit for it, then think about the great responsibility you are taking on.

First, when it comes to your own behavior, you must be completely different from what you are now. You must not blame God or other people; you must completely rid yourself of desire, and only avoid things that are within your control. You must not feel anger, resentment, envy, or pity. You must not see a girl as attractive, nor should you care about your reputation, be pleased by a boy, or be enticed by a piece of cake. Remember that other people build walls, live in houses, and hide in darkness when they do such things, and they have many ways to keep things hidden. A man can shut the door, place someone in front of the room, and tell them, "If anyone comes, say I'm not here, that I'm busy." But a Cynic must use modesty as his only protection; if he doesn't, he'll be shamefully exposed in his nakedness under the open sky. Modesty is his house, his door, his guard in front of the bedroom, and his darkness. He should have nothing to hide. If he tries to hide something, he loses the essence of being a Cynic, a person who lives openly under the sky, a free person. He starts to fear something outside of himself, he needs to hide, and he can't find a place to hide even if he wants to. And if by chance this public teacher gets caught, what kind of punishment will he face? When someone fears these things, how can they be bold enough to oversee others? It's impossible.

So first, you must purify your mind and your way of life. You should say to yourself, "My task is to work on my understanding, just as wood is to a carpenter and leather is to a shoemaker; my job is to correctly interpret appearances. The body means nothing to me; its parts mean nothing to me. Death? Let it come whenever it will, whether it's the death of the whole body or just a part of it. Run away, you say? But where? Can anyone throw me out of the world? No, they cannot. But wherever I go, the sun is there, the moon is there, the stars are there, dreams, omens, and communication with the gods are there."

Then, if you are prepared in this way, a true Cynic won't be satisfied just with this. He must also know that he is sent by Zeus as a messenger to people to teach them about what is truly good and bad, to show them that they have gone astray, searching for the essence of good and evil in the wrong places while ignoring where it really is. He is like a spy, just as Diogenes was taken to King Philip after the battle of Chaeronea as a spy. A Cynic is a spy of what is truly good and bad for people, and his duty is to carefully examine things and report back truthfully, without being frightened or confused by appearances.

A Cynic should be able to stand up and speak loudly if needed, like Socrates, who would ask people, "Men, where are you rushing to? What are you doing, you poor souls? You're like blind people wandering aimlessly. You're on the wrong path and have left the right one behind. You're searching for happiness and success where they don't exist, and when someone shows you where they are, you don't believe them. Why are you looking for them outside yourselves?" Socrates might ask, "In the body? It's not there. If you don't believe me, look at Myro and Ophellius. In possessions? It's not there. But if you doubt me, look at Croesus. Look at those who are rich now and see how their lives are filled with misery. In power? It's not there. If it were, then people who were consuls multiple times should be happy, but they aren't. Whom should we believe in these matters? You, who look from the outside and are dazzled by appearances, or the people themselves? What do they say? Listen to them when they groan, when they grieve, when they think they're more miserable and in greater danger because of their consulships and glory. Is it in royal power? No, it isn't. If it were, Nero and Sardanapalus would have been happy. But even Agamemnon wasn't happy, though he was better than Sardanapalus and Nero. While others are sleeping soundly, what is he doing?"

Agamemnon says: "Much from his head he tore his rooted hair: — Iliad, x 15 "I am perplexed," he says, "and Disturb'd I am," and "my heart out of my bosom Is leaping." —Iliad, x 91"

Epictetus explains that Agamemnon wasn't troubled by his possessions or his body. No, he was rich in gold and bronze. So, what was wrong with him? It was the part of him that deals with desires and aversions, the part that moves toward or away from things. That part had been neglected and was corrupt. He didn't understand the nature of the good he was made for or the nature of evil. He didn't know what was truly his and what belonged to others. When something belonging to others went wrong, he would say, "Woe to me, the Greeks are in danger!" His ruling faculty, the part that should guide him, was wretched, neglected, and uncared for. He worried, "The Greeks will be destroyed by the Trojans." But if the Trojans didn't kill them, wouldn't they still die eventually? "Yes, but not all at once," he might say. But what difference does it make? If death is an evil, whether people die all at once or one by one, it's still an evil. Is anything going to happen other than the separation of the soul and body? No, that's all. And if the Greeks die, is the door closed? Can't you still choose to die? Yes, you can. So, why do you lament and say, "Oh, you who are king and hold Zeus's scepter?" There is no such thing as an unhappy king, just as there is no such thing as an unhappy god. So what are you? In truth, you're just a shepherd, because you weep like shepherds do when a wolf takes one of their sheep. The people you govern are like sheep to you. And why did you come here? Was your desire in danger? Was your aversion? Was your ability to act or avoid acting threatened? "No," he says, "but my brother's wife was taken away." Wasn't it a gain to be rid of an adulterous wife? "But we'll be looked down upon by the Trojans!" Are the Trojans wise or foolish? If they're wise, why are you fighting them? If they're foolish, why do you care what they think?

So where is the good, if it's not in these things? Tell us, you who are a lord, a messenger, and a spy. It's not where you think it is or where you're looking for it. If you had chosen to seek it, you would have found it within yourselves, and you wouldn't be wandering off the right path, seeking what belongs to others as if it were your own. Turn your thoughts inward. Reflect on the ideas you already have. What kind of thing do you imagine the good to be? "Something that flows easily, that is happy, that isn't hindered." Isn't it also something great, valuable, and free from harm? In what should you look for something that flows easily, that isn't hindered? In something that serves or in something that's free? "In something that's free." So, is your body free, or is it a slave? "We don't know." Don't you realize that it's a slave to fever, gout, eye infections, dysentery, tyrants, fire, iron, and everything that's stronger than it? "Yes, it's a slave." How, then, can anything that belongs to the body be free from hindrance? And how can something be great or valuable if it's naturally dead, like earth or mud? Well then, do you possess nothing that's free? "Maybe nothing." Who can force you to agree to something that seems false? "No one." Who can force you not to agree to something that seems true? "No one." In this, you can see that there's something in you that's naturally free. But what about desire, aversion, or moving toward or away from something? Can you do any of these things without first receiving the impression that something is useful or necessary? "No one can." In these things, too, you have something that isn't hindered and is free. Miserable people, focus on this, take care of this, seek the good here.

"And how is it possible for a man who has nothing, who is naked, homeless, without a hearth, dirty, without a servant, without a city, to live a life that flows easily?" Look, God has sent you a man to show you that it's possible. Look at me, who has no city, no house, no possessions, no servant; I sleep on the ground; I have no wife, no children, no official post, only the earth and sky, and one poor cloak. And what do I lack? Am I not without sorrow? Am I not without fear? Am I not free? When did any of you see me fail to achieve what I desire or fall into something I wanted to avoid? Did I ever blame God or man? Did I ever accuse anyone? Did any of you ever see me with a sorrowful face? And how do I deal with those you're afraid of and admire? Don't I treat them like slaves? Who, when he sees me, doesn't think he's seeing his king and master?

This is the language of the Cynics, this is their character, this is their purpose. You might say, "No, but their characteristic is the little wallet, the staff, the big jaws, devouring everything they're given, storing it up, or unreasonably insulting everyone they meet, or showing off their shoulders as if it's something special." Do you see what you're getting into? First, take a mirror, look at your shoulders, observe your loins, and your thighs. You're about to compete in the Olympic Games, not in some small and insignificant contest. In the Olympic Games, you're not just allowed to be defeated and leave; first, you must be disgraced in front of the entire world, not just in front of Athenians, Spartans, or Nicopolitans. Next, you'll be whipped if you've entered the contest rashly, and before being whipped, you'll suffer thirst, heat, and swallow a lot of dust.

Reflect more carefully, know yourself, consult the divine, and don't attempt anything without God. If he advises you to proceed, be assured that he intends for you to become great or to receive many blows. For a Cynic, this amusing quality is part of the package: he must be flogged like a donkey, and when he's flogged, he must love those who flog him, as if he were the father and brother of all. You might say, "No, but if someone flogs you, stand in the public square and shout, 'Caesar, what am I suffering in this state of peace under your protection?' Let's bring the offender before the governor." But what is Caesar to a Cynic, or what is a governor, or anyone else except the one who sent the Cynic down here, whom he serves, namely Zeus? Does he call upon anyone other than Zeus? Isn't he convinced that whatever he suffers, it's Zeus who's training him? Hercules, when he was trained by Eurystheus, didn't think he was miserable; he confidently undertook everything he had to do. And would a Cynic, who's being trained by Zeus, call out and complain, he who's worthy of bearing Diogenes' scepter? Listen to what Diogenes says to passersby when he's sick with a fever, "Miserable people, won't you stop? You're going on such a long journey to Olympia to see athletes fight and destroy each other, but you won't stop to see the fight between a fever and a man?" Would such a man accuse God of treating him unfairly, a man who takes pride in his situation and claims to be an example to those who pass by? What could he accuse God of? For maintaining decent behavior? For making his virtue more evident? Well, and what does he say about poverty, death, and pain? How does he compare his own happiness to that of the great king (the king of Persia)? Or rather, he thought there was no comparison between them. Where there are disturbances, grief, fears, unsatisfied desires, and aversions to things that can't be avoided, how can there be a path to happiness? But where there are corrupt principles, those things must necessarily exist.

When the young man asked if, "When a Cynic falls ill and a friend invites him to stay at his house and be cared for, should the Cynic accept the invitation?" Epictetus replied: "And where will you find a friend of a Cynic? For the person who invites him should be like the Cynic to be worthy of being considered his friend. He should be a partner in the Cynic's scepter and royalty, and a worthy helper, if he wants to be considered worthy of the Cynic's friendship, like Diogenes was a friend to Antisthenes, and Crates was a friend to Diogenes. Do you think that if someone comes to a Cynic, greets him, and offers his house, he's a Cynic's friend, and the Cynic will think him worthy of taking him into his home? So, if you please, reflect on this too: rather look for a convenient place to bear your illness and where you'll be sheltered from the cold. But you seem to want to go to someone's house to be well-fed for a while. Why then do you think of attempting such a great thing as the life of a Cynic?"

"But," the young man asked, "Should marriage and having children, as a chief duty, be undertaken by the Cynic?" If we had a community of wise men, Epictetus replied, perhaps no one would readily apply himself to Cynicism. For whose sake should he undertake this way of life? However, if we suppose that he does, nothing would stop him from marrying and having children because his wife would be like him, his father-in-law would be like him, and his children would be raised like him. But in the present situation, which is like an army in battle formation, is it not appropriate for the Cynic to focus solely on serving God, able to move among people without being tied to common duties or entangled in the ordinary relationships of life, which, if neglected, would cause him to lose his character as an honorable and good man? And if he observes them, he will lose his role as the messenger, spy, and herald of God. Consider that he would have responsibilities toward his father-in-law, other relatives of his wife, and his wife herself (if he has one). Being a Cynic would also prevent him from caring for his family's illnesses and providing for their support. And that's just the beginning; there would be more distractions. Where now is that king, the one who devotes himself to public interests?

The people's guardian and so full of cares. —Iliad, ii 25

It is his duty to look after others, both the married and those with children, to see who treats his wife well and who doesn't, which families are well-managed and which aren't, going around like a doctor checking pulses. He might say to one, "You have a fever," to another, "You have a headache or gout," and to another, "Avoid eating," or, "Eat," or, "Don't bathe," and to another, "You need surgery or cauterization." How can he have time for this if he's tied to the duties of ordinary life? Isn't it his duty to provide clothes for his children and send them to school with writing materials? Shouldn't he also provide them with beds? For they can't be genuine Cynics from birth. If he doesn't do this, it would be better to expose the children as soon as they're born than to kill them in this way. Consider how we're reducing the Cynic's royalty, how we're stripping him of his kingship. "Yes, but Crates took a wife." You're talking about a special case due to love and a woman who was another Crates. But we're discussing ordinary marriages, those that aren't distracting, and we don't find that marriage in this world is especially suited to the Cynic.

How, then, shall a man maintain society? In the name of God, are those who introduce two or three noisy children into the world greater benefactors to society than those who oversee as much of humanity as possible, seeing what they do, how they live, what they pay attention to, and what they neglect contrary to their duty? Did those who left small children to the Thebans do them more good than Epaminondas, who died childless? And did Priam, who fathered fifty worthless sons, or Danaus or Aeolus, contribute more to the community than Homer? So, should the duties of a general or the work of a writer prevent a man from marrying or having children, and should such a man be judged to have chosen a childless life for no reason? And shouldn't the Cynic's kingship be considered an equivalent to having children? Don't we see his greatness, and don't we rightly admire the character of Diogenes? And instead of this, do we look at the present Cynics who are like dogs waiting at tables, imitating the Cynics of old in no way except perhaps in their crude behavior, but in nothing else? Such matters wouldn't have bothered us at all, nor would we have wondered if a Cynic chose not to marry or have children. Man, the Cynic is the father of all men; the men are his sons, the women are his daughters. He visits everyone with care and concern. Do you think he scolds people he meets out of idle meddling? He does it as a father, as a brother, and as the servant of the father of all, the servant of Zeus.

If you please, ask me also if a Cynic should engage in government. Fool, do you seek a greater form of governance than the one he's already engaged in? Do you ask if he should appear before the Athenians and discuss finances and supplies, he who must talk to all men, whether Athenians, Corinthians, or Romans, not about supplies, finances, peace, or war, but about happiness and misery, good fortune and bad fortune, slavery and freedom? When a man has taken on the responsibility of such a state, do you ask if he should engage in the administration of another state? Ask me also if he should hold a government office. Again, I'll say to you: Fool, what greater government could he exercise than the one he already exercises now?

A Cynic also needs to have a certain level of physical fitness because if he looks weak, thin, and pale, his words won't carry the same weight. He must not only prove to ordinary people that it's possible to be a good man without depending on the things they value, but he must also show through his own body that a simple and frugal life in the open air doesn't harm the body. "Look," he says, "I'm living proof of this, and my body is, too." That's what Diogenes did; he went about looking healthy and strong, and his appearance drew people's attention. But if a Cynic seems pitiful, he appears to be nothing more than a beggar. People turn away from him; they're offended by him. He shouldn't look dirty, so he doesn't repel people in that way either; his roughness should be clean and appealing.

A Cynic also needs natural charm and sharpness, and if he doesn't have these qualities, he's just a dull fellow and nothing more. He needs these qualities so that he can handle any situation that comes his way. That's why Diogenes responded to someone who asked, "Are you the

Diogenes who doesn't believe in the gods?" by saying, "How could that be when I think that you're hateful to the gods?" On another occasion, when Alexander the Great stood by him while he was sleeping and quoted Homer's line (Iliad, ii 24),

"A man, a counselor, should not sleep all night,"
Diogenes, still half-asleep, replied,
"The people's guardian and so full of cares."

But above all, a Cynic's ruling faculty must be purer than the sun; otherwise, he will be nothing more than a cunning, deceitful person because while he himself is entangled in some vice, he will criticize others. Consider how things are: Kings and tyrants rely on their guards and weapons to reprimand and punish wrongdoers, even if they themselves are bad. But a Cynic, instead of using weapons and guards, relies on his conscience to give him this power. When he knows that he has watched and worked for the good of humanity, that he has slept with a clear conscience, and that whatever thoughts he had were as a friend of the gods, as a servant, as a participant in Zeus's power, and that he's always ready to say,

"Lead me, O Zeus, and thou, O Destiny;"

and also, "If it so pleases the gods, so let it be," why shouldn't he have the confidence to speak freely to his brothers, his children, to all his kinsmen? That's why he's not a busybody or a meddler when he's in this state of mind; he's not interfering in others' affairs when he's overseeing human matters—he's looking after his own affairs. If that's not the case, you could also say that a general is a meddler when he inspects his soldiers, examines them, watches them, and punishes the disorderly. But if, while you have a stolen cake under your arm, you scold others, I'll say to you, "Why don't you go away into a corner and eat what you've stolen? What business do you have with other people's affairs? Who are you? Are you the bull of the herd or the queen of the bees? Show me the signs of your authority, like the ones they have by nature. But if you're just a drone claiming sovereignty over the bees, don't you think your fellow citizens will put you down, just as the bees do to drones?"

A Cynic must also have such endurance that he seems unfeeling to the average person, like a stone. No one insults him, no one strikes him, no one offends him, but he offers his body to anyone who wants to do what they will with it. He remembers that the weaker must be overpowered by the stronger in what they are weaker in; the body is weaker than many, and the weaker are overpowered by the stronger. So, he never enters into a contest in which he can be overpowered; instead, he immediately withdraws from things that belong to others. He doesn't claim things that are servile. But when it comes to his will and his use of appearances, you'll see how sharp his perception is, so much so that you might say Argus was blind compared to him. Is his assent ever rash? Is his movement toward an object hasty? Does his desire ever miss its mark? Does he ever encounter what he wants to avoid? Is his purpose ever unfulfilled? Does he ever find fault? Is he ever humiliated? Is he ever envious? These are the things he focuses all his attention and energy on; everything else, he treats with indifference. All is peaceful; no thief can take away his will, no tyrant can harm it. But what about his body? I say there is a threat. And his possessions? I say there is a threat. And what about government positions and honors? What does he care for them? When someone tries to frighten him with these things, he says, "Go away, look for children; masks are frightening to them, but I know they're just shells with nothing inside."

This is what you're considering. Therefore, if you please, I urge you in the name of God, delay your decision and first consider if you're prepared for it. Remember what Hector says to Andromache: "Go back inside and weave:

"War is the work of men Of all indeed, but specially 'tis mine." — Iliad vi 490

Hector knew his own strength and role in war, just as a Cynic must know whether he's truly ready for the challenges of such a life.

Chapter 23
To Those Who Read and Discuss Just to Show Off

First, decide who you want to be, and then do what matches that decision. This is true in almost everything. People who train for sports first decide what they want to be, and then they follow the right steps. If someone wants to run a long-distance race, they follow a specific diet, walking routine, and exercise plan. If someone wants to run a short sprint, their training is different. And if they want to compete in multiple events like the Pentathlon, their training will be even more varied. The same goes for the arts. If you are a carpenter, you will have certain tools and techniques; if you work with metal, you will have different ones. Whatever we do, if we don't have a clear goal, we'll end up doing it without purpose. And if we aim at the wrong goal, we'll miss the mark. There's a general goal that applies to everyone, and then there's a specific goal for each person. First, we must act as a human being. What does that mean? It means we shouldn't be like sheep, even though they're gentle, nor should we be destructive like wild beasts. But the specific goal depends on each person's way of life and will. A musician acts as a musician, a carpenter as a carpenter, a philosopher as a philosopher, and a speaker as a speaker.

So, when you say, "Come and listen to me read," make sure you're not doing it without a purpose. Then, if you find you have a purpose, think about whether it's the right one. Do you want to help others or just be praised? If you want to do good, that's one thing. But if you just want praise, remember what you've heard: "What's the value of praise from the many?" And that's true—praise doesn't make a musician better at music, nor does it help a mathematician. So, if you want to be useful, in what way? Tell us, so we can rush to your reading room. But can anyone be useful to others if they haven't first received something useful themselves? No, they can't. Just like someone can't be a good carpenter if they haven't learned carpentry, or a good shoemaker if they haven't learned how to make shoes.

If you want to know whether you've gained anything useful, show us your thoughts, philosopher. What does desire promise? It promises not to fail in what you want. What does avoiding something promise? It promises not to fall into what you don't want. Well, are you keeping these promises? Tell me the truth; but if you lie, I'll tell you the truth. Recently, when your listeners weren't that enthusiastic and didn't applaud you, you left feeling down. And when you were praised, you went around asking everyone, "What did you think of me?" "Wonderful, master," they might say. "But how did I handle that particular part?" Which part? "The part where I described Pan and the nymphs?" "Excellently." Then you tell me you're acting according to nature in your desires and aversions? Get out of here; try to convince someone else. Didn't you praise someone against your own opinion? Didn't you flatter someone just because they were a senator's son? Would you want your own children to be like that? I hope not. Then why did you praise and flatter him? "He's a smart young man and listens well to speeches." Why? "Because he admires me." Ah, there's your answer. But don't you think these same people secretly despise you? So, when someone who knows they haven't done anything good or even thought about it hears a philosopher say, "You have great natural talent, and you're honest and good-natured," what do you think they're really thinking? Probably something like, "This guy must need something from me." Or tell me, what action has shown that this person has a great mind? Look, he's been around you for a while, listening to your talks and readings; has he become more modest? Has he started reflecting on himself? Has he realized what a bad state he's in? Has he thrown away his arrogance? Is he looking for someone to teach him? Yes, but not someone to teach him how to live—he's looking for someone to teach him how to talk. That's why he admires you too. Listen to what he says: "This man writes beautifully, much better than Dion." That's a whole different thing. Does he say, "This man is modest, trustworthy, and free from disturbances?" Even if he did, I would ask him: "Since this man is trustworthy, tell me what that means." And if he couldn't tell me, I'd say: "First, understand what you're saying, and then speak."

You, who are in a bad state, craving applause and counting your listeners, do you really intend to be useful to others? "Today, a lot more people attended my talk. Yes, many, maybe five hundred." That's nothing; suppose there were a thousand—Dion never had so many listeners—How could he? And they understood what was said beautifully. "What's beautiful can move even a stone." See, these are the words of a philosopher. This is the mindset of someone who will do good for others; here's someone who has listened to talks, who has read about Socrates as Socratic, not just as the writings of Lysias and Isocrates. "I've often wondered by what arguments..." Not so, but "by what argument": this is more precise than that." What, have you read the words any differently than you read little poems? Because if you read them as you should, you wouldn't be focusing on such things; instead, you would be paying attention to these words: "Anytus and Melitus can kill me, but they cannot harm me." "And I am always of such a disposition as to pay regard to nothing of my own except to the reason which, after inquiry, seems to me the best."

So, who ever heard Socrates say, "I know something and I teach?" Instead, he would send different people to different teachers. That's why they would come to him and ask to be introduced to philosophers by him, and he would take them and recommend them. Not so; but as he accompanied them, he would say, "Come listen to me speak today at the house of Quadratus." Why should I listen to you? Do you want to show me that you can put words together cleverly? Go ahead, put them together, and what good will it do you? "But just praise me." What do you mean by praise? "Say to me, 'Admirable, wonderful.'" Fine, I'll say it. But if that's what praise is, whatever philosophers mean by the word "good," what do I have to praise in you? If it's good to speak well, teach me, and I'll praise you. "What then? Shouldn't a person listen to such things without pleasure?" I hope not. For my part, I don't even listen to a musician without pleasure. But should I stand

and play the lute just because of that? Listen to what Socrates says: "Nor would it be appropriate for a man of my age, like a young man composing speeches, to appear before you." Like a young man, he says. Because, in truth, this small art is a delicate thing: to choose words, put them together, and present them gracefully, and while doing so, to think, "There aren't many who can do these things." I swear by all that you value.

Does a philosopher invite people to hear him? Just as the sun draws people to it, or as food does, doesn't a philosopher also attract those who will benefit? What doctor invites a patient to be treated? Actually, I've heard that even doctors in Rome now invite patients, but when I lived there, patients invited the doctors. I invite you to come and hear that things are going badly for you, that you're taking care of everything except what you should be taking care of, and that you don't know what's good and bad and are unlucky and unhappy. A fine kind of invitation: and yet, if the philosopher's words don't have this effect on you, he might as well be dead, and so is the speaker. Rufus used to say, "If you have time to praise me, I'm speaking to no purpose." He used to speak in such a way that every one of us sitting there thought someone had accused him before Rufus: he touched on what was happening, and he showed every man's faults right in front of their eyes.

The philosopher's school, men, is like a doctor's office: you shouldn't leave it feeling pleased, but in pain. Because you're not in good health when you enter: one person has a dislocated shoulder, another has an abscess, a third has a fistula, and a fourth has a headache. Should I sit here and share little thoughts and exclamations so that you can praise me and then leave, one with his shoulder still dislocated, another with his head still aching, and a third with his fistula or abscess just as it was before? Is this why young men should leave home, leave their parents, friends, relatives, and property, just so they can say to you, "Wonderful!" when you're speaking? Did Socrates do this, or Zeno, or Cleanthes?

"What then? Isn't there a style of speaking that encourages people?" Who denies that? Just like there's a style for refuting arguments and teaching. But who ever added a fourth style to these, the style of showing off? What is the style of encouragement? It's the ability to show both one person and many the struggle they're engaged in, and that they're focusing on anything but what they truly want. Because they want things that lead to happiness, but they're looking for them in the wrong place. To do this, you don't need a thousand seats and a fancy pulpit, nor do you need to dress up in a fine robe or cloak and describe the death of Achilles. Stop, I beg you by the gods, stop ruining good words and good actions as much as you can. Nothing is more powerful in encouragement than when the speaker shows the listeners that they need him. But tell me, who, when they hear you preaching or speaking, becomes anxious about themselves or starts reflecting on their own life? Or, after leaving, says, "The philosopher really struck a chord with me; I must stop doing these things." Instead, don't they just say to someone else, "He spoke beautifully about Xerxes;" and another person says, "No, he spoke better about the battle of Thermopylae." Is this what it means to listen to a philosopher?

Chapter 24
We Should Not Be Moved by a Desire for Things Beyond Our Control

Don't let something that is against nature in someone else be a problem for you. You weren't made by nature to be sad because of others or to be unhappy because of others, but to be happy with them. If someone is unhappy, remember that it's their own fault. God made all people to be happy and free from disturbances. He gave each person certain things that are their own and other things that are not. Some things are subject to being blocked, forced, or taken away, and these things are not truly ours. But the things that can't be hindered are truly ours. God, like a caring father, made the nature of good and evil something that belongs to us.

But you might say, "I've parted from someone, and they are sad." Why did they think something that belonged to someone else was their own? Why, when they looked at you and felt joy, didn't they also realize that you are mortal and that it's natural for you to leave them or travel far away? Because they didn't think about these things, they now suffer the consequences of their own foolishness. But why do you, or for what reason, feel sorry for yourself? Is it because you didn't think about these things either? Have you, like people who don't think deeply, enjoyed everything as if you would always have them, whether it's places, people, or conversations? And now you're sitting and crying because you don't see the same people or live in the same places. Indeed, you deserve this, to be more miserable than crows and ravens who can fly wherever they want, change their nests, and cross the seas without crying or regretting their past conditions. "But they do this because they are irrational creatures," you might say. Was reason then given to us by the gods so that we could be unhappy and miserable, living our lives in sorrow and tears? Should all people be immortal? Should no one ever travel? Should we never leave our homes, but instead stay rooted like plants? And if any of our friends go away, should we just sit and cry? And when they come back, should we dance and clap our hands like little children?

Shouldn't we grow up now and remember what we've heard from the philosophers? If we didn't listen to them like they were just entertainers, they told us that this world is one city, that we are all made from the same substance, and that things must change over time. Some things must give way to others, some must dissolve, and others take their place. Some stay in the same place, and others move. All things are full of harmony, first with the gods and then with people, who are naturally meant to be one family. Some people must stay together, and others must be separated, finding joy in those who are with them and not grieving for those who are away. Besides having a noble character and disregarding things beyond his control, man also has the ability not to be fixed to one place but to go to different places at different times, sometimes out of necessity and other times just to see new things.

This is how it was for Ulysses, who saw "the cities of many men and learned their ways" (Iliad vi 490). Even before him, Hercules traveled the world, seeing both the lawless deeds and the good laws of people, casting out lawlessness and introducing good laws. And yet, how many friends do you think he had in Thebes, in Argos, in Athens? And how many friends did he make as he traveled? He even married when it seemed right to him, had children, and left them without regret or sadness because he knew that no one is truly an orphan. The true father, who cares for everyone, is always there. Hercules didn't just hear that Zeus was the father of men; he believed it deeply. He called Zeus his own father and looked to him in everything he did. Because of this, Hercules was able to live happily wherever he was. Happiness and longing for what isn't present can never go together. A happy person must have everything they desire, like someone who is full of food and has no thirst or hunger.

"But Ulysses longed for his wife and cried as he sat on a rock," you might say. Do you follow Homer and his stories in everything? Or if Ulysses did cry, then what was he but an unhappy man? And what good person is unhappy? If Zeus doesn't take care of his own citizens, making sure they are happy like himself, then everything is poorly managed. But it's not right to think this way. If Ulysses did weep and lament, then he wasn't a good man. For who is good if they don't know who they are? And who knows what they are if they forget that all things made by nature are perishable and that it's impossible for one person to always be with another? To desire impossible things is foolish and shows a slavish character, someone who is fighting against God in the only way they can—through their opinions.

"But my mother cries when she doesn't see me," you might say. Why hasn't she learned these principles? I'm not saying we shouldn't care that she's crying, but we shouldn't desire things that aren't ours. Another person's sorrow is their own, but my sorrow is mine. I will do everything in my power to stop my own sorrow, but I won't try to stop someone else's by all means. If I did, I would be fighting against God, opposing Zeus, and placing myself against his plan for the universe. The punishment for this disobedience isn't just something my children will pay for; I will pay for it too, by being disturbed, frightened by dreams, anxious at every piece of news, and having my peace depend on letters from others.

"Someone has arrived from Rome. I just hope there's no bad news." But what harm can happen to you where you are not? "Someone has come from Greece. I hope there's no bad news." This way, every place can be a source of trouble for you. Isn't it enough to be unfortunate where you are? Must you also be miserable about places across the sea, based on letters? Is this how your life is secure? "Well then, what if my friends have died in places far from me?" What have they suffered other than the natural fate of mortals? How can you want to live to old age and not see the death of anyone you love? Don't you know that over a long time, many different things must happen? One person will die of fever, another will be killed by a robber, and another will be taken by a tyrant. Such is the nature of life, and these are the people we live with in the world. Cold, heat, bad living conditions, travel, sea voyages, winds, and other circumstances can destroy one person, banish another, and send one on an embassy and another into an army. Will you sit there, anxious about all these things, lamenting, unhappy, and dependent on others—not just one or two people, but thousands upon thousands?

Did you learn this when you were with the philosophers? Didn't you learn that human life is like a battle, where one person must keep watch, another must go on reconnaissance, and another must fight? It's impossible for everyone to be in one place, nor would it be better if they were. But you neglect the orders of the general and complain when something harder than usual is asked of you. You don't realize what you're doing to the army by your actions. If everyone acted like you, no one would dig a trench, build a wall, keep watch, or expose themselves to danger, and the army would be useless. Similarly, if you're on a ship as a sailor, you should stick to your assigned place. If you're told to climb the mast, don't refuse. If you're told to go to the front of the ship, don't refuse. What captain would tolerate you? Wouldn't he throw you overboard as useless, an obstacle and a bad example to the other sailors? It's the same in life. Every person's life is like a battle, and it's long and varied. You must act like a soldier and follow the general's orders, even trying to anticipate what he wants. There's no comparison between this general and any other, neither in strength nor in superiority of character. You are in a high position, not a low one; you are always a senator. Don't you know that someone in such a position must spend little time on personal matters and often be away from home, either governing or being governed, fulfilling some duty, serving in war, or acting as a judge? And yet you tell me that you want to be like a plant, fixed to one place and rooted there? "Yes, because it's pleasant," you might say. Who says it isn't? But so is a good meal, or a beautiful woman. What else do those who seek pleasure as their end goal say? Don't you see what kind of people you're imitating? You're speaking like Epicureans and people who live only for pleasure. Yet, while you act like them and share their opinions, you still want to talk like Zeno and Socrates? Won't you stop borrowing from others things that don't suit you at all?

For what do they desire other than to sleep without disturbance, to yawn at their leisure when they wake up, to wash their face, to write and read whatever they like, to talk about trivial matters while being praised by their friends for anything they say, then to go for a short walk, bathe, eat, and sleep again in their usual way? Why should we even describe it further? You can easily imagine it. Now tell us how you want to spend your time, you who admire truth, Socrates, and Diogenes. What do you wish to do in Athens—the same as others, or something different? If so, why do you call yourself a Stoic? People who falsely claim to be Roman citizens are punished severely, and should those who falsely claim to follow something so great and honorable get away with it? No, this is not possible. The divine law is strong and inevitable, and it punishes the greatest crimes most severely. What does this law say? Let the person who pretends to be something they are not be a braggart, a vain person. Let the person who disobeys the divine order be base and a slave. Let them suffer grief, envy, and pity, and, in short, let them be unhappy and full of lament.

"Well then, do you want me to flatter a certain person? To go to their door?" If reason requires this for the sake of your country, family, or humanity, then why not go? You're not ashamed to go to the shoemaker when you need shoes or to the gardener when you need vegetables. Why should you be ashamed to go to a wealthy person when you need something? "But I don't feel any awe of a shoemaker," you might say. Then don't feel awe of the rich. "But I won't flatter the gardener," you might add. And don't flatter the rich. "How then shall I get what I want?" Do I tell you to go as if you're sure to get what you want? No, I only tell you to do what is fitting for you. "Then why should I still go?" So that you can say you've done your duty as a citizen, a brother, a friend. Remember, you went to the shoemaker and the vegetable seller, who have no power in anything great or noble, even if they charge a high price. You go to buy lettuce; it costs a penny, not a fortune. So it is here. The matter is worth going to the rich man's door for. Fine, I'll go. It's worth talking to him about. Fine, I'll talk with him. But do you also have to kiss his hand and flatter him with praise? No, that's not worth it. It's not good for me, the state, or my friends to do something that ruins a good citizen and a friend. "But you'll seem uninterested in the matter if you don't succeed." Have you forgotten why you went? Don't you know that a good person does nothing for appearances but only for doing what's right? "What's the benefit of doing right, then?" And what's the benefit of a man writing the name "Dion" correctly? The benefit is having written it correctly. "Is there no reward, then?" Do you seek a reward for doing what's right beyond the act itself? In the Olympic Games, you wish for nothing more, but it seems enough to be crowned. Does it seem so small and worthless to be good and happy? For these purposes, being introduced by the gods into this world, and it being your duty to undertake the work of a man, do you still need a nurse or a mother to care for you? Are you so easily influenced by the tears of foolish women, and do you become weak because of them? Will you never stop being a foolish child? Don't you know that the older a person is when they act like a child, the more ridiculous they are?

In Athens, did you visit anyone you wanted to? "Yes, I visited anyone I pleased." Then here too, be ready to see whom you please, but do it without being mean, neither with desire nor aversion, and your affairs will be well managed. But this doesn't depend on whether you go or stand at doors; it depends on what's inside you, on your opinions. When you've learned not to value external things that aren't under your control and to consider that none of them is truly yours, but that only your own judgments, opinions, and actions are yours, where is there any room left for flattery or meanness? Why do you still long for the peace of Athens and the familiar places? Wait a little, and you will become familiar with these new places too. Then, if you're so weak-minded, when you leave these places again, you'll cry and lament once more.

"How then shall I become kind-hearted?" By being noble and happy. It's not reasonable to be mean-spirited or to cry for yourself, or to depend on others, or to blame God or people. I urge you to become kind-hearted in this way, by following these rules. But if, because of what you call affection, you become a slave and wretched, there's no benefit in being affectionate. What stops you from loving someone as a person who is mortal, someone who might leave you? Didn't Socrates love his own children? He did, but as a free man, someone who remembered that he must first be a friend to the gods. Because of this, he didn't do anything unworthy of a good man, not even in his defense, nor when deciding his penalty, nor at any other time in his life as a senator or soldier. Yet we always find excuses for being weak, some for the sake of a child, others for a mother, or brothers. But it's not right for us to be unhappy because of any person. Instead, we should be happy because of all people, but especially because of God, who made us for this purpose.

Well, did Diogenes love no one? He was so kind and cared so much for all people that he willingly took on many labors and hardships for humanity. He did love people, but how? As a servant of God, caring for people but also being subject to God. Because of this, the whole world was his home, not just one place. When he was captured, he didn't regret leaving Athens or his friends there. He even became familiar with the pirates and tried to help them. Later, when he was sold, he lived in Corinth just as he had lived in Athens. He would have done the same if he had gone to another country. This is how freedom is acquired. For this reason, he used to say, "Ever since Antisthenes made me free, I have not been a slave." How did Antisthenes make him free? Listen to what Diogenes says: "Antisthenes taught me what is mine and what is not mine. Possessions are not mine, nor are family, servants, friends, reputation, familiar places, or way of life—all these belong to others. What then is truly mine? The use of appearances. This Antisthenes showed me, and I possess it free from any hindrance or compulsion. No person can block my way, no person can force me to use appearances in a way I don't choose." Who then has power over me? Is it Philip or Alexander, or the great king? How could they have power over me? For if a person is going to be overpowered by another, they must first be overpowered by things. If pleasure doesn't have power over someone, nor pain, nor fame, nor wealth, but that person is willing to spit out their own poor body and leave life when they choose, whose slave can they still be? But if Diogenes had loved living in Athens and was overpowered by that life, his affairs would have been at everyone's command. The stronger would have had the power to make him suffer. Do you think Diogenes would have flattered the pirates so that they might sell him to an Athenian, just so he could see the beautiful Piraeus, the Long Walls, and the Acropolis? In what condition would he have seen them? As a captive, a slave, and a weak person. And what good would that have done him? "No," you might say, "I would see them as a free man." Show me how you would be free. Imagine someone has caught you, takes you away from your familiar place, and says, "You are my slave because I can stop you from living as you wish. I can treat you harshly or kindly as I choose." On the other hand, you are cheerful and eager to return to Athens. What would you say to the person who treats you as a slave? What would you do to find someone to free you from slavery? Could you even look him in the face, or would you just beg to be set free? Man, you should go gladly to prison, eager to go before those who lead you there. Then I ask you, are you unwilling to live in Rome and desire to live in Greece? And when you must die, will you then also fill us with your tears because you won't see Athens or walk in the Lyceum? Did you go abroad for this? Was this why you sought someone to help you? What kind of help? To solve logical puzzles more quickly or to handle complex arguments? Is this why you left your brother, your country, your friends, and your family? So that you could return after learning these things? So you didn't go abroad to gain a steady mind, to be free from disturbance, to be safe from harm, to never complain about anyone, to accuse no one, and to ensure no one could wrong you, and so you could maintain your place in life without obstacles? This is a fine goal you've gone abroad for—logical puzzles and sophistry. If you like, take your place in the marketplace and sell them like medicines. Won't you even deny everything you've learned so that you don't give a bad name to your teachings as useless? What harm has philosophy done you? How has Chrysippus harmed you that you would prove through your actions that his teachings are useless? Were the troubles you had at home not enough, the ones that caused your pain and complaints, even if you hadn't gone abroad? Have you added more to the list? And if you make new friends, you'll have more reasons to complain, and the same if you grow attached to another country. Why then do you live just to surround yourself with new sorrows that make you unhappy? Then, I ask you, do you call this affection? What affection, man! If it's a good thing, it causes no harm; if it's bad, I have nothing to do with it. I'm made by nature for my own good, not for my own harm.

What then is the training for this? First and foremost, the highest and most important is this: when you enjoy something, enjoy it as if it's not one of those things that can't be taken away, but as something fragile, like a clay pot or a glass cup. That way, if it breaks, you'll remember what it was and won't be troubled. The same applies to people. If you kiss your child, your brother, or your friend, don't let your pleasure go unchecked. Hold it back, just like those who stand behind victorious generals and remind them they are mortal. You, too, remind yourself that the one you love is mortal and that what you love isn't truly yours. It has been given to you for the moment, not to be kept forever. It's like a fig or a bunch of grapes given to you at the right season. But if you want these things in the winter, you're a fool. So, if you long for your son or friend when it's not possible, know that you're wishing for a fig in winter. For just as winter comes to figs, so do all things in life come to an end according to nature. And further, when you're enjoying something, consider the opposite. What harm is there in saying to yourself while you kiss your child, "Tomorrow you will die," or to a friend, "Tomorrow you will leave, or I will, and we will never see each other again?" "But these are words of bad omen," you might say. And some charms are also considered bad omens, but because they're useful, I don't care. Let them be useful. But do you call something a bad omen just because it signifies something natural? Cowardice is a bad omen, so is a weak spirit, sorrow, grief, and shamelessness. These are bad omens, yet we shouldn't hesitate to speak them to protect ourselves from these things. Do you tell me that a name that signifies something natural is a bad omen? Then say that the reaping of grain is a bad omen, for it means the destruction of the grain, but not of the world. Say that the falling of leaves is a bad omen, and that it's bad for dried figs to replace fresh ones, and for grapes to turn into raisins. All these things are just changes from one state to another, not destruction, but part of a fixed plan and order. Leaving home is a small change. Death is a bigger change, not from being to nothingness, but to something that isn't now. "Shall I then no longer exist?" you might ask. No, you won't exist in the same way, but you'll become something else that the world now needs. For you came into existence not when you chose, but when the world needed you.

The wise and good person, remembering who they are, where they came from, and who created them, focuses only on this: how to fulfill their role according to the order of things and in obedience to God. Do you still want me to live? I will continue to live as free and noble as you intended. For you have made me free from obstacles in what is truly mine. But if you no longer need me, I thank you for the time I have stayed in your service, and now I leave, still obedient to you. How do I leave? As you please, as a free person, as your servant, as someone who understands your commands and prohibitions. And as long as I stay in your service, who do you want me to be? A prince or a private person, a senator or a commoner, a soldier or a general, a teacher or the head of a household? Whatever place and position you assign to me, as Socrates says, I will die ten thousand times rather than abandon it. And where do you want me to be? In Rome, Athens, Thebes, or Gyara? Just remember me wherever I am. If you send me to a place where I can't live according to nature, I will not leave life in disobedience to you, but as if you were giving me the signal to retreat. I do not leave you, far from it, but I see that you no longer need me. If I can live according to nature, I will seek no other place than where I am, or other people than those among whom I am.

Let these thoughts be with you day and night. Write them down, read them, talk about them with yourself and others. Ask someone, "Can you help me with this?" and then go to another and another. Then, if something happens that is against your wish, this thought will immediately comfort you: that it is not unexpected. It is a great thing to say in all situations, "I knew that I brought a mortal child into the world." For so you will also say, "I knew that I am mortal, I knew that I could leave my home, I knew that I could be thrown out, I knew that

I could be imprisoned." Then if you turn to yourself and ask where the event came from, you will immediately remember that it came from the world of things outside your control, things that are not yours. Then you will ask, "And who sent it?" The leader, the general, the state, the law. Give it to me, then, for I must always obey the law in everything. Then, when the thought of the situation pains you, for it is not within your power to prevent this, fight against it with reason and overcome it. Don't let it grow stronger or lead you to conclusions by creating images in your mind as it pleases. If you are in Gyara, don't imagine life in Rome, and how many pleasures were there for those who lived there, and how many there would be for those who returned to Rome. Instead, focus on how a person who lives in Gyara ought to live in Gyara like a person of courage. And if you are in Rome, don't imagine what life in Athens is like, but think only of life in Rome.

Then, instead of all other pleasures, substitute this one: the pleasure of knowing that you are obeying God, that not just in words but in actions, you are living as a wise and good person. What a thing it is to be able to say to yourself, "Now, whatever others may say solemnly in schools and may be judged to be saying in a strange way, this I am doing; and they are sitting and talking about my virtues, inquiring about me, and praising me. And of this, Zeus has willed that I shall receive proof from myself and shall know if he has a soldier such as he ought to have, a citizen such as he ought to have, and if he has chosen to show me to others as a witness of things beyond their control: Look, you fear without reason, you foolishly desire what you desire. Don't seek the good in things outside yourself; seek it within, or you won't find it." For this purpose, he leads me here and sends me there, shows me to people as poor, without power, and sick; sends me to Gyara, leads me to prison—not because he hates me, far from it, for who hates his best servants? Nor because he doesn't care about me, for he doesn't neglect even the smallest things. But he does this to exercise me and use me as an example to others. Being given such a task, do I still care about where I am, who I am with, or what people say about me? Should I not focus entirely on God and his instructions and commands?

With these thoughts always in mind, practicing them yourself, and keeping them ready, you will never lack comfort and strength. For it is not shameful to be without food, but it is shameful not to have enough reason to keep away fear and sorrow. Once you've freed yourself from fear and sorrow, will there be any tyrant for you, or a tyrant's guard, or attendants on Caesar? Or will any appointment to high office trouble you, or those who sacrifice in the Capitol when given important roles? How could these things bother you who have received such great authority from Zeus? Only, don't boast about it or make a show of it, but show it through your actions. And if no one notices, be satisfied that you are yourself in a healthy state and happy.

Chapter 25
To Those Who Stray From Their Purpose

Think about the goals you set for yourself at the beginning. Consider which ones you've achieved and which ones you haven't. Notice how you feel happy when you remember the goals you've met and feel upset about the ones you've missed. If it's possible, try to regain what you've lost. We shouldn't give up when we're in the middle of a big challenge; we must even be willing to take hits. The struggle we're facing isn't like wrestling or the Pancration, where both winners and losers can still have some merit or luck. No, this battle is for good fortune and happiness themselves.

Even if you've stepped out of the fight for good fortune and happiness, nothing stops you from getting back in. You don't have to wait four more years for the next Olympic Games. As soon as you're ready and motivated again, you can jump back into the fight. And if you give up again, you can still return to it once more. If you finally win, it's as if you've never given up. Just don't get into the habit of quitting so often that you start to enjoy it, like a bad athlete who goes around, defeated in every game, like quails who've run away from a fight.

If the sight of a beautiful young girl tempts me, well, hasn't that happened before? If I feel an urge to criticize someone, haven't I done that before, too? You talk as if you've escaped unharmed, just like someone who might say to a doctor who advises against bathing, "But haven't I bathed before?" If the doctor could respond, he might ask, "And what happened after your bath? Didn't you get a fever or a headache?" Likewise, when you recently criticized someone, didn't you act like a mean-spirited person, like a petty gossip? Didn't you reinforce that habit in yourself by repeating it? And when you were overpowered by that young girl's beauty, did you really come away unharmed? So, why do you bring up what you did before?

You should remember your past mistakes, just like a slave remembers the beatings they've received, and you should avoid making the same errors again. But unlike slaves, who remember because of the pain, what causes you to remember your mistakes? What punishment do you face for your faults? When have you ever been in the habit of avoiding bad behavior? Painful experiences, whether we like it or not, can be helpful to us.

Chapter 26
To Those Who Fear Want

Are you not embarrassed to be more fearful and cowardly than runaway slaves? When they escape from their masters, what do they depend on? What property do they have? What servants do they rely on? Don't they just steal a little to survive the first few days, and then figure out ways to keep themselves alive as they move from place to place, whether by land or sea? And have you ever heard of a runaway slave dying of hunger? But here you are, worried that you might run out of the things you need and staying awake at night because of it. How blind are you that you can't see where the lack of necessities leads?

"Well, where does it lead?" you ask. It leads to the same place that a fever or a falling rock would lead you—to death. Haven't you told your friends many times that you're not afraid of death? Haven't you read about it and even written about it? And how many times have you bragged that you were okay with the idea of dying?

"Yes, but my wife and children might go hungry too," you say. And where does their hunger lead them? Isn't it the same place? Don't they also face the same end? So why not look at that final destination with courage, knowing that both the richest people and the poorest people, kings and even tyrants, must all end up there? You might arrive at that place hungry, while they might arrive there stuffed from overeating and drinking.

Have you ever seen a beggar who wasn't old, even very old? They sleep outside in the cold, day and night, lying on the ground, eating only what's absolutely necessary, and somehow, they almost never die. Can't you write? Can't you teach children? Can't you be a guard at someone's door?

"But it's shameful to be in such a position," you say. Then first learn what things are truly shameful and then tell us that you're a philosopher. But until then, don't let anyone call you a philosopher.

Is it shameful for you to experience something that's not your fault, something you didn't cause, something that happened by chance, like a headache or a fever? If your parents were poor and didn't leave you anything, or if they're still alive but don't help you, is that shameful for you? Is this what you learned from philosophers? Didn't you learn that only the things that are truly shameful should be blamed, and only what's blameworthy deserves blame? Who do you blame for something that's not their fault, something they didn't do themselves? Did you make your father the way he is? Can you change him? Is that within your power? Then why should you wish for things that aren't within your control, or feel ashamed if you don't get them? Have you really spent your time studying philosophy by looking to others and hoping for things outside yourself?

Then go ahead and complain, cry, and worry that you won't have food tomorrow. Worry about your poor servants stealing from you, running away, or dying. Live your life in constant fear, you who have only approached philosophy in name and have shown by your actions that its teachings are useless and unprofitable. You've never sought stability, freedom from disturbance, or control over your emotions. You've never sought out a teacher for these purposes, but you've looked for many just to learn arguments. You've never truly asked yourself, "Can I handle this, or can't I? What should I do next?" Instead, you've acted as if all your affairs were secure and you could just sit back and focus on intellectual exercises.

Shouldn't you have gained something more from philosophy, and then protected it? Have you ever seen someone build a wall without also building a fort around it? Have you ever seen a guard posted with no door to watch? But you practice philosophy to prove—what? That you won't be confused by tricky arguments and won't be swayed—by what? Show me first what you hold onto, what you measure, or what you weigh. Show me the scales or the measuring stick you use. Or how long will you keep measuring dust? Shouldn't you be showing people the things that make them happy, the things that help them achieve their goals, and why we shouldn't blame anyone or complain about anything, but instead accept the way the universe works? Show me these things.

"Look, I'll show you: I'll solve some logical puzzles for you," you say. But that's just a tool, not the real measure. That's why you're now paying the price for neglecting true philosophy. You're trembling with fear, lying awake at night, consulting everyone for advice. And if your plans don't please everyone, you think you've done something wrong.

You're afraid of hunger, but it's not really hunger that you fear. You're afraid that you won't have someone to cook for you, someone to shop for you, someone to take off your shoes, someone to dress you, others to rub you down, and to follow you around. You're afraid that you won't have the life of a sick person who's pampered and waited on. But learn how healthy people live, how slaves live, how laborers live, how true philosophers live. Learn how Socrates lived, who had a wife and children. Learn how Diogenes lived, and how Cleanthes lived, who ran a school and also drew water for a living. If you want to live like them, you can do it anywhere and live with full confidence.

What should you have confidence in? In what's truly secure, in what can't be taken away: your own will. Why have you made yourself so useless that no one wants to take you into their home, no one wants to care for you? If someone found a useful and intact tool on the street, they would pick it up and consider it a valuable find. But no one will pick you up, and everyone will see you as a burden. Can't you even do the job of a dog or a rooster? Why do you want to keep living if this is what you are?

Does a good person worry that they won't have food? Blind people don't starve, neither do lame people. Should a good person starve? And a good soldier will always find someone to pay him, just like a laborer or a shoemaker does. So, will a good person be lacking in anything? Does God really neglect the things he's created—his servants, his witnesses—who he uses as examples for others to show that he exists and that he takes care of the world? Doesn't he show that a good person faces no real evil, whether in life or in death?

What if God doesn't provide a good person with food? What else is he doing but, like a good general, giving the signal to retreat? I obey, I follow, agreeing with the commander's orders and praising his actions. I came when he called me, and I will go when he tells me to leave. And while I'm alive, it's my duty to praise God by myself, with others, and with many people. God doesn't give me many things or an abundance of wealth. He doesn't want me to live luxuriously. He didn't even give that to Hercules, who was his own son. Another person, Eurystheus, was king of Argos and Mycenae, and Hercules obeyed orders, worked hard, and was tested. And what was Eurystheus in the end? He wasn't even king of himself, while Hercules was the ruler and leader of the whole earth and sea. He purified the world of lawlessness and brought in justice and holiness, and he did all this both naked and alone.

And when Ulysses was shipwrecked, did he lose hope? Did it break his spirit? No. How did he go to the maidens to ask for help, to beg— something that most people consider shameful?

"Like a lion bred in the mountains, trusting in his strength" — Odyssey vi 130

What was he relying on? Not on his reputation, wealth, or power, but on his own strength, which is his understanding of what's within our control and what's not. These are the only things that make people truly free, that free them from obstacles, that allow them to look confidently at the rich and powerful. This is the gift given to philosophers. But you won't come out strong and bold; instead, you'll be trembling over your trivial possessions and silverware.

Unhappy man, is this how you've spent your time until now?

"What if I get sick?" you ask. You will be sick in the way you ought to be.

"Who will take care of me?" you ask. God and your friends.

"I will lie on a hard bed," you say. But you will lie there like a man.

"I won't have a comfortable room," you complain. You will be sick in an uncomfortable room.

"Who will provide me with the necessary food?" you wonder. The same people who provide for others.

You will be sick like everyone else. And what will be the end of your sickness? Anything other than death?

Do you think that death is the worst thing that can happen to a person, or is it the fear of death that's truly terrifying? To overcome this fear, I advise you to practice reasoning, exercises, and reading. Only then will you understand that this is the way to become truly free.

Book IV

Chapter 1
On Freedom

Aperson is free who lives as they wish to live; who is neither subject to compulsion, nor to hindrance, nor to force; whose movements towards action are not impeded, whose desires reach their goal, and who does not fall into what they wish to avoid. Who, then, chooses to live in error? No one. Who chooses to live deceived, prone to mistake, unjust, unrestrained, or discontented? No one. Not one of the bad lives as they wish; nor are they then free. And who chooses to live in sorrow, fear, envy, pity, desiring and failing in their desires, attempting to avoid something but falling into it? Not one. Do we then find any of the bad free from sorrow, free from fear, who does not fall into what they wish to avoid, and who does not fail in what they wish to achieve? Not one; nor do we find any bad person free.

If a person who has been twice consul hears this, and if you add, "But you are a wise person; this is nothing to you," they will forgive you. But if you tell them the truth, and say, "You are no different from those who have been sold three times as far as not being a slave," what else should you expect but blows? For they will say, "What? I, a slave, I whose father was free, whose mother was free? I, who no man can purchase? I, who am of senatorial rank, a friend of Caesar, who have been consul, and who own many slaves?"—In the first place, most excellent senator, perhaps your father was also a slave in the same kind of servitude, and your mother, and your grandfather, and all your ancestors as well. But even if they were as free as possible, what is that to you? What if they were noble, and you are of a mean nature; if they were fearless, and you are a coward; if they had the power of self-restraint, and you do not?

"And what," you may say, "has this to do with being a slave?" Does it seem to you to be nothing to act unwillingly, under compulsion, with groans—does this have nothing to do with being a slave? "It is something," you say: "but who can compel me except Caesar, the lord of all?" Then even you have admitted that you have one master. But that he is the common master of all, as you say, should not console you at all: but know that you are a slave in a great household. So also, the people of Nicopolis are accustomed to exclaim, "By the fortune of Caesar, we are free."

However, if you please, let us not speak of Caesar for the moment. But tell me this: have you never loved anyone, a young girl, a slave, or someone free? "What does this have to do with being a slave or free?" Were you never commanded by the person you loved to do something you did not wish to do? Have you never flattered your little slave? Have you never kissed her feet? And yet, if someone compelled you to kiss Caesar's feet, you would think it an insult and excessive tyranny. What else, then, is slavery? Have you never gone out by night to some place you did not wish to go, spent money you did not wish to spend, uttered words with sighs and groans, or submitted to abuse and exclusion? But if you are ashamed to confess your own actions, look at what Thrasonides says and does, who, after having served in the military, perhaps more than you, went out by night, when Geta (a slave) does not venture out. But if Geta were compelled by his master, he would have cried out and gone out, lamenting his bitter slavery. Next, what does Thrasonides say? "A worthless girl has enslaved me, me whom no enemy ever did." Unhappy man, you are the slave of a girl, and a worthless girl at that. Why do you still call yourself free? Why do you talk of your military service? Then he calls for a sword and is angry with the person who, out of kindness, refuses it; and he sends presents to the girl who hates him, entreats, and weeps, and on the other hand, after having a little success, he is elated. But even then, how? Was he free enough neither to desire nor to fear?

Now consider the case of animals, how we apply the notion of liberty. People keep tame lions shut up and feed them, and some take them around; and who will say that this lion is free? Isn't it the fact that the more he lives at ease, the more he is in a slavish condition? And who, if they had perception and reason, would wish to be one of these lions? Well, when birds are caught and kept shut up, how much do they suffer in their attempts to escape? And some of them die of hunger rather than submit to such a life. And as many of them as live, barely live and with suffering waste away; and if they ever find any opening, they make their escape. So much do they desire their natural liberty, to be independent and free from hindrance. And what harm is there in this? What do you say? I am made by nature to fly where I choose, to live in the open air, to sing when I choose: you deprive me of all this, and say, what harm is it to you? For this reason, we shall say that only those animals are free which cannot endure capture but escape from captivity by death as soon as they are caught. So Diogenes also somewhere says that there is only one way to freedom, and that is to die content. And he writes to the Persian king, "You cannot enslave the Athenian state any more than you can enslave fish." How is that? Cannot I catch them? "If you catch them," says Diogenes, "they will immediately leave you, just like fish; for if you catch a fish, it dies; and if these men are caught, they will die too. What use, then, is the preparation for war?" These are the words of a free man who had carefully examined the matter, and, as was natural, had discovered it. But if you look for it in a different place than where it is, what wonder is it that you never find it?

The slave wishes to be set free immediately. Why? Do you think he wishes to pay money to the collectors of the twentieth tax? No; but because he imagines that so far, through not obtaining this, he is hindered and unfortunate. "If I shall be set free, immediately it is all happiness, I care for no one, I speak to all as an equal and like them, I go where I choose, and I come from any place I choose, and go where I choose." Then he is set free, and forthwith, having no place where he can eat, he looks for someone to flatter, someone with whom he shall sup. Then he either works with his body and endures the most dreadful things; and if he can obtain a manger, he falls into a slavery much worse than his former slavery. Or even if he becomes rich, being a man without any knowledge of what is good, he loves some little girl, and in his unhappiness laments and desires to be a slave again. He says, "What evil did I suffer in my state of slavery? Another clothed me, another gave me shoes, another fed me, another looked after me when I was sick; and I only did a few services for him. But now, wretched man that I am, what things I suffer, being a slave to many instead of to one. But however," he says, "if I shall acquire rings, then I shall live most prosperously and happily." First, to acquire these rings, he submits to what he is worthy of; then, when he has acquired them, it is again all the same. Then he says, "If I shall be engaged in military service, I will be free from all evils." He obtains military service. He suffers as much as a flogged slave, and nevertheless, he asks for a second service and a third. After this, when he has completed his career, and is made a senator, then he becomes a slave by entering the assembly, and he serves the finer and most splendid slavery—not to be a fool, but to learn what Socrates taught, what is the nature of each thing that exists, and that a man should not rashly adapt preconceptions to the various things that are. For this is the cause of all men's evils—their inability to adapt their general preconceptions to particular things. But we have different opinions about the cause of our evils. One man thinks that he is sick—not so, however, but the fact is that he does not adapt his preconceptions correctly. Another thinks that he is poor; another that he has a severe father or mother; and another again that Caesar is not favorable to him. But all this is one and only one thing—the inability to adapt preconceptions correctly. For who does not have a preconception of what is bad: that it is harmful, that it should be avoided, that it should in every way be guarded against? One preconception is not opposed to another, except when it comes to the matter of adaptation. What then is this evil, which is both harmful and something to be avoided? He answers, "Not being

Caesar's friend." He has missed the mark; he has failed to adapt correctly, and is confused, seeking things that are not relevant to the matter. For when he has succeeded in being Caesar's friend, he still has not found what he was looking for. For what is it that everyone seeks? To live securely, to be happy, to do everything as they wish, not to be hindered, nor compelled. When then he has become Caesar's friend, is he free from hindrance? Free from compulsion? Is he tranquil? Is he happy? Of whom shall we inquire? What more trustworthy witness have we than this very man who has become Caesar's friend? Come forward and tell us: When did you sleep more quietly, now or before you became Caesar's friend? Immediately, you hear the answer, "Stop, I beg you, do not mock me; you do not know what miseries I suffer, and sleep does not come to me. One comes and says, 'Caesar is already awake, he is now going forth'; then come troubles and cares." Well, when did you dine with more pleasure, now or before? Hear what he says about this too. He says that if he is not invited, he is pained; and if he is invited, he dines like a slave with his master, all the while being anxious that he does not say or do anything foolish. And what do you suppose he is afraid of? Being beaten like a slave? How could he expect anything so good? No, but as befits so great a man, Caesar's friend, he is afraid that he may lose his head. And when did you bathe more freely, and exercise more peacefully? Finally, which life do you prefer, your present or your former life? I swear that no one is so foolish or so ignorant of truth as not to lament his own misfortunes the closer he is in friendship to Caesar. Since then, neither those who are called kings live as they wish, nor the friends of kings, who then are truly free? Seek, and you will find; for you have aids from nature to discover the truth. But if you are not able to discover it by yourself, listen to those who have made the inquiry. What do they say? Does freedom seem to you a good thing? "The greatest good." Is it possible then for someone who possesses the greatest good to be unhappy or suffer misfortune? "No." Whomever you see unhappy, unfortunate, or lamenting, confidently declare that they are not free. "I do declare it." We have now moved away from buying and selling and similar arrangements concerning property: for if you have rightly agreed to these matters, if the great king (the Persian king) is unhappy, he cannot be free, nor can a minor king, nor a man of consular rank, nor one who has been twice consul. So be it.

Further, answer me this question too: does freedom seem to you something great, noble, and valuable? "How could it not?" Is it possible then that someone who possesses something so great, valuable, and noble can be mean? "It is not possible." When you see someone subject to another or flattering them against their own judgment, confidently declare that this person is not free; not only if they do this for a bit of supper but also if they do it for a governorship or a consulship. And call those who do these things for small matters little slaves, and those who do them for great matters great slaves, as they deserve to be called. "This is agreed upon." Do you think that freedom is independent and self-governing? "Certainly." Then, whoever it is in another's power to hinder or compel, declare that person is not free. And do not look, I beg you, at his grandfathers and great-grandfathers, or inquire about whether he was bought or sold. But if you hear him saying from his heart and with feeling, "Master," even if the twelve fasces precede him (as consul), call him a slave. And if you hear him say, "Wretch that I am, how much I suffer," call him a slave. If finally, you see him lamenting, complaining, or unhappy, call him a slave, even though he wears a praetexta. If he is doing none of these things, do not yet say he is free, but learn his opinions. Are they subject to compulsion or hindrance, or bad fortune? If you find them so, call him a slave who has a holiday during the Saturnalia: say that his master is away; he will return soon, and you will know what he suffers. "Who will return?" Whoever has power over anything the man desires, either to give it to him or take it away. "So then we have many masters?" We do: for we have circumstances as masters before our present masters, and these circumstances are many. Therefore, it is necessary that those who have power over any of these circumstances must be our masters. For no one fears Caesar himself, but they fear death, banishment, loss of property, prison, and disgrace. Nor does anyone love Caesar unless Caesar is a person of great merit, but they love wealth, the office of tribune, praetor, or consul. When we love, hate, and fear these things, those who have power over them must be our masters. Therefore, we adore them even as gods; for we think that what can give us the greatest benefit is divine. Then we wrongly assume that a certain person has the power of conferring the greatest benefits; therefore, he is something divine. For if we wrongly assume that a certain person has the power of conferring the greatest benefits, it is a necessary consequence that the conclusion from these premises must be false.

What then makes a person free from hindrance and makes them their own master? For wealth does not do it, nor consulship, nor provincial government, nor royal power; but something else must be found. What then is it that, when we write, makes us free from hindrance and unimpeded? The knowledge of the art of writing. What then is it in playing the lute? The science of playing the lute. Therefore in life also, it is the science of life. You have heard this in a general way, but examine it in parts. Is it possible for someone who desires things that depend on others to be free from hindrance? No. Is it possible for them to be unimpeded? No. Therefore, they cannot be free. Consider this: do we have nothing in our power, or do we have all things, or are some things in our power and others in the power of others? "What do you mean?" When you want your body to be whole, is it in your power or not? "It is not in my power." When you want it to be healthy? "Neither is this in my power." When you want it to be beautiful? "Nor is this." Life or death? "Neither is this in my power." Your body, then, belongs to another, subject to anyone stronger than yourself. "It does." But your estate, is it in your power to have it when you please, as long as you please, and in the way you please? "No." And your slaves? "No." And your clothes? "No." And your house? "No." And your horses? "Not one of these things." And if you wish for your children to live, or your wife, or your brother, or your friends, is it in your power? "This too is not in my power."

So, do you have nothing that is your own, nothing that depends on you alone and cannot be taken away, or do you have something of the kind? "I do not know." Look at the matter this way and examine it. Can anyone make you agree with something false? "No one." In the matter of agreement, then, you are free from hindrance and obstruction. "Agreed." Well, and can anyone force you to desire something you do not wish? "He can, for when he threatens me with death or imprisonment, he compels me to desire to avoid it." If you despise death and imprisonment, do you still care what he says? "No." Is then the despising of death your own act or not? "It is my act." It is your own act then to desire to move toward something: or is it not so? "It is my own act." But to desire to avoid something, whose act is that? This too is your act. "What if I try to walk, but someone stops me?" What part of you does he stop? Does he stop your power of agreeing? "No, but he stops my poor body." Yes, as he would stop a stone. "Agreed, but I no longer walk." And who told you that walking is your own act, free from hindrance? I said that this only was free from hindrance: the desire to move, but where there is a need for the body and its cooperation, you heard long ago that nothing is your own. "Agreed to this also." And who can compel you to desire what you do not wish? "No one." And to plan or decide, or in short, to use the appearances that present themselves—can anyone compel you? "He cannot do this, but he will stop me from obtaining what I desire." If you desire something that is your own, and one of the things that cannot be stopped, how will he stop you? "He cannot in any way." Who then tells you that he who desires things that belong to others is free from hindrance?

"Must I then not desire health?" By no means, nor anything else that belongs to another: for what is not in your power to obtain or keep when you wish, belongs to another. Keep, then, not only your hands but even your desires far from it. If you do not, you have surrendered yourself as a slave; you have subjected your neck, if you admire anything that is not your own, to everything that depends on others' power and is perishable, to which you have conceived a liking. "Is not my hand my own?" It is a part of your own body, but it is by nature earth, subject to hindrance, compulsion, and the slave of everything stronger. And why do I say your hand? You should hold your entire body as a poor ass loaded, as long as it is possible, as long as you are allowed. But if there is pressure and a soldier seizes it, let it go, do not resist, nor complain; if you do, you will be beaten, and still lose the ass. But when you should feel this way about the body, consider what remains to be done about everything else provided for the body's sake. When the body is an ass, all other things are bits belonging to the ass: packsaddles, shoes, barley, fodder. Let these also go: get rid of them faster and more readily than the ass.

When you have prepared yourself this way, and practiced this discipline—to distinguish what belongs to another from what is your own, what is subject to hindrance from what is not, to concern yourself with the things free from hindrance, and not concern yourself with the things that are not free—do you still fear any man? No one. For what will you be afraid of? About the things that are your own, in which the nature of good and evil consists? And who has power over these things? Who can take them away? Who can impede them? No one can, no more than they can impede God. But will you be afraid about your body and possessions, things that are not yours, things that in no way concern you? And what else have you been studying from the beginning but to distinguish between your own and not your own, the things that are in your power and not in your power, the things subject to hindrance and not subject? Why did you come to the philosophers? Was it so that you may still be unfortunate and unhappy? You will then, as I have supposed you to do, be without fear and disturbance. And what is grief to you? For fear comes from what you expect, but grief from what is present. But what more will you desire? For of the things that are within the power of the will, as being good and present, you have a proper and regulated desire: but of the things that are not in the power of the will, you do not desire any one, and so you do not allow any place for what is irrational, impatient, or excessively hasty.

When you are this way towards things, what man can still be formidable to you? For what has a man that is formidable to another, either when you see him or speak to him or finally are conversant with him? Not more than one horse has with respect to another, or one dog to another, or one bee to another bee. Things indeed are formidable to every man, and when any man can give these things to another or take them away, then he too becomes formidable. How then is a fortress demolished? Not by the sword, not by fire, but by opinion. For if we demolish the fortress within the city, can we also demolish the one of fever, or that of beautiful women? Can we, in a word, demolish the fortress within us and cast out the tyrants within us, whom we have daily over us, sometimes the same tyrants, other times different tyrants? But with this, we must begin, and with this, we must demolish the fortress and eject the tyrants by giving up the body, the parts of it, the faculties of it, the possessions, the reputation, magisterial offices, honors, children, brothers, friends, by considering all these things as belonging to others. And if tyrants have been ejected from us, why do I still enclose the fortress by a wall of circumvallation, at least on my account; for if it still stands, what does it do to me? Why do I still eject the guards? For where do I perceive them? Against others, they have their fasces, and their spears, and their swords. But I have never been hindered in my will, nor compelled when I did not will. And how is this possible? I have placed my actions in obedience to God. Is it his will that I shall have a fever? It is my will also. Is it his will that I should move toward something? It is my will also. Is it his will that I should obtain something? It is my wish also. Does he not will? I do not wish. Is it his will that I die, that I be put to the rack? It is my will then to die, it is my will then to be put to the rack. Who then can still hinder me contrary to my judgment, or compel me? No one more than they can hinder or compel Zeus.

This is how the more cautious travelers act. A traveler has heard that the road is infested by robbers; he does not venture to enter it alone but waits for the companionship on the road either of an ambassador, a quaestor, or a proconsul, and when he has attached himself to such persons, he goes along the road safely. So in the world, the wise man acts. There are many bands of robbers, tyrants, storms, difficulties, losses of what is dearest. Where is there any place of refuge? How shall he pass along without being attacked by robbers? What company shall he wait for to pass along safely? To whom shall he attach himself? To what person generally? To the rich man, to the man of consular rank? And what is the use of that to me? Such a man is stripped himself, groans, and laments. But what if the fellow companion himself turns against me and becomes my robber? What shall I do? I will be a friend of Caesar: when I am Caesar's companion, no one will wrong me. First, to become illustrious, what things must I endure and suffer? How often and by how many must I be robbed? Then, if I become Caesar's friend, he too is mortal. And if Caesar, from any circumstance, becomes my enemy, where is it best for me to retire? Into a desert? Well, does fever not come there? What shall be done then? Is it not possible to find a safe companion, a faithful one, strong, secure against all surprises? Thus he considers and perceives that if he attaches himself to God, he will make his journey safely.

How do you understand "attaching yourself to God?" In this sense: that whatever God wills, a man also shall will; and what God does not will, a man also shall not will. How then shall this be done? In what other way than by examining the actions and administration of God? What has he given to me as my own and in my power? What has he reserved to himself? He has given me the things that are in the power of the will: he has put them in my power free from impediment and hindrance. How was he able to make the earthy body free from hindrance? He could not, and so he subjected to the revolution of the whole possessions, household things, house, children, wife. Why then do I fight against God? Why do I will what does not depend on the will? Why do I will to have absolutely what is not granted to me? But how should I will to have things? In the way, they are given and as long as they are given. But he who has given takes away. Why then do I resist? I do not say I will be a fool if I use force against one who is stronger, but I will first be unjust. For whence had I things when I came into the world? My father gave them to me. And who gave them to him? And who made the sun? And who made the fruits of the earth? And who made the seasons? And who made the connection of men with one another and their fellowship?

Then after receiving everything from another and even yourself, are you angry and do you blame the giver if he takes anything from you? Who are you, and for what purpose did you come into the world? Did he not introduce you here, did he not show you the light, did he not give you fellow workers, and perceptions and reason? And as who did he introduce you here? Did he not introduce you as subject to death, and as one to live on the earth with a little flesh, to observe his administration, and to join him in the spectacle and the festival for a short time? Will you not then, as long as you have been permitted, after seeing the spectacle and the solemnity, when he leads you out, go with adoration of him and thanks for what you have heard and seen? "No; but I would still enjoy the feast." The initiated too would wish to be longer in the initiation; and perhaps also those at Olympia to see other athletes; but the solemnity is ended: go away like a grateful and modest man; make room for others: others also must be born, as you were, and being born, they must have a place, and houses, and necessary things. And if the first do not retire, what remains? Why are you insatiable? Why are you not content? Why do you contract the world? "Yes, but I would have my little children with me and my wife." What, are they yours? Do they not belong to the giver and to him who made you? Will you not give up what belongs to others? Will you not give way to him who is superior? "Why then did he introduce me into the world on these conditions?" And if the conditions do not suit you, depart. He has no need of a spectator who is not satisfied. He wants those who join the festival, those who take part in the chorus, so they may rather applaud, admire, and celebrate with hymns the solemnity. But those who cannot bear trouble, and the cowardly, he will not unwillingly see absent from the great assembly; for they did not, when they were present, behave as they ought to at a festival nor fill up their place properly, but they lamented, found fault with the deity, fortune, their companions; not seeing both what they had and their powers, which they received for contrary purposes, the powers of magnanimity, of a generous mind, manly spirit, and what we are now inquiring about—freedom. "For what purpose then have I received these things?" To use them. "How long?" As long as he who has lent them chooses. "What if they are necessary to me?" Do not attach yourself to them, and they will not be necessary: do not say to yourself that they are necessary, and they are not necessary.

This study you ought to practice from morning to evening, beginning with the smallest things and those most liable to damage: with an earthen pot, with a cup. Then proceed in this way to a tunic, a little dog, a horse, a small estate in land; then to yourself, your body, the parts of your body, your children, your wife, your brothers. Look all around and throw these things from you (which are not yours). Purge your opinions so that nothing clings to you of the things that are not your own, that nothing grows to you, that nothing gives you pain when it is torn from you; and say, while you are daily exercising yourself as you do in the school, not that you are philosophizing, for this is an arrogant expression, but that you are presenting as an asserter of freedom: for this is really freedom. To this freedom, Diogenes was called by Antisthenes, and he said that he could no longer be enslaved by anyone. For this reason, when he was taken prisoner, how did he behave towards the pirates? Did he call any of them master? And I do not speak of the name, for I am not afraid of the word, but of the state of mind by which the word is produced. How did he reprove them for feeding their captives badly? How was he sold? Did he seek a master? No, but a slave. And when he was sold, how did he behave towards his master? Immediately he argued with him and told his master that he should not be dressed as he was, nor shaved in such a way; and about the children, he told them how they should be raised. And what was strange about this? For if his master had bought a wrestling teacher, would he have employed him in the exercises of the palestra as a servant or as a master? And so if he had bought a physician or an architect. And so in every matter, it is absolutely necessary that he who has skill must be the superior of him who does not. Whoever then generally possesses the science of life, what else must he be than a master? For who is the master on a ship? The person who steers the helm. Why? Because the person who does not obey him suffers for it. "But a master can give me stripes." Can he do it then without suffering for it? So I also used to think. But because he cannot do it without suffering for it, for this reason, it is not in his power: and no one can do what is unjust without suffering for it. And what is the penalty for someone who puts their slave in chains? What do you think that is? The fact of putting the slave in chains; and you will also admit this if you choose to maintain the truth, that man is not a wild beast, but a tame animal. For when is a vine doing badly? When it is in a condition contrary to its nature. When is a rooster? Just the same. Therefore a man also is so. What then is a man's nature? To bite, to kick, to throw into prison, and behead? No; but to do good, to cooperate with others, to wish them well. At that time then, he is in a bad condition, whether you choose to admit it or not, when he is acting foolishly.

"Socrates then did not fare badly?" No, but his judges and his accusers did. "Nor did Helvidius at Rome fare badly?" No, but his murderer did. "How do you mean?" The same as you do when you say that a rooster has not fared badly when he has gained the victory and been severely wounded; but that the rooster has fared badly when he has been defeated and is unhurt; nor do you call a dog fortunate, who neither pursues game nor works, but when you see him sweating, when you see him in pain and panting violently after running. What paradox (unusual thing) do we utter if we say that the evil in everything is what is contrary to its nature? Is this a paradox? Do you not say this in the case of all other things? Why then, in the case of man only, do you think differently? But because we say that the nature of man is tame (gentle), social, and faithful, you will not say that this is a paradox. It is not. What then is it a paradox to say that a man is not hurt when he is whipped, put in chains, or beheaded? Does he not, if he suffers nobly, come off even with increased advantage and profit? But is he not hurt, who suffers most pitifully and disgracefully, who in place of a man becomes a wolf, or viper, or wasp?

Well then, let us summarize the things that have been agreed on. The person who is not restrained is free, to whom things are exactly as they wish them to be; but one who can be restrained, compelled, hindered, or thrown into any circumstances against their will, is a slave. But who is free from restraint? One who desires nothing that belongs to others. And what are the things that belong to others? Those that are not in our power either to have or not to have, or to have of a certain kind or in a certain manner. Therefore, the body belongs to another, the parts of the body belong to another, possession (property) belongs to another. If then you are attached to any of these things as your own, you will pay the penalty, which is proper for someone who desires what belongs to another. This road leads to freedom; this is the only way of escaping from slavery, to be able to say at last with all your soul:

"Lead me, O Zeus, and thou, O destiny,
The way that I am bid by you to go."
— Iliad vi 490

But what do you say, philosopher? The tyrant summons you to say something that does not suit you. Do you say it or not? Answer me. "Let me consider." Will you consider now? But when you were in the school, what was it that you used to consider? Did you not study what things are good and what are bad, and what things are neither one nor the other? "I did." What then was our opinion? "That just and honorable acts were good; and that unjust and disgraceful acts were

bad." Is life a good thing? "No." Is death a bad thing? "No." Is prison?
"No." But what did we think about mean and faithless words and
betrayal of a friend and flattery of a tyrant? "That they are bad." Well
then, you are not considering, nor have you considered nor deliberated.
For what is the matter for consideration? Is it whether it is appropriate
for me, when I have the power, to secure for myself the greatest of
good things and not avoid the greatest evils? A fine inquiry indeed, and
necessary, and one that demands much deliberation. Man, why do you
mock us? Such an inquiry is never made. If you really imagined that
base things were bad and honorable things were good, and that all
other things were neither good nor bad, you would not even have
approached this inquiry, nor have come near it; but immediately you
would have been able to distinguish them by the understanding as you
would do (in other cases) by the vision. For when do you inquire if
black things are white, if heavy things are light, and do not comprehend
the manifest evidence of the senses? How then do you now say that
you are considering whether things that are neither good nor bad ought
to be avoided more than things that are bad? But you do not possess
these opinions, and neither do these things seem to you to be neither
good nor bad, but you think that they are the greatest evils; nor do you
think those other things (mean and faithless words, etc.) to be evils,
but matters which do not concern us at all. For thus, from the
beginning, you have accustomed yourself. "Where am I? In the schools:
and are any listening to me? I am discoursing among philosophers."
But I have gone out of the school. Away with this talk of scholars and
fools. Thus a friend is overpowered by the testimony of a philosopher;
thus a philosopher becomes a parasite; thus he lets himself for hire for
money; thus, in the senate, a person does not say what he thinks; in
private (in the school), he proclaims his opinions. You are a cold and
miserable little opinion, suspended from idle words as from a hair. But
keep yourself strong and fit for the uses of life, and be initiated by being
exercised in action. How do you hear (the report)? I do not say that
your child is dead, for how could you bear that? But that your oil is
spilled, your wine drunk up? Do you act in such a way that one standing

by you while you are making a great noise, may say this only: "Philosopher, you say something different in the school. Why do you deceive us? Why, when you are only a worm, do you say that you are a man?" I should like to be present when some philosophers lie with a woman, that I might see how they are exerting themselves, and what words they are uttering, and whether they remember their title of philosopher, and the words they hear, say, or read.

And what is this to liberty? Nothing else than this: whether you who are rich choose or not. And who is your evidence for this? Who else than yourselves? Who have a powerful master (Caesar), and who live in obedience to his nod and motion, and who faint if he only looks at you with a scowling countenance; you who court old women and old men, and say, "I cannot do this: it is not in my power." Why is it not in your power? Did you not lately contend with me and say that you are free? "But Aprulla has hindered me." Tell the truth then, slave, and do not run away from your masters, nor deny, nor venture to produce anyone to assert your freedom, when you have so many evidences of your slavery. And indeed, when a man is compelled by love to do something contrary to his opinion (judgment), and at the same time sees the better, but has not the strength to follow it, one might consider him still more worthy of excuse as being held by a certain violent and in a manner a divine power. But who could endure you who are in love with old women and old men, and wipe the old women's noses, and wash them and give them presents, and also wait on them like a slave when they are sick, and at the same time wish them dead, and question the physicians whether they are sick unto death? And again, when to obtain these great and much admired magistracies and honors, you kiss the hands of these slaves of others, so you are not the slave even of free men. Then you walk about before me in stately fashion as a praetor or a consul. Do I not know how you became a praetor, by what means you got your consulship, who gave it to you? I would not even choose to live, if I must live by help of Felicion and endure his arrogance and servile insolence; for I know what a slave is, who is fortunate, as he thinks, and puffed up by pride.

"You then," someone may say, "are you free?" I wish, by the Gods, and pray to be free; but I am not yet able to face my masters; I still value my poor body; I value greatly the preservation of it entire, though I do not possess it entirely. But I can point out to you a free man so that you may no longer seek an example. Diogenes was free. How was he free? Not because he was born of free parents, but because he was himself free because he had cast off all the handles of slavery, and it was not possible for any man to approach him, nor had any man the means of laying hold of him to enslave him. He had everything easily loosed, everything only hanging to him. If you laid hold of his property, he would have rather let it go and be yours than he would have followed you for it; if you had laid hold of his leg, he would have let go his leg; if of all his body, all his poor body; his intimates, friends, country, just the same. For he knew from whence he had them and from whom, and on what conditions. His true parents indeed, the Gods, and his real country he would never have deserted, nor would he have yielded to any man in obedience to them and their orders, nor would any man have died for his country more readily. For he was not used to inquire when he should be considered to have done anything on behalf of the whole of things (the universe, or all the world), but he remembered that everything that is done comes from there and is done on behalf of that country and is commanded by him who administers it. Therefore see what Diogenes himself says and writes: "For this reason, he says, Diogenes, it is in your power to speak both with the King of the Persians and with Archidamus the king of the Lacedaemonians, as you please." Was it because he was born of free parents? I suppose all the Athenians and all the Lacedaemonians because they were born of slaves, could not talk with them (these kings) as they wished, but feared and paid court to them. Why then does he say that it is in his power? Because I do not consider the poor body to be my own, because I want nothing, because law is everything to me, and nothing else is. These were the things that permitted him to be free.

And that you may not think that I show you the example of a man who is a solitary person, who has neither wife nor children, nor country, nor friends, nor kinsmen, by whom he could be bent and drawn in various directions, take Socrates and observe that he had a wife and children, but he did not consider them as his own; that he had a country, as long as it was fit to have one, and in such a manner as was fit; friends and kinsmen also, but he held all in subjection to law and obedience to it. For this reason, he was the first to go out as a soldier, when it was necessary, and in war, he exposed himself to danger most unsparingly; and when he was sent by the tyrants to seize Leon, he did not even deliberate about the matter, because he thought it was a base action, and he knew he must die (for his refusal), if it so happened. And what difference did that make to him? For he intended to preserve something else, not his poor flesh, but his fidelity, his honorable character. These are things that could not be assailed nor brought into subjection. Then when he was obliged to speak in defense of his life, did he behave like a man who had children, who had a wife? No, but he behaved like a man who has neither. And what did he do when he was ordered to drink the poison, and when he had the power of escaping from prison, and when Crito said to him, "Escape for the sake of your children," what did Socrates say? Did he consider the power of escape as an unexpected gain? By no means: he considered what was fit and proper; but the rest he did not even look at or take into the reckoning. For he did not choose, he said, to save his poor body, but to save that which is increased and saved by doing what is just, and is impaired and destroyed by doing what is unjust. Socrates will not save his life by a base act; he who would not put the Athenians to the vote when they clamored that he should do so, he who refused to obey the tyrants, he who discoursed in such a manner about virtue and right behavior. It is not possible to save such a man's life by base acts, but he is saved by dying, not by running away. For the good actor also preserves his character by stopping when he ought to stop, better than when he goes on acting beyond the proper time. What then shall the children of Socrates do? "If," said Socrates, "I had gone off to Thessaly, would you have taken care of them; and if I depart to the world below, will there be no man to take care of them?" See how he gives death a gentle name and mocks it. But if you and I had been in his place, we should have immediately answered as philosophers that those who act unjustly must be repaid in the same way, and we should have added, "I shall be useful to many, if my life is saved, and if I die, I shall be useful to no one." For, if it had been necessary, we should have made our escape by slipping through a small hole. And how in that case should we have been useful to anyone? Where would they have been staying? Or if we were useful to people while we were alive, should we not have been much more useful to them by dying when we ought to die, and as we ought? And now Socrates, being dead, is no less useful to people, and even more useful, by the memory of what he did or said when he was alive.

Think of these things, these opinions, these words: look at these examples if you want to be free if you desire the thing according to its worth. And what is the wonder if you buy so great a thing at the price of so many and so great things? For the sake of what is called liberty, some hang themselves, others throw themselves down precipices, and sometimes even whole cities have perished. And will you not, for the sake of true, unassailable, and secure liberty, give back to God the things he has given when he demands them? Will you not, as Plato says, study not to die only, but also to endure torture, exile, and scourging, and in a word to give up all that is not your own? If you do not, you will be a slave among slaves, even if you are ten thousand times a consul; and if you make your way up to the Palace (Caesar's residence), you will still be a slave; and you will feel that perhaps philosophers speak words that are contrary to common opinion (paradoxes), as Cleanthes also said, but not words contrary to reason. For you will know by experience that the words are true and that there is no profit from the things that are valued and eagerly sought by those who have obtained them; and to those who have not yet obtained them, there is an imagination that when these things come, all that is good will come with them. Then, when they come, the feverish feeling is the same, the tossing to and fro is the same, the satiety, the desire for things that are not present; for freedom is acquired not by the full possession of the things that are desired, but by removing the desire. And that you may know that this is true, as you have labored for those things, so transfer your labor to these; be vigilant for the purpose of acquiring an opinion that will make you free; pay court to a philosopher instead of to a rich old man; be seen about a philosopher's doors: you will not disgrace yourself by being seen; you will not go away empty nor without profit if you go to the philosopher as you ought, and if not (if you do not succeed), try at least: the attempt is not disgraceful.

Chapter 2
On Familiar Intimacy

First of all, make sure you never get so close to your old friends or anyone you used to hang out with that you start doing the same things they do again. If you don't stick to this, you'll end up hurting yourself. But if you start to think, "They might think I'm being unfriendly, and they won't like me as much," remember that everything has a price. You can't stay the same person if you stop doing what they do. So, you have to choose: do you want to stay as you were and keep their affection, or do you want to grow and be different, even if it means they don't treat you the same?

If you think it's better to improve yourself, then focus on that and don't let anything else distract you. No one can make real progress if they're always torn between two choices. But if you decide to stick to your old ways, then you'll miss out on both— you won't get better, and you won't keep what you had before. When you used to care about things that weren't important, you pleased your friends. But you can't be the best at both, and the more you focus on one, the more you'll fall behind in the other.

For example, if you stop drinking with your old drinking buddies, you won't be as fun for them as you used to be. So, you have to choose: do you want to be a heavy drinker and keep their friendship, or do you want to be sober and maybe lose their affection? You also can't expect to be as well-liked as before if you stop singing with the same people you used to sing with. Here too, you have to decide which you prefer. If you think it's better to be modest and behave properly, then let go of the other stuff—don't engage with those people anymore. But if you find that this doesn't suit you, then go all in the other way: become someone who chases after pleasure and acts accordingly, and you'll get what you want.

You might even jump up in the theater and shout out praise for the dancer. But remember, you can't be two completely different characters at once. You can't be both Thersites, who was known for being ugly and mean, and Agamemnon, who was tall, handsome, and respected by others. If you choose to be like Thersites, then you have to accept being unattractive and bald. If you want to be like Agamemnon, then you have to be noble, strong, and care for those who follow you.

Chapter 3
What To Aim at in Exchange

Keep this idea in mind whenever you lose something that's outside of your control: think about what you gain in return. If what you gain is more valuable, never say, "I've lost something." For example, if you get a horse instead of a donkey, or an ox instead of a sheep, or if you gain the chance to do a good deed instead of receiving money, or if you gain peace of mind instead of idle gossip, or if you gain modesty instead of crude talk. If you remember this, you will keep your character the way it should be. But if you don't, you'll lose important opportunities, and no matter how hard you work on yourself, you'll end up wasting your efforts and destroying what you've built. It only takes a small mistake to lose everything, just like a ship captain only needs to turn the ship slightly the wrong way to cause it to crash, even if he didn't do it on purpose but just wasn't paying enough attention. The same thing can happen with your life: if you just "fall asleep" on your duties for a moment, everything you've worked on can disappear.

So, pay attention to what's happening around you, and stay alert. What you're trying to protect is no small thing. It's your modesty, honesty, consistency, freedom from emotions, calmness, and in short, your liberty. Ask yourself, "What will I trade these things for? Is it worth it?" If you do give them up, see what you're getting in return. Maybe I have decency, and someone else has a powerful job like being a tribune or a praetor. But I don't cheer when it's not appropriate, and I won't stand up where I shouldn't, because I'm free and I follow God willingly. I don't seek anything else—not my body, not possessions, not a high position, not even a good reputation. Because God doesn't want me to seek those things. If He wanted them to be good for me, He would have made them so. But since He didn't, I can't go against His will.

Always protect what is truly good for you, and in everything else, behave in a way that's reasonable and consistent. If you don't, you'll be unhappy, you'll fail at everything, and you'll face obstacles. These are the laws given by God, and we should follow them—not the laws made by people like Masurius and Cassius.

Chapter 4
To Those Who Want to Live a Peaceful Life

Remember that not only the desire for power and wealth makes us lowly and dependent on others, but even the desire for peace, free time, travel, and learning can do the same.

Always keep in mind that it's not just wanting power and riches that can make us feel weak and controlled by others, but even wanting peace, leisure, travel, or learning can also put us in the same position.

For to speak plainly, whatever the external thing may be, the value which we set upon it places us in subjection to others.

To put it simply, whatever external thing we place high value on makes us dependent on others.

What then is the difference between desiring to be a senator or not desiring to be one; what is the difference between desiring power or being content with a private station; what is the difference between saying, "I am unhappy, I have nothing to do, but I am bound to my books as a corpse"; or saying, "I am unhappy, I have no leisure for reading"?

So, what's the difference between wanting to be a senator or not wanting to be one? What's the difference between wanting power or being content with a simple life? What's the difference between saying, "I'm unhappy because I have nothing to do but read," or saying, "I'm unhappy because I don't have time to read"?

For as salutations and power are things external and independent of the will, so is a book.

Just like greetings and power are external things beyond our control, so is a book.

For what purpose do you choose to read? Tell me.

Why do you choose to read? Tell me.

For if you only direct your purpose to being amused or learning something, you are a silly fellow and incapable of enduring labor.

If your purpose is just to amuse yourself or learn something, you're being foolish and unable to handle real effort.

But if you refer reading to the proper end, what else is this than a tranquil and happy life?

But if you read to achieve a peaceful and happy life, what else could it be?

But if reading does not secure for you a happy and tranquil life, what is the use of it?

If reading doesn't bring you peace and happiness, what's the point of it?

"But it does secure this," the man replies, "and for this reason I am vexed that I am deprived of it."

You might say, "But it does bring me peace and happiness, and that's why I'm upset when I can't read."

And what is this tranquil and happy life, which any man can impede, I do not say Caesar or Caesar's friend, but a crow, a piper, a fever, and thirty thousand other things?

But what kind of peaceful and happy life can be so easily disturbed—not just by Caesar or Caesar's friend, but by something as small as a crow, a noisy musician, a fever, or any number of little things?

But a tranquil and happy life contains nothing so sure as continuity and freedom from obstacle.

True peace and happiness should be steady and uninterrupted.

Now I am called to do something: I will go then with the purpose of observing the measures (rules) which I must keep, of acting with modesty, steadiness, without desire and aversion to things external;

If I'm called to do something else, I'll go and do it, keeping in mind the rules I must follow, acting with modesty, calmness, without strong desires or dislikes for external things;

and then that I may attend to men, what they say, how they are moved;

I'll pay attention to what people say and how they react;

and this not with any bad disposition, or that I may have something to blame or to ridicule;

but I won't do this with a bad attitude or just to find something to blame or mock;

but I turn to myself, and ask if I also commit the same faults.

Instead, I'll turn inward and ask if I make the same mistakes.

How then shall I cease to commit them?

How can I stop making these mistakes?

Formerly I also acted wrong, but now I do not: thanks to God.

I used to do wrong too, but now I don't, thanks to God.

Come, when you have done these things and have attended to them, have you done a worse act than when you have read a thousand verses or written as many?

So, after you've done all this and paid attention to it, have you really done something worse than when you've read or written a thousand verses?

For when you eat, are you grieved because you are not reading?

When you eat, do you get upset because you're not reading?

Are you not satisfied with eating according to what you have learned by reading, and so with bathing and with exercise?

Aren't you content with just eating as you've learned from reading, and the same goes for bathing and exercising?

Why then do you not act consistently in all things, both when you approach Caesar, and when you approach any person?

Why not act the same way in all things, whether you're meeting with Caesar or anyone else?

If you maintain yourself free from perturbation, free from alarm, and steady; if you look rather at the things which are done and happen than are looked at yourself;

If you stay calm, free from fear, and steady; if you focus more on what's being done and happening rather than on yourself;

if you do not envy those who are preferred before you; if surrounding circumstances do not strike you with fear or admiration, what do you want? Books?

If you don't envy those who are ahead of you; if the things around you don't make you feel fear or awe, what more do you need? Books?

How or for what purpose? for is not this (the reading of books) a preparation for life? and is not life itself (living) made up of certain other things than this?

Why? What for? Isn't reading books just preparation for life? And isn't life itself made up of more than just this?

This is just as if an athlete should weep when he enters the stadium, because he is not being exercised outside of it.

This is like an athlete crying when he enters the stadium because he's not still training outside.

It was for this purpose that you used to practice exercise; for this purpose were used the halteres (weights), the dust, the young men as antagonists; and do you seek for those things now when it is the time of action?

You trained for this moment; you used weights, dust, and sparring partners for this; and now, when it's time to act, do you still want those things?

This is just as if in the topic (matter) of assent when appearances present themselves, some of which can be comprehended, and some cannot be comprehended, we should not choose to distinguish them but should choose to read what has been written about comprehension (κατάληψις).

It's like in matters of understanding when some things can be grasped and others can't, instead of trying to figure them out, you'd rather just read about comprehension.

What then is the reason of this? The reason is that we have never read for this purpose, we have never written for this purpose, so that we may in our actions use in a way conformable to nature the appearances presented to us;

Why is this? It's because we've never read or written with the purpose of using what we learn in our actions, in a way that aligns with nature;

but we terminate in this, in learning what is said, and in being able to expound it to another, in resolving a syllogism, and in handling the hypothetical syllogism.

instead, we stop at just learning what's said, being able to explain it to others, solving a logical problem, and handling a hypothetical situation.

For this reason where our study (purpose) is, there alone is the impediment.

That's why, wherever our study is focused, that's where the obstacles are.

Would you have by all means the things which are not in your power?

Do you want to have things that aren't within your control?

Be prevented then, be hindered, fail in your purpose.

Then be ready to be blocked, hindered, and fail in your purpose.

But if we read what is written about action (efforts), not that we may see what is said about action, but that we may act well:

But if we read what's written about action not just to see what's said, but to actually act well:

if we read what is said about desire and aversion (avoiding things), in order that we may neither fail in our desires, nor fall into that which we try to avoid;

if we read about desire and avoiding things so that we neither fail in our desires nor fall into what we try to avoid;

if we read what is said about duty, in order that remembering the relations (of things to one another) we may do nothing irrationally nor contrary to these relations;

if we read about duty so that, by remembering how things are related, we don't do anything irrational or contrary to these relations;

we should not be vexed in being hindered as to our readings, but we should be satisfied with doing the acts which are conformable (to the relations),

then we wouldn't be upset about being hindered from reading, but we would be content with doing actions that are in line with these relations,

and we should be reckoning not what so far we have been accustomed to reckon: "Today I have read so many verses, I have written so many;"

and we wouldn't be counting how many verses we've read or written today;

but (we should say), "Today I have employed my action as it is taught by the philosophers; I have not employed my desire; I have used avoidance (ἐκκλίσει) only with respect to things which are within the power of my will;

but instead, we'd say, "Today I've acted according to what the philosophers teach; I haven't let desire control me; I've only avoided things that are within my control;

I have not been afraid of such a person, I have not been prevailed upon by the entreaties of another; I have exercised my patience, my abstinence, my cooperation with others;"

I haven't been afraid of anyone, I haven't given in to anyone's pleas; I've practiced patience, self-control, and cooperation with others;"

and so we should thank God for what we ought to thank him.

and so we should thank God for the things we should be thankful for.

But now we do not know that we also in another way are like the many.

But right now, we don't realize that in another way, we're just like everyone else.

Another man is afraid that he shall not have power: you are afraid that you will.

Another person fears they won't have power, while you fear that you will.

Do not do so, my man; but as you ridicule him who is afraid that he shall not have power, so ridicule yourself also.

Don't be like that, my friend; and just as you might laugh at someone who fears not having power, you should also laugh at yourself.

For it makes no difference whether you are thirsty like a man who has a fever, or have a dread of water like a man who is mad.

Because it doesn't matter if you're thirsty like someone with a fever or if you're afraid of water like someone who's mad.

Or how will you still be able to say as Socrates did, "If so it pleases God, so let it be?"

How will you be able to say, like Socrates did, "If it pleases God, then let it be?"

Do you think that Socrates if he had been eager to pass his leisure in the Lyceum or in the Academy and to discourse daily with the young men, would have readily served in military expeditions so often as he did;

Do you think Socrates, if he had been eager to spend his free time in the Lyceum or the Academy talking with young men every day, would have so easily gone on military expeditions as often as he did?

and would he not have lamented and groaned, "Wretch that I am; I must now be miserable here, when I might be sunning myself in the Lyceum?"

And wouldn't he have complained and groaned, saying, "Poor me, I have to suffer here when I could be relaxing in the Lyceum?"

Why, was this your business, to sun yourself? And is it not your business to be happy, to be free from hindrance, free from impediment?

But was it really his job to just sun himself? Isn't it more important to be happy, free from obstacles, and free from hindrances?

And could he still have been Socrates, if he had lamented in this way: how would he still have been able to write Paeans in his prison?

And could he still be Socrates if he complained like that? How would he have been able to write hymns in his prison?

In short remember this, that what you shall prize which is beyond your will, so far you have destroyed your will.

In short, remember this: if you value anything beyond your control, you've already destroyed your will.

But these things are out of the power of the will, not only power (authority), but also a private condition: not only occupation (business), but also leisure.

But these things—power, a private life, work, and leisure—are all beyond your control.

"Now then must I live in this tumult?"

"So now do I have to live in this chaos?"

Why do you say tumult?

Why do you call it chaos?

"I mean among many men."

"I mean among many people."

Well what is the hardship?

But what's so hard about that?

Suppose that you are at Olympia: imagine it to be a panegyris (public assembly), where one is calling out one thing, another is doing another thing, and a third is pushing another person; in the baths there is a crowd: and who of us is not pleased with this assembly, and leaves it unwillingly?

Imagine you're at Olympia, at a public gathering where one person is shouting one thing, another person is doing something else, and someone else is pushing people around; in the baths, there's a crowd: but who among us doesn't enjoy this kind of gathering and leaves it reluctantly?

Be not difficult to please nor fastidious about what happens.

Don't be hard to please or picky about what happens.

"Vinegar is disagreeable, for it is sharp; honey is disagreeable, for it disturbs my habit of body. I do not like vegetables.

"Vinegar is unpleasant because it's sharp; honey is unpleasant because it upsets my stomach. I don't like vegetables.

So also I do not like leisure; it is a desert: I do not like a crowd; it is confusion."

In the same way, I don't like leisure; it's boring: I don't like crowds; they're chaotic."

But if circumstances make it necessary for you to live alone or with a few, call it quiet, and use the thing as you ought: talk with yourself, exercise the appearances (presented to you), work up your preconceptions.

But if you have to live alone or with just a few people, call it peace and use it as you should: talk with yourself, think about the things that appear to you, and challenge your assumptions.

If you fall into a crowd, call it a celebration of games, a panegyris, a festival: try to enjoy the festival with other men.

If you find yourself in a crowd, call it a celebration, a festival: try to enjoy the festival with others.

For what is a more pleasant sight to him who loves mankind than a number of men?

Because what's more pleasant to someone who loves people than seeing a lot of people?

We see with pleasure herds of horses or oxen: we are delighted when we see many ships: who is pained when he sees many men?

We enjoy watching herds of horses or oxen, and we're happy when we see many ships: who gets upset when they see a lot of people?

"But they deafen me with their cries."

"But their noise deafens me."

Then your hearing is impeded. What then is this to you?

So your hearing is blocked. But what does that have to do with you?

Is then the power of making use of appearances hindered?

Is your ability to make use of what appears to you hindered?

And who prevents you from using according to nature inclination to a thing and aversion from it; and movement towards a thing and movement from it?

Who's stopping you from naturally being drawn to or away from something; from moving toward or away from it?

What tumult (confusion) is able to do this?

What chaos can stop you from doing this?

Do you only bear in mind the general rules: what is mine? what is not mine? what is given (permitted) to me? what does God will that I should do now? what does he not will?

Just keep in mind the general rules: What's mine? What isn't mine? What's allowed for me? What does God want me to do now? What doesn't He want?

A little before he willed you to be at leisure, to talk with yourself, to write about these things, to read, to hear, to prepare yourself.

Earlier, He wanted you to have leisure, to talk with yourself, to write about these things, to read, to listen, to prepare yourself.

You had sufficient time for this.

You had enough time for this.

Now he says to you: Come now to the contest, show us what you have learned, how you have practiced the athletic art.

Now He says to you: Come to the contest, show us what you've learned, how you've practiced the art of living.

How long will you be exercised alone?

How long will you keep training alone?

Now is the opportunity for you to learn whether you are an athlete worthy of victory, or one of those who go about the world and are defeated.

Now is the chance to find out if you're an athlete worthy of victory, or just someone who wanders around getting defeated.

Why then are you vexed?

So why are you upset?

No contest is without confusion.

No contest is without some chaos.

There must be many who exercise themselves for the contest, many who call out to those who exercise themselves, many masters, many spectators.

There will be many who train for the contest, many who shout at those who train, many coaches, many spectators.

"But my wish is to live quietly."

"But I want to live quietly."

Lament then and groan as you deserve to do.

Then go ahead and complain and groan, as you deserve to.

For what other is a greater punishment than this to the untaught man and to him who disobeys the divine commands: to be grieved, to lament, to envy, in a word to be disappointed and to be unhappy?

What greater punishment is there for an ignorant person or someone who disobeys the divine commands than to be sad, to complain, to envy, in short, to be disappointed and unhappy?

Would you not release yourself from these things?

Don't you want to free yourself from these things?

"And how shall I release myself?"

"How can I free myself?"

Have you not often heard that you ought to remove entirely desire, apply aversion (turning away) to those things only which are within your power, that you ought to give up everything: body, property, fame, books, tumult, power, private station?

Haven't you often heard that you should get rid of all desires, that you should only turn away from things within your control, and that you should give up everything: your body, property, reputation, books, chaos, power, and your social status?

For whatever way you turn, you are a slave, you are subjected, you are hindered, you are compelled, you are entirely in the power of others.

No matter where you turn, you're a slave, you're controlled, you're blocked, you're forced, you're completely at the mercy of others.

But keep the words of Cleanthes in readiness:

But keep these words of Cleanthes ready:

Lead me, O Zeus, and thou necessity. —Iliad vi 490.

"Lead me, O Zeus, and Destiny."

Is it your will that I should go to Rome? I will go to Rome.

Do you want me to go to Rome? I'll go to Rome.

To Gyara? I will go to Gyara.

To Gyara? I'll go to Gyara.

To Athens? I will go to Athens.

To Athens? I'll go to Athens.

To prison? I will go to prison.

To prison? I'll go to prison.

If you should once say, "When shall a man go to Athens?" you are undone.

If you ever say, "When can I go to Athens?" you're already lost.

It is a necessary consequence that this desire, if it is not accomplished, must make you unhappy;

Because if this desire isn't fulfilled, it will make you unhappy;

and if it is accomplished, it must make you vain, since you are elated at things at which you ought not to be elated;

and if it is fulfilled, it will make you vain, because you'll be happy about things you shouldn't be happy about;

and on the other hand, if you are impeded, it must make you wretched because you fall into that which you would not fall into.

and on the other hand, if you're blocked, it will make you miserable because you'll end up in situations you didn't want to be in.

Give up then all these things.

So give up all these things.

"Athens is a good place."

"Athens is a nice place."

But happiness is much better; and to be free from passions, free from disturbance, for your affairs not to depend on any man.

But happiness is much better; and being free from passions, free from disturbances, and not depending on anyone else for your well-being.

"There is tumult at Rome and visits of salutation."

"There's chaos in Rome and people visiting each other."

But happiness is an equivalent for all troublesome things.

But happiness makes up for all the trouble.

If then the time comes for these things, why do you not take away the wish to avoid them?

So when the time comes for these things, why don't you just let go of the desire to avoid them?

What necessity is there to carry a burden like an ass, and to be beaten with a stick?

Why do you need to carry a burden like a donkey and get beaten with a stick?

But if you do not so, consider that you must always be a slave to him who has it in his power to effect your release, and also to impede you, and you must serve him as an evil genius.

But if you don't do this, remember that you'll always be a slave to whoever has the power to either free you or block you, and you'll serve him as if he were a wicked spirit.

There is only one way to happiness, and let this rule be ready both in the morning and during the day and by night: the rule is not to look towards things which are out of the power of our will, to think that nothing is our own, to give up all things to the Divinity, to Fortune;

There's only one path to happiness, and keep this rule in mind morning, noon, and night: don't focus on things outside of your control, don't think that anything belongs to you, and give everything up to God and Fate;

to make them the superintendents of these things, whom Zeus also has made so;

let them manage these things, just as Zeus has made them managers;

for a man to observe that only which is his own, that which cannot be hindered;

focus only on what's yours, what can't be stopped;

and when we read, to refer our reading to this only, and our writing and our listening.

and when we read, let it be for this purpose only, and the same goes for writing and listening.

For this reason I cannot call the man industrious if I hear this only: that he reads and writes;

That's why I can't call someone hardworking just because they read and write;

and even if a man adds that he reads all night, I cannot say so, if he knows not to what he should refer his reading.

and even if they say they read all night, I still can't say they're hardworking if they don't know why they're reading.

For neither do you say that a man is industrious if he keeps awake for a girl; nor do I.

Because you wouldn't call someone hardworking if they stay up all night for a girl, and neither would I.

But if he does it (reads and writes) for reputation, I say that he is a lover of reputation.

But if someone reads and writes for fame, I'd say they're just a lover of fame.

And if he does it for money, I say that he is a lover of money, not a lover of labor;

And if they do it for money, I'd say they're a lover of money, not of hard work;

and if he does it through love of learning, I say that he is a lover of learning.

and if they do it because they love learning, I'd say they're a lover of learning.

But if he refers his labor to his own ruling power, that he may keep it in a state conformable to nature and pass his life in that state, then only do I say that he is industrious.

But if they direct their work towards maintaining their mind in line with nature and living their life in that state, then I'd say they're truly hardworking.

For never commend a man on account of these things which are common to all, but on account of his opinions (principles);

Because you should never praise someone for things everyone does, but for their principles;

for these are the things which belong to each man, which make his actions bad or good.

because these are what belong to each person, and these make their actions good or bad.

Remembering these rules, rejoice in that which is present, and be content with the things which come in season.

By keeping these rules in mind, enjoy what's happening now, and be content with things that come at the right time.

If you see anything which you have learned and inquired about occurring to you in your course of life, be delighted at it.

If you notice something happening in your life that you've learned about, be happy about it.

If you have laid aside or have lessened bad disposition and a habit of reviling; if you have done so with rash temper, obscene words, hastiness, sluggishness;

If you've managed to reduce or get rid of a bad attitude or a habit of complaining, if you've done the same with anger, cursing, impatience, or laziness;

if you are not moved by what you formerly were, and not in the same way as you once were, you can celebrate a festival daily, today because you have behaved well in one act, and tomorrow because you have behaved well in another.

if you're no longer affected by the things that used to bother you, and not in the same way as before, then you can celebrate every day—today because you acted well in one way, and tomorrow because you did well in another.

How much greater is this a reason for making sacrifices than a consulship or the government of a province?

Isn't this a much better reason to be thankful than getting a high office or governing a province?

These things come to you from yourself and from the gods.

These things come from both yourself and the gods.

Remember this: who gives these things and to whom, and for what purpose.

Remember who gives these things, to whom, and why.

If you cherish yourself in these thoughts, do you still think that it makes any difference where you shall be happy, where you shall please God?

If you hold on to these thoughts, do you still think it matters where you'll be happy or where you'll please God?

Are not the gods equally distant from all places?

Aren't the gods just as close to all places?

Do they not see from all places alike that which is going on?

Don't they see everything equally from all places?

Chapter 5
To Those That are Contentious and Brutal

A wise and good person never fights with anyone, and as much as possible, they prevent others from fighting too. We see a great example of this in the life of Socrates. He not only avoided fights himself but also stopped others from quarreling when he could. Look at Xenophon's Symposium to see how many arguments Socrates settled, how he handled people like Thrasymachus, Polus, and Callicles, and how he managed to deal with his wife and son when they were difficult or tried to argue with him.

Socrates understood that no one can control what another person thinks or decides. He only cared about controlling what was in his power. And what was that? It wasn't about making others act a certain way because that's beyond his control. Instead, it was about making sure he lived according to nature, doing what was right, no matter what others did. This is what a wise and good person always aims for. It's not about being the commander of an army or getting married, but if these things happen, the goal is to keep your inner peace and integrity.

If you wish that your son or wife wouldn't make mistakes, you're wishing for something that's out of your control. Learning what you can control and what you can't is the key. So, if you understand this, how can there be any room for quarrels? Are you surprised when bad things happen or when people act badly? Shouldn't you expect bad people to act even worse than they do? If someone insults you, be thankful they didn't hit you. If they hit you, be thankful they didn't wound you. And if they wound you, be thankful they didn't kill you.

Why should someone who hasn't learned that people should love each other act differently? Your neighbor might throw stones, but does that mean you did something wrong? If your belongings are broken, remember that you are not your possessions—you are a free mind. If you're like a wolf, you'll want to bite back and throw more stones. But if you're a person, you should look inside yourself to see what kind of person you are.

Just like a horse is unhappy when it can't run, a person is unhappy when they lose their integrity and honesty. We should pity a person who loses these things, not for losing their belongings or land, because those aren't truly theirs—they belong to others. We should care about the character and principles with which a person was born, just like we care about the stamp on a coin. If the stamp is that of Trajan, we accept it, but if it's Nero's, we reject it as counterfeit. The same goes for people: if a person has qualities like kindness, sociability, and tolerance, we accept them as a fellow citizen and neighbor. But if they are full of anger and resentment, then they are not truly a person.

Should you worry about being despised by those who don't know you? What does their opinion matter? No true craftsman cares about the opinion of someone who doesn't understand their craft. And if people are more hostile to you because of your good nature, why does that bother you? Can they harm your will or prevent you from seeing things as they truly are? No, they can't. So why be disturbed or show fear? Instead, show them that you are at peace with everyone, no matter what they do, and laugh at those who think they can harm you. They don't know who you really are or where your true good and evil lie, because they can't touch what's really yours.

In the same way, people who are safe in a strong city mock those who try to attack it, saying, "Look at all the effort they're wasting! Our walls are strong, and we have enough supplies for a long time." In the same way, nothing can truly harm you if your beliefs are strong. No wall or body is as strong as a person's beliefs, and nothing outside of you can truly harm you if you don't let it.

If you choose to protect the things that truly matter—like your beliefs and principles—then you will remain safe. Remember that it's not the things that happen to you that hurt you, but your opinions about those things. This is the real battle, the real civil war within yourself. What made Eteocles and Polynices enemies was nothing else than their opinions about royal power and exile—thinking one was the worst evil and the other the greatest good.

This understanding is what helped Socrates manage his household and deal with a difficult wife and son. He didn't care when his wife poured water on his head or trampled on a cake sent to him because he knew these things didn't truly matter. He remained in control of his will, knowing that no one could truly harm him unless he allowed it.

These beliefs bring love in a household, harmony in a state, peace between nations, and gratitude to God. They make a person cheerful and confident in all circumstances, knowing that external things are beyond their control and not truly important. We can write and talk about these ideas, but often we don't truly believe in them. We're like the Spartans who are brave at home but cunning and deceitful when they go abroad. We are lions in the classroom, but foxes outside of it.

Chapter 6
To Those Who are Distressed at Being Pitied

Someone might say, "It makes me sad when people pity me." But ask yourself, is it really your problem if someone else pities you, or is it their problem? Can you actually stop them from feeling pity? You might think, "I can show them that I don't need their pity." But are you sure you don't deserve pity, or are you just pretending? You might believe you don't need pity, but people don't pity you for the reasons you think. They pity you because you're poor, don't hold important jobs, or because of sickness and death.

Now, are you ready to convince everyone that none of these things are really bad and that a poor person without a fancy job can still be happy? Or are you going to try to show off that you're rich and powerful? The second option is something a boastful or foolish person would do. Think about what it would take to keep up that appearance. You'd need to hire servants, buy fancy dishes, and display them publicly, even if it's always the same set. You'd need to wear fancy clothes and try to look more handsome and noble than you really are. You'd need to show that you're friends with important people and try to get invited to their homes or at least make people think you dine with them.

If you choose this path just to avoid being pitied, you'll have to do all these things. But the first path, trying to change everyone's mind about what is truly good or bad, is impossible and would take forever. Even Zeus hasn't convinced everyone about what is truly good or bad. Do you think you can do it? The only person you can truly convince is yourself. But if you haven't even convinced yourself, how can you hope to convince others?

How long have you lived with yourself? How much power do you have to convince yourself? Who is closer to you or more interested in your well-being than you are? Yet, you still haven't fully convinced yourself. Are things not upside down right now? Haven't you been trying to learn how to be free from grief, to avoid being disturbed, to avoid feeling low, and to be free?

Haven't you heard that there's only one way to achieve this? You need to give up worrying about things that are not within your control, admit that they belong to others, and not let them trouble you. What others think about you—whether they pity you or not—is not something you can control. So why let it bother you?

Won't you stop worrying about others and focus on being your own student and teacher? Other people will decide for themselves whether they want to live in a way that goes against nature. But for you, no one is closer to you than yourself. Why do you listen to philosophers, agree with them, but still feel no relief? Are you really so foolish? In other areas, you've learned quickly—whether it's reading, wrestling, or solving problems. Has reason not convinced you?

From the beginning, you've chosen what's rational, and you read, listen, and write about these things. You haven't found any stronger reason than living according to nature. So what's missing? Have you not completely gotten rid of your wrong opinions? Have you not practiced applying the right opinions to real-life actions, but instead let them rust like unused armor?

You don't just settle for learning in exercises or in reading and writing. You analyze logical arguments and even create your own. But when it comes to the teachings that can actually free you from grief, fear, and passion, you don't practice them. You care more about what others think of you and whether they see you as someone worth noticing or someone who is happy.

Wretched man, look at what you're saying about yourself. What do you think you are, in your opinions, desires, and actions? Do you care more about what others think of you than about how you see yourself? Are you pained because people don't pity you in the way you think they should? If you're pained by pity, don't you make yourself deserving of it? If you care about being pitied, how are you not an object of pity?

Remember what Antisthenes said: "It's a royal thing, O Cyrus, to do right and be spoken of poorly." —Iliad vi 490. If your head is healthy, but people think you have a headache, what does it matter? If you're free from fever, but people pity you as if you had one, does it affect you? You could even say with a sad face, "Yes, I've been ill for a long time," while secretly laughing at their pity.

Why can't you do the same when people pity you for being poor? If you have the right opinion about poverty, why should their pity bother you? If you're not in power but have the right opinion about power, why care if others pity you? Let them look after themselves. You're not hungry or cold, but because they might be, they think you are too. Should you go around announcing, "Don't be mistaken, I'm fine. I don't worry about poverty or power, I only care about having the right opinions. That's what I care about."

What foolish talk this is. How can you claim to have the right opinions when you're not content with what you are, but are bothered by how others see you?

You might say, "But others will get more and be preferred to me." Isn't it reasonable for those who work hard to get more in the areas they've worked on? They've worked for power, and you've worked on your opinions. They've worked for wealth, and you've worked on using the right perspectives. See if they are better at what you've worked on. Are they less disappointed in their desires? Do they avoid things better than you do? Are they better at aiming their actions, at behaving properly as men, sons, parents, or in other roles?

If they have power and you don't, remind yourself that you didn't work for power, while they did. It's unreasonable to think that you should have more of what you haven't worked for.

"But since I care about right opinions, it's more reasonable for me to have power," you might say. Yes, in the area of opinions, you should have more. But in the area where they've worked harder, they should have more. It's like thinking that because you have the right opinions, you should be better at archery than an archer, or better at metalwork than a smith. If you want power, focus on it, and then lament if you don't get it.

Right now, you're saying you focus on one thing, but you actually want another. You can't mix these different pursuits. Each day, some people wake up thinking about who to flatter, who to please, and how to gain favor. They might lie or deceive to achieve their goals. But if you've focused on using the right opinions, then each morning, ask yourself, "What do I need to do today to be free from passion and disturbance? What am I? A body? A piece of property? No, I'm a rational being."

Reflect on your actions. Have you done anything unfriendly or unsocial? Have you done everything you should have done? There's a big difference in what people desire, what they do, and what they wish for. Yet you still expect to share equally in things you haven't worked for while they have. And you're surprised when they pity you? But they don't mind if you pity them because they believe they have what's good, and you don't. That's why you're not satisfied with what you have and want what they have.

If you were truly convinced that you possess what is truly good, you wouldn't care what others say about you.

Chapter 7
On Freedom From Fear

What makes a tyrant so scary? You might say it's the guards, their swords, the people who stay close to him, and those who keep others out. But why isn't a child scared if you bring them to the tyrant, even when he's surrounded by his guards? Is it because the child doesn't understand what's happening? So, if someone does understand what guards are and that they carry swords, but goes to the tyrant because they want to die and think it will be easier if someone else kills them, are they still afraid of the guards? No, because they actually want what the guards can do.

Now, if someone doesn't want to die or live at all costs, but only lives as long as they're allowed, what stops them from approaching the tyrant without fear? Nothing. If someone feels the same way about their possessions as that person felt about their body, or feels the same way about their children and spouse, and if they are so upset or hopeless that they don't care whether they own these things or not, like kids who play with toys and fight over the game but don't care about the toys themselves, then this person doesn't care about the stuff (possessions) but only about enjoying and using them. So, what tyrant or guards or swords can scare this person?

If someone can become so indifferent to these things because of madness or the Galilaeans can become like this out of habit, is it possible that no one can learn from reason and understanding that God made everything in the universe perfect and free from obstacles, and that every part of it works for the good of the whole? While other animals can't understand how the world works, human beings, who are rational, have the ability to think about these things and understand their place in the universe, and that it's right for the parts to serve the whole. And besides being naturally noble, big-hearted, and free, humans see that some things around them are within their control and free from obstacles, while other things are beyond their control and can be blocked by others. The things that are free from obstacles are within our will, while those that can be blocked are beyond our control.

For this reason, if someone believes that their happiness and well-being come from things that are free from obstacles and under their control, they will be free, successful, happy, safe, big-hearted, pious, and grateful to God for everything. They won't complain about or blame the things that are beyond their control. But if someone thinks their happiness and well-being depend on external things that are beyond their control, they will inevitably be blocked, hindered, and become a slave to those who control the things they desire and fear. Such a person must inevitably become irreligious because they think God is harming them, unjust because they always demand more than what's fair, and cowardly and weak.

What stops a person who understands these things clearly from living with a light heart, easily handling life, quietly waiting for whatever happens, and calmly dealing with what has already happened? Would you ask me to endure poverty? Come and see what poverty is like when it finds someone who knows how to handle it well. Do you want me to have power? Give me power, and I'll take the trouble that comes with it too. How about exile? Wherever I go, I'll be fine because it wasn't the place that made me happy, but my beliefs, which I'll take with me wherever I go. No one can take them from me; they're mine alone, and as long as I have them, I'm content, no matter where I am or what I'm doing. But now, it's time to die. Why do you say "to die" like it's a tragic event? Just say what it really is: it's time for the body to break down into the things it was made from. And what's so scary about that? What's going to disappear from the universe? What new or amazing thing is going to happen? Is this why a tyrant is scary? Is this why guards with big, sharp swords seem intimidating? Tell this to others, but I've thought about all these things. No one has power over me. I've been set free; I know what's right, and no one can make me a slave. I know who I am, and I know who my real judges are. You think you control my body? What does that matter to me? You think you control my property? What does that matter to me? You think you control my exile or my chains? Well, I'll leave all of that and even my poor body when you say so. Test your power, and you'll see how far it goes.

So, who am I supposed to fear now? Those who guard the tyrant's bedchamber? Are they supposed to do something to me? Lock me out? If they find out I want to get in, then let them lock me out. Why do I go to the door then? Because I think it's my role, while the play lasts, to take part in it. So how do I avoid getting locked out? Because unless someone lets me in, I choose not to go in. I'm always content with what happens because I believe that what God chooses is better than what I choose. I'll follow Him as a servant and a follower. I have the same goals as He does, the same desires. In other words, I want what He wants. There's no way to lock me out, but there is for those who try to force their way in. Why don't I try to force my way in? Because I know nothing good is being handed out inside to those who get in. But when I hear someone called lucky because Caesar honors them, I ask, what exactly did they get? A province to govern? Did they also get the right opinion on how to govern? The office of a Prefect? Did they also get the ability to do the job well? Why do I still try to get inside Caesar's chamber? A man throws out dried figs and nuts, and the children grab them and fight each other for them. Adults don't, because they think it's a small thing. But if a man threw out shells, even the children wouldn't grab them. Provinces are given out: let the children worry about that. Money is given out: let the children worry about that. Praetorships and consulships are given out: let the children scramble for them, let them be shut out, beaten, and kiss the hands of the giver, of the slaves. But to me, these are just dried figs and nuts. So what? If you don't get them while Caesar is tossing them around, don't be upset. If a dried fig falls into your lap, take it and eat it; that's how much value it has. But if I have to bend down and turn one over, or get turned over by someone else, and flatter those who got inside Caesar's chamber, then a dried fig isn't worth the trouble, nor is anything else that's not really good, which the philosophers have taught me not to value.

Show me the guards' swords. Look how big they are and how sharp. So what do these big and sharp swords do? They kill. And what does a fever do? The same thing. And what does a falling tile do? The same thing. Should I be amazed at these things, worship them, and walk around as a slave to all of them? I hope not. But when I've learned that everything that comes into existence must also disappear, so the universe doesn't stop or get stuck, I no longer care whether a fever, a tile, or a soldier ends my life. But if I have to choose between them, I know the soldier will do it with less trouble and faster. So, when I neither fear what a tyrant can do to me nor want anything he can give, why am I still amazed? Why am I still confused? Why do I fear the guards? Why am I happy if he talks to me nicely and receives me? Why do I tell others how he talked to me? Is he a Socrates? Is he a Diogenes that his praise should prove my worth? Have I been eager to copy his morals? But I keep playing along and go to him, and serve him as long as he doesn't ask me to do something foolish or unreasonable. But if he says to me, "Go and bring Leon of Salamis," I say to him, "Find someone else because I'm not playing anymore." (The tyrant says): "Take him to prison." I go; that's part of the game. "But your head will be cut off!" Does the tyrant's head always stay in place, and the heads of those who obey him? "But you will be thrown out unburied." If the corpse is me, I'll be thrown out; but if I'm different from the corpse, then speak more accurately according to the truth, and don't try to scare me. These things are scary to children and fools. But if someone has entered a philosopher's school and still doesn't know what they are, they deserve to be full of fear and to flatter those they used to flatter. If they haven't learned yet that they're not just flesh, bones, or muscles, but the mind that uses these body parts and controls them and understands the world, then they deserve to be afraid.

"Yes, but this kind of talk makes us despise the laws." And what kind of talk makes people more obedient to the laws? Things that are under the control of a fool aren't laws. And yet, see how this kind of talk makes us act the way we should, even towards these foolish people; because it teaches us not to seek the things they can surpass us in. This talk teaches us to give up our bodies, our property, our children, parents, and siblings, and to let go of everything except our opinions, which even Zeus has willed to be each person's private property. Where is the disobedience to the law here? Where is the foolishness?

Where you are stronger, I let you win; but where I am stronger, you should let me win, because I've studied this, and you haven't. It's your study to live in houses with fancy floors, to have servants at your beck and call, to wear fine clothes, to have many hunters, musicians, and actors. Do I want any of these things? Have you studied opinions and your own rational mind? Do you know what it's made of, how it's put together, how it works, and what powers it has? Then why are you upset if someone who has studied these things better than you has the advantage? But these things are the most important. And who stops you from working on these things and taking care of them? Who has a better supply of books, more free time, and more people to help you? Just turn your attention to these things at last, even if only for a little while, to your own mind. Think about what it is that you have, where it came from, this thing that uses all your other abilities, tests them, chooses, and rejects. But as long as you focus on external things, you'll have those things better than anyone else, but you'll have your mind just as you choose to have it: neglected and filthy.

Chapter 8
To Those Who Hastily Assume the Character of Philosophers

Never praise or blame someone just because they do something that most people do. Don't assume they are skilled or unskilled because of it. By doing this, you will avoid being too quick to judge or being unfair. For example, if someone bathes very quickly, is that wrong? No, it's not. But what does it mean? It just means they bathe quickly. Does it mean everything they do is done well? Not at all. Only actions that come from good thinking are done well; those that come from bad thinking are done poorly. So, until you understand why a person does something, don't praise or blame them for it. But it's hard to know a person's thoughts just by looking at their actions.

If you see someone using a hammer, do you automatically assume they're a carpenter? No. What about someone who sings—do you assume they're a musician? Not necessarily. Now, if you see someone wearing a philosopher's cloak and growing a beard, do you assume they're a philosopher? Just because they dress like one doesn't mean they are one. So, if you see someone who looks like a philosopher acting foolishly, don't say, "Look at what that philosopher is doing!" Instead, you should say, "This person isn't really a philosopher." If we did this in other professions, we would never say, "Carpenters are bad at their job," just because we saw one person using a hammer poorly. We'd say, "This person isn't a good carpenter."

But when it comes to philosophy, people do the opposite. If they see someone acting against what a philosopher teaches, they don't take away the title of philosopher. Instead, they assume that person is a philosopher and conclude that philosophy itself must be useless.

Why does this happen? Because we value the skills of a carpenter or musician and judge them based on their actions, but we don't value philosophy the same way. We judge philosophers only by their appearance, which leads to confusion. Other professions don't take their name from what they wear but from their skills and the tools they use. What is the tool of a philosopher? Is it a cloak? No, it's reason. What is the goal of a philosopher? Is it to wear a cloak? No, it's to have correct thinking.

Before you judge a philosopher for acting wrongly, first see if they are doing what they profess. But now, when you see someone acting inappropriately, you say, "Look at the philosopher," as if the name "philosopher" belongs to someone who behaves badly. But you wouldn't say, "Look at the carpenter," if you knew a carpenter was cheating or overeating. You understand, to some degree, what a philosopher should be, but you get confused and don't pay attention.

Even those who call themselves philosophers often start by focusing on things that don't really matter. As soon as they put on the cloak and grow a beard, they say, "I am a philosopher." But no one says, "I am a musician," just because they've bought a guitar, and no one says, "I am a blacksmith," just because they've put on an apron. The tools are made for the art, and the name comes from the art, not the tools.

Euphrates said it well: "I tried for a long time to be a philosopher without anyone knowing it. And this helped me because when I did something good, I knew I did it for myself, not for an audience. I ate well, composed myself well, walked properly—all for myself and God. If I did something wrong, I didn't endanger philosophy or hurt others by my actions. For this reason, people who didn't know me were surprised that I spent so much time with philosophers but wasn't one myself. What harm was there in being known as a philosopher by my actions and not by outward signs?"

See how I eat, drink, sleep, and deal with challenges. See how I control my desires, how I avoid things I shouldn't want, how I handle my relationships, both natural and acquired. See how I live free from confusion and obstacles. Judge me by these things if you can. But if you're so blind that you can't recognize a good blacksmith unless you see him with a hammer, then what does it matter if I'm not recognized by such a foolish judge?

Socrates wasn't known as a philosopher by most people. They would come to him and ask to be introduced to philosophers. Was Socrates upset about this? Did he say, "Don't you know that I'm a philosopher?" No, he would take them to meet other philosophers, satisfied with simply being a philosopher himself. He didn't need to be seen as one. He didn't care if people didn't think he was a philosopher because he focused on what really mattered to him.

What is the job of a good and honorable person? Is it to have many students? Not at all. Those who care about that can focus on it. Was Socrates' job to study difficult ideas? Others can handle that. So, what was Socrates focused on? He was focused on what could harm or benefit him. If anyone could harm him, he wasn't doing anything. If he was waiting for someone else to help him, he was nothing. If he wanted something and didn't get it, he was unlucky. He challenged anyone to this contest, and I don't think he would have refused a challenge from anyone.

What do you think? Did Socrates go around saying, "I'm a great man"? Not at all. That would be the act of a fool, saying, "I'm free from worry and disturbance. My friends, while you're all anxious and upset about trivial things, I'm the only one free from all troubles." Is it not enough for you to be free from pain unless you announce it to everyone? Do you need to gather those suffering from headaches, fevers, and other ailments and say, "Look at me! I'm free from all pain"? This is empty boasting unless you can immediately show them how to be free from pain too and offer your own health as an example.

That's the true Cynic, honored by Zeus with the scepter and crown, who says, "Look, people, you're searching for happiness and peace in the wrong places. I'm sent by God to show you by example. I have no property, house, wife, children, bed, coat, or tools, and yet I'm healthy and happy. Test me, and if you see that I'm free from trouble, I'll tell you how I've been cured." This is noble and kind. But it's the job of Zeus or someone he chooses to serve this purpose, to always act in a way that supports the truth of virtue and doesn't undermine it.

But now, some people are drawn to philosophy as someone with a bad stomach might be drawn to food they can't digest. They rush towards the symbols of philosophy, like the cloak and beard, and argue with anyone who crosses their path. If they see someone in a warm coat, they'll pick a fight with them. Man, first, learn to handle the cold. Make sure your desires are not like those of a sick person or a pregnant woman. First, try to keep your philosophy to yourself for a while. Just as fruit needs time to grow and ripen, you need time to develop before you're ready to show yourself. If a plant sprouts too soon, it will wither and die in the cold. You, too, are like a plant that has grown too quickly. The cold will kill you because you've rushed into fame too soon. You think you're something special, but you're just a fool among fools. You've been harmed by the cold, even if you think you're still thriving.

Let us grow naturally. Why do you expose us before we're ready? Why do you force us? We're not yet strong enough to face the world. Let the roots grow, then the first joint, then the second, and then the third. Only then will the fruit naturally appear, even if I don't choose for it to happen. Who, having developed such great principles, doesn't recognize their own power and move towards the right actions? A bull doesn't need anyone to tell him to fight when he sees a predator. A dog doesn't need to be told to chase a wild animal. If I have the qualities of a good person, why should I wait for someone else to push me to act? Right now, I don't have those qualities, believe me. So why do you want me to wither before my time, as you have?

Chapter 9
To Someone Who Has Lost Their Sense of Shame

When you see someone else with power, remember that you don't have the desire for power. When you see someone who is rich, think about what you have instead of money. If you have nothing in place of riches, you might feel unhappy. But if you don't want riches, understand that you have something more valuable than wealth. If someone else has a beautiful wife, remember that you're lucky not to crave a beautiful wife. Do these things seem small to you? Think about how much those who are rich, powerful, or with beautiful spouses would give to be able to not care about wealth, power, or even those they love.

Do you understand how a thirsty person with a fever feels? It's nothing like how a healthy person feels thirst. A healthy person stops being thirsty after drinking, but a sick person feels nauseated after drinking, may vomit, and ends up even thirstier. Wanting and having wealth, power, or a beautiful spouse can be like that—leading to jealousy, fear, indecent thoughts, and bad behavior.

You might ask, "What have I lost?" My friend, you used to be modest, and now you're not. Haven't you lost something? Instead of reading wise philosophers like Chrysippus and Zeno, you're now interested in stories of people who seduce women. Haven't you lost something? Instead of admiring Socrates and Diogenes, you admire someone who can attract and corrupt the most women. You want to appear handsome and make efforts to look good, even though you aren't. You like to show off fancy clothes to attract women, and you think finding some fancy hair oil makes you happy. But before, you didn't care about any of this. You were more interested in good conversation, noble people, and high-minded ideas. You used to sleep, walk, and dress like a good man. Now, can you really say you've lost nothing?

Do people only lose money? Isn't losing modesty a loss? Isn't losing decent behavior a loss? If someone has lost these things, haven't they suffered a loss? Maybe you don't think these things matter. But there was a time when you believed losing these was the only real loss, and you were determined not to be disturbed from living a good life.

Now, nobody is disturbing you from living well except yourself. Fight with yourself, bring yourself back to decency, modesty, and freedom. If someone had told you that I was forced to become an adulterer, dress like you do, or use perfumed oils, wouldn't you have been outraged and wanted to defend me? Now, will you not defend yourself? And how much easier is it to help yourself? There's no need to hurt anyone, chain anyone up, insult anyone, or go to court. All you need to do is talk to yourself, the person who's easiest to persuade. Nobody has more power over you than you do.

First, condemn what you're doing. Then, after you've condemned it, don't give up on yourself. Don't be like weak-spirited people who, after giving in once, completely give up and let themselves be swept away like they're caught in a flood. Look at what trainers do with boys. If a boy falls, they say, "Get up and try again until you're strong." Do the same with yourself. Be assured that nothing is more adaptable than the human soul. You just need to exercise your will, and it can be corrected. On the other hand, if you're careless, you'll ruin everything. Ruin and help both come from within.

You might ask, "What do I gain?" What greater gain is there than this? You'll go from being shameless to modest, from being disorderly to orderly, from being untrustworthy to faithful, from being reckless to self-controlled. If you seek anything more than this, keep doing what you're doing—but not even a god can help you now.

Chapter 10
What We Should Disregard and What We Should Value

People's difficulties mostly come from things outside their control. They feel helpless about these external things. They ask questions like, "What should I do?" or "How will this turn out?" or "Will this happen?" or "Will that happen?" These are the kinds of questions people ask when they focus on things they can't control.

But who ever asks, "How can I make sure I don't believe something that's false?" or "How can I keep myself from turning away from what's true?" If someone is good enough to worry about these kinds of things, I would tell him, "Why are you worried? These things are within your control. Be confident; don't rush into agreeing with something before you've thought it through properly."

On the other hand, if someone is anxious about wanting something but afraid he won't get it, or if he fears ending up with something he's trying to avoid, I would first give him a big hug because he's thinking about his own life and actions instead of worrying about things outside of himself that others usually fuss over. Then I would say to him, "If you don't want to end up wanting something you can't have or trying to avoid something but failing, then don't desire things that belong to others or try to avoid things that aren't under your control. If you don't follow this rule, you're going to end up frustrated by not getting what you want and stuck with what you don't."

What's so hard about this? Where is there any reason to ask, "How will this turn out?" or "What will happen next?"

Isn't what happens outside your control? Yes, it is. And isn't the nature of good and bad based on things that are within your control? Yes, it is. So, can anyone stop you from handling things the right way, according to nature? No, they can't. So, stop asking, "How will it be?" No matter how it turns out, you'll handle it well, and the outcome will be good for you.

Imagine if Hercules said, "How can I make sure I don't run into a big lion?" or "How can I avoid meeting a wild boar?" or "How can I keep from running into bad people?" Why would he care about that? If a big boar shows up, he'll have a bigger challenge to overcome. If bad people show up, he'll get rid of them and make the world a better place.

You might say, "But what if I die in the process?" Then you'll die doing something noble. Since everyone has to die someday, isn't it better to be found doing something worthwhile, like helping others or being kind?

But if I can't be found doing great things, at least let me be found doing something within my control, like improving myself, practicing using my thoughts wisely, working on staying calm, and treating people the right way. If I succeed in these areas, then I'll move on to the next goal: making sure my judgments about things are correct.

If death finds me while I'm busy doing these things, that's enough for me. I can stretch out my hands to God and say, "I've used the tools you gave me to understand your plan and follow it. I haven't disrespected you with my actions. See how I've used my thoughts and beliefs? Have I ever blamed you? Have I ever been unhappy with what happens, or wished things were different? Have I ever tried to go against the natural order of things? I'm thankful that you gave me life, and I'm grateful for everything you've given me. I'm content with the time I've had, and now I return everything to you."

Isn't this a good way to live? And isn't it a good way to die?

But to be able to say these things, you have to let go of some other things. You can't want to be a powerful leader and also be able to live this way. If you want things that belong to others, you lose what's truly yours. That's just how things work—nothing is free.

And where's the surprise in that? If you want to be a leader, you'll have to stay awake at night, run around pleasing people, flatter everyone, exhaust yourself by standing at the doors of important people, say and do things that don't suit a free person, and give gifts to many people. And what do you get in return? You get a position where you can give orders a few times, host some games, and throw fancy dinners. Or if you disagree, show me what else there is besides these things.

On the other hand, if you want peace of mind, freedom from worry, a good night's sleep, to be truly awake when you're awake, and to fear nothing, then you'll need to give something up and put in some effort. But if you lose something while focusing on these things, or if something you value is wasted or someone else gets what you thought you deserved, will you immediately get upset? Or will you consider what you've gained in return and realize how much you've received in exchange?

Do you expect to get something so valuable for nothing? And how could you? You can't focus on both external things and your inner self. If you want external things, you'll have to give up working on your inner self. If you don't, you'll lose both because you're trying to do two things at once.

You might spill oil or break household items. So what? But you'll remain calm. A fire might destroy your books, but you'll still treat situations the right way. "But I'll have nothing to eat," you might say. If you're that unfortunate, then death is like a safe harbor where you can find refuge. Death is a safe harbor for everyone, which is why life isn't so hard. Whenever you choose, you can leave, and you won't have to endure any more suffering.

So why worry? Why lose sleep over things? After thinking about what's truly good and bad, you should say, "These are within my power, and no one can take them from me or force bad things on me against my will."

Then you can rest easy, knowing that what truly matters is safe. As for the things that belong to others, let those who get them worry about them. I can only control what's mine, and I'll do my best with that. Everything else is up to the one who controls everything.

When a person understands this, they don't toss and turn at night worrying about what might happen. They don't regret losing a friend like Patroclus or Antilochus or Menelaus, because they knew from the beginning that no friend is immortal. They didn't fool themselves into thinking their friend would outlive them and take care of their children. If you did think that, you were foolish. Why blame yourself or cry like a child?

You might say, "But my friend used to serve my meals." Well, he did that because he was alive. But now he's gone, so someone else will serve you. If that person dies, you'll find another.

If the pot you cook your meals in breaks, does that mean you'll starve because you lost your favorite pot? No, you'll go out and buy a new one.

And if you say, "No greater ill than this could happen to me," like it says in the Iliad, remember that it's not the loss that hurts you. You just need to stop blaming your situation and realize that these things happen to everyone.

Do you think Homer wrote these stories to show us that even the strongest, richest, and most handsome people, when they don't have the right mindset, can still be miserable?

Chapter 11
On Cleanliness

Some people wonder whether caring for others is part of human nature. But I think those same people would have no doubt that a love for cleanliness is definitely part of human nature. If humans are different from animals in any way, it's this. When we see an animal cleaning itself, we often say with surprise, "That animal is acting like a human!" On the other hand, if a person criticizes an animal for being dirty, we immediately excuse the animal by saying, "Well, it's not a human." So we believe there's something special in humans, something we first received from the Gods. Because the Gods are naturally pure and free from corruption, the more humans use their reason, the more they are drawn to cleanliness and purity. But since it's impossible for human nature to be completely pure, because we are made up of different materials, reason is used to make us love cleanliness as much as possible.

The first and highest form of cleanliness is in the soul, and the same goes for impurity. You can't see the impurity of the soul the way you can see dirt on the body. But when it comes to the soul, what could make it dirty except for its own bad judgments? The actions of the soul include moving toward or away from something, feeling desire or aversion, preparing, planning, and agreeing to something. So, what makes these actions dirty and impure? Nothing else but the soul's bad judgments. Therefore, the impurity of the soul is its bad opinions, and to purify the soul, we must plant good opinions in it. A soul is pure when it has good opinions because only then is it free from disturbance and pollution in its actions.

We should try to do the same with our bodies, as much as we can. It's natural for mucus to flow from the nose, given how the human body is made. That's why nature provided us with hands and nostrils to remove it. If someone doesn't wipe away the mucus, they aren't behaving like a human. It's also natural for our feet to get muddy and dirty when we walk through dirty places. That's why nature provided us with water and hands. It's impossible to eat without leaving some food stuck in the teeth, so nature tells us to clean our teeth. Why? So that you behave like a human and not like a wild animal or a pig. It's also natural for sweat and tight clothing to leave dirt on the body that needs to be cleaned off. That's why we have water, oil, hands, towels, scrapers, and other tools to clean our bodies. But if you don't act this way, think about it: even a blacksmith will remove rust from his tools, and you would clean a plate before eating if you weren't completely impure and dirty. So, why wouldn't you wash your body and keep it clean? Why not? I'll tell you: first, to act like a human being; and second, so that you won't be unpleasant to those around you. You do something similar in this matter, and you don't even realize it: you think you deserve to stink. Fine, go ahead and stink. But do you think those who sit beside you, those who eat with you, or those who kiss you deserve the same? Either go live in a desert, where you belong, or live by yourself and smell yourself. It's only fair that you alone should have to deal with your own filth. But when you're in a city, behaving so thoughtlessly and foolishly, what kind of person do you think you're being? If nature had given you a horse, would you neglect it? Now think that you've been entrusted with your own body as if it were a horse. Wash it, wipe it down, and take care that no one turns away from you or avoids you. But who wouldn't avoid a dirty, smelly person whose skin is filthy more than they would avoid someone covered in muck? That smell is from outside; it's put on him. But the other smell is from neglect, coming from within, almost as if the body is rotting.

"But Socrates rarely washed." Yes, but his body was clean and beautiful, so much so that the most handsome and noble people loved him and preferred to be near him rather than those with the best physical appearance. He could choose not to bathe or wash himself if he wanted, yet even using water rarely had an effect. "—The Clouds," line 102. But Aristophanes says: "Those who are pale, unshod, 'tis those I mean." For Aristophanes claimed that Socrates walked on air and stole clothes from the gym. However, all who have written about

Socrates provide the exact opposite testimony: they say he was not only pleasant to listen to but also pleasant to look at. The same was written about Diogenes. For we shouldn't let the appearance of the body discourage people from philosophy. Just as a philosopher should show that he is cheerful and calm, he should also show that in matters related to the body: "See, people, that I have nothing, that I want nothing. See how I live without a home, without a city, and if it happens that I am an exile and without a hearth, I live more freely and happily than all those of noble birth and the rich. But look at my poor body too and observe that it isn't harmed by my tough way of living." But if someone like this says to me, with the appearance and face of a condemned person, "What God would persuade me to take up philosophy if it makes people like this?" Far from it; I wouldn't choose to do so, even if I were to become wise. I would rather a young person just starting out in philosophy come to me with their hair neatly trimmed than dirty and scruffy because this shows a certain sense of beauty and a desire for what is proper. Where they think beauty lies, they strive to find it. All they need is to be shown where true beauty is and told: "Young person, you seek beauty, and that's good. You must know that it grows in the part of you where your rational mind is. Look for it where your desires and aversions are because that's where your higher nature resides. The body is just earth, so why waste time on it? If you learn nothing else, time will teach you that the body is nothing." But if someone comes to me covered in filth, dirty, with a mustache down to their knees, what can I say to them? What can I use to change their mind? What resemblance can I use to guide them? Can I tell them that beauty isn't about being covered in muck but lies in the rational mind? Does this person even care about beauty? Does he have any idea of it in his mind? Go and talk to a pig, and tell it not to roll in the mud.

For this reason, Xenocrates' words also affected Polemon, since he was a lover of beauty. Polemon had some inclination towards beauty, but he was looking for it in the wrong place. Even animals that live with humans aren't dirty. Does a horse ever roll in the mud? Does a well-bred dog? No, but pigs, dirty geese, worms, and spiders do, creatures that are banished farthest from human society. Do you, as a human, want to be like a worm or a spider? Will you never wash yourself, even just a little? Will you not clean off the dirt from your body? Will you not be clean so that those who are with you will enjoy your company? But do you enter temples with us in this state, where it's not even allowed to spit or blow your nose, while you are a heap of spit and snot?

Does anyone demand that you decorate yourself? Far from it; the only decoration needed is the natural one—your rational mind, your opinions, your actions. As for your body, it only needs to be clean enough not to offend others. But if someone tells you that you shouldn't wear clothes dyed with purple, would you then smear dirt on your cloak or tear it? "But how can I keep a clean cloak?" you ask. Man, you have water—wash it. Here is a youth worthy of love, here is an old man worthy of loving and being loved in return, someone trustworthy enough to teach your children. Would you want this teacher to give lessons while sitting on a dung heap? Let this not be so: every mistake comes from something in human nature; but this (neglect of cleanliness) is close to being something against human nature.

Chapter 12
On Attention

When you have let your attention slip for a short time, do not think that you can regain it whenever you choose. Instead, keep in mind that because of the mistake you made today, your situation will be worse for everything that follows. First, and what is most troubling, is that you develop a habit of not paying attention; then you form a habit of postponing your attention. By continually postponing it, you keep pushing away the happiness of life, proper behavior, and living according to nature. If delaying attention is useful, then completely abandoning attention would be even more useful; but if it's not useful, then why don't you keep your attention steady?

"Today I choose to play." Well then, shouldn't you play with attention? "I choose to sing." What stops you from singing with attention? Is there any part of life where attention isn't needed? Will you do anything in life worse by paying attention to it, or better by not paying attention at all? What in life is done better by those who do not use attention? Does a carpenter work better by not paying attention to what he's doing? Does a ship's captain manage his ship better by ignoring it? Is any smaller task done better by inattention? Don't you see that once you've let your mind go, it's no longer within your power to bring it back to proper behavior, modesty, or moderation? You end up doing whatever comes into your mind, following your impulses.

So, to what things should I pay attention? First, focus on the general principles and always have them ready. Without these principles, do not sleep, do not get up, do not drink, do not eat, and do not interact with others. Remember that no one has control over another person's will; only your own will contains good and bad. No one else has the power to bring me good or to cause me harm—only I have control over myself in these matters. Once these things are secured, why should I be worried about external things? What tyrant should I fear, what disease, what poverty, or what offense from another person?

Well, I did not please a certain person. Is it my job to please them, to be judged by them? No. So why should I worry about them? But this person is considered important. Let them concern themselves with that, as will those who think so. But I have someone I should please, someone I should obey—God, and those who are closest to Him. He has placed me in charge of myself and has given me control over my own will, along with rules for how to use it correctly. When I follow these rules in reasoning, I don't care about what anyone else says. In tricky arguments, I do not care about anyone else's opinion. So why, in more important matters, do I get annoyed by those who criticize me? What causes this disturbance? Nothing but the fact that I haven't been disciplined in this area. All knowledge looks down on ignorance and the ignorant. This applies not only to sciences but even to the arts. Bring forth any shoemaker you like, and he will mock those who don't know his craft. The same goes for any carpenter.

First, we should have these rules ready and never act without them. We should keep our minds focused on this goal: not to pursue anything external or anything that belongs to others or is under their control, but to act according to the rules of the one who has the power. We should pursue only what is within the power of our will, and everything else as allowed. Next, we should remember who we are and what our name is, and strive to direct our actions according to the roles we play in life. For example, when is it the right time to sing, when is it the right time to play, and in whose presence? What will be the outcome of our actions? Will our companions lose respect for us? Will we lose respect for them? When should we joke, and whom should we tease? On what occasion should we agree with others, and with whom? And finally, how can we maintain our own character while agreeing with others? But whenever you stray from these rules, there is immediate damage— not from anything external, but from the action itself.

So, is it possible to be completely free of faults if you do all this? It is not possible, but it is possible to aim constantly at being free of faults. We should be satisfied if, by never neglecting our attention, we can at least avoid some mistakes. But when you say, "Tomorrow I will start paying attention," you must realize that you are really saying, "Today I will be shameless, careless about time and place, and mean-spirited. Today, others will have the power to hurt me. Today, I will be angry and jealous." Look at all the bad things you allow yourself to do. If it is good to pay attention tomorrow, how much better is it to do so today? If it is in your interest to pay attention tomorrow, it is even more important to do so today, so that you'll be able to do it tomorrow as well, and not put it off again until the day after tomorrow.

Chapter 13
To Those Who Easily Share Their Secrets

When someone seems to talk openly and honestly about their own affairs, why do we often feel compelled to share our own secrets with them? It might seem unfair to listen to someone else's affairs without sharing our own in return. We might also think that if we don't share our own stories, we won't seem honest or open. People often say, "I've told you all about myself; why won't you tell me something about yourself? Is that fair?" We also tend to believe that we can safely trust someone who has already shared their secrets with us. We think that this person wouldn't reveal our secrets because they wouldn't want us to reveal theirs. This is how careless people often get trapped by soldiers in Rome. A soldier might sit next to you in plain clothes and start speaking badly about Caesar. Then, thinking that the soldier is trustworthy because he started the criticism, you share your own thoughts. After that, you get arrested and taken away in chains.

Something similar happens to us in other situations. If someone confidently shares their affairs with me, does that mean I should share mine with anyone I meet? No, because if I'm the kind of person who knows how to keep quiet, I won't tell anyone else what I've heard. But the other person might go out and tell everyone what I shared. If I find out about this, and if I'm the same type of person, I might want to get revenge by revealing what they told me, causing trouble for both of us. But if I remember that no one can truly harm another, and that everyone's actions affect themselves, then I won't act like them. Even so, I still suffer because of my own foolishness in talking too much.

"True, but it's unfair if you've heard someone's secrets and don't share your own in return." Did I ask you for your secrets? Did you share your affairs with me on the condition that I must share mine too? If you're a chatterbox who thinks everyone is your friend, should I be like that too? Why should I be reckless just because you were? It's like if I had a barrel that was watertight, and you had one with a hole in it. You come to me and ask to store your wine in my barrel, but then you complain that I didn't store my wine in yours. How is that fair? You trusted your affairs to someone who is trustworthy and discreet, someone who understands that only their own actions can harm or benefit them, and that external things don't matter. Should I then trust my affairs to you, someone who has no control over their own will and might even betray me for a bit of money or some small favor, like Medea who would kill her own children? How is that fair? But if you show me that you are trustworthy, discreet, and steady, and that you have good principles, then I won't wait for you to ask—I will come to you myself and ask you to hear my affairs. After all, who wouldn't want to use a good barrel? Who wouldn't value a kind and trustworthy advisor? Who wouldn't be happy to have someone who is willing to share the burden of their troubles and help lighten the load?

"True, but I trust you; you don't trust me." First of all, you don't really trust me; you're just a chatterbox who can't keep anything to yourself. If you truly trusted me, you would only tell me your affairs. But instead, whenever you see someone who seems available, you sit down and say, "Brother, I have no better or dearer friend than you; please listen to my affairs." And you do this even with people you barely know. But if you really trusted me, it would be clear that you trust me because I'm trustworthy and discreet, not because I've shared my affairs with you. Let me have the same opinion about you. Show me that sharing your affairs makes you trustworthy and discreet. If that were true, I'd go around telling my affairs to everyone if that would make me trustworthy and discreet. But that's not how it works, and this situation requires a special set of principles. If you see someone who is focused on things outside their control and lets those things dictate their will, you must understand that this person is easily influenced by thousands of things. They don't need physical torture to force them to reveal what they know. Even a slight nod from a girl, the flattery of someone connected to Caesar's court, the desire for a government position, or an inheritance—any of these things could sway them. So, remember as a general rule that discussions about secret matters require trust and matching principles. But where can we easily find that nowadays? If you can't answer that, let someone show me a person who can say, "I care only about the things that are truly mine, the things that cannot be taken away, the things that are naturally free. This is what I believe is good; as for everything else, let them be as they are. I do not concern myself."

Translated by Tim Zengerink

The Nicomachean Ethics

Aristotle

Book 1

Every art and every study, as well as every action and choice, is believed to aim at some good. For this reason, the good has been rightly described as what everything seeks. However, there is a difference among these goals: some are activities, while others are products that come from these activities. When there are goals separate from the actions, the products are naturally seen as better than the activities. Since there are many types of actions, arts, and sciences, their goals are many as well. The goal of medicine is health, that of shipbuilding is a ship, that of strategy is victory, and that of economics is wealth. But when different arts are connected under one skill—like bridle-making and the other arts related to horse equipment fall under the skill of riding, and this, along with all military activities, falls under the skill of strategy—it is clear that the goals of the master skills are better than those of the subordinate ones. After all, the subordinate actions are done for the sake of the higher goals. It doesn't matter whether the activities themselves are the goals or if they lead to something else, as is the case with the sciences mentioned.

Now, if there is one ultimate goal of everything we do, something we desire for its own sake (and not for the sake of something else), and if we don't choose everything for some other reason (which would go on forever, making our desires pointless), then this ultimate goal must be the greatest good. Knowing this should have a huge effect on our lives. Wouldn't we, like archers aiming at a target, be more likely to hit the right mark? If this is true, then we must try to figure out what this goal is and which of the sciences or abilities it belongs to. It seems to belong to the most authoritative art, the one that truly leads all others. Politics appears to be this type of art because it decides which sciences should be studied in the state and which subjects different classes of citizens should learn and how much they should learn. We see that even the most important skills, like strategy, economics, and rhetoric, fall under politics. Since politics uses the other sciences and makes laws about what we should and should not do, its goal must include the goals of all other sciences. This means the goal of politics must be the good for humanity. Even if the greatest good is the same for one person as it is for a state, the good of the state is greater and more complete. Whether we are trying to achieve or preserve the good, it's better to do it for a whole nation or for city-states than for one person. These are the goals our study focuses on since we are discussing political science in one sense of the term.

Our discussion will be enough if it is as clear as the topic allows. Precision shouldn't be expected the same way in every discussion, just as it's not expected in every craft. Fine and just actions, which political science studies, can vary greatly and be seen differently by different people. This leads some to think they exist only because of custom, not nature. Goods also vary in this way because they can sometimes bring harm to people. For example, people have been ruined because of their wealth, and others because of their courage. So, when speaking about such topics and using such ideas, we should be satisfied with indicating the truth roughly and in general terms. When discussing things that are only mostly true and starting with similar ideas, we can't expect perfect conclusions. Therefore, each statement should be accepted in the spirit it is given. It is the mark of an educated person to look for precision in each subject only as far as the topic allows. It is clearly foolish to expect mathematical certainty from a speechmaker and to demand scientific proof from a storyteller.

Each person judges well what they know, and they are good judges of the things they are familiar with. So, the person who is trained in a subject is a good judge of that subject, and the person with a well-rounded education is a good judge in general. This is why a young person isn't the best audience for lessons on political science. They are inexperienced in life's actions, which are the starting point for these discussions. Also, since young people tend to follow their emotions, their study will be useless because the goal is not knowledge but action. It doesn't matter whether they are young in years or young in character.

The problem isn't age but living in a way where they pursue each passing desire as their emotions guide them. For such people, as with those who are lacking self-control, knowledge brings no benefit. But for those who want to live and act based on reason, knowledge about these subjects will be very useful.

These thoughts about the student, the kind of treatment to expect, and the purpose of our study can serve as our introduction.

Let's return to our study and, considering that all knowledge and every pursuit aims at some good, ask what we say political science aims at and what the highest good achievable by action is. In words, there is broad agreement: most people and those of higher understanding say that it is happiness. They agree that living well and doing well are the same as being happy. But they disagree about what happiness is. Many people don't agree with the wise on this. Most think it's something obvious like pleasure, wealth, or honor. However, they often change their minds—thinking happiness is health when they're sick or wealth when they're poor. Still, knowing they don't know, they admire those who speak of great ideas beyond their understanding. Some believe that there is another good beyond these obvious ones, something that exists on its own and causes the goodness of all other things. It may not be necessary to examine every opinion ever held, but it is enough to look at those that are most common or seem worth considering.

Let's not forget, though, that there's a difference between arguments from first principles and arguments toward first principles. Plato was right to ask whether we are coming from or going toward first principles. It's like a race where you either run from the starting line to the turn or from the turn back to the starting line. We must begin with what is known, but knowledge can mean two things: what is known to us and what is known without conditions. We should begin with what is known to us. So, anyone who wants to understand what is noble, just, and generally related to political science must have been brought up with good habits. The facts are the starting point, and if these are clear enough to him, he won't need the reasoning right away.

A person who has been well brought up has or can easily gain these starting points. As for someone who neither has them nor can get them, let him listen to the words of Hesiod:

"Best of all is the one who knows everything for himself;
Good is he who listens to wise advice from others;
But he who neither knows nor listens to others
Is a useless fool."

Let's now return to the main point of our discussion. Looking at how people live, most people—especially those of lower desires— seem to equate the good, or happiness, with pleasure. This is why they love a life of enjoyment. There are, we might say, three main types of life: the life of pleasure, the political life, and the contemplative life. Most people are quite base in their tastes, preferring a life suitable for animals, but they get this idea because many powerful people share the same desires.

Looking at the main types of life, people of higher refinement and active nature tend to identify happiness with honor. Roughly speaking, this is the goal of the political life. However, honor seems too shallow to be what we are truly looking for, as it depends more on those who give honor rather than the one who receives it. But the good we seek should be something that belongs to a person and can't be easily taken away. Furthermore, people seem to seek honor to be assured of their goodness. They seek honor from wise people who know them and value their virtue. Clearly, then, virtue is better than honor, at least according to these people. One might even say that virtue, rather than honor, is the true goal of the political life. Yet, even this seems incomplete because having virtue is compatible with being asleep or inactive, and it can even exist alongside great suffering and misfortune. But no one would call a person happy if they were living like that unless they were just stubbornly defending their argument. But enough about this—it has been discussed at length in other debates. The third type of life is the contemplative life, which we will discuss later.

The life of money-making is one pursued out of necessity, and wealth is clearly not the good we are searching for. Wealth is useful for getting something else. So, we might instead say that the earlier-mentioned things (like pleasure and honor) are true goals because they are loved for themselves. But it's clear that even these aren't the ultimate goals. Many arguments have been made to support them, but we should now move on from this subject.

Next, we should consider the idea of the universal good and carefully examine what it means. This inquiry is made difficult by the fact that the idea of Forms has been introduced by friends of ours. Still, it is better—and indeed our duty—to pursue the truth even if it means criticizing ideas that are dear to us, especially since we are philosophers and lovers of wisdom. While both truth and friends are important, piety demands we honor truth above our friends.

Those who introduced the idea of Forms did not propose Ideas for categories that included levels of priority and order. For this reason, they did not suggest there was an Idea for all numbers. But the term "good" is used in different ways in different categories, such as substance, quality, and relation. Substance is more fundamental in nature than relation because relation is like an offshoot or an accident of being. So, there cannot be one common Idea of good across all these categories. Furthermore, "good" has many meanings, just like "being" does. It is used for substances like God and reason, for qualities like the virtues, for quantities like moderation, and for relations like usefulness. It is also used for time, like the right moment, and for place, like the right location. Clearly, it cannot be one thing present in all cases. If it were, it could not be used in all these different categories. Also, since each science studies one thing, there would be one science of all goods, but instead, we see many sciences studying things within the same category. For example, strategy studies opportunity in war, and medicine studies opportunity in illness. Medicine also studies moderation in food, while gymnastics studies moderation in exercise.

One might also ask what is meant by "the thing itself," as when we say "man himself" or a particular man, the definition of man is the same. If they are both men, they don't differ in that respect. The same should be true of "good itself" and particular goods—they shouldn't differ as far as their goodness is concerned. Furthermore, something doesn't become better just because it lasts longer. Something that lasts a day isn't necessarily less good than something that lasts forever. The Pythagoreans seem to give a better explanation of the good when they place "the One" in the column of goods. This is the view that Speusippus seems to have followed.

But we should discuss these things elsewhere. However, we should consider that the Platonists haven't been talking about all goods. They say that the goods we pursue for themselves are good in relation to a single Form, while things that produce or preserve these goods, or prevent their opposites, are only secondarily called good. Clearly, then, goods must be spoken of in two ways: some are good in themselves, and others are good because they lead to these. Let's separate goods that are good in themselves from those that are useful and see if the former are all good because of one Idea. What kind of things would we call good in themselves? Is it things we pursue even when they are not connected to other things, like knowledge, sight, and certain pleasures and honors? Certainly, even if we pursue these for something else, we would still place them among things that are good in themselves. Or, is nothing good in itself except the Form of good? If that's the case, the Form would be empty. But if the things we've mentioned are good in themselves, then there must be some common quality that makes them all good, just like there is something common in both snow and white lead that makes them white. But when we consider things like honor, wisdom, and pleasure, their goodness seems to come from different sources. So, the good is not one single thing that applies to all these different cases.

Then, what do we mean by the good? It's not like things that only have the same name by chance. Are goods one because they come from one good or because they all contribute to one good? Or are they one by analogy? Certainly, reason is in the soul just as sight is in the body, and so on in other cases. But maybe we should leave these subjects for now. Perfect accuracy about them belongs to another area of philosophy. The same goes for the idea of the universal good. Even if there is one good that applies to all goods or exists on its own, it clearly can't be achieved by humans. But right now, we're looking for something that can be achieved. Still, some might think it's worth recognizing this idea of the universal good as a way to better understand the goods we can achieve. If we know the universal good, we can use it as a guide to help us achieve the goods that are good for us. This argument sounds reasonable, but it seems to go against the methods used in the sciences. All sciences aim at some good and try to supply what is missing, but they don't start by studying the universal good. It's hard to believe that experts in different fields don't know about such a great help as the universal good. It's also difficult to see how a carpenter or a weaver would benefit in their craft by knowing about the universal good, or how someone who understands the Idea of the good would be a better doctor or general. A doctor seems to study not general health, but the health of a particular person. After all, it's individuals that doctors treat. But we've said enough about these topics for now.

Let us once again focus on the idea of the good we are trying to find, and ask what it could be. It seems to vary depending on different actions and skills. For example, in medicine, strategy, and other arts, it differs. So what is the good in each case? Surely, it is the thing for which everything else is done. In medicine, it's health; in strategy, it's victory; in architecture, it's a house; and in other areas, it's something else. In every action and effort, it is the end goal, because it is for this goal that people do everything else they do. So, if there is one goal for everything we do, this goal will be the good we can achieve through action. And if there are more than one, these will be the goods we can achieve through action.

This reasoning leads us, in a different way, to the same point. But we should try to explain this more clearly. Since there are clearly multiple goals, and we choose some of them (for example, wealth, flutes, or tools) for the sake of something else, it is clear that not all goals are final ends. The highest good is clearly something final. So, if there is only one final end, that will be what we are looking for. If there are more than one, the most final of these will be what we are searching for. We say that what is worthy of being pursued for its own sake is more final than something pursued for another reason, and what is never desired for something else is more final than things desired both for themselves and for another reason. Therefore, we call "final" without any limits that which is always desired for itself and never for something else.

Happiness, more than anything else, seems to be this kind of thing. We always choose it for ourselves, not for something else. But honor, pleasure, reason, and every virtue we choose for themselves (because even if nothing else came from them, we would still choose each one of them), yet we also choose them because they lead to happiness. Happiness, on the other hand, no one chooses for the sake of these or for any other reason.

From the perspective of self-sufficiency, the same result appears. The final good is thought to be self-sufficient. Now, by self-sufficient, we do not mean something that only one person needs, like someone living alone, but also something for their family, friends, and fellow citizens, because humans are social beings. But we must set a limit to this, because if we include our ancestors, descendants, and friends' friends, we will be dealing with an infinite chain. Let us leave this for another time and now define self-sufficient as that which, when alone, makes life desirable and complete, lacking nothing. We believe happiness to be like this. We also think it is the most desirable thing of all, not just one good thing among others. If it were one of many, even the smallest addition would make it more desirable, because the added good would make it better, and greater good is always more desirable.

So, happiness is something final and self-sufficient, and it is the goal of action.

However, saying that happiness is the highest good might seem obvious, and people might still want a clearer explanation of what it really is. We could explain it more clearly if we could first figure out the function of a human being. Just as for a flute-player, sculptor, or artist, and generally for all things that have a purpose or activity, the good is thought to reside in that purpose, so it seems to be with humans, if they also have a function. Do the carpenter and the leatherworker have specific functions or tasks, but not humans? Were we born without a purpose? Or, just as the eye, hand, and foot have functions, does humanity, too, have a specific role apart from these? What might it be? Life itself seems common to both plants and animals, but we are searching for what is unique to humans. Therefore, let's rule out the life of nutrition and growth. The next possibility is a life of perception, but this also seems to be shared with horses, oxen, and every animal. What remains is the active life of the part of us that has reason. One part of reason follows principles, and the other part has and exercises them. Since "life of reason" has two meanings, we should clarify that we mean life in the sense of activity because that seems to be the truer meaning of the term. If the function of a human is an activity of the soul that follows or implies a rational principle, and if we say that both a person and a good person share the same function— like a lyre and a good lyre-player—and if, in all cases, the function is the same but excellence makes it better, then we must add to this definition the idea of performing that function well. For example, the function of a lyre-player is to play the lyre, and the function of a good lyre-player is to do so skillfully. If this is the case, and if the function of a person is a kind of life, this life will involve actions of the soul that follow a rational principle, and the function of a good person will be to perform these actions nobly and well. Since any action is performed well when it is done in line with its excellence, human good turns out to be activity of the soul in accordance with virtue. If there are many virtues, the good follows the best and most complete ones.

But we must add "throughout a complete life." One swallow does not make a summer, nor does one day. Likewise, one good day or short time does not make someone blessed and happy.

Let this be a rough outline of the good. We should first sketch it out roughly, then fill in the details later. It seems that anyone can carry on and explain something that has been well outlined, and time is a good helper in such tasks. The growth of the arts happens this way—anyone can add what is missing. We should also remember what has been said before and not seek the same level of precision in all subjects. Instead, in each area, we should aim for the kind of accuracy that fits the topic. A carpenter and a mathematician study the right angle in different ways. The carpenter looks at how useful it is for his work, while the mathematician is interested in what it actually is. We must act the same way in all subjects, ensuring that our main task does not get bogged down by minor questions. Nor should we always demand to know the cause of everything. Sometimes, it's enough that the facts are well-established, especially in the case of first principles. First principles are the most important thing. We come to know them in different ways—some by induction, others by observation, habit, or other methods. But we should try to understand each principle in the right way, putting effort into explaining them clearly, as they greatly influence everything that follows. The beginning is said to be more than half of the whole, and many of the questions we ask are cleared up by it.

We must also consider this matter in light of both our conclusions and what is commonly believed. When our view is correct, all the facts fit together, but when it is wrong, the facts start to clash. Goods have been divided into three types: some are external, some are related to the soul, and some to the body. We consider those related to the soul as the truest goods, and we classify actions and activities of the soul in this category. Therefore, our argument must be correct according to this view, which is an old one agreed upon by many philosophers. It is also correct because we define the goal in terms of certain actions and activities. This places it among goods of the soul, not among external goods. Another common belief that fits our account is that a happy person lives well and acts well because we have basically defined happiness as living and acting well. The traits that are usually associated with happiness all seem to match our definition of it. Some people say happiness is virtue, some say it's practical wisdom, while others believe it's a kind of philosophical wisdom. Some say it's one or all of these things, either with or without pleasure. Others include external prosperity. Many of these ideas have been held by both ordinary people and important thinkers, and it's unlikely that all of them are completely wrong. Instead, they are probably right in at least one way, or even in most ways.

Our account fits with those who say that happiness is virtue or a specific virtue, because virtuous activity belongs to virtue. However, there is an important difference between putting the highest good in having virtue or in using it, in the state of mind or in the action itself. The state of mind might exist without leading to any good results, like when someone is asleep or otherwise inactive, but action cannot. If someone is engaged in virtuous activity, they will act, and act well. Like in the Olympic Games, it is not the most beautiful or strongest people who win crowns, but those who actually compete. It is some of these who are victorious. Likewise, it is those who act that win the good things in life.

Their life is also naturally pleasant. Pleasure is a state of the soul, and to each person, what they love is pleasant to them. For example, a horse is pleasant to someone who loves horses, and a spectacle is pleasant to someone who loves sights. In the same way, just actions are pleasant to someone who loves justice, and virtuous actions are pleasant to someone who loves virtue. For most people, their pleasures conflict with each other because their pleasures are not naturally pleasant, but for lovers of the noble, the things that are naturally pleasant are also pleasant to them. Virtuous actions are like this. So for them, these actions are pleasant in themselves, and also naturally pleasant. Therefore, their life does not need any extra pleasure to make it enjoyable—it is already pleasant. Also, a person who does not enjoy doing noble things is not truly good. No one would call someone just if they didn't enjoy acting justly, or call someone generous if they didn't enjoy generous acts. This applies to all other virtues as well. If this is true, then virtuous actions are naturally pleasant. They are also good and noble, and have all these qualities to the highest degree, because a good person judges them to be so. Their judgment is as we have described. So happiness is the best, noblest, and most pleasant thing in the world. These qualities are not separated from one another, as in the old inscription at Delos:

The noblest is what is most just, the best is health, but the most pleasant thing is to get what you desire.

All these qualities belong to the best activities, and we believe that one or all of these activities are connected with happiness.

But as we said, happiness also needs external goods. It is either impossible or difficult to do noble deeds without the proper resources. In many cases, we use friends, wealth, and political power as tools, and there are some things that, if missing, take away from happiness. For example, good birth, good children, and beauty. A person who is very ugly or poorly born, or who is isolated and without children, is unlikely to be very happy. A person would be even less likely to be happy if they had very bad children or friends, or if they lost good children or friends to death. So, as we said, happiness seems to need a certain level of good fortune. This is why some people connect happiness with luck, while others link it with virtue.

For this reason, people also ask whether happiness is something we learn or develop through habit or some other kind of training, or whether it comes from divine intervention or luck. If it is a gift from the gods, it would make sense that happiness is something they give, as it is the best thing a person can have. But this question might be better for another discussion. Even if happiness is not a gift from the gods but instead comes as a result of virtue or some kind of learning or training, it still seems to be one of the most godlike things. The reward and goal of virtue seem to be the best things in the world, something divine and blessed.

According to this view, happiness will also be widely shared because everyone who has the potential for virtue can achieve it with the right study and effort. If it is better to be happy because of our actions rather than because of chance, it makes sense that this is the way it works. Everything that depends on nature is as good as it can be, and the same goes for anything that relies on art or reason. This is especially true when it depends on the best cause of all. It would be a very poor arrangement if the greatest and most noble thing in life were left to chance.

The answer to this question is also clear from the definition of happiness. We said that happiness is a virtuous activity of the soul, of a certain kind. Of the other goods, some must exist beforehand as conditions for happiness, and others are helpful and useful as tools. This agrees with what we said at the beginning. We said the goal of political science is the best end, and political science focuses on making the citizens good and capable of noble actions.

It makes sense, then, that we do not call an ox, horse, or any other animal happy because none of them can take part in this kind of activity. For this reason, a boy is not happy either, because he is not yet able to act this way due to his age. When we call boys happy, it is because of the hopes we have for their future. As we said, not only is complete virtue needed for happiness, but also a complete life, because many changes and chances happen throughout life. The most fortunate people may experience great misfortune in old age, like Priam in the Trojan story. No one would call someone who ended their life in misery happy.

Should we not call anyone happy while they are still alive, as Solon says, and wait until they die to judge? But even if we accept this idea, does that mean someone is happy only when they're dead? Isn't that an odd thing to say, especially since we believe that happiness involves activity? If we don't call a dead person happy, and Solon didn't mean that, maybe what he meant is that once someone dies, we can safely say they were blessed because they are no longer at risk of misfortune. However, this raises another question. We think good and bad things can still happen to a dead person, just like they can happen to someone who is alive but unaware of them—like when children or descendants experience good or bad fortunes, or receive honors or dishonors.

This creates a problem. What if a man lived a happy life and died in a way that honored his life, but later his descendants faced many hardships or some did well while others did not? The closeness of the relationship between the man and his descendants can also vary a lot. It would seem strange if the dead person's happiness changed based on what happens to their descendants—sometimes being happy and other times being sad. But it also seems strange if their descendants' fortunes had no effect on the dead person's happiness.

Let's go back to the main problem. Maybe looking at it again will help us solve this issue. If we must wait until a person dies to call them happy, not because they are happy now but because they were happy before, this seems like a paradox. How could we not call someone happy while they're alive, if happiness is something that belongs to them at that time? We might hesitate to call living people happy because life is full of changes, and happiness seems like something that should be stable and not easily altered. One person might experience many ups and downs in life. If we judged them based on every turn of events, we might call them happy at one moment and unhappy the next, making happiness seem as changeable as a chameleon. But maybe it's wrong to let a person's happiness depend so much on their changing fortunes. Happiness doesn't depend on things like wealth or power but on a person's virtuous actions, which define happiness.

This discussion actually supports our definition of happiness. No part of a person's life is as lasting as their virtuous actions. These actions are thought to last even longer than knowledge of the sciences. Among these actions, the most valuable ones last the longest because happy people tend to live their lives consistently in line with virtue. This may be why we don't forget them. So, we can say the happy person will remain happy throughout their life because they will always or most often be engaged in virtuous activities and contemplation. They will handle life's ups and downs with nobility and grace, especially if they are truly good and morally strong.

Many things in life happen by chance, but these events differ in importance. Small strokes of good or bad luck don't affect life much, but if many big events turn out well, they can make life happier. Not only do they add beauty to life, but the way a person handles these events can show their nobility and goodness. On the other hand, if these events go badly, they can harm happiness because they bring pain and can stop people from doing many things. Even then, a person's nobility can still shine through when they endure great misfortunes with dignity—not by ignoring the pain, but by showing greatness of soul.

If, as we said, a person's actions define their life, a truly happy person can never become miserable. They won't do things that are disgraceful or mean. We believe that a truly good and wise person will handle whatever life brings in the best possible way, like how a good general uses the army he has or a good shoemaker works with the leather he's given. The same goes for all other craftsmen. If this is true, a happy person cannot become miserable, although they may not reach the highest level of happiness if they face extreme misfortunes like those of Priam.

A truly happy person is not constantly changing in their happiness. They won't lose their happiness easily or because of ordinary bad luck. Only a series of very great misfortunes could shake their happiness. Even if they do face many great misfortunes, they won't regain their happiness quickly. If they regain it at all, it will only be after a long period of time and after they've had many great successes.

So, should we not say that someone is happy if they live according to complete virtue and have enough external goods—not just for a short time, but for their entire life? Or should we add that they must also die in a way that reflects how they lived? The future is unknown to us, but happiness, as we've said, is the final goal and something complete in every way. If this is true, we will call happy those among the living who meet these conditions and who will continue to do so, but we will only call them truly happy once their life is complete. That settles these questions.

The idea that the fortunes of a person's descendants and friends don't affect their happiness at all seems a bit harsh and goes against what people generally believe. But since there are many events, and these events can vary greatly in how much they matter, it would take too long to go through each one in detail. A general outline should be enough. Just as some of the misfortunes a person experiences have a bigger impact on their life than others, the same is true for the misfortunes of their friends and descendants. It also makes a difference whether these misfortunes happen to people who are alive or those who are already dead. For example, in a tragedy, it matters whether horrible deeds happen on stage or are just talked about. Whether or not the dead are affected by the fortunes of the living is something people still debate. It seems that if good or bad things do reach the dead, the effects are weak or small, or at least not enough to make a happy person unhappy or change the situation of someone who is blessed. The fortunes of friends and descendants may have some impact on the dead, but only in a way that doesn't make the happy unhappy or cause any major change in their state.

Now that we've answered those questions, let's consider whether happiness is something to be praised or something to be valued. It's clear that happiness isn't just a potential thing. Everything that is praised seems to be praised because it's a certain kind of thing and is related to something else. For example, we praise a just or brave person because of their actions and what they do. We praise someone strong or fast because they are good at something important. This is clear when it comes to the gods, too. It seems strange to compare the gods to human standards, but we do this in praise because praise involves comparing one thing to another. However, we don't praise the best things, we value them more highly. Instead of praising the gods and the most godlike humans, we call them blessed and happy. The same goes for good things like happiness. No one praises happiness in the same way they praise justice. Instead, they call it blessed because it's more divine and better than things that are praised.

Eudoxus seems to have been right in arguing that pleasure is the highest good. He believed that the fact that pleasure, though good, is not praised shows that it is better than the things that are praised. He thought that God and the good were similar because all other things are judged in comparison to them. Praise is fitting for virtue because virtue leads people to do good deeds, but we celebrate virtuous acts themselves. This might be something that those who study praise and celebration focus on, but for us, it's enough to understand that happiness is something to be valued and complete. This seems clear because happiness is the first principle. It is the reason we do everything we do, and we consider the first principle of anything to be the most valuable and divine.

Since happiness is an activity of the soul according to perfect virtue, we need to examine what virtue is. Maybe this will help us better understand the nature of happiness. The true student of politics is thought to study virtue above all things because they want to make their fellow citizens good and obedient to the law. This is shown by lawgivers like those in Crete and Sparta, and others like them. If this inquiry belongs to political science, then it fits with our overall plan. But clearly, the virtue we need to study is human virtue because the good we are looking for is human good, and the happiness we are concerned with is human happiness. By human virtue, we don't mean bodily virtue but virtue of the soul, since happiness is also an activity of the soul. If this is true, the student of politics must know something about the soul, just as a doctor must know about the body if they are to heal it. And politics is more important than medicine. Even the best doctors spend much time learning about the body. So, the student of politics must study the soul, but only enough to answer the questions we are discussing. Going deeper would require more precision than our purpose demands.

Some things about the soul are already discussed well enough in other works, and we can use them here. For example, people say that one part of the soul is irrational, and one part follows reason. Whether these parts are physically separate, like parts of the body, or only separated in how we define them, doesn't matter for our current discussion.

Of the irrational part, one part seems to be shared by all living things and is responsible for nutrition and growth. This is the power of the soul we find in all plants and animals, including humans. It's more reasonable to think of this as a common power than to assign different powers to different creatures. The excellence of this part of the soul seems to be shared by all living things, not just humans. This part of the soul seems to be most active during sleep, and since goodness and badness aren't obvious during sleep, there's a saying that happy people are no better off than unhappy people for half of their lives. This happens naturally because sleep is when the soul is inactive in the part where it can be good or bad. However, perhaps some movements of the soul happen during sleep, and in that case, the dreams of good people might be better than those of others. But let's leave this topic aside for now, as the nutritive part of the soul has no part in human excellence.

There seems to be another irrational part of the soul that, in a way, listens to reason. For example, we praise the rational part of a person who has self-control and the person who lacks it. We praise the part of their soul that listens to reason because it guides them in the right direction toward the best things. But we also find another part of the soul that seems naturally opposed to reason and fights against it. Just as paralyzed limbs may move in the opposite direction when we try to move them, so it is with the soul. The impulses of those who lack self-control often pull them in opposite directions. In the body, we can see what goes wrong, but in the soul, it's less visible. However, we must assume that the soul, too, has something that goes against reason. Exactly how it is distinct from other parts of the soul doesn't concern us right now.

Even this part of the soul seems to listen to reason in some way. In a person with self-control, it obeys reason, and in the brave and temperate person, it listens even more closely to reason. In these people, the irrational part and the rational part speak with the same voice.

So, the irrational part of the soul seems to have two parts. The part responsible for nutrition doesn't follow reason at all, while the part responsible for desires and appetites does, in a way, listen to and obey reason. This is the same way we talk about following the advice of a father or a friend, not in the same way we discuss following a mathematical rule. The fact that the irrational part of the soul listens to reason is shown by how we give advice, reproof, or encouragement. If we say this part of the soul listens to reason, then the part of the soul that follows reason and the part that doesn't will each have two parts. One part follows reason strictly, while the other part follows reason like a person follows the guidance of their father.

Virtue is also divided into two kinds based on this difference. Some virtues are intellectual, and others are moral. For example, wisdom, understanding, and practical judgment are intellectual virtues, while generosity and temperance are moral virtues. When we talk about someone's character, we don't say they are wise or have understanding, but that they are good-tempered or temperate. Yet, we also praise the wise person for their state of mind. States of mind that deserve praise are called virtues.

Book 2

Virtue, as we know, is of two types: intellectual and moral. Intellectual virtue mainly comes from teaching, which is why it requires both experience and time. Moral virtue, on the other hand, comes from habit, which is why the word for moral virtue (ethike) comes from the word for habit (ethos). This shows that none of the moral virtues are naturally within us, because nothing that exists by nature can develop a habit that goes against its nature. For example, a stone, which naturally moves downward, can't be trained to move upward, even if you throw it up ten thousand times. The same goes for fire—it naturally rises and can't be trained to move downward. In the same way, nothing that behaves naturally in one way can be trained to behave in the opposite way. So, virtues don't come to us by nature or against nature. Instead, we are naturally able to acquire them, but they are perfected through habit.

For all things that come to us naturally, we first have the potential for them, and only later do we actually use them. This is clear with the senses: we didn't develop our ability to see or hear by using these senses many times. On the contrary, we had them before we used them. But we develop virtues by practicing them, just like with skills. For the things we need to learn before we can do them, we learn by doing them. For example, we become builders by building, and we become musicians by playing music. In the same way, we become just by doing just acts, temperate by doing temperate acts, and brave by doing brave acts.

This idea is also supported by what happens in cities. Lawmakers make citizens good by forming good habits in them. This is the goal of every lawmaker, and those who fail at this miss their target. This is the difference between a good and bad constitution.

In addition, the same causes that produce a virtue can also destroy it, just like with skills. A person becomes a good or bad musician by playing well or poorly. The same applies to builders and all other trades. People become good or bad at their craft based on how well they practice it. If this weren't true, there would be no need for teachers, and everyone would simply be born good or bad at their craft. The same goes for virtues. By behaving a certain way in our interactions with others, we become either just or unjust. By behaving a certain way when faced with danger, and by getting used to feeling either fear or confidence, we become either brave or cowardly. The same is true for our desires and feelings of anger: some people become temperate and calm, while others become self-indulgent and irritable, based on how they act in different situations. In short, our character develops from our repeated actions. That's why the actions we take must be of a certain kind, because our character reflects the differences in our actions. It makes a huge difference whether we develop good or bad habits from a young age.

Since we aren't trying to gain theoretical knowledge (like in other studies), but instead to become good, we must focus on actions—specifically, how we should do them. The way we act shapes the kind of character we develop, as we've already said. We all agree that we must act according to the right rule, and we'll discuss what this rule is later and how it connects to the other virtues. But for now, we should agree that when we talk about conduct, we are speaking in general terms, and we shouldn't expect exact details. Just like in matters of health, what is good for us doesn't have a strict set of rules. The same goes for specific cases, which are even less precise, as they don't follow any strict laws or rules. It's up to each individual to decide what is appropriate for the situation, just like a doctor or a navigator must do in their work.

Even though this is the nature of our discussion, we can still provide some help. First, let's consider that things can be destroyed by either deficiency or excess. This is true for both strength and health. To better understand this, we can look at things we can sense. For example, both too much or too little exercise can destroy strength, and both too much or too little food or drink can destroy health. However, the right amount of these things will both produce and maintain strength and health. The same is true for temperance, courage, and the other virtues. A person who runs from everything or fears everything becomes a coward. A person who is afraid of nothing and faces every danger becomes reckless. A person who indulges in every pleasure and avoids none becomes self-indulgent. Meanwhile, a person who avoids every pleasure, like someone who is insensitive, also misses the mark. So, temperance and courage are destroyed by both excess and deficiency, but they are maintained by moderation.

The same things that help virtues grow can also destroy them. This is true for all things we can sense. For example, strength comes from eating well and exercising, and strong people are better able to continue doing these things. The same is true for the virtues. By avoiding pleasures, we become temperate, and once we've become temperate, we are better able to avoid pleasures. The same applies to courage. By getting used to facing frightening things and standing our ground, we become brave, and once we are brave, we are more capable of standing our ground in the face of danger.

We can use pleasure and pain as a sign of our character. A person who avoids bodily pleasures and takes joy in doing so is temperate, while a person who is bothered by this is self-indulgent. A person who stands firm in the face of fear and either takes joy in doing so or is not troubled by it is brave, while a person who is troubled by it is a coward. Moral excellence is connected to pleasure and pain because we do bad things for pleasure and avoid noble things because they cause us pain. That's why we should be brought up from a young age, as Plato suggests, to take pleasure in the right things and feel pain for the right things. This is the proper way to be educated.

If the virtues are connected to our actions and feelings, and every action and feeling is tied to pleasure and pain, then virtue must also be connected to pleasure and pain. This is further proven by the fact that punishments use pleasure and pain, and punishment is a kind of cure.

Cures work through opposites, so this shows the importance of pleasure and pain in shaping our character.

As we mentioned earlier, every state of the soul is influenced by the things that can make it better or worse. People become bad by chasing the wrong pleasures or avoiding the wrong pains, either at the wrong time or in the wrong way. This is why some people define virtues as being free from emotion and stillness. However, this definition isn't quite right because it doesn't include important details like doing things at the right time, in the right way, and for the right reasons. We assume that excellence in virtue means doing what is best in relation to pleasure and pain, while vice is doing the opposite.

We can also see that virtue and vice deal with these same things through other facts. There are three things we can choose and three things we can avoid: the noble, the beneficial, and the pleasant, as well as their opposites, the disgraceful, the harmful, and the painful. The good person tends to make the right choices in all of these areas, while the bad person makes the wrong choices, especially when it comes to pleasure. This is because pleasure is something all animals experience, and it is connected to all of our choices. Even the noble and beneficial things can feel pleasant.

Pleasure has been with us since we were born, which is why it's hard to remove it from our lives. We use pleasure and pain to measure our actions—some people more than others. For this reason, our whole study must focus on these feelings, because how we feel pleasure and pain has a big impact on our actions.

It's harder to fight against pleasure than against anger, as Heraclitus said, but both art and virtue deal with difficult things. Goodness is even better when it is more challenging. For this reason, both virtue and political science deal with pleasure and pain. A person who uses pleasure and pain correctly will be good, while a person who uses them incorrectly will be bad.

So, we can say that virtue is connected to pleasure and pain, and that it is strengthened by the actions that created it. If these actions are done differently, it can be destroyed. The actions that created virtue are the same ones that maintain it.

Some might ask what we mean when we say that we become just by doing just acts and temperate by doing temperate acts. After all, if people are doing just or temperate acts, aren't they already just and temperate? This seems to be like saying that if people follow the rules of grammar or music, they are already grammarians or musicians.

But this isn't even true for the arts. It's possible to follow the rules of grammar by chance or at someone's suggestion. A person is only a grammarian if they not only follow the rules but also understand them and apply them with knowledge.

The same goes for the virtues. The products of the arts have their value in themselves, so it's enough that they have a certain quality. But if acts of virtue have the right qualities, that doesn't mean they are done with justice or temperance. The person doing the act must also be in the right state when they do it. First, they must know what they are doing. Second, they must choose to do it, and choose it for its own sake. Third, their action must come from a firm and unchanging character. These conditions don't apply to the arts. In the arts, knowledge is enough, but for virtue, knowledge is only a small part. The other conditions are far more important and come from repeatedly doing just and temperate acts.

Actions are called just and temperate when they are the kinds of actions a just or temperate person would do. But just because someone does these actions doesn't mean they are just or temperate themselves. Instead, they must do them in the way a just or temperate person would do them. So it is true that we become just by doing just acts, and we become temperate by doing temperate acts. Without doing these things, no one would ever become good.

Most people, however, don't do these things. Instead, they turn to theory, thinking that by studying philosophy, they will become good. They behave like patients who listen carefully to their doctors but don't follow any of the instructions. Just as these patients will never be healthy this way, people will never improve their character by simply studying philosophy.

Next, we need to consider what virtue is. Since the things that are found in the soul are divided into three types—passions, faculties, and states of character—virtue must be one of these. By passions, I mean things like appetite, anger, fear, confidence, envy, joy, friendship, hatred, longing, and pity—in general, any feelings that come with pleasure or pain. By faculties, I mean the things that make us able to feel these emotions, like the ability to feel anger, pain, or pity. By states of character, I mean the way we relate to our emotions—whether we manage them well or poorly. For example, we manage anger poorly if we feel it too strongly or too weakly, and we manage it well if we feel it moderately. The same goes for all the other emotions.

Virtue and vice, however, are not passions. We are not called good or bad because of our passions, but because of our virtues or vices. We also aren't praised or blamed for simply feeling a certain way. A person isn't praised for feeling fear or anger, nor is someone blamed for feeling angry. Instead, we are praised or blamed for how we manage our virtues or vices.

Also, we don't choose to feel emotions like anger or fear, but virtues involve choice. In respect to our passions, we are said to be moved, but in respect to our virtues and vices, we are said to be in a certain state.

For these reasons, virtues are not faculties. We aren't called good or bad for simply having the capacity to feel emotions. Also, our faculties are natural, but we aren't naturally good or bad. We've already discussed this. So, if virtues are neither passions nor faculties, they must be states of character.

This explains what virtue is in terms of its category.

We also need to explain what kind of state virtue is. Every virtue brings something into good condition and helps it do its work well. For example, the virtue of the eye makes the eye and its work good. The virtue of a horse makes it good and capable of running, carrying its rider, and facing enemies. If this is true in every case, then the virtue of a person is the state of character that makes a person good and helps them do their work well.

We've already explained how this happens, but we can also clarify this by considering the specific nature of virtue. In everything that is continuous and divisible, we can take more, less, or an equal amount, either in terms of the thing itself or in relation to us. The equal amount is a middle point between excess and deficiency. The middle point in the object is equally distant from the extremes, and this is the same for everyone. But the middle point in relation to us is different. It is neither too much nor too little, and this varies for each person. For example, if ten pounds of food is too much and two pounds is too little, the middle point for one person might be six pounds, but that might still be too much or too little for another person. The same applies to running or wrestling. A skilled person will avoid both excess and deficiency and aim for the middle point, not in the object, but in relation to themselves.

If this is true for all the arts, where the best work is done by aiming for the middle point, then virtue must also aim for the middle. We often say that good works of art can't have anything added or taken away, because excess and deficiency ruin the work, while the middle point preserves it. Good artists focus on this in their work, and since virtue is better and more exact than art, it must aim at the middle as well. I'm referring to moral virtue here, which deals with emotions and actions. In both, there can be excess, deficiency, and a middle point. For example, we can feel fear, confidence, desire, anger, pity, and pleasure too much or too little, and in both cases, this is bad. But to feel them at the right time, in the right way, and for the right reasons is to find the middle point, and this is what virtue aims for. The same is true for actions. In all actions, excess is a kind of failure, as is deficiency, while the middle point is praised and successful. Since being praised and being successful are qualities of virtue, virtue is a kind of middle.

It's easy to fail in many ways because evil is limitless, as the Pythagoreans said, while good is limited. It's easier to miss the target than to hit it, which is why excess and deficiency are signs of vice, while the middle point is a sign of virtue.

People can be good in only one way, but they can be bad in many ways.

Virtue, then, is a state of character that involves choice and lies in a middle point, which is determined by reason and by how a wise person would determine it. It is a middle point between two vices: one of excess and one of deficiency. In both emotions and actions, vices go too far or not far enough, while virtue finds and chooses the middle.

However, not all actions or emotions have a middle point. Some are inherently bad, such as spite, shamelessness, and envy. In terms of actions, things like adultery, theft, and murder are always wrong, no matter how they are done. You can't be right with these actions by committing adultery with the right person, at the right time, and in the right way. These actions are always wrong. There is no middle point for unjust, cowardly, or indulgent actions. It would be absurd to think that there could be a middle, an excess, or a deficiency in such things. Just as there is no excess or deficiency of temperance or courage, since the middle point is actually an extreme, there is no middle, excess, or deficiency for the actions we mentioned. They are always wrong, no matter how they are done. There is no middle point for actions that are inherently bad.

We need to apply what we've discussed to specific situations. General statements about behavior apply broadly, but when it comes to actions, specific examples are more accurate since actions involve individual situations. We'll take our examples from our list. When it comes to feelings like fear and confidence, courage is the middle ground. Those who are too fearless don't have a name, while people with too much confidence are called reckless, and those with too much fear and too little confidence are called cowards.

For pleasures and pains (mainly pleasures), the middle is called temperance, and the excess is self-indulgence. People who are deficient in feeling pleasure are rare and don't have a common name, but we'll call them "insensible."

When it comes to giving and taking money, the middle is called generosity, and the excess and deficiency are wastefulness and stinginess. Wasteful people spend too much and take too little, while stingy people take too much and spend too little. (We're giving a summary here and will explain these more precisely later.) When dealing with larger amounts of money, we call the middle magnificence, and the excess is called tastelessness or vulgarity, while the deficiency is called meanness. These are different from generosity, which deals with smaller amounts, and we'll explain the differences later.

When it comes to honor and dishonor, the middle is proper pride. Too much pride is vanity, and too little is humility. Just as generosity relates to magnificence, dealing with small and large amounts, proper pride relates to honors, with some people aiming for small honors and others for large ones. You can desire honor in the right way, too much, or too little. The person who wants too much honor is called ambitious, while the person who wants too little is unambitious. The middle person doesn't have a specific name, but the extreme positions are often labeled ambition. Because these people are at the extremes, they both claim to be in the middle. That's why we sometimes call people ambitious and other times unambitious, and sometimes praise one group or the other. We'll explain this later, but for now, let's continue.

Anger also has a middle, an excess, and a deficiency. Though these don't have clear names, we call the person in the middle good-tempered. The person who gets too angry is irascible, and the person who doesn't get angry enough is inirascible (not easily angered).

There are three other qualities that are similar but slightly different because they deal with how we interact with others. One is about truthfulness, and the other two deal with being pleasant, either through joking or in everyday life. We'll discuss these to show that in everything, the middle is good, while the extremes are bad and deserve blame. Many of these qualities don't have names, but we'll create some for clarity. When it comes to truthfulness, the middle is honesty, the excess is exaggeration, and the deficiency is false modesty. In terms of joking and amusement, the middle is ready-wittedness, the excess is buffoonery (being overly silly), and the deficiency is boorishness (being dull or boring). When it comes to being pleasant in everyday life, the middle is friendliness, the excess is flattery (if done for personal gain) or being overly agreeable (without an ulterior motive), and the deficiency is being quarrelsome or surly (constantly unpleasant).

Some traits, like shame, are not virtues but are still praised. For example, someone who feels shame at everything is overly bashful, while someone who never feels shame is shameless. The middle is modesty. Righteous indignation is the middle between envy and spite, and these traits relate to how we feel about other people's fortunes. A person with righteous indignation is upset by undeserved good fortune, an envious person is upset by all good fortune, and a spiteful person is happy when others suffer. We'll explain these traits more later. When it comes to justice, which has multiple meanings, we'll explore its types and how it relates to the idea of the middle. We'll also discuss rational virtues in a similar way.

There are three kinds of dispositions: two vices (excess and deficiency) and one virtue, which is the middle. They are all opposed to each other in some way. The extreme states are opposed to each other and to the middle, just as something large is bigger than something small, but both are larger and smaller than something equal. For example, a brave person might seem reckless to a coward and cowardly to a reckless person. Similarly, a temperate person might seem self-indulgent to someone who is insensible and insensible to someone who is self-indulgent. The same goes for someone who is generous; they may seem wasteful to someone stingy and stingy to someone wasteful. Because of this, people at the extremes tend to accuse those in the middle of being at the opposite extreme.

Since these states are opposed, the greatest opposition is between the two extremes, not between the extremes and the middle, because the extremes are farther apart. For example, recklessness might seem somewhat similar to bravery, and wastefulness to generosity, but the extremes are furthest from each other, and opposites are defined by how far apart they are.

In some cases, one extreme is more opposed to the middle than the other. For example, it's not recklessness (the excess) but cowardice (the deficiency) that is most opposed to bravery. Likewise, it's not insensibility (the deficiency) but self-indulgence (the excess) that is most opposed to temperance. This happens for two reasons. First, one extreme is often closer to the middle than the other, so we focus on the extreme that's farther away. For example, recklessness seems more similar to bravery, while cowardice seems more different. Second, people naturally tend toward certain extremes, and we oppose the one we tend toward more. Since we're more likely to seek pleasure, self-indulgence (an excess) is more opposed to temperance than insensibility (a deficiency).

So, moral virtue is a middle between two extremes, one involving excess and the other deficiency. It focuses on finding the middle ground in both feelings and actions. This shows that being good is not easy. It's hard to find the middle in everything, just like it's hard to find the exact center of a circle. Anyone can get angry or spend money, but doing it in the right way, for the right reasons, and at the right time is much harder. That's why being good is rare, praiseworthy, and noble.

To aim for the middle, we should first move away from what's most opposed to it, just like Calypso advises in The Odyssey, "Steer the ship away from the waves." Since one extreme is usually more wrong than the other, and hitting the middle is very difficult, the next best thing is to choose the lesser of two evils. The best way to do this is to think about where we tend to go wrong, and steer ourselves in the opposite direction. This will help us get closer to the middle, like straightening a bent stick.

We also need to be especially careful with pleasure, because it's something we don't judge fairly. We should treat pleasure like the elders treated Helen of Troy, blaming her for the chaos she caused. By rejecting pleasure in this way, we're less likely to make mistakes. If we do this, we'll be able to hit the middle.

But this is difficult, especially in specific situations. For example, it's hard to say exactly when and for how long it's right to be angry or whom we should be angry with. Sometimes we praise people for being mild and not getting angry, and other times we praise them for getting angry and being brave. A person who only deviates a little from the right path isn't criticized, but someone who deviates a lot is noticed and blamed. However, it's hard to say exactly where the line is, and that's something that depends on experience. What's clear is that the middle is always praiseworthy, and we should lean toward either excess or deficiency as needed to stay as close to the middle as possible.

Book 3

Since virtue is concerned with feelings and actions, and praise or blame is given for feelings and actions that are voluntary, while those that are involuntary receive pardon or sometimes pity, it is important to know the difference between voluntary and involuntary actions. This distinction is necessary for understanding virtue and is also useful for lawmakers when deciding on rewards and punishments. We consider actions involuntary if they happen due to force or ignorance. An action is considered forced if its cause is completely outside the person, and they contribute nothing to it, like being carried somewhere by a strong wind or by other people who have control over them.

However, there are actions done out of fear of greater harm or to achieve a noble goal (for example, if a tyrant orders someone to do something shameful, threatening to kill their family unless they comply). It's debated whether such actions are voluntary or involuntary. The same question arises with throwing goods overboard during a storm. In general, nobody would throw their goods away voluntarily, but if doing so would save their life and the lives of their crew, any sensible person would choose to do it. These actions are a mix of voluntary and involuntary, but they are closer to being voluntary because they are chosen as the best option at that moment. The decision at the time of the action makes it voluntary. The person acts voluntarily because the source of movement that controls their body is within them, and they have the power to do or not do these things. Therefore, while these actions might seem involuntary in some ways, they are more voluntary when considering the circumstances.

People are sometimes praised for such actions, especially when they endure something bad or shameful for the sake of a noble cause. On the other hand, they may be blamed if they go through terrible things for no good reason. Some actions aren't praised, but people might be excused for them when they are forced to do things that push beyond what human nature can withstand. In some cases, however, there are things that should never be done, no matter how extreme the circumstances, and people should face death instead of committing such acts. For instance, the story of Euripides' Alcmaeon being forced to kill his mother seems absurd. It can be difficult to determine what is worth enduring and at what cost, and it's even harder to stick to those decisions. Usually, people are expected to endure pain, while the things they are forced to do are seen as disgraceful. As a result, people are either praised or blamed for how they respond when faced with force.

So, what kinds of actions should be called forced? We can say that actions are truly forced when the cause comes entirely from outside, and the person does not contribute anything to them. However, actions that are undesirable on their own, but are chosen because they bring about some benefit, and where the cause comes from the person, are in themselves involuntary but are now voluntary because of the circumstances. They are more like voluntary actions because in specific cases, the individual acts voluntarily. It's hard to say what should be chosen and what shouldn't be, as there are many differences depending on the situation.

If someone were to say that pleasant and noble goals have the power to force us, then all actions would be considered forced because people do everything for these goals. But those who act under force do so unwillingly and with pain, while those who act for pleasure or nobility do so willingly and with joy. It would be strange to blame outside circumstances for disgraceful actions while praising oneself for noble ones. It seems, then, that forced actions are those where the cause is outside the person, and the person contributes nothing.

Not everything done out of ignorance is involuntary. Only actions that cause regret or pain are involuntary. Someone who acts out of ignorance but feels no regret about what they did isn't considered to have acted involuntarily, since they didn't know what they were doing, but they also aren't called voluntary, because they don't feel pain over their actions. If someone acts out of ignorance and later regrets it, they are considered to have acted involuntarily. But if they don't regret it, they are not considered involuntary actors, though we might say they acted without knowing.

Acting out of ignorance is different from acting while being ignorant. For example, someone who is drunk or angry is not acting out of ignorance, but they are acting without full knowledge of their actions.

Every wicked person is ignorant of what they should and shouldn't do, and it's this kind of mistake that leads people to become unjust or bad in general. However, the word "involuntary" is not used when someone is ignorant of what benefits them personally, because acting from mistaken judgment doesn't make an action involuntary—it makes someone wicked. Rather, involuntary actions arise from ignorance of specific circumstances related to the action. This is where pity and pardon come in, as someone who is unaware of these particulars acts involuntarily.

It's helpful to understand what specific things someone can be ignorant of. A person can be ignorant of who they are, what they are doing, who or what they are affecting, what tool they are using, or what result they expect their action to bring. Additionally, they might not know how they are doing something, such as whether they are acting gently or violently. No one can be ignorant of all of these things without being mad. It's especially hard for someone to be ignorant of themselves. However, someone might be unaware of what they are doing, like saying something without realizing it or not knowing they were revealing a secret, as Aeschylus did with the mysteries. Or someone might accidentally discharge a weapon while only intending to show how it worked. Someone might mistake a person for an enemy, as Merope did, or think a spear has a safety tip when it doesn't, or believe a rock is light and harmless when it's not. A person might give someone a drink to heal them but accidentally cause harm, or they might try to tap someone in sparring and actually wound them. Ignorance could relate to any of these aspects of an action, and the person is seen as acting involuntarily, especially if they were unaware of the most important details, such as the goal of the action. Additionally, if the action was painful and caused regret, it is considered involuntary.

Since actions done by force or ignorance are involuntary, voluntary actions are those where the cause lies within the person, and they are aware of the specifics of what they are doing. It seems wrong to say that actions done out of anger or desire are involuntary. If that were true, animals and children would never act voluntarily, and we'd have to say that noble actions are done voluntarily while bad actions are done involuntarily. But this doesn't make sense because the same source—anger or desire—causes both types of actions. It would be strange to call actions involuntary when they are driven by desires we should have, like the desire for health or learning. Also, involuntary actions are usually painful, but actions that come from desire are generally pleasurable. There isn't much difference between mistakes made from calculation and mistakes made from anger, as both are considered human traits. Therefore, actions driven by anger or desire are still our actions, and it would be strange to call them involuntary.

Now that we have distinguished between voluntary and involuntary actions, we need to discuss choice. Choice is thought to be closely connected with virtue and is a better way of understanding character than actions are.

Choice seems to be voluntary, but it is not the same thing as voluntary action. Voluntary actions are more widespread. Both children and animals can act voluntarily, but they cannot make choices. We might describe actions done suddenly as voluntary, but we wouldn't say they are done by choice.

People who say that choice is the same as appetite, anger, wish, or a kind of opinion are wrong. Choice is not shared by animals, but appetite and anger are. An impulsive person acts on appetite, but not on choice. A self-controlled person acts with choice, but not appetite. Appetite can be opposed to choice, but not to itself. Appetite is concerned with pleasure and pain, while choice is not.

Anger is even less connected with choice because actions done out of anger are thought to be less deliberate.

Choice is also not the same as wish, though they are related. We can wish for impossible things, like immortality, but we don't choose them because choosing implies a belief that the action can be accomplished. We might wish for something we have no control over, like a particular athlete winning a competition, but we don't choose it. Choice is focused on actions we believe we can achieve ourselves. We wish for goals, but we choose the means to reach them. For instance, we wish to be healthy, but we choose the actions that make us healthy. We wish to be happy, but we don't choose happiness in the same way. Choice is connected to things that are in our power.

Choice is also different from opinion. Opinion deals with all kinds of subjects, even things that are impossible or eternal. It is judged based on whether it is true or false, while choice is judged based on whether it is good or bad.

We don't become good or bad people just by having certain opinions, but we do by making certain choices. Opinions are about what is true or false, while choices are about what we pursue or avoid. Opinion is praised for being accurate, while choice is praised for aiming at the right target. When we choose, we focus on what we know to be good, while opinions are often about things we are unsure of. Some people make good choices but have bad opinions, and others have good opinions but make bad choices because of their character. Whether opinion comes before or alongside choice is not important here. What matters is that they are not the same thing.

So, what exactly is choice, if it's not any of the things we've discussed? Choice seems to be voluntary, but not all voluntary actions involve choice. Could it be something that follows deliberate thinking? Choice involves reasoning and thought. Even the word "choice" suggests that it involves selecting something over other options.

Do we deliberate about everything, and is everything something we can deliberate about, or are there some things we can't? We should probably say that only what a sensible person would deliberate about is something worth deliberating on, not what a fool or madman would think about. For instance, no one deliberates about things that are eternal, like the material universe or whether the diagonal of a square is equal to its side. Similarly, we don't deliberate about things that involve movement but always happen the same way, whether by necessity or nature or some other cause, like the solstices or the rising of the stars. Nor do we deliberate about things that happen differently each time, like droughts or rain, or about random events like finding treasure.

We also don't deliberate about all human matters. For example, no Spartan deliberates about what the best government for the Scythians would be. These things can't be influenced by our efforts. We deliberate about things that are within our power and that we can actually do. Everything else, like nature, necessity, or chance, is not up to us. People deliberate about things they can do by themselves. For example, there's no need to deliberate about exact sciences, like writing letters of the alphabet—we know how to do that. But we do deliberate about things that involve our efforts and don't always have a fixed outcome, like medical treatment or making money. We deliberate more about navigation than about gymnastics, because navigation hasn't been worked out as exactly. We also deliberate more about the arts than the sciences because we tend to have more doubts about arts.

Deliberation deals with things that usually happen in a certain way but where the outcome is unclear, or things where there is uncertainty. We ask others to help us deliberate on important matters when we don't trust ourselves to make the right decision.

We don't deliberate about ends, only about means. A doctor doesn't deliberate whether he should heal people, nor does an orator deliberate whether he should persuade people. A statesman doesn't wonder whether he should create law and order. They take their goals for granted and think about how to reach them. If there are several ways to reach the goal, they deliberate about which way is best and easiest. If there's only one way, they think about how to use that method and what steps are needed to achieve it. It's like solving a geometry problem—the person who deliberates breaks down the problem into steps. Deliberation is a form of investigation, though not all investigation is deliberation, such as mathematical studies. What comes last in deliberation seems to come first in the process of doing things. If something seems impossible, like if money is needed but can't be obtained, we stop deliberating. If something seems possible, we try to do it.

By 'possible,' I mean something that can be done through our own efforts, and this includes things we can achieve with the help of friends since the source of the action is still within us. Sometimes we deliberate about tools, other times about how to use them. In the same way, we deliberate about the means to achieve our goal and how to use those means. As was said earlier, human beings are the source of their own actions. Deliberation is about the things a person can do themselves, and actions are done for the sake of something else. The end goal is not something we deliberate about, only the means to achieve it. We don't deliberate about basic facts, like whether something is bread or if it has been baked properly. Those are matters of perception. If we were always deliberating, we'd never stop.

The same thing is both deliberated about and chosen. However, the thing we choose is already decided upon because it's what we concluded after deliberating. We stop investigating how to act when we've traced the source of the action back to ourselves. The part of ourselves that rules is what makes the choice. This can be seen in ancient governments, as described by Homer. Kings would announce their decisions to the people.

The object of choice is something within our power that we desire after deliberating. So, choice is a deliberate desire for things that are in our control. Once we've deliberated, we desire things in line with our deliberation.

We've now given an outline of choice, explained what kinds of things it deals with, and shown that it concerns the means to an end.

Wish is for the end. Some people think it's for what is truly good, while others think it's for what seems good. Those who say it's for the good must admit that what a person who doesn't choose rightly wishes for isn't really a wish. If they wish for something bad, then it wasn't a true object of wish. Those who say wish is for what seems good must admit that there's no single natural object of wish—only what seems good to each person. Different things seem good to different people, and sometimes even opposite things seem good.

If these ideas seem unsatisfying, we could say that the true good is the object of wish for everyone, but for each person, their wish is based on what seems good to them. The truly good thing is wished for by the good person, while anything could be wished for by a bad person. This is like the way healthy things are good for healthy bodies, but other things might seem healthy to someone who is sick. The good person sees the truth in everything, while others don't. Different people have different ideas of what is noble and what is pleasant, but perhaps what makes a good person different is that they see the truth in these matters. People often make mistakes because of pleasure, thinking something is good when it isn't. This is why we sometimes choose pleasure as though it were good and avoid pain as though it were evil.

The end is what we wish for, and the means to that end are what we deliberate about and choose. Actions that concern the means to an end must be voluntary and based on choice. The exercise of virtues involves choosing the right means, so virtue is in our control, just like vice. If we can choose to act, then we can also choose not to act. So if doing the right thing is in our power, then not doing the wrong thing is also in our power, and vice versa.

If it's within our power to do noble or base acts and we can choose not to do them, then being good or bad is also in our power.

The saying that "no one is wicked voluntarily or happy involuntarily" is partly false and partly true. No one is involuntarily happy, but wickedness is voluntary. Otherwise, we would have to deny that a person is the cause of their own actions, just as they are the cause of their children. If it's clear that actions come from within us, then the actions whose source is within us must also be in our control and voluntary.

This is supported by individuals and by lawmakers, who punish people for wicked acts (unless they were forced or acted out of ignorance that wasn't their fault). They honor people who do noble acts, as if to encourage them and discourage others. No one encourages people to avoid things that are out of their control, like being hot or in pain. We will experience these things anyway. In fact, we punish people for ignorance when it's their fault, like doubling penalties for drunkenness. The person had the power not to get drunk, and their drunkenness caused their ignorance. We also punish people for not knowing the law when they should know it. We assume they could have avoided ignorance if they had been more careful.

A person might say that all people desire what seems good, but they can't control how things seem to them. The way things appear depends on their character. But if people are responsible for their own state of mind, then they are also responsible for how things appear to them. If not, then no one is responsible for their bad actions, and everyone does bad things because they are ignorant of the true end, thinking they will get what is best. It's like being born with an eye for seeing what is truly good—some people are naturally gifted with this, and others are not.

Whether it's natural or not, virtue is voluntary because the good person chooses the right means voluntarily. Vice is also voluntary because the bad person's actions also depend on themselves, even if not their end goal. If the virtues are voluntary, then vices must be voluntary too, since we are responsible for our character and how we see things.

We've described the virtues in general—they are means, states of character, and involve doing the acts by which they are produced. They are in our control and voluntary, following the right rule. Actions and states of character are not voluntary in the same way, though. We control our actions from beginning to end if we know the facts. But while we control the start of our character, its development is less obvious, just like with illnesses. Because it was in our power to act a certain way, our character is voluntary.

Let's now look at the individual virtues, explain what they are about, how they work, and how many there are. Let's start by discussing courage.

It has already been shown that courage is about how we handle feelings of fear and confidence. Clearly, the things we fear are the terrible things, and these are, without a doubt, evils. That is why people often define fear as expecting something bad to happen. We fear all kinds of evils, like disgrace, poverty, illness, loneliness, and death, but not all of these are what a brave person deals with. In fact, it is right and honorable to fear certain things, and it would be wrong not to fear them—such as disgrace. A person who fears disgrace is seen as good and modest, while someone who doesn't fear it is shameless. Sometimes people mistakenly call a shameless person brave because they don't fear disgrace, and in a way, they seem like the brave person, since a brave person is also fearless. However, things like poverty and illness are not the kinds of things we should fear, and they don't come from vice or wrongdoing. Yet, even someone who is unafraid of these things is not considered brave. We sometimes still call them brave because of a similarity—just as some people who are cowards in war can still be generous and confident when it comes to losing money.

A man is not a coward if he fears his wife or children being insulted, or if he fears envy or similar things. Nor is someone brave just because they stay confident when they are about to be beaten. So, what kinds of terrible things does the brave person face? Surely, it is the most frightening things, because no one is more likely to stand firm against something truly terrifying than the brave person. Death is the most terrible thing of all because it is the end, and once someone is dead, nothing can be good or bad for them anymore. However, even the brave person does not face death in every situation, like at sea or when dealing with illness. In what situations, then? Surely, in the most noble ones. The noblest deaths are those that happen in battle because they occur in the greatest and most honorable danger. These deaths are honored both in city-states and at royal courts. So, a brave person is one who is unafraid of a noble death and of all situations that involve death, especially those in war, which are the most honorable of these situations. Even at sea or in sickness, the brave person is fearless, but in a different way from the sailor, for example. The brave person has lost hope for safety and dislikes the thought of dying this way, while sailors are more hopeful because of their experience. We show bravery when there is a chance to demonstrate skill or when dying is noble, but these situations do not offer either.

What is frightening is not the same for all people, but we can say that there are some things that are beyond human strength and terrifying for everyone—at least for anyone sensible. However, the frightening things that are not beyond human strength vary in size and degree, and the same is true for the things that give us confidence. The brave person is as fearless as a human can be. Therefore, while they will fear things within human strength, they will face them properly and as the rule of honor dictates, because the purpose of virtue is honor. But it is possible to fear these things either too much or too little, or to fear things that aren't actually frightening at all. The mistakes people make involve fearing what they shouldn't, fearing in the wrong way, or fearing at the wrong time, and the same goes for the things that give us confidence. The brave person faces and fears the right things, at the right time, and for the right reasons, while also feeling confidence in the right way and under the right conditions. This person is brave because they act according to what is right and how the rule directs. In everything, the goal is to match our actions to the state of character. This applies to the brave person as well. Courage is noble, and so the goal is noble too, because everything is defined by its goal. Therefore, the brave person endures and acts courageously for the sake of a noble goal.

For those who go to extremes, the person who has no fear of anything has no name (as we've already said, many character traits have no names), but this person would be like a madman or someone insensible if they feared nothing—not even earthquakes or storms, as it is said the Celts do not. A person who is overly confident in the face of real dangers is rash. The rash person is seen as boastful, pretending to be brave. They want to appear brave just like the brave person, so they imitate bravery when they can. Because of this, most rash people are a mix of rashness and cowardice. They act confident in certain situations but fail to stand firm against truly frightening things. The person who fears too much is a coward because they fear what they shouldn't, or they fear things in the wrong way. All these descriptions apply to the coward, who also lacks confidence. However, the coward's excessive fear is especially noticeable in painful situations. The coward is a despairing person, fearing everything, while the brave person is the opposite. Confidence is a sign of hopefulness. So, the coward, the rash person, and the brave person deal with the same situations, but they react to them differently: the first two overreact or underreact, while the third holds the right balance. Rash people are eager for danger ahead of time, but back out when faced with it. Brave people, on the other hand, are calm beforehand but ready when the time comes for action.

As we have said, courage is about finding the right balance between fear and confidence in the situations we've described. The brave person chooses or endures things because it is noble to do so or because it would be shameful not to. However, dying just to escape poverty, heartache, or any other painful situation is not the act of a brave person. In fact, it's cowardly, because it shows weakness in the face of hardship, and such a person faces death not because it's noble, but just to avoid suffering.

Courage is like this, but the name also applies to five other types of behavior.

First, there is the courage of a citizen-soldier, which is most like true courage. Citizen-soldiers seem to face danger because of the punishments they'd receive by law or the shame they'd face if they didn't, and also because of the honors they gain from acting bravely. This is why the bravest nations are those where cowards are dishonored and the brave are rewarded with respect. This type of courage is what Homer describes in characters like Diomede and Hector:

"First will Polydamas heap disgrace on me," and

"For Hector will speak to the Trojans,

'Tydeides was afraid and fled from my face.'"

This courage is the closest to true courage because it comes from virtue. It is based on feelings of shame, the desire for honor, and avoiding disgrace, which is shameful. We might put in this same category those who are forced by their leaders to fight. They are inferior, though, because they do what they do not out of shame but out of fear, and they are not avoiding disgrace but avoiding pain. They are forced by their rulers, as Hector says:

"But if I spy any coward hanging back from the fight,
That man will have no hope to escape the dogs."

The people who assign these men to their positions and beat them if they retreat do the same thing, as do those who put trenches behind the troops to prevent escape. All of these methods are forms of compulsion. But true bravery comes from acting nobly, not from being forced to act.

The second kind of courage is based on experience in certain situations. This is why Socrates thought that courage was knowledge. Different people show this in different situations, but professional soldiers show it in war. There are often false alarms in battle, and these soldiers are familiar with them, which makes them appear brave. Their experience gives them confidence because they know how to use their weapons well and have the best ones for both attack and defense. Therefore, they fight like armed men against unarmed men or like trained athletes against beginners. In these cases, it isn't the bravest who fight best, but those who are the strongest and in the best condition. However, professional soldiers often turn cowardly when the danger is too great and they are outnumbered or outmatched. They are the first to flee, while citizen-soldiers die where they stand, as happened at the temple of Hermes. For the citizen-soldier, running away is disgraceful, and death is better than living with shame. The professional soldiers, on the other hand, always expected to be the stronger ones, so when they realize they're not, they run away. They fear death more than disgrace, which is not how a brave person behaves.

Third, some people act bravely because of passion. They charge into danger like wild animals attacking those who have wounded them, and this is sometimes mistaken for bravery. Brave people also act with passion because passion drives us to rush into danger. This is why Homer uses phrases like "put strength into his passion" or "aroused their spirit" or "hard he breathed panting" and "his blood boiled." All these expressions suggest the stirring of passion. Brave people, however, act for honor, and passion helps them, but wild animals act out of pain. They attack because they've been hurt or because they are afraid. For example, if they're in the woods, they don't approach anyone. Wild animals are not brave because they rush into danger without thinking of the risks—they act out of pain and passion. If that were bravery, even a donkey would be brave when it's hungry, because no amount of beating can drive it away from food. Lust also drives adulterers to take risks. So, being driven by pain or passion doesn't make someone brave. The kind of bravery that comes from passion seems the most natural, and it would be true bravery if it were combined with choice and a noble goal.

Men, like animals, feel pain when they are angry and feel pleasure when they take revenge. Those who fight for these reasons are aggressive, but not truly brave, because they don't act for honor or according to the rules—they act out of strong emotion. They are somewhat like brave people, but not exactly.

Fourth, optimistic people are not brave either, though they seem confident in danger because they have won many times and defeated many enemies. They are similar to brave people because both feel confident, but brave people are confident for the right reasons, while optimistic people are confident because they think they are the strongest and cannot be hurt. Drunk people also behave this way— they become overly confident. However, when things don't go as they expected, they run away. A truly brave person faces dangers that are real and terrifying because it is noble to do so, and shameful not to. This is why it is considered braver to remain calm and fearless in sudden emergencies rather than in situations that are expected. In unexpected situations, actions come more from a person's character, because there is less time to prepare. Expected actions may be planned and calculated, but sudden actions must come from a person's state of character.

Fifth, people who are unaware of the danger may also appear brave, but they are not far removed from optimistic people, except that they lack the same self-confidence. Optimistic people can hold their ground for a while, but those who realize the danger or suspect that things are different from what they thought, flee, as happened with the Argives when they mistook the Spartans for Sicyonians.

So, we have described the character of truly brave people and those who are only thought to be brave.

Although courage involves feelings of both confidence and fear, it deals more with fear. Someone who remains calm and acts as they should in the face of fear is considered braver than someone who simply feels confident. Bravery is about facing what is painful, and because of this, courage is justly praised. It is harder to face pain than to resist something pleasant.

Even though the goal of courage is something pleasant, it is often hidden by the painful circumstances that come with it. This is similar to athletic competitions. Boxers aim for the pleasant outcome—the victory and honors—but the blows they take along the way are painful and exhausting. Because the pain and effort are great, the pleasant goal seems small and insignificant. In the same way, death and wounds are painful and something the brave person does not want, but they face them because it is noble to do so and shameful not to. The more virtuous and happier a person is, the more painful the thought of death will be because life is most valuable to them, and they know they are losing the greatest goods. This is painful, but it makes them even braver, because they still choose noble deeds in war at this cost. So, not all virtues are pleasant when practiced, except in the sense that they reach their goal. The best soldiers may not always be those with the greatest virtue, but those who have nothing else good in their lives. These people are willing to face danger and even sell their lives for small rewards.

This, then, is a summary of courage. It is not hard to understand its nature, at least in outline, from what has been said.

Now that we've talked about courage, let's discuss temperance, since these seem to be the virtues of the parts of us that aren't controlled by reason. We've said that temperance is about finding balance when it comes to pleasures (it's less concerned with pains and not in the same way), and self-indulgence also deals with the same things. So, let's now figure out what kind of pleasures temperance and self-indulgence are concerned with. We can distinguish between physical pleasures and those of the mind, such as the love of honor or learning. People who love these things enjoy them with their mind, not their body. But those who are focused on these pleasures aren't called temperate or self-indulgent. Similarly, those who enjoy other types of non-physical pleasures, like those who love hearing or telling stories or spend their days on random things, are called gossips, but not self-indulgent. The same goes for people who are upset about losing money or friends—they aren't called self-indulgent either.

Temperance is related to physical pleasures, but not all of them. For example, those who enjoy looking at things like colors, shapes, or paintings aren't called temperate or self-indulgent, even though it's possible to take pleasure in them in the right amount, or too much, or too little.

The same goes for things we hear. No one calls someone self-indulgent for enjoying music or acting too much, and those who enjoy these things appropriately aren't called temperate either.

We also don't use these terms for those who enjoy smells, unless it's in a certain way. For instance, we don't call someone self-indulgent for enjoying the smell of apples, roses, or incense, but we do call them self-indulgent if they enjoy the smell of perfume or rich food. This is because self-indulgent people like these smells since they remind them of the things they crave. You can even see other people, when they're hungry, enjoying the smell of food, but it's the self-indulgent person who loves this kind of thing because it's what they crave.

There aren't any animals other than humans who enjoy these kinds of senses, except accidentally. For example, dogs don't enjoy the smell of a hare, but they enjoy eating it, and the smell just tells them the hare is nearby. Similarly, a lion doesn't enjoy the sound of an ox, but enjoys eating it; the ox's sound just tells the lion the ox is near, which makes it seem like the lion enjoys the sound. And it's the same when the lion sees a stag or goat—it's not the sight that pleases the lion, but the meal that's coming.

Temperance and self-indulgence, however, are concerned with the kinds of pleasures that humans share with other animals, which seem more basic and animal-like. These are the pleasures of touch and taste. But even taste doesn't play a big role here, since taste is about recognizing flavors, which is what wine tasters or chefs do. Self-indulgent people don't enjoy making these distinctions; they enjoy the physical pleasure, which always comes through touch—whether with food, drink, or sexual contact. This is why a certain glutton once wished his throat were as long as a crane's, because he wanted to enjoy the contact for longer. So, the sense most connected to self-indulgence is the sense of touch, which is the most common of all the senses. Self-indulgence is rightly criticized because it connects us more to our animal side than to our human side. To love these kinds of pleasures more than anything else is animal-like. Even of the pleasures of touch, the most acceptable ones have been eliminated, like the pleasure that comes from rubbing in the gym or the heat that results from it. The kind of touch a self-indulgent person enjoys doesn't affect their whole body, just certain parts.

Some desires seem to be natural to everyone, while others are unique to individuals and are learned. For example, the desire for food is natural, because anyone who is hungry craves food, and the same goes for drink, and for love, especially if someone is young and strong, as Homer says. But not everyone craves the same type of food or love, and that's what makes personal desires seem more individual. However, these personal desires still have a natural element, because different things are more pleasing to different types of people, and some things are more pleasing to everyone than others.

With natural desires, most people make mistakes in only one way—by going too far. To eat or drink more than necessary until you're overfull is to go beyond what your body naturally needs, since natural desire is about filling a lack. People who do this are called gluttons, which suggests they fill their stomachs beyond what is right. It's people with a very servile character who behave this way. But with personal desires, people make many mistakes in many different ways. For example, someone who is "fond of something" might like it too much, or like something they shouldn't, or like it more than most people do. Self-indulgent people go wrong in all these ways. They either enjoy things they shouldn't because they're harmful, or they enjoy the right things but do so more than they should or more than most people.

Clearly, then, overindulgence with pleasure is self-indulgence and is wrong. But with pain, it's not like courage where you're praised for facing it or blamed for avoiding it. The self-indulgent person is called that because they are more upset than they should be when they don't get something pleasant, even though their upset is caused by the pleasure they crave. The temperate person, on the other hand, is praised for not being upset when something pleasant is absent or when they have to avoid it.

The self-indulgent person craves all pleasant things or at least the most pleasant ones, and they are led by their desires, even if it means sacrificing everything else. That's why they are upset both when they don't get what they want and even while they're still craving it (because desire itself involves pain). But it seems ridiculous to be upset in the pursuit of pleasure. People who don't enjoy pleasure as much as they should are rare, because that level of insensitivity is not human. Even other animals can tell the difference between different kinds of food and enjoy some more than others. If there were someone who found no pleasure in anything, they would be something very different from a human. This type of person doesn't have a name because they almost never exist.

The temperate person, however, takes a balanced approach to these things. They don't enjoy the things the self-indulgent person does, or if they do, they enjoy them less. They also don't crave what they shouldn't, or if they do, they don't crave it too much or feel pain when it's absent, or they do so only to a small degree and at the right times. Instead, they enjoy the things that bring health or good condition, and they do so in moderation. They may enjoy other pleasant things as well, but only if they don't interfere with health or nobility or go beyond what they can afford. A person who ignores these limits loves pleasure more than it's worth. The temperate person, however, is the kind of person who follows the right rules.

Self-indulgence is more voluntary than cowardice because it's driven by pleasure, while cowardice is driven by pain. Pleasure is something we choose, and pain is something we avoid. Pain messes with the person who feels it, while pleasure doesn't. That's why self-indulgence is more voluntary and also more blameworthy. It's easier to get used to the things that lead to self-indulgence because there are many of them in life, and getting used to them doesn't involve any danger. But the opposite is true for terrifying things.

Cowardice seems voluntary in some ways but not others. Cowardice itself is painless, but in specific situations, pain causes us to act, such as when we throw down our weapons or disgrace ourselves in other ways. In these cases, it seems like our actions are done under pressure. But for the self-indulgent person, specific acts are voluntary because they act out of desire, even though the overall state of being self-indulgent is less voluntary. No one desires to be self-indulgent.

The term self-indulgence is also used for childish faults because these resemble the things we've been discussing. It doesn't matter which one was named after the other for our purposes—the point is that childish faults are called after self-indulgence. This comparison isn't a bad one because the desire for what is base and which grows quickly should be kept in check. This is especially true for appetite and children, since children live by their appetites and have the strongest desires for pleasure. If this part of ourselves is not controlled by reason, it can go too far. In an irrational being, the desire for pleasure is never satisfied, even if it tries every source of gratification, and the more it indulges its appetite, the stronger the desire grows. If these appetites are powerful, they can even drive out reason. That's why they should be limited and few, and they should not conflict with reason—this is what we call a controlled state. Just as a child should follow the guidance of a tutor, our appetites should follow reason. In a temperate person, the appetites should align with reason, because both aim at what is noble. The temperate person desires the right things, in the right way, and at the right time. This is what reason tells us to do.

And this concludes our discussion of temperance.

Book 4

Let's now talk about liberality. It seems to be the balance when it comes to wealth. A liberal person is praised not for their skills in war, or for being moderate, or for making legal decisions, but for how they give and receive wealth, especially for how they give it. By "wealth," we mean anything that is valued by money. Prodigality and stinginess are extremes related to wealth. We call someone stingy when they care too much about money, but sometimes we use the word "prodigal" in a more complicated way. We call people prodigal when they lack self-control and spend money on things that are indulgent. That's why these people are considered to have poor character, as they show more than one vice. So, this is not the proper way to use the word "prodigal." A prodigal person has one bad trait: wasting their wealth. A prodigal person is ruining themselves, and since life depends on having some wealth, wasting it is like ruining your own life.

This is how we'll understand the word "prodigality" here. Now, anything that can be used can either be used well or poorly, and wealth is something useful. Anything useful is best used by someone who has the virtue related to it. So, wealth will be best used by someone who has the virtue related to wealth—this is the liberal person. Spending and giving seem to be how wealth is used, while taking and keeping it are about possession. So, it's more important for a liberal person to give to the right people than to take from the right sources, or to avoid taking from the wrong ones. Doing good is more virtuous than receiving good, and doing what's noble is better than not doing something shameful. Giving is clearly a way of doing good and acting nobly, while taking is more about receiving good or avoiding shameful behavior. We feel grateful toward someone who gives, not to someone who simply doesn't take, and we praise givers more. It's also easier not to take than to give, as people are more likely to give too little of what's theirs than to take from others. Givers are called liberal, but those who don't take aren't praised for being liberal—they're praised for being just. Those who take aren't really praised at all. Liberality is one of the most loved virtues because liberal people are generous, and their generosity is helpful, depending on their giving.

Virtuous actions are noble and done for the sake of nobility. The liberal person, like all virtuous people, will give for the sake of nobility and will do it rightly. They will give to the right people, the right amounts, at the right time, and in the right way. They will also do it with pleasure, or at least without pain, since virtuous acts are either pleasant or not painful. A person who gives to the wrong people, or not for the sake of nobility but for some other reason, is not considered liberal. And someone who gives with pain is not liberal either because they value their wealth more than the noble act, and this isn't typical of a liberal person.

A truly liberal person also won't take from wrong sources, as this doesn't fit with someone who doesn't care too much about wealth. They also won't be eager to ask for things because it's not typical of someone who gives to others to want benefits for themselves. They will, however, take from the right sources, like their own wealth, not because it's noble but out of necessity—so they can continue to give. They won't neglect their own property, as they use it to help others. They won't give to just anyone, but will give to the right people at the right time, when it is noble to do so. It's very typical of a liberal person to give too much, leaving little for themselves. This is because a liberal person doesn't focus on their own needs. The term "liberality" relates to a person's resources. Being liberal isn't about the number of gifts but about the character of the giver, and this depends on how much wealth they have. So, someone who gives less can still be more liberal if they have less to give.

People who inherited their wealth, rather than earning it, are often thought to be more liberal. First, because they've never experienced a lack of resources, and second, because people tend to value what they've created themselves, just like parents love their children. A liberal person usually doesn't become wealthy because they're not focused on taking or keeping wealth but on giving it away. They don't value wealth for its own sake but as a way to give. This leads to the common complaint that the people who deserve wealth the most often have the least of it. But it's not surprising because wealth, like anything else, can't be had without effort. Even so, a liberal person won't give to the wrong people or at the wrong time, because that wouldn't be true liberality. If they spent money on the wrong things, they wouldn't have anything left for the right causes.

As we've said, a liberal person spends according to their means and on the right things. A person who goes beyond this is called prodigal. We don't call rulers prodigal because it's hard for them to spend more than they have. Liberality is a balance in giving and receiving wealth. A liberal person will give and spend the right amount, on the right things, whether big or small, and do so with pleasure. They will also take the right amounts from the right sources. Since virtue is a balance between both, the liberal person will do both as they should. Proper giving and taking go hand in hand, while improper giving and taking don't happen together. If a liberal person ends up spending in a way that isn't right or noble, they will feel some pain, but only a little, and as they should. Virtue involves feeling both pleasure and pain at the right things and in the right way.

A liberal person is easy to deal with in money matters because they don't care too much about money. They get more upset if they haven't spent on something they should have, rather than feeling bad about spending on something they shouldn't have. They don't agree with the saying of Simonides.

A prodigal person also makes mistakes here because they aren't pleased or upset by the right things or in the right way. This will become clearer as we continue. Prodigality and stinginess are extremes when it comes to giving and taking. Prodigality goes too far in giving and doesn't take enough, while stinginess falls short in giving and takes too much, except in small things.

The traits of prodigality don't often go together because it's hard to keep giving if you're not taking. Private individuals quickly run out of money if they keep giving, and these are the people we usually call prodigal. Still, a person like this seems much better than a stingy person. Prodigality can be cured with age or poverty, and this can help the person move toward a middle state. Prodigal people have some traits of a liberal person because they give and don't take, even though they don't do these things well. If they learned to do these things properly, they could become liberal because they would then give to the right people and avoid taking from the wrong sources. This is why prodigals are thought to have a less bad character—it's not evil to give too much and take too little, but it is foolish. A person like this is considered much better than a stingy person because they benefit others, while a stingy person benefits no one, not even themselves.

Most prodigals, however, do take from the wrong sources, and in this way, they're similar to stingy people. They take because they want to keep spending, but their resources run out quickly, so they're forced to find money from other places. Since they don't care about honor, they take from any source, however wrong. Their giving isn't liberal because it's not noble, and it's not done properly. Sometimes they give to the wrong people, like flatterers, and neglect those with good character. Because of this, most prodigals are also self-indulgent, spending their money on pleasures instead of living for what's noble.

The prodigal person, if left unchecked, will continue this way. But with guidance, they can become more balanced. Meanness, on the other hand, is harder to cure. Old age and hardship tend to make people stingy. Most people are more interested in gaining money than giving it. Stinginess comes in many forms and seems to cover many different behaviors.

It has two parts: not giving enough and taking too much. Not all stingy people are the same, though. Some people take too much, while others don't give enough. People we call "miserly" or "stingy" don't give much but don't covet other people's property either. Some of these people hoard money to avoid doing anything shameful in the future. Others avoid taking from others because they know that if they do, others will take from them. So, they prefer to neither give nor take.

There are others who take from any source, like people in shady businesses, pimps, or moneylenders who charge high interest. These people take more than they should and from the wrong places. Their love of gain is their main fault. They'll accept a bad reputation if it means they can make money, even if it's just a little. People who make big gains from wrong sources, like tyrants who rob cities or temples, aren't called stingy—they're called wicked or unjust. But gamblers and thieves are considered stingy because they love gain and endure shame for the sake of money. They're both willing to take from wrong sources, making them greedy.

Meanness is considered the opposite of liberality. It's worse than prodigality, and people are more likely to be stingy than prodigal.

This covers liberality and its opposing vices.

It seems fitting to discuss magnificence next. This also deals with wealth, but it's different from liberality. It doesn't cover all uses of wealth but focuses on spending large amounts. As the name suggests, magnificence involves spending on a grand scale. However, the scale depends on the situation. For example, outfitting a ship is not the same as leading a sacred procession. Magnificence is about spending appropriately for the person and the occasion. A person who spends properly on small or moderate things isn't called magnificent, but the person who spends properly on big things is. A magnificent person is liberal, but a liberal person isn't necessarily magnificent. The lack of magnificence is called stinginess, while the excess is called vulgarity or bad taste. These vices don't involve spending too much on the right things but spending extravagantly on the wrong things. We'll discuss these vices more later.

A magnificent person is like an artist who knows how to spend large amounts in a tasteful way. As we said earlier, a person's character is shown by their actions and their goals. The magnificent person spends large amounts appropriately, and the result is fitting. The result should match the expense, or even surpass it. The magnificent person spends for honor's sake, which is true of all virtues. They will do so gladly and generously because careful calculation is a sign of stinginess. They'll focus on making the result as beautiful as possible, rather than on how cheaply it can be done. The magnificent person must also be liberal. A liberal person spends what they should, but a magnificent person does this on a grander scale, creating something even more impressive. Possessions and works of art aren't valuable in the same way. A possession's value is based on its cost, while a work of art's value comes from its beauty and greatness. Magnificence applies to spending on important and honorable things, like offerings to the gods, temples, or public projects. Magnificent people spend their money to support the city or the people, not for themselves.

A magnificent person will also make their house reflect their wealth because even a house is a public symbol. They prefer to spend on things that last because those are the most beautiful. They spend appropriately on everything. What's right for gods is not the same as what's right for humans, and what's right in a temple is different from what's right in a tomb. Each expenditure has its own greatness. What's most magnificent is spending a large amount on something great, but what's magnificent in one case may be small in another. The magnificent person makes sure everything they create matches the size of the expense.

The person who goes too far and is vulgar spends too much on the wrong things, showing bad taste. They might host a dinner party on the scale of a wedding banquet or use purple robes for a comedy, like they do in Megara. They do these things not for honor but to show off their wealth, thinking they'll be admired. Where they should spend a lot, they spend too little, and where they should spend a little, they spend too much. The stingy person, on the other hand, spends too little on everything. After spending a lot, they'll ruin the result by skimping on a small detail. They always try to spend as little as possible and regret even that.

Both vulgarity and stinginess are vices, but they don't bring as much disgrace because they aren't harmful to others or very shameful.

The goods that come from fortune, such as wealth and power, are also thought to add to a sense of pride. People who are well-born, wealthy, or powerful are considered worthy of honor because they are in a better position than others. When someone has something good that sets them apart, they are usually honored more. This is why people with these advantages tend to be prouder since others honor them for these things. However, in reality, only a truly good person deserves honor. A person who has both virtue and good fortune is seen as even more deserving of honor. But those who have wealth and power without virtue have no right to make great claims or to be called "proud" because true pride requires perfect virtue.

People without virtue often become disdainful and arrogant when they have good fortune. Without virtue, it's hard to handle the advantages of fortune with grace. They look down on others because they think they are better, and they act however they please. These people try to imitate a proud person, but they don't really understand what true pride is. The proud person looks down on others in a just way because they know their true worth, while most people look down on others for no good reason.

A proud person does not rush into small or trivial dangers, nor do they enjoy danger for its own sake, because they value only a few things. But they will face great dangers, and when they do, they won't hesitate to risk their life, knowing that sometimes life isn't worth living under certain conditions. A proud person is the kind who gives help to others but is ashamed of receiving help, because giving is a sign of superiority, while receiving is a sign of inferiority. When they do receive help, they tend to return the favor with even greater kindness, making the original giver feel indebted to them, which allows the proud person to stay in control of the relationship. They also tend to remember the help they have given but not the help they've received because the giver is superior, and the proud person always wants to be in a superior position. This is why Thetis didn't remind Zeus of the help she gave him, and why the Spartans didn't talk about how they helped the Athenians but focused on what they had received.

A proud person also doesn't ask for much from others, if anything, but is quick to give help when needed. They act with dignity toward people who are in high positions or who are fortunate, but they are humble toward people of the middle class. It's difficult to be superior to those in high positions, but easy to be above those in lower positions, and it isn't seen as rude to act superior to the powerful, but it would be rude to act that way toward the weak. A proud person doesn't aim for the things that others value or excel in, and they are often slow to act unless something great and honorable is at stake. They don't do many things, but the things they do are great and worthy of note.

A proud person must also be open about their feelings, whether love or hate. Hiding one's feelings or caring more about what others think than about the truth is seen as cowardly. A proud person speaks and acts openly because they are confident and don't need to hide anything. They tell the truth unless they are using irony to mock those who are beneath them. A proud person won't revolve their life around someone else unless that person is a friend because that would be like being a servant. For this reason, flatterers are seen as having no self-respect, and people who lack self-respect often become flatterers.

A proud person isn't easily impressed because nothing seems great to them. They don't hold onto grudges because that's not what proud people do—they overlook wrongs. They don't gossip, either about themselves or about others, because they don't care to be praised, nor do they care to blame others. Similarly, they aren't in the habit of praising others and don't speak ill of their enemies unless out of a sense of superiority.

When it comes to small or necessary matters, a proud person doesn't complain or beg for favors. This is because they don't take such things too seriously. A proud person would rather have beautiful but useless things than useful and profitable ones because this better fits their self-sufficient character.

A slow and deliberate step, a deep voice, and calm speech are all seen as traits of a proud person. Someone who takes few things seriously won't be in a hurry, and someone who thinks nothing is great won't get easily excited. A shrill voice and fast movements come from being in a rush or getting excited.

This, then, is the proud person. The person who falls short of this is overly humble, and the person who goes too far is vain. However, neither of these types of people is considered bad, just mistaken. An overly humble person denies themselves what they deserve, even if they are worthy of good things, and this shows a lack of self-awareness. If they knew their worth, they would seek out the things they are worthy of since these things are good. These people aren't thought to be foolish but rather too shy. However, this attitude can make them worse because people usually aim for what matches their worth, and these overly humble people avoid noble actions and even good things because they feel unworthy.

On the other hand, vain people are foolish because they don't know themselves. They attempt to do honorable things they aren't capable of, and then they fail. They also like to show off with fancy clothes and outward displays, and they talk about their good fortune as if that will make them more honorable. However, being overly humble is more opposed to pride than vanity because it's both more common and worse.

Pride, then, is concerned with great honor, as we've said. There seems to be another virtue related to honor that is like generosity compared to magnificence. Neither deals with the grand scale, but both guide us to act rightly in smaller matters. Just as there is a balance in giving and receiving wealth, there is a balance in seeking honor. Some people want honor too much or from the wrong sources, while others don't seek honor even for noble reasons. Sometimes we praise the ambitious person as someone who loves what is noble, and other times we praise the unambitious person for being moderate and self-controlled.

It's clear that there is more than one way to be "fond of" honor. When we praise ambition, we are thinking of someone who loves honor more than most people, and when we blame it, we are thinking of someone who loves it too much. Since the balance here doesn't have a name, it seems like the extremes compete to take its place. However, just as people can desire more honor than they should or less than they should, it's also possible to desire the right amount, and this state of character is praised. This balanced state doesn't have a name, but it is still virtuous. It seems unambitious compared to ambition and ambitious compared to being unambitious. This is true of other virtues as well.

Good temper is a balance when it comes to anger. The middle state doesn't have a name, and the extremes don't have clear names either, but we place good temper in the middle, although it leans toward the side of not being angry enough. The excess of anger might be called "irascibility" because the emotion involved is anger, but there are many causes for anger.

A person who gets angry at the right things, with the right people, in the right way, at the right time, and for the right length of time is praised. This is the good-tempered person because good temper is praised. A good-tempered person is calm and doesn't act on their emotions. They get angry only as the situation requires, but they tend to lean more toward being too calm than being too angry. A good-tempered person is not vengeful and tends to be forgiving.

On the other hand, those who don't get angry when they should are blamed. People who don't get angry in the right way or with the right people at the right time are seen as foolish because it seems like they don't care or don't feel pain when they are wronged. Since they don't get angry, they are also seen as unlikely to defend themselves. People who endure insults or allow their friends to be insulted are seen as weak.

The excess of anger can show up in many ways. A person might get angry with the wrong people, at the wrong things, too often, too quickly, or for too long. Not all of these traits show up in the same person because too much anger can destroy itself. Quick-tempered people tend to get angry too fast and with the wrong people or for the wrong reasons, but their anger doesn't last long, which is their best trait. They don't hold back their anger, so they express it quickly and then it's over.

People who are choleric, or quick to anger, get angry at everything and everyone, earning their name. Sulky people are harder to calm down and hold onto their anger for a long time. They don't express their anger right away, so it builds up inside them, and they won't feel better until they get revenge. If they don't, they carry the anger with them because no one knows they are upset, and that takes time to process. These people are difficult for both themselves and their close friends to be around. We call people bad-tempered if they are angry at the wrong things, too much, and for too long, and if they can't be calmed down until they have punished someone.

Good temper is more opposed to the excess of anger than to the lack of it because excessive anger is more common (since revenge is more natural to humans), and bad-tempered people are harder to live with.

It's clear from what we've already said that it's not easy to define exactly how much anger is appropriate, with whom, about what, or for how long. It's hard to say at what point right action becomes wrong. We don't blame someone who strays only a little, either toward too much anger or too little. Sometimes we praise people who seem too calm, calling them good-tempered, and sometimes we praise people who seem too angry, calling them strong and capable of leadership. It's hard to say exactly how far someone can go before they are blamed, and this depends on the situation and requires good judgment. However, it's clear that the middle state is praiseworthy—being angry in the right way, at the right time, with the right people. The extremes are blameworthy, either a little or a lot, depending on how far someone goes. Clearly, the middle state is best.

In social life, some people are seen as too eager to please. These people always agree with others and never cause conflict because they think it's their job to avoid upsetting anyone. On the other hand, people who argue about everything and don't care if they upset others are seen as rude and argumentative. It's clear that both of these extremes are wrong, and the balanced approach is better—where someone is pleasant and helpful, but also stands up for what is right. This middle state doesn't have a name, but it is similar to friendship. The person who holds this middle position is like a good friend, but without the emotional attachment of friendship. This person acts rightly not because they love or hate anyone, but because they are a good person. They act the same way toward both close friends and strangers, though they adjust their behavior to fit each relationship. They don't treat everyone the same but respond to each person appropriately, based on what's right.

This person tries to bring pleasure to others and avoid causing pain when it's honorable and good to do so. But if their actions would bring dishonor or harm to someone, they will choose to cause a little pain instead of agreeing with something wrong. This person will act differently toward those in higher positions and those in lower ones, and they will adjust their behavior depending on the situation.

This balanced person doesn't have a name, but people who are too eager to please are called "obsequious," and those who do it for personal gain, like money, are called "flatterers." People who argue all the time are called "contentious" or "churlish." These extremes seem to be opposites, and the middle state is without a name.

There's also a balance when it comes to boasting. The person who tells the truth about themselves without exaggeration or understatement is in the middle. The boaster, however, claims to have qualities they don't really have or exaggerates what they do have. On the other hand, the overly modest person downplays their qualities or denies them. Both of these extremes are wrong, but the person who tells the truth about themselves is praiseworthy.

Each person acts and speaks according to their character. A truthful person speaks and lives in a straightforward way because of their character, not for some other purpose. Lying is generally seen as bad, and truth is seen as good. Therefore, the truthful person is praised, while both the boaster and the overly modest person are criticized, though the boaster is usually seen as worse.

Now, let's discuss the boaster first. We aren't talking about someone who breaks promises or lies in serious matters—that falls under justice. We're talking about someone who is truthful in everyday life because of their character. This kind of person is seen as fair because they value the truth, and if they avoid lying even when nothing important is at stake, they are likely to be truthful when something important is on the line.

A boaster is seen as someone who claims more than they have, especially when they do it to gain something. The boaster who seeks fame or honor is less blameworthy than the one who does it for money, but both are wrong. A boaster who exaggerates their skills for money, like pretending to be a doctor or fortune-teller, is more blameworthy because they are lying for personal gain.

On the other hand, someone who is overly modest and downplays their good qualities is seen as more likable. This person isn't lying for personal gain but is avoiding showing off. However, if someone downplays their qualities too much, especially things that are obvious, they are seen as deceitful, and this can be a form of boastfulness in disguise.

The person who finds the middle ground—neither exaggerating nor downplaying their qualities—is the one who deserves praise. Both the boaster and the overly modest person are wrong, but the boaster is the worse of the two.

In life, there is also a balance between seriousness and playfulness. Some people are too serious, while others are too eager to joke around. A person who jokes too much and doesn't care if they hurt others is seen as vulgar, while someone who can't take a joke or make one is seen as rude or unapproachable. The person who finds the middle ground is considered witty because they know how to say the right thing at the right time, and their humor is appropriate for the situation.

A well-bred person's jokes are different from those of a vulgar person. You can see this difference in old and new comedies. The old comedies often focused on indecency, while the newer ones rely more on clever humor. This shows the difference between good taste and poor taste.

The person who jokes well does so in a way that is fitting for a well-bred person. They don't seek to hurt others with their humor, and their jokes are enjoyable for the listener. This person will also only make jokes that are appropriate and avoid ones that are mean-spirited.

The person who finds the right balance in humor is praiseworthy. The person who jokes too much and in bad taste is like a buffoon, while the person who can't take a joke is no fun to be around. Relaxation and amusement are important parts of life, but they need to be done in the right way.

So, these middle states in life are three in number, all dealing with how we interact with others in words and actions. They differ in that one is about truth, while the other two are about being pleasant.

Shame, however, is not a virtue. It's more like a feeling than a state of character. Shame is a kind of fear of dishonor, like how people feel fear in the face of danger. For example, people blush when they feel ashamed, just like they turn pale when they are afraid. Both are physical reactions, and this is more characteristic of a feeling than a character trait.

Shame is more appropriate for young people because they live more by their feelings and are more likely to make mistakes. Young people who feel shame are praised because it shows they care about their mistakes. However, we wouldn't praise an older person for feeling shame because we expect them to avoid actions that would make them feel ashamed. A good person doesn't need to feel shame because they don't do bad things, and shame is only felt when someone does something wrong. Feeling ashamed of bad actions doesn't make you a good person. It's better to avoid bad actions altogether.

So, while shame might be a good thing in certain situations, it's not the same as a virtue. A good person won't do anything shameful, so they don't need to feel shame. We'll talk more about continence and other related states later, but for now, let's move on to justice.

Book 5

When talking about justice and injustice, we need to (1) look at what actions they focus on, (2) figure out what kind of balance justice is, and (3) understand what extremes justice lies between. We will follow the same path as we did in previous discussions.

We know that everyone sees justice as a way of thinking that makes people want to do the right thing and act fairly. They also see injustice as a way of thinking that makes people act unfairly and desire what's unfair. Let's start with that. This is different from how we view science and skills. A science or skill can relate to opposite things, but a state of character only leads to one type of result. For example, being healthy means we only do things that are good for our health, like walking in a healthy way.

Often, we understand one thing by comparing it to its opposite, or by looking at the people who show these qualities. For example, (A) if we know what good health is, we can also understand bad health. (B) We know good health from those who are healthy, and vice versa. If good health means firm flesh, then bad health would mean flabby flesh, and something that creates firmness would be considered healthy. If one opposite is unclear, the other usually is too. For example, if the word "just" is unclear, "unjust" will be too.

The terms "justice" and "injustice" can have more than one meaning, but because the meanings are so close, we often don't notice. This is different from words with very different meanings, like how "kleis" can mean a collarbone or the tool to lock a door. Let's look at the different meanings of "an unjust person." We call both the lawbreaker and the greedy, unfair person unjust, so it's clear that both law-abiding and fair people are just. So, the just person is both law-abiding and fair, while the unjust person is both lawless and unfair.

Since the unjust person is greedy, they focus on certain goods—not all goods, but those that affect success or failure. These are always good in general, but they're not always good for a specific person. People often pray for and chase these things, but they should really pray that these things are good for them, and they should choose what is good for them specifically. The unjust person doesn't always choose the bigger thing, but sometimes they choose the smaller, especially when it's something bad. Since the smaller evil is still considered somewhat good, and greed focuses on the good, the unjust person is seen as greedy. They are also unfair, which is true in both cases.

Since the lawbreaker is unjust and the law-abiding person is just, all lawful actions are, in a way, just actions. The laws, set up by legislators, are considered lawful, and we say each of these actions is just. The laws are meant to benefit everyone or the best people or those in power, depending on the case. So, in one sense, we call those actions just that help create and maintain happiness and its parts for the whole community. The law tells us to act bravely, like not running away from danger or giving up our weapons. It also tells us to act with self-control, like not committing adultery or giving in to every desire, and to be good-tempered, like not hitting others or speaking badly of them. The law does this for other virtues and vices too, commanding some actions and forbidding others. A well-made law does this well, while a hastily made law does it less effectively. So, this kind of justice is complete virtue, but not in every sense—only when it comes to how we treat others. That's why justice is often seen as the greatest virtue, and there's a saying that "justice holds all virtues." It's considered complete virtue because it involves practicing all virtues, and it's complete because the person who has it uses it both for themselves and in their interactions with others. Many people can be virtuous in their own lives but not with others. This is why people say, "power reveals the person," because a ruler has to deal with others and be part of a community.

This is also why justice is called "another's good," since it's about treating others well. The worst person is someone who acts badly toward both themselves and their friends, while the best person isn't the one who's only good to themselves, but the one who's good to others. This is harder to do. Justice, in this sense, isn't just part of virtue—it's the whole of virtue, and the same goes for injustice. The difference between virtue and justice is clear from what we've said. They are the same, but their essence isn't the same. Justice is about how we treat others, while virtue is about the kind of person we are.

What we are studying now is justice as a part of virtue because we believe there is a kind of justice like that. The same goes for injustice in the particular way we're looking at it.

There is this kind of justice, and we can see it when we notice that someone can do wrong without being greedy, like throwing away their shield out of cowardice or speaking harshly out of anger. But when someone acts greedily, they are unjust, even if they don't show these other vices. So, there's another kind of injustice that's just part of the wider idea of injustice, which means "against the law." For example, if someone commits adultery for money and gains from it, they are unjust. But if someone does it because of their desires and loses money or gets punished, they are more self-indulgent than unjust. The person who profits from it is unjust but not self-indulgent, showing that greed is linked to injustice.

All other unjust acts are connected to some other vice. Adultery is linked to self-indulgence, leaving a comrade in battle is tied to cowardice, and hitting someone is linked to anger. But when someone gains from their actions, it's not connected to any specific vice except injustice. So, there's another, specific type of injustice, which is part of the broader kind because it shares the same basic idea. Both forms of injustice relate to others, but the specific one is about honor, money, safety, or all three, driven by the pleasure of gaining something. The general kind of justice involves all the things that matter to a good person.

It's clear, then, that there are different kinds of justice, and that one is separate from full virtue. We need to understand its type and differences.

We divided injustice into lawbreaking and unfairness, and justice into law-abiding and fairness. Lawbreaking connects to the broader sense of injustice, but unfairness is different from lawbreaking, like a part is different from the whole. All unfair acts are lawbreaking, but not all lawbreaking acts are unfair. So, injustice in the sense of unfairness is just a part of the wider idea of injustice, and the same goes for justice. This is why we need to talk about specific justice and injustice.

The kind of justice that covers all virtues and the injustice that covers all vices toward others can be set aside for now. We already know how "just" and "unjust" are used in this broad sense. Most of the laws focus on what's virtuous overall. The law tells us to practice every virtue and avoid every vice. Laws that aim to create virtue overall are those made for the common good. But when it comes to making an individual a good person in general, we need to figure out whether that's the role of politics or something else. It may not be the same thing to be a good person and a good citizen in every state.

When it comes to specific justice and what's just in this sense, (A) one type is about dividing things like honor, money, or anything else that people share in a society, where people can get either equal or unequal parts. (B) The other type deals with making things right between people in transactions. These can be divided into two groups: (1) some transactions are voluntary, like buying, selling, lending, and renting, which are voluntary because they start by choice, and (2) some are involuntary, like theft, adultery, poisoning, bribery, and murder. These can be either done in secret or violently, like physical assault or robbery.

(A) We've shown that both unjust people and unjust actions are unfair or unequal. So, it's clear that there's something in between these two extremes, and that's what's equal. In any case where there's a more and a less, there's also something that's equal. If injustice is inequality, then justice is equality, as people generally think. Since equality is in the middle, justice must also be in the middle. Equality means at least two things are being compared, so justice is both about balance and being equal for certain people. Equality is in the middle of greater and less, and it involves two people and the things being compared. If the people are unequal, they won't receive equal shares, and this is what causes conflicts. People argue when equals get unequal shares, or unequals get equal shares. This is clear because rewards should be given based on merit. Everyone agrees that justice in distribution must be based on some type of merit, though people don't all agree on what kind. Democrats say merit is based on being free, oligarchs say it's based on wealth or noble birth, and aristocrats say it's based on excellence.

So, justice is a kind of proportional equality, and proportion applies not just to numbers but to relationships between things. Proportion means the ratios are equal, and it always involves at least four terms. Continuous proportions can involve repeating terms, like saying, "as line A is to line B, so is line B to line C." Here, B is mentioned twice, so there are still four terms. Justice involves at least four terms, where the ratio between one pair is the same as the ratio between the other. As A is to B, so C is to D, and similarly, as A is to C, B is to D. So, the whole is in the same ratio to the whole. This kind of proportion makes distribution fair, and when terms are matched this way, justice is achieved. This fairness is the balance between the extremes, and injustice violates this balance. Mathematicians call this kind of proportion "geometrical" because it keeps the same ratio between parts and the whole.

So, what's just is proportional, and what's unjust breaks that proportion. When someone acts unjustly, they get too much, and the person treated unjustly gets too little of what's good. In the case of bad things, the reverse is true. The person with the lesser evil is considered to have more good because the lesser evil is better to choose than the greater one, and what's worth choosing is good. Therefore, the lesser evil is considered a greater good.

This, then, is one type of justice.

The other type is about correcting wrongs in both voluntary and involuntary dealings between people. This form of justice is different from the kind that deals with sharing common goods. The justice that deals with sharing is always based on a certain proportion (for example, in dividing up the money of a business partnership, it will be based on the amount each partner contributed). The injustice here happens when someone breaks this proportion. But justice in dealings between people is about equality, and injustice is about inequality—not in the same proportion as before, but in equal parts. It doesn't matter if a good person cheats a bad person, or a bad person cheats a good person, or if a good or bad person commits adultery. The law only looks at the wrong that was done and treats both people as equal—if one person is wrong and the other was wronged, if one person caused harm and the other received it. Since this type of injustice creates inequality, the judge's job is to restore equality. For example, if one person was wounded and the other did the wounding, or one person was killed and the other did the killing, the harm and the act are unequal. The judge's role is to equalize this by giving a penalty, taking away from what the wrongdoer gained. Even if the wrongdoer didn't gain in every situation (like wounding someone), we still call the harm "gain" for the wrongdoer and "loss" for the victim. After the judge determines the extent of the harm, one person is seen as having lost, and the other as having gained. Therefore, justice is the middle ground between gain and loss, and justice will correct things so that both sides are equal.

This is why, when people argue, they go to a judge. To go to the judge is to seek justice because a judge is like a living form of justice. People seek the judge as a neutral party, and in some places, they even call judges mediators because they believe that if they get a fair middle ground, they will get justice. So, justice is a middle point, and since the judge aims for fairness, justice is also a middle point. The judge tries to restore equality, like dividing a line into two unequal parts and taking from the longer part to make both sides equal. When the whole is divided equally, then people say they have what is rightfully theirs. The equal part is the middle point between the larger and smaller parts, according to simple mathematical equality.

This is also why justice is called "sikaion" because it means splitting something into two equal parts. It's similar to calling a judge "sikastes," which means a divider or equalizer. When you take something from one equal part and add it to the other, one part ends up being greater than the other by two units; if nothing had been added to the larger part, it would only be bigger by one unit. So, one part exceeds the middle by one unit, and the middle exceeds the smaller part by one unit. This helps us understand how much we must take from the bigger part and how much we must add to the smaller part. We need to add to the smaller part what the middle exceeds it by, and take from the larger part what exceeds the middle.

Let's say the lines AA', BB', and CC' are equal. If we take a segment AE from line AA' and add a segment Cd to line CC', the whole line DCC' will exceed the line EA' by the segments CD and CF, and therefore it also exceeds the line Bb' by the segment CD. (See diagram.)

The terms "loss" and "gain" come from voluntary exchanges, like buying and selling. To have more than your share is called gaining, and to have less is called losing. When people get neither more nor less than their fair share, they say they have what's rightfully theirs, and that they neither lose nor gain.

Justice, then, is the middle point between gaining and losing, specifically in cases that aren't voluntary. Justice is about having the same amount before and after the event.

Some people think that equality in return, or reciprocity, is always just, like the Pythagoreans believed. They defined justice as reciprocity. But reciprocity doesn't always fit either distributive or corrective justice—though people think Rhadamanthus' justice was based on this idea:

"If someone suffers what they caused, justice is done."

However, reciprocity and corrective justice don't always align. For example, (1) if an official has wounded someone, they shouldn't be wounded in return, and if someone wounds an official, they should be punished more than just being wounded. Also, (2) there's a big difference between acts done on purpose and acts done by accident. But in business, reciprocity works—people exchange fairly based on what's agreed. This proportional exchange keeps society together. People try to give back either good for good or bad for bad. If they can't do this, they feel powerless, like slaves. If they can't return good for good, no exchange happens, and without exchange, society can't function. This is why the temple of the Graces is important—it encourages people to give back favors. Grace means helping someone who helped you, and sometimes taking the lead in showing kindness first.

Fair exchange is based on proportion. Let's say A is a builder, B is a shoemaker, C is a house, and D is a shoe. The builder should receive shoes from the shoemaker and give the shoemaker a house in return. First, there must be proportional equality in what's being exchanged, and then the trade happens. If the work of one person is better than the other, the trade isn't equal, and the agreement doesn't hold. This applies to all professions. For example, two doctors don't trade with each other; instead, a doctor trades with a farmer or another person who provides a different service. Their work is different and unequal, so they need to find a way to balance it.

This is why money exists—it acts as a way to compare everything. It's like an intermediate that measures the value of all goods. It allows us to determine how many shoes are worth a house or how much food is worth a house. The number of shoes that trade for a house depends on the value of the builder's work compared to the shoemaker's work. Without money, there would be no exchange, and without exchange, people wouldn't interact. Proportion can't happen unless things are made equal. So, everything has to be measured by something, and that's why money was created.

In truth, it's not easy to make such different things equal, but they can be made equal enough by looking at how much they're needed. Money represents demand, and because of this, it allows things to be compared. That's why it's called "nomisma" (money)—because it exists by law (nomos) and can be changed or made useless if people decide. So, reciprocity happens when the value of the goods is equal— when the shoemaker's work equals the builder's work. We don't compare them after they've been traded, but while they still have their goods. This makes them equal partners. If not for this balance, no trade would happen.

Money ensures people can exchange even if they don't need something right now, by acting as a guarantee for future trade. Even though the value of money can change, it's usually more stable than goods. Because of this, everything needs a price so that trade can always happen. If there's trade, people can work together.

Money, as a measure, makes things equal by allowing them to be compared. Without money, there wouldn't be exchange, and without exchange, people couldn't cooperate. Although it's impossible to make such different things truly equal, they can be made comparable based on demand. Money acts as this comparison because everything is measured by money.

Let's say A is a house, B is ten minae, and C is a bed. If A is worth five minae, the house is half of B. If C is a bed worth one-tenth of B, then it's clear how many beds are worth one house—five. It didn't matter if people exchanged five beds for a house or the value of five beds in money.

Now, we have defined what is just and unjust. It's clear that just action is a middle point between acting unjustly and being treated unjustly. One person gets too much, and the other gets too little. Justice is a balance, but not in the same way as other virtues—it relates to an intermediate amount, while injustice is about the extremes. A just person does what is fair by choice and will share fairly with others, giving neither more good to themselves nor more harm to others. This fairness follows a proportion. Injustice, on the other hand, involves either taking too much or too little of what's good or bad, which leads to imbalance.

Justice helps create equality by making sure everyone gets what they deserve. Injustice causes either excess or lack, and just action is about finding that middle ground.

Acts done out of anger are rightly judged not to be done with evil intent. It's not the person acting in anger who starts the wrongdoing, but the person who made them angry. Also, the argument isn't whether the action happened or not, but whether it was fair. It's the clear unfairness that causes the anger. People don't argue about whether the act occurred, as they might in business disputes where one of the two parties must be dishonest—unless they forgot. But they agree on the fact and argue about who is in the right. A person who deliberately hurts another knows they've done so, so one person believes they were wronged while the other disagrees.

If someone harms another on purpose, they act unjustly. These are the actions of an unjust person if they violate fairness or equality. Likewise, someone is just when they act fairly by choice, but they act fairly if they simply act voluntarily.

Some involuntary actions are excusable, and others are not. Mistakes that people make because they don't know any better or due to ignorance are excusable. However, mistakes made not because of ignorance, but because of an unnatural or uncontrollable passion, are not excusable.

Since we have defined what it means to suffer and do injustice, we can now ask if Euripides' strange words hold any truth:

"I killed my mother, that's my story in short.
Were you both willing, or both unwilling?"

Is it really possible to be treated unjustly on purpose, or is suffering injustice always the opposite—something involuntary—just as doing injustice is voluntary? Is suffering injustice always involuntary, or can it be voluntary at times? The same question can be asked for being treated fairly: all fair actions are voluntary, so it seems reasonable that both being treated unfairly and being treated fairly could be either voluntary or involuntary. But it seems strange, even in the case of being treated fairly, that it could always be voluntary, since some people are treated fairly against their will.

Another question we might ask is whether everyone who suffers something unjust is being treated unjustly, or if it's like taking action.

In both doing and receiving, it's possible to experience justice or injustice by accident. Doing something unjust isn't the same as acting unjustly, just as suffering something unjust isn't the same as being treated unjustly. The same is true for acting justly and being treated fairly. It's impossible to be treated unjustly if the other person isn't acting unjustly, or to be treated fairly if they aren't acting fairly.

Now, if acting unjustly means deliberately harming someone, and 'deliberately' means knowing the person you're acting on, the tool you're using, and how you're doing it, then someone who harms themselves because they lack self-control does it voluntarily. This means they can also be treated unjustly on purpose, which raises the question of whether someone can treat themselves unjustly. A person may harm themselves on purpose due to a lack of self-control while being harmed by someone else who also acts deliberately, so it's possible to be treated unjustly on purpose.

Or perhaps our definition is wrong. Should we add to 'harming another on purpose' the idea that it must also be 'against the will of the person being harmed'? In that case, a person may be harmed on purpose and suffer an unjust act on purpose, but no one is treated unjustly on purpose, because no one wants to be treated unjustly—not even the person who lacks self-control. They act against their own will since no one wants what they don't think is good, even though the person without self-control does things they believe they shouldn't.

Also, a person who gives away their possessions, like how Homer says Glaucus gave Diomede "armor of gold for bronze, worth a hundred oxen for nine," is not treated unjustly. Though giving is within his power, being treated unjustly isn't, because someone else must treat him unjustly. So, it's clear that being treated unjustly is not something done willingly.

Two questions still remain: whether it's the person who gives someone more than their share who acts unjustly, or the person who gets too much, and whether it's possible to treat yourself unjustly.

These questions are connected. If the first case is true—that the one who distributes unfairly is unjust but not the person who receives too much—then if a person gives another more than they give themselves, knowing and choosing to do so, they treat themselves unjustly. This is what modest people seem to do, since the virtuous person tends to take less than their share. Or is this view too simple? Maybe they receive more of some other good, like honor or dignity. We can solve this by applying the same rule we use for unjust action: the person isn't treated unjustly if it's what they wanted, so they don't suffer injustice, though they may suffer harm.

It's clear that the one who distributes unfairly acts unjustly, but not always the person who gets too much. Injustice belongs to the person who deliberately acts unfairly, not the one who receives the unfair share. The responsibility lies with the person who makes the decision, and in this case, that's the distributor, not the recipient. Also, the word 'act' has different meanings: lifeless objects, a hand, or a servant carrying out an order can be said to 'kill,' but it's not really them acting unjustly, even though they carry out an unjust action.

If the distributor made their judgment in ignorance, they don't act unjustly according to the law, and their decision isn't legally unjust, though it may be unjust in another sense (since legal justice and natural justice are different). But if the distributor knowingly makes an unfair judgment, they are trying to get something extra, either gratitude or revenge. In this case, they get too much, just like if they had taken part of the spoils. It doesn't matter if what they get is different from what they distribute; for example, if they give out land but aim to receive money from it.

People think that it's easy to act unjustly, and so being just must be easy too. But it's not. It's easy to sleep with someone else's wife, hurt someone, or take a bribe. But doing these things as part of a bad character is neither easy nor within everyone's control. Similarly, people think it takes no great wisdom to know what's just and unjust, because understanding the laws isn't hard. But how actions should be done and goods divided fairly—that's harder to know than what's good for health. Even though knowing that honey, wine, or medicine can help is easy, knowing how, to whom, and when to use them requires the skill of a doctor.

For this reason, people think that being unjust can come as easily to a just person as it does to an unjust one. The just person would be even better at unjust actions because they know what to do. For example, they could sleep with someone or harm their neighbor, and the brave person could throw away their shield and run from danger. But to act cowardly or unjustly isn't just doing those things—it's doing them because of a bad character, just as being a doctor doesn't mean simply using or not using a knife, but knowing how to heal in the right way.

Just actions occur between people who share good things and can have too much or too little of them. Some beings, like the gods, can't have too much of them, and to others, like those who are beyond help, not even a little share is good—it harms them. But to others, these goods are helpful up to a certain point, so justice is a human concept.

Next, we'll talk about fairness and what it means to be fair. Fairness and justice seem to be neither entirely the same nor completely different. We sometimes praise fairness and fair people, so we use the term to praise other virtues as well. But when we think about it, it seems strange that fairness could be different from justice yet still praiseworthy. If they are different, then either justice or fairness can't be good. If both are good, they must be the same.

These thoughts give rise to questions about fairness. All of them are somewhat correct and not in opposition. Fairness is better than one type of justice, but it's still a kind of justice. Fairness isn't different in kind, just better in a certain way. The same thing can be just and fair, and while both are good, fairness is better. The reason we face this problem is that fairness corrects legal justice. All laws are general, but sometimes it's impossible to make a general law fit every case. The law takes the most common case, knowing that it won't always be right. This isn't the fault of the law or the lawmaker—it's because of the nature of human affairs. So, when the law speaks in general terms, but a specific case doesn't fit, fairness comes in to correct the mistake. Fairness allows us to make the decision that the lawmaker would have made if they were present and knew the situation.

Fairness is better than this kind of justice, though not better than justice in an absolute sense. It corrects errors that arise from the general nature of the law. This is why not everything can be decided by law— sometimes we need to make exceptions. Laws are like the flexible lead rulers used to make molds, which bend to fit the stone rather than staying rigid. In the same way, judgments are made to fit the facts.

It's clear now what fairness is and that it's a kind of justice, but better in certain ways. It's also clear who the fair person is—the one who chooses and acts fairly, not insisting on their rights to an extreme but often taking less than their share even when the law is on their side. This quality is fairness, which is a kind of justice, not a separate virtue.

Whether a person can treat themselves unjustly is clear from what we've said. One type of just actions is those based on virtue that are required by law. For example, the law doesn't allow suicide, and what it doesn't allow, it forbids. A person who harms another on purpose breaks the law and acts unjustly, knowing both the person they harm and the tool they use. So, if someone stabs themselves in anger, it goes against the right way to live, and the law doesn't permit it. They act unjustly, but toward whom? Surely toward the state, not themselves. They suffer willingly, but no one is treated unjustly willingly. This is why the state punishes suicide—because it's considered unjust to the state.

Also, in the sense of acting unjustly where a person acts unjustly but isn't completely bad, it's not possible to treat oneself unjustly. This is different from the first sense. The unjust person in this case is bad in a particular way, like a coward, not bad in every way. Their unjust action doesn't show full wickedness. In this case, it would mean that the same thing could be both added to and taken from the same person at the same time, which is impossible—justice and injustice always involve more than one person.

Additionally, unjust actions are voluntary and chosen. But if a person harms themselves, they are both the one suffering and the one causing the suffering at the same time. So, it's impossible to treat yourself unjustly. Besides, no one commits injustice without specific actions, and no one can commit adultery with their own spouse or steal from their own house.

The question of whether a person can treat themselves unjustly is solved in the same way as the question of whether a person can be treated unjustly willingly.

It's clear that both suffering injustice and acting unjustly are bad. One means getting less than the fair amount, and the other means getting more, similar to how health is the goal in medicine. But acting unjustly is worse, because it involves vice and deserves blame. Vice is either complete and absolute or close to it, though not every voluntary unjust action shows full injustice as a character trait. Being treated unjustly doesn't involve vice in oneself. In itself, being treated unjustly is less bad, but it can sometimes lead to a worse outcome. Theory doesn't care about that—it calls pleurisy a worse illness than a small injury, though the injury could become worse if it leads to being captured or killed.

Metaphorically, there is a kind of justice between a person and themselves, though not in the strict sense. It's like the justice between a master and servant or husband and wife. These relationships show how the rational part of the soul relates to the irrational part. People believe that a person can be unjust to themselves because these parts of the soul can conflict. This leads people to think there is a kind of justice between the parts of a person, like between ruler and ruled.

This is our account of justice and the other moral virtues.

Book 6

Since we have previously said that one should choose what is in the middle, not the extreme of too much or too little, and that this middle point is decided by the correct rule, let's discuss what these correct rules are. In all the states of character we have mentioned, as well as in other areas, there is a goal the person with the right rule aims for, and they either increase or decrease their actions to hit that goal. There is a standard that defines these middle points, which we call the balance between too much and too little, and this standard follows the right rule. But even though this statement is true, it's not very clear. It's like when we say in other areas of knowledge that we should not do too much or too little, but act in a balanced way as the right rule dictates. If someone only knew that, they wouldn't be much wiser, just as we wouldn't know what kind of medicine to use if someone only told us, "use what the medical art prescribes, as practiced by those who know it." That's why, when it comes to the soul, it's necessary not only to make the true statement but also to understand what the right rule is and what standard sets it.

We divided the virtues of the soul into two kinds: those related to character and those related to intellect. Now that we've talked in detail about moral virtues, let's talk about the others, starting with some comments about the soul. We said before that the soul has two parts: one part follows rules or reason, and the other part is irrational. Let's now make another distinction within the part that follows reason. There are two parts here as well: one part thinks about things that don't change, and the other thinks about things that can change. Since the things they focus on are different, the parts of the soul that deal with them must also be different. The part that deals with what doesn't change can be called the scientific part, and the part that deals with what can change can be called the calculating part. This is because calculating and reasoning are the same thing, and we never calculate about things that don't change. So, the calculating part is a part of the soul that deals with rational principles.

Next, we need to understand what the best state of these two parts is, as that will be their virtue. The virtue of anything is related to its proper function. In the soul, three things control action and truth: sensation, reason, and desire.

Sensation doesn't start any actions. This is clear because animals can sense things but don't take actions the way humans do. In the same way that thinking can affirm or deny something, desire can lead to pursuit or avoidance. Since moral virtue is about choosing, and choice is thoughtful desire, both the reasoning must be correct and the desire must be right for the choice to be good. The desire should go after what the reasoning points to. This kind of thinking and truth is practical. For the thinking that is contemplative (not practical or productive), the good state is truth, and the bad state is falsehood. But in the part that is both practical and rational, the good state is when truth and right desire work together.

The source of action (not its goal) is choice, and choice comes from desire and reasoning toward a goal. This is why choice can't exist without reason and intellect or without a moral state. Good and bad actions need both intellect and character to happen. But intellect by itself doesn't cause anything to happen. Only the kind of intellect that has a goal and is practical leads to action. This kind of intellect even controls the intellect that produces things because anyone who makes something does it for a goal. The thing they make isn't the ultimate goal, but good action is. So, choice is either reason driven by desire or desire driven by reason, and this leads to action. This is why humans act. (It's important to note that nothing in the past can be chosen. No one chooses to have destroyed Troy, for example, because we don't deliberate about the past, only about the future, which can still change. As Agathon said:

"Even God cannot change what is done.")

The work of both intellectual parts is truth. Therefore, the best state for each part is the one that leads to truth, and that is their virtue.

Let's start from the beginning and talk about these states again. The ways the soul holds on to truth through affirmation or denial are five in number: art, scientific knowledge, practical wisdom, philosophical wisdom, and intuitive reason. We don't include judgment and opinion because they can be wrong.

Now, what exactly is scientific knowledge? If we are going to be precise and not just rely on similarities, we say that scientific knowledge is knowing something that cannot be otherwise. For things that could be different, we don't know whether they exist once they are out of our sight. Scientific knowledge deals with things that must be as they are, and therefore, it deals with things that are eternal. Things that are necessary are all eternal, and eternal things don't have a beginning or an end. Science is also thought to be teachable, and its object is something that can be learned. All teaching comes from what is already known, as we explain in Analytics. Teaching can happen either by induction or by syllogism. Induction starts from specifics and leads to a general understanding, and syllogism starts from general truths. The starting points of syllogisms are not proven by more syllogisms; they are learned through induction. So, scientific knowledge is a state where we can prove things, and it has the other characteristics that we explain in Analytics. Scientific knowledge occurs when a person believes something in the right way and knows the starting points of their argument. Otherwise, they only know things incidentally.

Let this be our explanation of scientific knowledge.

Both things that are made and things that are done are part of the variable. Making and acting are different. We can trust even the discussions outside of our own school on this. The capacity to act and the capacity to make are also different. Therefore, making isn't the same as acting, and acting isn't the same as making. Architecture, for example, is an art and is essentially the capacity to make something. Art is the ability to make, based on a correct understanding of how to do it. All art deals with creating something—figuring out how something can come into being that might or might not exist. The origin of this creation lies in the maker, not the thing being made. Art isn't about things that exist by necessity or nature, as those things originate from themselves. Since making and acting are different, art is about making, not acting.

In some way, both chance and art deal with the same objects. As Agathon said, "art loves chance, and chance loves art." Art, then, is the ability to make something by following correct reasoning, while lack of art is the opposite—it involves incorrect reasoning. Both art and chance deal with things that can vary.

Now let's talk about practical wisdom. We can understand what it is by considering who we think has it. A person with practical wisdom is able to think well about what is good and beneficial for themselves, not just in one specific area like health or strength, but in terms of living a good life overall. We also give credit to people who have practical wisdom in a specific area when they can figure out the best way to reach a good goal that is not the object of any art. So, in the general sense, a person who can deliberate well has practical wisdom. No one deliberates about things that don't change or about things they can't control. Since scientific knowledge involves proving things, and there's no proof of things that change (since they could be otherwise), practical wisdom can't be scientific knowledge or art. It's not science because the things we can do might be otherwise, and it's not art because making and acting are different. Practical wisdom must be the ability to act well concerning what is good or bad for humans. Making has an end beyond itself, but action is an end in itself. That's why we say people like Pericles had practical wisdom—because they could see what was good for themselves and for others in general. We consider those who are good at managing households or states to have this wisdom. (This is also why we call temperance "sophrosune," which means it preserves practical wisdom. It helps preserve the kind of judgment we've described. Not all judgments are ruined by pleasure and pain—only those about what should be done. The starting point for actions lies in the goal they aim for. But someone who is corrupted by pleasure or pain can no longer see why they should choose certain actions. Vice destroys the cause of action.)

So, practical wisdom is the ability to act well concerning human goods. While there is excellence in art, there is no such thing as excellence in practical wisdom. In art, a person who makes mistakes on purpose is better than one who makes mistakes by accident, but in practical wisdom, the opposite is true, just as it is with the virtues. Practical wisdom is a virtue, not an art. There are two parts of the soul that can reason, and practical wisdom is the virtue of the part that forms opinions. Opinion is about things that can change, and so is practical wisdom. But practical wisdom isn't just reasoning. This is shown by the fact that reasoning can be forgotten, but practical wisdom cannot be.

Scientific knowledge is about things that are universal and necessary, and it deals with what can be proven. All scientific knowledge comes from first principles, but the first principles themselves cannot be the objects of science, art, or practical wisdom. Scientific knowledge deals with things that can be demonstrated, and art and practical wisdom deal with things that can change. First principles also can't be the objects of philosophical wisdom because philosophers need to prove things about them. So, if the mental states that give us truth are scientific knowledge, practical wisdom, philosophical wisdom, and intuitive reason, and first principles aren't objects of the first three, then it must be intuitive reason that grasps them.

Wisdom has two meanings. In the arts, we call people wise when they are highly skilled, like Phidias in sculpture or Polyclitus in making statues. Here, wisdom simply means excellence in art. But we also think some people are wise in general, not just in one specific area. As Homer says in Margites:

"The gods made him neither a digger nor a ploughman,
Nor wise in anything else."

So, wisdom must be the highest form of knowledge. The wise person must know not only what follows from first principles but also the first principles themselves. Wisdom must be intuitive reason combined with scientific knowledge of the highest things, which is as complete as it can get.

We're talking about the highest things because it would be strange to think that politics or practical wisdom is the best kind of knowledge since humans aren't the best things in the universe. If what is healthy or good is different for humans and fish, but what is white or straight is always the same, we can say that what is wise is the same for all but practical wisdom differs. It applies to those things that are concerned with themselves. That's why we say that some animals have practical wisdom when they can take care of their own lives. It's also clear that philosophical wisdom and politics are not the same. If philosophical wisdom were about a person's own interests, there would be many different kinds of philosophical wisdom, just as there are many different kinds of medicine, one for each kind of being.

But if someone argues that humans are the best of animals, this doesn't change the point. There are other things that are much more divine than humans, such as the heavenly bodies. So, philosophical wisdom is scientific knowledge combined with intuitive reason about the highest things in nature. That's why we say that people like Anaxagoras and Thales had philosophical wisdom, even though they were often ignorant of what was good for themselves. They knew remarkable, admirable, difficult, and divine things, but they were useless because they didn't focus on human goods.

Practical wisdom, on the other hand, is concerned with human things and things that can be deliberated about. We say that practical wisdom involves deliberating well, but no one deliberates about things that can't change or that don't have an end goal. The person who is good at deliberating is the one who can aim at the best outcome for humans, based on reason, from the things that can be done. Practical wisdom isn't just about general truths; it must also deal with specific details. Practice deals with specific things. That's why someone with experience may be more practical than someone with theoretical knowledge. For example, a person may know that light foods are easy to digest, but if they don't know what kinds of food are light, they can't create a healthy diet. However, someone who knows that chicken is light food will be better at creating a healthy diet.

Practical wisdom is about action, so we should have both general and specific knowledge, or at least specific knowledge. But even within practical wisdom and philosophical wisdom, there are different kinds of control.

Political wisdom and practical wisdom are the same kind of state of mind, but their essence is different. The practical wisdom involved in managing a city includes legislative wisdom, which is concerned with creating laws, while the political wisdom that deals with specific actions is known simply as 'political wisdom.' This kind of wisdom deals with actions and decisions since laws are meant to guide individual actions. This is why people involved in this art are said to 'participate in politics,' just as manual workers are said to 'do things.'

Practical wisdom is mostly identified with the type that deals with a person's own life, and this is generally called 'practical wisdom.' Other types include household management, legislation, and politics. Politics can be divided into two parts: deliberative and judicial. Knowing what is good for oneself is one kind of knowledge, but it is very different from other types. The person who knows and focuses on their own interests is considered to have practical wisdom, while politicians are often seen as meddling in other people's affairs. This is reflected in the words of Euripides:

"How could I be wise, when I could have had
An equal share among the soldiers,

Instead of aiming too high and doing too much?"

People who think this way believe that one should look out for their own good, and they think this is the right thing to do. This belief is where the idea that such people have practical wisdom comes from. But maybe one's own good can't exist without household management or some form of government. Additionally, knowing how to manage your own affairs isn't easy and requires investigation.

What has been said is supported by the fact that while young people can become experts in geometry, mathematics, and other similar subjects, it's believed that a young person cannot have practical wisdom. The reason is that practical wisdom deals not only with general ideas but also with specific situations, which come from experience. A young person doesn't have experience because experience comes with time. We might also wonder why a boy can become a mathematician but not a philosopher or a physicist. It's because the things studied in mathematics exist in theory, while the first principles of philosophy and physics come from experience. Young people don't have firm beliefs about these first principles; they only know the words. But the nature of mathematical objects is clear to them.

Additionally, mistakes in deliberation can be about either general principles or specific details. For example, someone might not know that all water that weighs heavy is harmful, or they might not realize that this specific water weighs heavy.

It's clear that practical wisdom is not the same as scientific knowledge. Practical wisdom, as we've said, is about specific facts because the things to be done are specific in nature. It is different from intuitive reason. Intuitive reason deals with general starting points, which can't be explained, while practical wisdom focuses on specific facts. These facts aren't known through scientific knowledge but through perception—a perception similar to how we recognize that a certain shape is a triangle. In this way, there is a limit, just as there is with general rules. But this kind of perception is closer to practical wisdom, though it's different from the perception that involves the senses.

There's a difference between inquiry and deliberation. Deliberation is a specific kind of inquiry. We need to understand what excellence in deliberation is and whether it's a form of scientific knowledge, opinion, skill in guessing, or something else. It isn't scientific knowledge because people don't inquire about things they already know. But good deliberation involves inquiring and thinking carefully. It also isn't a skill in guessing because guessing doesn't involve reasoning and happens quickly, while people take time to deliberate. We say that people should act quickly once they've finished deliberating but should deliberate slowly. Quick thinking is different from excellence in deliberation because it's more like guessing. Excellence in deliberation also isn't the same as opinion. But since someone who deliberates badly makes mistakes, while someone who deliberates well does so correctly, excellence in deliberation must involve correctness. This correctness is different from knowledge or opinion. There's no such thing as correct knowledge (since knowledge doesn't include error), and correctness of opinion is the same as truth. At the same time, everything that is a matter of opinion is already decided. Excellence in deliberation involves reasoning. The only option left is that it's the correctness of thinking. Opinion is not the same as inquiry because it has already reached a conclusion, while someone who is deliberating is still searching and calculating.

Excellence in deliberation means being correct in deliberation. So, we need to first understand what deliberation is and what it deals with. Since there are different kinds of correctness, it's clear that excellence in deliberation is not just any kind of correctness. For example, a person without self-control or a bad person, if they are clever, may achieve their goal through deliberation. But they will have ended up with something harmful. To deliberate well is considered a good thing because it means being correct in achieving good ends. However, (1) it's possible to reach something good through incorrect reasoning, by using false premises. This means that even if someone achieves the right result, they didn't reach it in the right way, so this isn't excellence in deliberation. (2) It's also possible to achieve a result after long deliberation, while someone else might reach it more quickly. In the first case, we don't yet have excellence in deliberation, which is about being correct in terms of the goal, the method, and the timing. (3) Additionally, it's possible to deliberate well either in a general sense or about a specific goal. Excellence in deliberation in the general sense is when someone achieves a goal that is good in general, while excellence in deliberation in a specific sense is when someone succeeds in reaching a particular goal. (4) If it's true that people with practical wisdom are good at deliberating, then excellence in deliberation will be about correctly determining what leads to the goals that practical wisdom recognizes.

Understanding and goodness of understanding, which make people known as having good judgment, are not exactly the same as opinion or scientific knowledge. If they were, everyone would have good understanding. Nor are they part of specific sciences like medicine or geometry. Understanding isn't about things that are always true and unchangeable, nor is it about everything that comes into existence. It deals with things that can be questioned and deliberated about. So, it deals with the same objects as practical wisdom. But understanding and practical wisdom aren't the same. Practical wisdom leads to decisions, as its goal is to determine what should or shouldn't be done. Understanding, on the other hand, only makes judgments. Understanding and good understanding are the same thing. Having understanding isn't the same as having or gaining practical wisdom. Just as learning is called understanding when it's the use of knowledge, understanding is about using opinion to judge what others say about matters related to practical wisdom—and doing so correctly. The term 'understanding' has come from the ability to grasp scientific truth, and we often use it to describe that ability.

Judgment, which makes people known as having good judgment or as sympathetic judges, is the ability to correctly recognize what is fair. This is shown by the fact that we say the fair person is also a person of good judgment. Fairness is closely related to good judgment in certain matters, and judgment is about correctly recognizing what is fair. Correct judgment is the ability to recognize what is true.

All the states we've discussed seem to come together. When we talk about judgment, understanding, practical wisdom, and intuitive reason, we give credit to the same people for having these qualities. We say that they have reached an age of wisdom and possess practical wisdom and understanding. All these qualities deal with specifics, or what we might call ultimate things. Being a person of understanding and good judgment means being able to make decisions about the matters that practical wisdom deals with. What is fair is something that all good people recognize in their dealings with others. Everything we need to do in life involves specifics or ultimate things. People with practical wisdom must know specific details, and understanding and judgment are also about things that need to be done. These are ultimate things. Intuitive reason deals with ultimate things in both directions. It deals with both the first principles and the last conclusions. The intuitive reason that we use in demonstrations grasps the first, unchangeable principles, while the intuitive reason we use in practical matters grasps the final, changeable fact, or the minor premise. These variable facts are the starting points for reaching a goal, and we understand universals by looking at specifics. So, we must have a perception of these facts, and this perception is intuitive reason.

This is why these qualities are thought to be natural abilities. No one is considered a natural philosopher, but people are thought to have natural judgment, understanding, and intuitive reason. We believe these qualities come with age, and a person's natural development brings with it judgment and intuitive reason. This suggests that these qualities come from nature. Intuitive reason is both the starting point and the end. Demonstrations are based on intuitive reason and are about intuitive reason.

This is why we should listen to the sayings and opinions of experienced and older people, as well as people with practical wisdom. Their experience has given them insight, and they see things clearly.

We've now explained what practical and philosophical wisdom are and what they deal with. We've also said that each is a virtue of a different part of the soul.

We might wonder about the usefulness of these mental qualities. (1) Philosophical wisdom doesn't seem to deal with anything that makes a person happy, since it isn't concerned with things that come into being. Practical wisdom, on the other hand, does deal with things that make a person happy. But why do we need it? Practical wisdom deals with things that are just, noble, and good for humans. These are the things a good person does, but knowing about them doesn't make us better at doing them. Just as knowing what is healthy doesn't make us better at creating health (since health comes from the state of the body, not from the art of medicine), knowing what is just doesn't necessarily help us act justly. (2) If we say that a person should have practical wisdom to help them become good, practical wisdom is still useless for people who are already good. It's also useless for people who don't have virtue because it doesn't matter whether they have practical wisdom or follow the advice of someone who does. In the same way, we want to be healthy, but we don't need to learn the art of medicine to become healthy. (3) It also seems strange that practical wisdom, which is inferior to philosophical wisdom, would be in charge of it. This seems to be implied by the fact that the art that produces something also controls and commands it.

These are the questions we need to consider. So far, we've only mentioned the difficulties.

(1) First, we should say that these mental states are worth choosing for their own sake, even if they don't produce anything, because they are the virtues of the two parts of the soul.

(2) Secondly, these states do produce something, but not in the same way that the art of medicine produces health. Philosophical wisdom produces happiness, not by making something, but by existing and being used. Since it's part of virtue as a whole, possessing and using philosophical wisdom makes a person happy.

(3) Additionally, a person can only achieve their purpose through both practical wisdom and moral virtue. Virtue helps us aim at the right goals, and practical wisdom helps us find the right way to achieve them. (The fourth part of the soul—the part that deals with nutrition—doesn't have a virtue like this because it doesn't have control over what it does.)

(4) As for the idea that practical wisdom doesn't help us do what is noble and just, let's start by discussing something else. We've said that some people do just actions without being truly just. This includes people who follow the laws but do so unwillingly, out of ignorance, or for reasons other than the actions themselves. Even though they do the right things, they don't do them because they are good. To be truly good, a person must be in the right state when they act—they must choose to do good and do it for its own sake. Virtue helps us make the right choices, but knowing what to do to carry out those choices belongs to another ability.

We need to pay attention to this and explain it more clearly. There is an ability called cleverness, which helps people achieve the goals they aim for. When the goal is good, cleverness is praiseworthy, but when the goal is bad, cleverness is just smartness. This is why we call people with practical wisdom clever or smart. Practical wisdom isn't the same as cleverness, but it can't exist without it. This insight into practical matters doesn't develop without the help of virtue. This is because the reasoning behind actions starts with an understanding of what is good, but only good people can fully understand this. Wickedness leads us astray and makes us misunderstand the starting points for action.

It's clear that it's impossible to have practical wisdom without being good.

We must now consider virtue again. Virtue is related to cleverness in the same way that practical wisdom is related to cleverness. They aren't the same, but they are similar. Natural virtue is like cleverness, while virtue in the full sense is like practical wisdom. People believe that certain character traits are natural. From the moment we are born, we might naturally be just, self-controlled, or brave, or have other moral qualities. But we still look for something else—something better. Both children and animals have these natural traits, but without reason, these traits can be harmful. It's like a strong body that moves without sight—it can fall badly because it can't see. But once reason is added, everything changes. The person still has the same natural traits, but now they are true virtues in the full sense.

In the part of us that forms opinions, there are two kinds of qualities: cleverness and practical wisdom. Similarly, in the moral part of us, there are two types of virtues: natural virtue and true virtue, and true virtue involves practical wisdom. This is why some people say that all virtues are forms of practical wisdom. Socrates was partly right and partly wrong. He was wrong to think that all virtues were forms of practical wisdom, but he was right to say that virtues include practical wisdom. This is supported by the fact that when people define virtue, they say it's a state of character and then add that it follows the right rule. The right rule is the one that follows practical wisdom. So, people seem to sense that true virtue is the kind that follows practical wisdom.

But we need to go a little further. Virtue isn't just the state that follows the right rule—it's the state that involves the right rule. Practical wisdom is the right rule about these matters. Socrates thought that virtues were rules or principles because he believed they were all forms of knowledge. We, however, believe that virtues involve a rational principle.

It's clear from what has been said that it's not possible to truly be good without practical wisdom, and you can't have practical wisdom without moral virtue. This also disproves the argument that the virtues can exist separately from each other. Some might argue that a person is not naturally equipped for all virtues, so they might have one virtue but not yet have developed another. This can happen with natural virtues, but not with the kind of virtues that make a person fully good. When a person has practical wisdom, they will have all the virtues. Even if practical wisdom didn't have any practical use, we would still need it because it is the virtue of this part of ourselves. It's also clear that we can't make the right choices without practical wisdom any more than we can without virtue. One helps us determine the right goal, and the other helps us do the things that lead to that goal.

However, practical wisdom isn't higher than philosophical wisdom, which is the higher part of us. It's like how medicine isn't above health—it doesn't use health but helps bring it about. Practical wisdom gives instructions for the sake of philosophical wisdom, but it doesn't command it. Saying practical wisdom is higher than philosophical wisdom would be like saying that politics rules the gods just because it gives orders about the state's affairs.

Book 7

Let's start fresh and explain that there are three kinds of bad character traits to avoid: vice, lack of self-control, and being brutish. There are opposites to two of these traits. One is called virtue, and the other is self-control. As for being brutish, the opposite would be a kind of superhuman virtue, something heroic and almost divine. Homer shows this when Priam says about Hector that he was so good:

"For he didn't seem like the child of a mortal man but as if he was born from a god."

So, if people say that humans can become like gods by having an excess of virtue, then the state of being godlike must be the opposite of being brutish. This is because, just like a brute doesn't have vice or virtue, a god doesn't either. A god's state is higher than virtue, and a brute's state is different from vice.

Now, since it's rare to find a godlike person—using a term from the Spartans, who called someone 'godlike' when they admired them greatly—it's also rare to find a brutish person among humans. You mainly find them among barbarians, though some people develop brutish qualities because of disease or deformity. We also call people who are extremely wicked 'brutish.' We'll talk more about this type of character later. While we've already discussed vice, now we need to talk about lack of self-control and weakness (or softness), as well as self-control and endurance. We need to look at these as neither exactly the same as virtue or wickedness nor as a completely different category. As always, we should look at the facts and, after addressing the difficulties, try to prove that most of the common ideas about these traits are true—or at least the majority of them and the most trustworthy ones. If we can refute objections and leave the common beliefs untouched, we will have proven our case well enough.

Both self-control and endurance are seen as good and praiseworthy, while lack of self-control and softness are seen as bad and blameworthy. The same person can be considered either self-controlled and sticking to their decisions or lacking self-control and abandoning them. A person who lacks self-control knows what they're doing is wrong but gives in to passion, while a self-controlled person knows their desires are wrong but refuses to follow them because of their reasoning. Everyone calls a person with self-control and endurance 'temperate.' Some think that a person with self-control is always temperate, while others disagree. Some also use the terms 'self-indulgent' and 'lacking self-control' interchangeably, while others make a distinction between the two. Some say that a person with practical wisdom cannot lack self-control, while others claim that even some practically wise and clever people can lack self-control. People also say that someone can lack self-control not just with physical desires but also with anger, the desire for honor, and the desire for profit. These are the things people say.

Now we can ask how someone who makes the right judgment can still lack self-control. Some say it's impossible for someone to act this way when they have knowledge because, as Socrates thought, it would be strange if knowledge could be overpowered and controlled like a slave. Socrates completely disagreed with the idea of lack of self-control. He believed there was no such thing because he said that no one acts against what they believe is best—they only do wrong because of ignorance. But this view clearly goes against what we observe, so we must investigate what happens with such a person. If they act out of ignorance, how exactly are they ignorant? It's clear that the person who lacks self-control doesn't think, before they give in, that they should act this way. But some people agree with some of Socrates' points but not all of them. They accept that knowledge is stronger than anything else, but they don't think that someone acts against what they think is best. Instead, they say that the person who lacks self-control doesn't have knowledge when they're overpowered by their desires; they only have an opinion.

But if it's just an opinion and not true knowledge, if it's not a firm conviction but a weak one, like someone who hesitates, we can understand why they fail to stick to it against strong desires. However, we don't feel the same way about wickedness or other bad states. So, is it practical wisdom that's overpowered? That would be the strongest state of all, but that idea doesn't make sense. It would mean that the same person could be both practically wise and lack self-control, but no one would say that a practically wise person would willingly do the worst things. Besides, we've already shown that a practically wise person is someone who acts (because they're concerned with real-world situations) and has all the other virtues.

Furthermore, if self-control means having strong, bad desires, then a temperate person can't be self-controlled, and a self-controlled person can't be temperate. This is because a temperate person wouldn't have bad or excessive desires, but a self-controlled person must have them. If the desires are good, then the state of resisting them would be bad, so not all forms of self-control would be good. If the desires are weak and not bad, there's nothing impressive about resisting them, and if they're weak and bad, there's still nothing great about resisting them.

Additionally, if self-control means sticking to every opinion, then it would be a bad thing, especially if it means sticking to false opinions. And if lack of self-control means abandoning every opinion, then there could be a good form of lack of self-control, like in Sophocles' play "Philoctetes," where Neoptolemus is praised for not sticking to the plan Odysseus convinced him to follow because he was upset about telling a lie.

Moreover, there's a problem with certain clever arguments. These arguments are designed to create paradoxes in an opponent's viewpoint to make the person who proves the paradox seem clever. But these arguments can confuse us. For example, one argument might suggest that foolishness combined with lack of self-control could be a kind of virtue. The reasoning is that a person who lacks self-control acts against what they believe is right, but they wrongly believe that something good is bad and that they shouldn't do it. So, as a result, they end up doing the good thing and avoiding the bad one.

Further, a person who chooses to pursue what is pleasant through careful thought might seem better than someone who does it out of lack of self-control. The first person is easier to correct because they might be persuaded to change their mind. But with a person who lacks self-control, we might say, "When water chokes you, what do you wash it down with?" If they had been persuaded that what they were doing was right, they would have stopped when they were persuaded to change their mind. But now, they act even though they've been persuaded to do something different.

Finally, if lack of self-control and self-control apply to everything, then who exactly is lacking self-control in the general sense? No one seems to lack control in every way, yet we still call some people lacking self-control without qualification. These are the kinds of difficulties we face. Some of these points must be disproven, while others should be accepted, as solving these difficulties is the key to finding the truth.

We should first ask if people who lack self-control act knowingly or not, and in what way they act knowingly. Then, we should ask what kinds of things the self-controlled and the uncontrollable person are concerned with—whether they deal with all pleasures and pains or just certain ones. We should also ask if self-control and endurance are the same thing or different, and we should approach the other relevant questions similarly. Our starting point is whether a person is self-controlled or lacking self-control because of the specific things they desire or because of their attitude toward them, or perhaps because of both. The next question is whether lack of self-control and self-control apply to every type of thing or just some. A person who lacks self-control in the general sense doesn't apply this to every object. They are mostly concerned with the same things as a self-indulgent person, but they differ in how they approach them. One person is led by their choices, thinking they should always pursue immediate pleasure, while the other person doesn't think so but still pursues it.

As for the idea that it's opinion and not knowledge that people act against when they lack self-control, that doesn't make a difference. Some people have firm opinions and don't hesitate but feel as if they know for sure. If the idea is that people with opinion are more likely to act against their judgment because their convictions are weaker, we can respond that there's not much difference between knowledge and opinion in this respect. Some people are just as convinced of their opinions as others are of their knowledge. This is shown by the views of Heraclitus. But since we use the word 'know' in two ways—for a person who has knowledge but isn't using it and for a person who is using it—it makes a difference whether someone has knowledge but isn't exercising it or is exercising it when they act wrongly. The latter case seems strange, but not the former.

Also, since there are two kinds of premises, a person can have both premises but still act against their knowledge, provided they are only using the universal premise and not the particular one. This is because particular actions are what must be done. There are also two types of universal terms: one applies to the person acting, and the other applies to the object. For example, "dry food is good for everyone" and "I am a person," or "this food is dry." But whether the person knows "this food is such and such," the person who lacks self-control either doesn't have that knowledge or isn't using it. So there's a big difference between these types of knowledge, and knowing in one way but acting incontinently wouldn't seem strange, while knowing in the other way would be extraordinary.

There's also a way that people can have knowledge without using it, which is like when someone is asleep, mad, or drunk. This is similar to the state of people under the influence of their desires. It's obvious that anger, sexual desire, and other such passions can change our bodily condition and can even make some people act mad. So, we can say that people who lack self-control are like people who are asleep, mad, or drunk. The fact that they use language based on knowledge doesn't prove anything. Even people under these passions can recite scientific proofs or poetry by Empedocles. Those who have just started learning something can repeat the words but don't yet fully understand it. They haven't made the knowledge part of themselves, and that takes time. So we should think that when people in a state of lack of self-control use language, it's no different from an actor reciting lines on a stage.

We can also think about the cause by considering human nature. One opinion is universal, and the other is about particular facts. When both opinions are combined, the soul must accept the conclusion. In cases of practical decisions, the person must immediately act. For example, if "everything sweet should be tasted" and "this is sweet," the person who can act and isn't prevented must immediately act. When the universal opinion is present and tells the person not to taste, but the opinion that "everything sweet is pleasant" and "this is sweet" is active, and when appetite is also present, one opinion tells the person to avoid the sweet thing, but appetite leads them toward it. This is why a person acts against self-control, not because of a contrary opinion but because of appetite. This also explains why animals don't lack self-control—they don't have universal judgments but only imagination and memory of particular things.

The explanation for how ignorance is removed and the person who lacks self-control regains knowledge is the same as for someone who is drunk or asleep. This is something for natural scientists to explain. Since the last premise is about a particular object and it leads to action, the person in a state of passion either doesn't have this knowledge or has it in the sense that knowing doesn't mean fully understanding, like a drunken person reciting the lines of a poem. And because this final term is not universal and isn't an object of scientific knowledge like the universal term, it seems that Socrates was right in saying that true incontinence doesn't arise in the presence of proper knowledge. The problem lies in perceptual knowledge, not in true knowledge.

This is enough to answer the question of how people can act with or without knowledge and how it's possible to act incontinently even when they have knowledge.

We should now discuss whether some people are generally lacking in self-control or whether all of them are lacking in a particular sense, and if so, what kinds of things they are concerned with. It's clear that both people with self-control and people who lack it, as well as people with endurance and those who are soft, are concerned with pleasures and pains.

Some pleasures come from things that are necessary, while others are desirable for their own sake but can be excessive. The bodily pleasures are necessary, such as those related to food and sexual desire. These are the same physical pleasures we mentioned earlier when talking about temperance and self-indulgence. The other pleasures aren't necessary but are still desirable, like victory, honor, wealth, and other good and enjoyable things. So, people who go to excess with these latter pleasures, going against what they know is right, aren't called lacking self-control without qualification. Instead, we say they lack self-control "with respect to money, gain, honor, or anger," because they are different from those who lack self-control in general, and we call them this way because of their resemblance to those who do.

For example, Anthropos (Man) won a contest at the Olympic Games. While the general definition of 'man' didn't differ much from his specific case, it was still different. We can see this because incontinence in general or in relation to physical pleasure is blamed as both a fault and a vice, but no one blames the people who lack control in other respects like that.

As for those who lack self-control with respect to bodily pleasures, which are the same pleasures that temperance and self-indulgence are concerned with, the person who pursues too much pleasure and avoids pain—whether it's hunger, thirst, heat, cold, or other physical sensations—against their better judgment and without choice is called lacking self-control, not with a specific qualification like "with respect to anger," but simply lacking self-control. This is confirmed by the fact that we call people 'soft' with regard to these pleasures, but not with regard to any of the others. That's why we group together the person lacking self-control with the self-indulgent person, and the self-controlled person with the temperate one, but we don't do this with other types of people. This is because they are all concerned with the same pleasures and pains, though they don't respond to them in the same way. Some people make deliberate choices, while others don't.

This is why we should call someone self-indulgent if they seek too much pleasure without having much appetite, or avoid moderate pain, rather than someone who does this because of strong desires. What would the first person do if they also had strong desires and suffered greatly from missing the "necessary" things?

Now, some desires and pleasures are connected to things that are generally good and noble. Some pleasant things are naturally worth choosing, while others are the opposite, and some fall in between, like wealth, profit, victory, and honor. People aren't blamed for being drawn to these things, for desiring or loving them, but for wanting them in the wrong way—that is, for going to excess. This is why people who go against what's right and either are controlled by or pursue one of the naturally noble and good things, like honor or love for children and parents, aren't considered bad. These things are good, and people who focus on them are praised. But there can still be excess, like in the case of Niobe who fought against the gods, or someone as devoted to their father as Satyrus, nicknamed "the filial," who was considered silly for it. So, there's no wickedness connected to these things because they are naturally worth choosing for their own sake. But still, excess is harmful and should be avoided. Similarly, there's no incontinence with these things, because incontinence is not just something to avoid, it's also something blameworthy. But because the feeling is similar, people use the term "incontinence" and add what it refers to, just like we call someone a bad doctor or actor without saying they're completely bad. In the same way, we don't call it incontinence without a qualifier, because these conditions aren't entirely bad, but only like badness. So, it's clear that true incontinence and continence are connected with the same things as temperance and self-indulgence. We use the word incontinence with anger because of the similarity, and this is why we say "incontinent in respect of anger," just like we say "incontinent in respect of honor or gain."

Some things are naturally pleasant. Of these, some are pleasant without exception, while others are pleasant only to specific types of people or animals. There are other things that aren't naturally pleasant, but (1) some become pleasant because of damage to the body, (2) some because of habits, and (3) some because of bad natures. Given this, we can find similar traits in these types of people, like we do in the first type. These are the brutish traits, like in the case of the woman who, they say, rips open pregnant women and eats the babies, or the things that savage tribes near the Black Sea are said to enjoy—like raw meat or human flesh, or even lending their children to each other to eat. Or there's the story of Phalaris.

These traits are brutish, but others come from disease or sometimes madness, like the man who sacrificed and ate his mother, or the slave who ate the liver of his companion. Other cases are bad habits, like pulling out one's hair, biting nails, or even eating coal or dirt, and also pederasty. These can be caused by nature in some people, and in others, they develop as bad habits from childhood.

People whose nature causes them to act this way aren't considered incontinent, just like we don't call women incontinent because they take the passive role in sex. Nor do we call those who act this way because of bad habits incontinent. These habits go beyond vice, just like brutishness does. A man with these habits doesn't experience normal continence or incontinence, but something that's only similar. A man with this problem in regard to anger is called incontinent in anger, but not simply incontinent. All extreme states—whether of foolishness, cowardice, self-indulgence, or bad temper—are either brutish or caused by disease. A man who's naturally afraid of everything, even the squeak of a mouse, is brutish in his cowardice, while a man who feared a weasel did so because of illness. In the case of foolish people, those who are naturally thoughtless and live by their senses are brutish, like some remote barbarian tribes, while others are foolish because of disease (like epilepsy) or madness. Some of these traits only show up sometimes, and people aren't always controlled by them. For example, Phalaris might have resisted the urge to eat a child or avoided unnatural sexual urges. But it's also possible for people to be controlled by these feelings, not just to have them. Just like human wickedness is called wickedness, but not simply wickedness—it's called brutish or diseased. In the same way, some types of incontinence are brutish or diseased, but only the type connected to human self-indulgence is simply incontinence.

It's clear, then, that incontinence and continence are connected to the same things as self-indulgence and temperance. Incontinence related to other things is a different type of incontinence, called incontinence only by metaphor and not in the true sense. Also, incontinence related to anger is less shameful than incontinence related to desires, as we'll now explain. Anger seems to listen to reason in some way, but it mishears it, like hasty servants who run off before they've heard everything, and then mess up the instructions, or like dogs that bark just because they hear a knock, without checking to see if it's a friend. Anger, because it's hot and quick, hears but doesn't really understand an order, and it rushes to take revenge. Reason or imagination tells us that we've been insulted, and anger, reasoning that such things should be resisted, boils up immediately. On the other hand, desire jumps to enjoy something when reason or perception only says that it's pleasant. So, anger follows reason in a way, but desire doesn't. That's why incontinence connected to desires is more shameful, because someone who's incontinent in anger is in some way defeated by reason, while someone controlled by desire is defeated by appetite and not by reason.

Also, we forgive people more easily for following natural desires, because we forgive them more easily for following common desires that everyone has, as long as they aren't excessive. Anger and bad temper are more natural than desires for excessive, unnecessary things. For example, there's the man who defended hitting his father by saying, "Yes, but he hit his father, and he hit his, and" (pointing to his child) "this boy will hit me when he's grown up; it's a family tradition." Or the man who, when being dragged along by his son, asked him to stop at the doorway, because he himself had only dragged his father that far.

Also, those who plot against others are more blameworthy. An angry person doesn't usually plot, and neither does anger itself—it's open. But the nature of desire is like what the poets say about

Aphrodite, the "cunning daughter of Cyprus," or Homer's description of her "embroidered girdle":

"And in it is the whisper of seduction,
which steals the wits of the wisest,
however sensible they are."

If this type of incontinence is worse than the type related to anger, then it's both incontinence in the strict sense and, in a way, vice.

Also, no one commits an act of violence because of anger without feeling pain, but everyone who acts violently because of anger feels pain, while someone who acts violently for pleasure does it with enjoyment. If acts done out of anger are the most justifiable, then incontinence driven by desire is worse because there's no justice in violent acts driven by desire.

It's clear, then, that incontinence connected to desire is more shameful than incontinence connected to anger, and continence and incontinence are tied to bodily desires and pleasures. But we need to understand the differences among these pleasures. As we said earlier, some are human and natural in both kind and amount, while others are brutish or result from illness and disease. Temperance and self-indulgence are only concerned with the first type of pleasure. That's why we don't call animals temperate or self-indulgent, except metaphorically, and only if one species of animal is more wanton, destructive, or greedy than another. Animals can't choose or plan; they're simply deviations from the norm, like how madmen deviate from normal humans. Brute behavior is less evil than vice, even though it's scarier, because there's no better part to corrupt in animals as there is in humans. Comparing a lifeless object to a living one in terms of badness is like comparing injustice itself to an unjust person. Both are bad, but a bad person will do far more evil than a brute.

When it comes to pleasures, pains, desires, and dislikes that arise from touch and taste, which temperance and self-indulgence are mostly concerned with, people can either be defeated by even the easiest of these, or they can resist the hardest ones. When it comes to pleasures, incontinence and continence are the relevant traits, while when it comes to pain, softness and endurance are the terms. Most people fall somewhere in the middle, though they often lean toward the worse traits.

Since some pleasures are necessary while others aren't, and since the necessary ones are only necessary to a point, but excesses of them aren't, the person who seeks out too many pleasures or pursues necessary things to an extreme, and does this by choice, for their own sake and not for some other result, is self-indulgent. This person is unlikely to regret their actions and is therefore incurable, because someone who can't regret their actions can't be fixed. The person who doesn't pursue them enough is the opposite of self-indulgent. The person who is in the middle is temperate. Similarly, there's a person who avoids physical pain, not because they're overwhelmed by it, but because they choose to. (Some people are drawn to certain acts because of the pleasure involved, others because they want to avoid the pain that comes from the desire for pleasure, so these types of people are different.) Now, we'd think worse of someone with no desire, or weak desires, if they did something disgraceful than we would if someone did it under the influence of strong desire. We'd also think worse of someone who hit someone else, not in anger, than if they did it out of anger. For what would they have done if they had been strongly affected? This is why the self-indulgent person is worse than the incontinent one. Of these states, softness is a kind of weakness, and self-indulgence is the opposite. The incontinent person is opposed by the continent one, while the soft person is opposed by the person of endurance. Endurance means resisting, while continence means conquering, and resisting and conquering are different, just like not being defeated is different from winning. This is why continence is better than endurance. A person who fails to resist things most people can handle is soft and effeminate. Effeminacy is also a type of softness. This kind of person drags their cloak to avoid the pain of lifting it, and pretends to be sick without thinking they're miserable, though the person they're imitating really is miserable.

The same goes for continence and incontinence. If someone is defeated by violent and overwhelming pleasures or pains, it's not surprising. We're even willing to forgive them if they tried to resist, like Theodectes' Philoctetes when bitten by a snake, or Carcinus' Cercyon in the Alope, or like people who try not to laugh but burst out in laughter anyway, like what happened to Xenophantus. But it's surprising when someone is defeated by, and can't resist, pleasures or pains that most people can handle, when it's not due to heredity or illness, like the softness that runs in the Scythian kings, or the softness that's more common in women than in men.

The person who loves amusement is thought to be self-indulgent, but is really soft. Amusement is a form of rest, since it's a break from work, and the person who loves amusement is one of those who go to excess with it.

There are two types of incontinence: impulsiveness and weakness. Some people, after deciding what's right, fail to stick to their decision because of their emotions. Others, because they don't deliberate at all, are led by their emotions. Some people, like those who first tickle others but don't get tickled themselves, if they've already seen what's coming and have stirred up their rational mind, aren't defeated by their emotions, whether the emotion is pleasant or painful. It's quick and excitable people who suffer the most from impulsive incontinence. Quick people, because they're so fast, and excitable people, because their passions are so strong, don't wait for reasoning to catch up, because they tend to follow their imagination.

The self-indulgent person, as we've said, is unlikely to regret their actions, because they stick to their choices. But the incontinent person is more likely to regret. This is why, contrary to how we initially framed the issue, the self-indulgent person is incurable, while the incontinent person can be cured. Wickedness is like a disease, like dropsy or tuberculosis, while incontinence is like epilepsy. Wickedness is a lasting problem, while incontinence comes and goes. In general, incontinence and vice are different in nature. Vice doesn't realize its own nature, but incontinence does. Of incontinent people, those who temporarily lose control are better than those who have reason but fail to follow it. The latter are defeated by weaker emotions and don't act without thinking first, unlike the former. The incontinent person is like someone who gets drunk easily and quickly on a small amount of wine, less than what most people would need.

It's clear, then, that incontinence isn't the same as vice (though in some cases it might be). Incontinence goes against choice, while vice aligns with choice. However, both lead to similar actions. As Demodocus said of the Milesians, "The Milesians aren't without sense, but they do senseless things." Similarly, incontinent people aren't criminals, but they do criminal acts.

Since the incontinent person tends to pursue excessive bodily pleasures against their better judgment, while the self-indulgent person pursues them because that's just who they are, it's easier to persuade the incontinent person to change, while it's harder to change the self-indulgent person. Virtue and vice either preserve or destroy the first principle, and in actions, the final cause is the first principle, just like in math the hypotheses are the first principles. In neither case does reasoning teach the first principles. Here, it's virtue, either natural or developed by habit, that teaches the right opinion about the first principle. A temperate person is like this. The opposite is the self-indulgent person.

But there's a person who is driven by passion and acts against the right rule. Their passion controls them so they don't follow the right rule, but it doesn't control them to the point where they believe they should pursue such pleasures without limit. This is the incontinent person, who is better than the self-indulgent person and not entirely bad, because the best part of them, the first principle, is still intact. Opposite to them is the person who sticks to their beliefs and isn't swayed by passion. From these points, it's clear that the latter state is good, and the former is bad.

Is someone continent if they stick to any rule or choice, or if they stick to the right rule? Is someone incontinent if they abandon any rule or choice, or if they abandon the right rule and the correct choice? We raised this question earlier. Or is it true that people only incidentally stick to any rule or choice, but in reality, they stick to the true rule and right choice, and abandon what is wrong? If someone chooses this for the sake of that, they're really choosing the latter, but only incidentally the former. When we speak without any qualification, we mean what is true in itself. Therefore, in a sense, the continent person sticks to any opinion, and the incontinent person abandons any opinion, but without qualification, the continent person sticks to the true opinion.

Some people are very stubborn and stick to their own opinions. We call these people "strong-headed." These people are hard to convince at first, and even after that, they don't easily change their minds. They are similar to people who have self-control, just like a person who wastes money is somewhat like a generous person, and a reckless person is a little like someone who is brave. But there are many differences between them. The strong-headed person doesn't give in to their feelings or desires, while someone with self-control might be convinced sometimes. The strong-headed person refuses to listen to reason. They still have desires, and many of them are led by their pleasures. These stubborn people are usually opinionated, ignorant, or rude, and their opinions are influenced by feelings of happiness or sadness. They feel proud if they don't change their minds, like they've won something, but they feel disappointed when their decisions are rejected, much like how sometimes a law can lose its power. In this way, they are more like people who can't control themselves than those who can.

However, some people don't stick to their decisions, not because they lack self-control, but for other reasons, like Neoptolemus in Sophocles' play Philoctetes. He changed his mind not because of shameful pleasure, but because of a good reason—he thought telling the truth was the right thing to do, even though Odysseus had convinced him to lie. So, not everyone who changes for pleasure is self-indulgent or bad; only those who do it for shameful reasons are.

There are also people who enjoy physical things less than they should and don't follow the proper path. A person who is somewhere between this kind of person and one who lacks self-control is a person with self-control. The person without self-control breaks the rules because they enjoy physical things too much, while the other breaks the rules by not enjoying them enough. The person with self-control, however, follows the rules and doesn't let either extreme affect them. Since self-control is good, both of these opposite states must be bad, as they usually seem to be. But because the other extreme is less common, we often think that self-control is only the opposite of self-indulgence, just as temperance is the opposite of self-indulgence.

Since many words are used similarly, we also use the word "self-control" to describe both a person with self-control and a temperate person. Both of these types of people don't do anything against the rules because of physical pleasures. The person with self-control still has bad desires but doesn't act on them, while the temperate person doesn't feel any pleasure that goes against the rules. The self-indulgent person and the person without self-control are similar, too. Both pursue physical pleasures, but the self-indulgent person believes they should, while the person without self-control does not.

A person cannot be wise and lack self-control at the same time. A person who has wisdom is also good in terms of character. A wise person not only knows what is right but can also act on it, while the person without self-control cannot. However, it's possible for a clever person to lack self-control. This is why some people mistakenly believe a clever person is wise, even if they lack self-control. Cleverness and wisdom are similar in how they think, but they are different in their purpose. The person without self-control is not like someone who fully understands the truth but more like someone who is asleep or drunk.

They act willingly in some way, knowing what they are doing and why, but they are not evil because their purpose is still good. In this way, they are only halfway to being bad. They are not criminals because they don't act out of malice. Of the two types of people without self-control, one type can't stick to their decisions after thinking things through, and the other doesn't think things through at all. So, a person without self-control is like a city that has good laws but doesn't follow them, like in Anaxandrides' joke, "The city made a law but doesn't care about laws." The wicked person is like a city that follows its laws, but those laws are bad.

Self-control and the lack of it deal with extremes compared to what is normal for most people. The person with self-control sticks to their decisions more than most people, and the person without self-control sticks to them less than most people can.

Among the types of people without self-control, those who act quickly are easier to fix than those who think things through but fail to follow their own decisions. People who lack self-control because of habit are easier to change than those who are naturally this way because it's easier to change a habit than to change one's nature. Even though habits are hard to break because they become like nature, as the poet Evenus says:

"I say that habit is just long practice, my friend, And it becomes people's nature in the end."

We have now explained what self-control, lack of self-control, endurance, and softness are, and how these states are connected to one another.

The study of pleasure and pain belongs to the political philosopher because it helps us understand what is good and bad in the purest sense. It's important to examine these things because we said that virtue and vice are tied to pleasures and pains. Most people also say that happiness includes pleasure, which is why we call happy people "blessed," using a word that suggests enjoyment.

Some people think that no pleasure is a good thing in itself, while others think that some pleasures are good, but most are bad. A third view is that even if all pleasures are good, the best thing in the world is not pleasure. The arguments for these views include: (1) Every pleasure is a process toward a natural state, and no process is the same as its result, like how building a house is not the same as the house itself. (2) A temperate person avoids pleasure. (3) A wise person seeks freedom from pain, not pleasure. (4) Pleasures get in the way of thinking, especially intense pleasures like sexual pleasure. (5) There is no art of pleasure, and all good things come from some kind of art. (6) Both children and animals seek pleasure.

The arguments for the idea that not all pleasures are good include: (1) Some pleasures are shameful, and (2) Some pleasures are harmful to health. Finally, the argument that the best thing isn't pleasure is based on the idea that pleasure is a process, not an end result.

These are the main points of these arguments. But these reasons don't necessarily prove that pleasure isn't a good thing, or even the best thing. First, good things can be good in different ways—some are simply good, while others are good for certain people. In the same way, natural states and the actions that come from them can be divided this way, too. Some things that seem bad might only be bad for some people or for a short time, but not bad in general. Others only seem like pleasures, but they actually involve pain and are just healing processes, like what happens to sick people.

Also, there are two types of good things: activities and states of being. The processes that restore us to our natural state are only pleasant by accident. The pleasure comes from the part of our nature that isn't damaged. Some pleasures, like those from contemplation, don't involve pain or desire at all. This shows that the other pleasures are only accidental because people don't enjoy the same things when they are healthy as when they are recovering. When they're recovering, they enjoy even things that are sharp or bitter, which aren't naturally pleasant.

It's also wrong to say that pleasure is always a process. Pleasures are more like activities that come from a natural state. Some people confuse pleasure with process because they think activities are processes, but they are not.

The argument that some pleasures are bad because they can harm your health is like saying that health is bad because some healthy things are bad for making money. Both are bad in certain ways, but not bad overall. Even thinking can sometimes harm your health.

Pleasures that come from the activity of practical wisdom don't get in the way, but foreign pleasures do. For example, the pleasures of learning and thinking help us do those activities better.

The fact that there is no art of pleasure is because there is no art for any other activity either—just for the ability to do them. But people think that the arts of cooking and perfume-making are arts of pleasure.

The arguments that temperate people avoid pleasure and that wise people seek a painless life, and that animals and children seek pleasure, are all answered in the same way. We've already pointed out in what way pleasures are good or not. Both animals and children seek the wrong kind of pleasures, the ones that involve desire and pain—bodily pleasures. Wise people seek calmness and freedom from these desires. That's why temperate people avoid bodily pleasures, though they still have pleasures of their own.

It's also widely agreed that pain is bad and something we should avoid. Some pain is bad without question, and other kinds of pain are bad because they get in the way of our lives. The opposite of something bad is good, so pleasure must also be good. Speusippus' argument that pleasure is opposed to both pain and good things, like how more is opposed to less and equal, doesn't work because he wouldn't say that pleasure is a kind of evil.

Even if some pleasures are bad, that doesn't mean the highest good can't be a pleasure. Just like how the highest good can be a kind of knowledge, even though some kinds of knowledge are bad. If happiness is the unimpeded activity of our natural state, and activities are pleasant, then the highest good might well be a pleasure. This is why all people think the happy life is also a pleasant one. No activity is perfect when it is blocked, and happiness is the most perfect state. That's why the happy person needs physical and external goods, not because happiness depends on them, but to avoid being hindered. People who say a person being tortured on the rack can still be happy because they are good are mistaken.

We need external things to be happy, which is why some people think good fortune is the same as happiness. But it isn't. Even good fortune, when it goes too far, can get in the way, and then it's no longer good fortune. Happiness has a limit when it comes to external things.

Finally, the fact that all animals and people pursue pleasure suggests that pleasure is somehow the highest good. Even though not everyone seeks the same pleasures, and not all pleasures are good, everyone still seeks pleasure because it is part of our nature. Bodily pleasures are common and shared by all, which is why people think they are the only pleasures.

It's also clear that if pleasure is not good, the happy person wouldn't need it. But if pleasure isn't a good, then pain can't be bad either, and the good person's life wouldn't be any more pleasant than anyone else's life. If their activities aren't more pleasant, why would they avoid pain?

Regarding bodily pleasures, some people think noble pleasures should be chosen but not bodily ones, like those the self-indulgent person pursues. But why, then, are the opposite of these pains considered bad? Necessary pleasures are good, even if not as good as noble ones, because their opposite, pain, is bad.

We also need to explain why bodily pleasures seem more desirable than they really are. First, it's because they relieve pain. People experience so much pain that they seek extreme bodily pleasure to get rid of it. Relief from pain makes these pleasures seem better than they are. Also, some pleasures come from a bad nature or bad habits, like those of animals or bad people. Others are meant to cure a problem, but being healthy is better than getting healthy. These pleasures only seem good because they are part of a healing process.

Second, some people pursue intense pleasures because they can't enjoy anything else. They create artificial desires, like thirst, just to satisfy them. When these desires aren't harmful, it's okay, but when they are harmful, it's bad. These people can't enjoy the more subtle pleasures because their nature is restless. Young people and those with a lot of energy are always in need of release. Their bodies are always uncomfortable because of their unique makeup, and they are driven by strong desires. This is why they seek intense pleasures and become self-indulgent. But pleasures that don't come with pain can't be excessive. These are the natural pleasures that are good on their own, not by accident.

When we talk about things that are pleasant by accident, we mean those that act as cures. We think these processes are pleasant because they help fix something that is wrong in our nature. Natural pleasures, on the other hand, are those that stimulate healthy parts of our nature.

There isn't one thing that is always pleasant because our nature isn't simple. We have another part to us since we are mortal creatures. So, if one part of us is doing something, it can feel unnatural to the other part of our nature. When both parts are balanced, what we do doesn't feel either painful or pleasant. If our nature were simple, the same action would always be the most enjoyable. This is why God experiences a single and simple pleasure all the time. There's not only an activity of movement but also an activity of stillness, and pleasure is found more in rest than in movement. But, as the poet says, "change in all things is sweet," and this is because of some kind of flaw. Just like how a flawed person is always changing, a nature that constantly needs change is flawed because it's not simple or good.

We've now talked about continence and incontinence, and about pleasure and pain—what each of these is and how some of them are good and others are bad. What's left is to discuss friendship.

Book 8

After everything we've discussed, it makes sense to now talk about friendship, because it is either a virtue or involves virtue, and it is essential for living well. No one would want to live without friends, even if they had all other good things in life. Even rich people and those with power are thought to need friends the most. What good is success without people to help and share it with, especially with friends, who deserve it the most? How can success be maintained without friends to protect it? The more success someone has, the more they are at risk of losing it. In times of poverty and misfortune, people feel that friends are their only source of comfort. Friendship helps young people avoid mistakes, and it supports older people by taking care of their needs and helping with the things they can't do because of weakness. Friendship also inspires people in their prime to do great things—"two people working together." With friends, people are better at both thinking and acting. Parents naturally feel friendship for their children, and children for their parents. This is true not just for humans but also for birds and most animals. People of the same race also feel friendship for each other, especially among humans, which is why we praise those who love humanity. We even notice this when we travel and see how every person seems to be connected to others. Friendship also seems to be what holds communities together, and lawmakers seem to value friendship even more than justice. Unity is something like friendship, and lawmakers strive for this, while removing division as their greatest enemy. When people are friends, they don't need justice, but when they are just, they still need friendship. The highest form of justice is thought to be something like friendship.

Friendship is not only necessary, but also noble. We praise those who love their friends, and it is considered a good thing to have many friends. We also believe that good people are the same people who make good friends.

There is much debate about friendship. Some say that friendship is based on similarity, and that similar people become friends. This is where sayings like "like attracts like" and "birds of a feather flock together" come from. Others, however, say, "two of a trade never agree." People have also asked deeper questions about this, like Euripides' saying that "dry land loves rain, and the sky filled with rain loves to fall to earth," or Heraclitus' idea that "what is opposite helps" and "the best harmony comes from different notes" and "all things are born from conflict." Empedocles, along with others, says the opposite: "like attracts like." These are physical questions that we can leave for now because they aren't part of this discussion. Let's focus on the human aspects, like whether friendship can form between any two people, or whether wicked people can be friends. Is there only one type of friendship, or are there different kinds? Those who believe there is only one kind of friendship say this because they think friendship can vary in degree. But even things that are different in kind can vary in degree. We've already discussed this point before.

The kinds of friendship may become clearer if we first understand what it is that people love. Not everything is loved—only what is lovable. The lovable is something that is good, pleasant, or useful. Something useful is what brings about some good or pleasure. So, the good and the useful are loved as ends. Do people love the good itself, or what is good for them? These things sometimes conflict. The same goes for what is pleasant. It's believed that each person loves what is good for themselves, and that what is good is lovable in general, but what is good for each person is lovable for them specifically. But each person doesn't love what is truly good for them, but what seems good to them. This difference doesn't matter much, though; we just have to say that "the lovable" is "what seems lovable."

There are three main reasons why people love something. We don't call the love of non-living things friendship, because it's not mutual love, and we don't wish good things for the non-living object itself. For example, it would be silly to say you wish wine well; if you wish anything for it, it's that it stays good so you can enjoy it. But for a friend, we should wish what is good for them for their sake. If someone wishes good for another person, but the feeling isn't returned, we call this goodwill, not friendship. Goodwill becomes friendship only when the feeling is returned and recognized. Many people feel goodwill toward those they've never met but believe to be good or useful. If this feeling is returned, they seem to have goodwill for each other, but we can't really call them friends if they don't know how the other person feels. To be friends, people must recognize that they both have goodwill and wish good for each other for one of the reasons mentioned.

These reasons are different from each other, and so are the types of love and friendship that come from them. There are three kinds of friendship, based on the three things that are lovable. For each of these, there is mutual and recognized love, and those who love each other wish each other well for the reason they love one another. People who love each other for their usefulness don't love each other for who they are, but for the good they get from each other. The same goes for those who love for pleasure—they don't love someone for their character but because they find them enjoyable. So, people who love for usefulness love for what is good for themselves, and those who love for pleasure love for what is pleasant to themselves. They don't love the person for who they are, but for how they are useful or enjoyable. These types of friendships are only based on circumstances. The loved person isn't loved for who they are, but for providing some good or pleasure. These friendships end easily if the person is no longer pleasant or useful.

What is useful doesn't last, and it always changes. When the reason for the friendship disappears, so does the friendship, because it only existed for a particular purpose. This kind of friendship is most common among older people, because at that age, people look for what is useful, not what is pleasant. Younger people, or those in their prime, seek friendships based on utility, too. These people don't spend much time together because they don't always enjoy each other's company. They only need each other when they are useful. They only find each other pleasant when they expect to get something good in the future. Friendships between host and guest also fall into this category.

Friendships between young people, on the other hand, seem to be based on pleasure. Young people live by their emotions and mostly chase what is pleasant to themselves at the moment. But as they grow older, their pleasures change. This is why young people become friends quickly and lose friendships just as fast. Their friendship changes with whatever they find enjoyable, and their pleasures change quickly. Young people also fall in love easily because most of their romantic friendships are based on emotions and the pursuit of pleasure. This is why they fall in love quickly and fall out of love just as fast, sometimes in a single day. But these people do want to spend their days and lives together, because this is how they fulfill the purpose of their friendship.

Perfect friendship is the friendship between good people who are alike in virtue. These friends wish well to each other because they are good, and they are good people themselves. People who wish well to their friends for their friends' sake are the truest friends. They do this because of who they are, not because of any outside factor. So, their friendship lasts as long as they are good—and goodness is something that lasts. These friends are good in general and good to each other, because good people are both good overall and useful to each other. They are also pleasant to each other because good people are pleasant in general and pleasant to each other. Each person finds their own activities and those of similar people enjoyable, and the actions of good people are either the same or similar. Such a friendship is permanent because it has all the qualities that friendship should have. All friendship is based on the desire for something good or pleasant—whether that good or pleasure is abstract or something the friend enjoys—and is based on a certain similarity. In the case of good people, all the qualities of friendship we've discussed belong to them because of who they are. For this kind of friendship, the other qualities are similar in both friends, and what is good without qualification is also pleasant without qualification. These are the most lovable qualities. Love and friendship, then, are found most often and in their best form between good people.

It is natural for such friendships to be rare because people like this are hard to find. Also, this kind of friendship takes time and familiarity to form. As the saying goes, people can't know each other until they've "eaten salt together." They can't become friends or be friends until each has been found lovable and trustworthy. Those who quickly show signs of friendship may want to be friends, but they aren't true friends until they both recognize the other as lovable and know this to be true. A desire for friendship can form quickly, but real friendship takes time.

This kind of friendship is perfect in both how long it lasts and in all other ways. In it, each friend gives and receives the same thing, or something similar to what they give. This is how things should be between friends. Friendships based on pleasure are similar to this kind of friendship, because good people also find each other pleasant. Friendships based on utility are also similar because good people are useful to each other, too. Friendships between lesser people tend to last longer when both friends get the same thing from each other, like pleasure, and also when they get this from the same source. This happens with witty people, for example, but not with lovers. Lovers do not enjoy the same things—the lover enjoys seeing their beloved, and the beloved enjoys receiving attention. When youth fades, the friendship often fades, too, because one no longer finds pleasure in seeing the other, and the other no longer receives attention. But many lovers stay together when they come to love each other's character through familiarity, especially if their characters are alike. Those who love each other for utility or pleasure are less likely to be true friends and less likely to stay friends for long. Those who are friends for utility part ways when they no longer benefit from each other, because they didn't love each other but loved the profit they gained.

When it comes to friendship for pleasure or utility, even bad people can be friends, or a good person can be friends with a bad person, or someone who is neither good nor bad can be friends with any kind of person. But when it comes to friendship for its own sake, only good people can truly be friends because bad people don't take pleasure in each other unless they get something from it.

Friendship between good people is the only type that cannot be harmed by slander. It's hard to believe bad things about someone you've known and trusted for a long time. Among good people, you find trust, the belief that "he would never wrong me," and all the other qualities that make true friendship. But in the other kinds of friendship, these problems can easily arise. People use the word "friend" even when their relationship is based on utility, like how alliances between states are made for mutual advantage. Friendships based on pleasure are like the friendships between children. So, we should probably call these people friends, too, and say that there are different kinds of friendship. The highest and truest form is the friendship between good people, but the other types are friendships by analogy. They are friends because of something good and something like what we find in true friendship, since even pleasure is good to those who love pleasure. These two kinds of friendship (pleasure and utility) are rarely combined, and people don't usually become friends for both pleasure and utility at the same time. Things that are only related by chance don't often come together.

Friendship is divided into these kinds. Bad people can be friends for the sake of pleasure or utility because they are alike in that way, but good people are friends for each other's sake because of their goodness. These are true friends, while the others are friends only by coincidence and because they resemble true friends.

Just as with virtue, some people are called good because of their character, while others are called good because of their actions. The same is true for friendship. Those who live together enjoy each other's company and help each other, but those who are apart or asleep aren't performing the activities of friendship, though they are ready to do so. Distance doesn't destroy friendship, but it stops the activity of it. However, if the distance lasts too long, people can forget their friendship. This is why people say, "out of sight, out of mind." Older people and sour people don't seem to make friends easily because they aren't very pleasant, and no one can spend time with someone who is unpleasant. Nature avoids what is painful and seeks what is pleasant. People who like each other but don't spend time together seem to have goodwill for each other rather than real friendship. There's nothing more characteristic of friends than living together. Even people who need something from others want their company, and those who are perfectly happy still want to spend their time with friends. Solitude is not good for these people. But people can't live together if they aren't pleasant and don't enjoy the same things, as friends who are companions do.

The truest friendship, as we've said many times, is the friendship of good people. What is good or pleasant without qualification is lovable and desirable, and for each person, what is good or pleasant to them is lovable. The good person is lovable and desirable to another good person for both reasons. It seems that love is a feeling, while friendship is more of a character trait. You can love non-living things, but friendship involves mutual choice, and choice comes from character. People wish good things for those they love, for their sake, not just because of a feeling but because of their character. When you love a friend, you love what is good for yourself, because a good person, in becoming a friend, also becomes a good thing for their friend. Each person loves what is good for themselves and returns this love equally with goodwill and pleasantness. Friendship is said to be based on equality, and this is most true in the friendship of good people.

Friendship doesn't easily form between sour or older people because they aren't as good-natured and don't enjoy company as much. These are considered the most important qualities for forming friendship. This is why younger people make friends more quickly than older people. It's because people don't become friends with those they don't find pleasant. The same goes for sour people—they don't make friends quickly. But these people may still have goodwill for each other because they wish each other well and help each other when needed. However, they aren't truly friends because they don't spend time together or enjoy each other's company. These two things are considered the most important parts of friendship.

You can't be a true friend to many people, just as you can't be in love with many people at once. Love is an intense feeling, and by nature, it can only be directed toward one person. It's also hard for many people to please the same person greatly, or to be considered good in the eyes of the same person. It also takes time to get to know someone and become familiar with them, and that's difficult to do with many people. However, when it comes to friendship based on utility or pleasure, it's possible to be friends with many people because many people can be useful or pleasant, and these kinds of relationships don't require as much time.

Of these two kinds of friendship, the one based on pleasure is more like true friendship, especially when both people get the same things from each other and enjoy each other's company, like in the friendships of young people. There is more generosity in these friendships. Friendships based on utility are more common among business-minded people. Those who are perfectly happy don't need friends for utility, but they do need friends for pleasure. They want to live with someone, and while they can endure what is painful for a short time, no one could put up with pain forever, not even if it came from something good. This is why they look for friends who are pleasant. Perhaps they should find friends who are both pleasant and good for them. That way, they will have all the qualities that friends should have.

People in positions of power tend to have friends who fall into two different groups: some are useful, and some are fun to be around. It's rare to find someone who is both useful and fun. They don't look for people whose fun side comes with virtue or whose usefulness is aimed at good things. Instead, they look for funny, witty people to entertain them, and other friends they choose are good at doing what they're told. These qualities rarely go together in one person.

We've already said that a good person is both fun and useful. However, a good person doesn't usually become friends with someone higher in status unless that person is also better in virtue. If they aren't, there's no equality in the friendship because one person isn't better in both ways. But finding someone who is better in both ways is not easy.

Still, the friendships we've talked about are about equality. Friends give and receive the same things from each other and want the same things for each other. Or, they might trade one thing for another, like fun for usefulness. However, we've already said that these types of friendships are less true and don't last as long.

People think these are friendships because they seem similar to friendships based on virtue. One involves fun, and the other involves usefulness. Both fun and usefulness are also part of virtuous friendships. However, these friendships don't last long and are not as strong against gossip and rumors as virtuous friendships are. So, they don't seem like true friendships because they are different from friendships based on virtue in many ways.

There's another type of friendship that involves inequality, like the friendship between a father and son, an older person and a younger person, or between a husband and wife. These friendships are also different from each other. The relationship between a parent and child isn't the same as the one between a ruler and a subject, and even a father's relationship with his son isn't the same as the son's relationship with his father. The same goes for husbands and wives. Each person has different roles and virtues, and they love each other for different reasons. This means the love and the friendship are different as well.

In these friendships, each person doesn't give or receive the same things from the other, and they shouldn't expect to. But when children give their parents what they owe them for bringing them into the world, and parents give their children what they need, these friendships will be lasting and excellent. In friendships where there is inequality, the love should also be unequal. The person who is better should be loved more than they love, and the more useful person should be loved more as well. When the love matches the merit of each person, a kind of equality is created, which is what we expect in friendship.

However, equality in friendship doesn't seem to work the same way as it does in justice. In justice, what's most important is proportional equality—each person gets what they deserve based on their merit. But in friendship, equal amounts of love and affection come first, and proportional merit comes second. This becomes clear when there's a big difference in virtue, wealth, or anything else between two people. They stop being friends because they no longer expect to be. This is especially clear with the gods, who are far greater than us in every way. It's also true for kings because people who are much lower in status don't expect to be friends with kings, just like ordinary people don't expect to be friends with the best or wisest people.

It's hard to say exactly how much difference two people can handle before they stop being friends. Friendship can still survive even if one person becomes a little different, but when one person becomes too different—like the difference between people and gods—friendship is no longer possible. This is why people wonder whether friends really want the greatest good for their friends, like becoming gods. If a friend becomes a god, they won't be friends anymore, and that wouldn't be a good thing for them. The answer is that a friend wants good things for their friend as long as they stay the same person they are now. So, they want the greatest good for their friend, but only as long as they stay human. But not every great thing; each person mostly wants the best things for themselves.

Most people seem to want to be loved more than they want to love. This is because of ambition, and it's why many people love flattery. The flatterer acts like a friend who is lower in status and pretends to love more than they are loved. Being loved is similar to being honored, which is something most people aim for. But people don't want honor for its own sake. Most people enjoy being honored by important people because they believe it will help them get what they want in the future. So, they like honor because it's a sign that good things will come. People who want honor from good people, or people who know them well, aim to confirm their own belief in their goodness. They enjoy honor because it makes them believe they are good based on what others think.

On the other hand, people enjoy being loved just for the sake of being loved. This makes it seem like being loved is better than being honored, and friendship seems to be desirable in itself. But it seems that loving is more important than being loved, as shown by how much mothers love their children. Some mothers give their children to others to raise, and as long as they know their children are okay, they love them even if they don't get love in return. They are happy just to see their children do well. Mothers still love their children even if the children don't know enough to return their love.

Since friendship depends more on loving, and people who love their friends are praised, it seems like loving is the main virtue of friendship. Only those who love in the right way can have lasting friendships, and only their friendships last over time.

This is also how unequal people can still be friends; their love can be made equal. Equality and similarity are what friendship is about, especially when it comes to people who are similar in virtue. Virtuous people are steady and loyal to each other. They don't ask for or offer bad favors, and they even stop each other from doing wrong. Good people try to keep themselves and their friends from doing anything bad.

Wicked people, however, are not steady. They don't even stay the same as themselves. They become friends for a short time because they enjoy each other's wickedness. Friendships based on usefulness or pleasure last longer because the friends continue to enjoy each other's company or benefit from each other. Friendships based on usefulness seem to happen most easily between opposites, like rich and poor, or ignorant and knowledgeable, because people want what they lack, and each gives something different in return. This can also be true in the case of lovers, where one is beautiful, and the other isn't.

Sometimes lovers seem ridiculous when they demand to be loved as much as they love, especially if they aren't equally lovable. Their demand might make sense if they were equally lovable, but if they aren't, it's silly. Still, opposites don't always seek each other out on purpose, but more by accident. What people really want is something in the middle, because that's what's best for them. For example, it's better for something dry not to become wet, but to reach a balanced, in-between state. The same goes for hot and cold and other opposites. We don't need to get too deep into this because it's not really the focus of our discussion.

Friendship and justice seem to focus on the same things and apply to the same people, as we said at the beginning. In every group, there seems to be some kind of justice and some kind of friendship. People call their fellow travelers and soldiers their friends, and the same goes for those they are connected to in other types of groups. The extent of their connection is the extent of their friendship, just as the extent of their connection determines how much justice exists between them. The saying "friends share everything" is true because friendship depends on sharing. Brothers and close friends share everything, but other friends share specific things—some more, some less. Friendships can be more or less true friendships, just like there are different levels of justice. The duties parents owe to their children aren't the same as those brothers owe each other, and the duties of close friends aren't the same as those of fellow citizens. The same is true for other kinds of friendship.

Because of this, there's also a difference in what it means to act unjustly toward each type of friend. It's worse to cheat a close friend than a fellow citizen, and worse not to help a brother than a stranger. It's also worse to hurt a father than anyone else. The demands of justice seem to grow stronger as the friendship becomes closer, which shows that friendship and justice apply to the same people and work in similar ways.

All kinds of groups are like smaller parts of a political community. People come together in groups for some specific advantage, to get something they need for their lives. This is also why political communities originally formed and why they still exist—people want what's best for the whole group. This is what lawmakers focus on when they create laws, and they call just what benefits everyone. Other groups aim for specific advantages, like sailors trying to make money on a voyage or soldiers trying to win a war. People in villages or religious groups act the same way. Some groups form for the sake of pleasure, like religious gatherings or social clubs. These groups exist for offering sacrifices and socializing.

But these groups are still part of the larger political community, which aims not just for short-term benefits but for what's good for life as a whole. They offer sacrifices, arrange gatherings, and assign honors to the gods, all while giving themselves some time to relax and enjoy life. These activities usually happen after the harvest when people have the most free time. So, all groups seem to be part of the larger political community, and the type of friendship depends on the type of group.

There are three main types of government, and each has a corrupted version of it. The good types are monarchy, aristocracy, and government based on property, which is often called "timocracy," although some people call it a "polity." Of these, monarchy is the best, and timocracy is the worst. The corrupted version of monarchy is tyranny. Both are types of one-man rule, but they are very different. A tyrant rules for his own benefit, while a king rules for the benefit of his people. A man is only a king if he doesn't need anything for himself and is better than his subjects in every way. A man like this doesn't have to worry about himself, so he focuses on what's good for his people. A king who doesn't act like this is just a king in name only.

Tyranny is the exact opposite of this. A tyrant only cares about himself. This is why tyranny is the worst form of government—it's the opposite of the best. Monarchy turns into tyranny when a bad king becomes a tyrant. Aristocracy turns into oligarchy when the rulers become corrupt. They divide the wealth of the city unfairly, keeping most of it for themselves and giving important jobs to the same small group of people. In this way, a few bad people end up in power instead of the best people. Timocracy turns into democracy because democracy is just timocracy taken a step further. Timocracy is government by the majority, and in democracy, everyone is considered equal if they meet the property requirement. Democracy is the least bad of the corrupted forms because it's only a small step away from timocracy.

These are the changes that governments are most likely to go through because they are the easiest and smallest transitions.

You can see examples of these types of governments even in households. The way a father deals with his children is like a monarchy because the father cares for them. This is why Homer calls Zeus "father." The ideal of monarchy is for it to be like a father's rule. However, in Persian families, the father's rule is more like a tyranny because they treat their sons like slaves. Tyranny is also like the way a master rules over his slaves because it's only for the master's benefit. This might seem like a proper form of government, but the Persian version is corrupt because different types of relationships should be governed in different ways.

The relationship between a man and his wife is like an aristocracy because the husband rules based on his worth. In matters where he should lead, he does, but in areas that suit his wife's abilities, he lets her handle them. If the husband tries to rule over everything, the relationship becomes more like an oligarchy because he's not ruling based on what's right. Sometimes, the wife rules because she's an heiress, and in that case, her rule is based on wealth and power rather than virtue, like in an oligarchy. The relationship between brothers is like timocracy because they are mostly equal, except for differences in age. If the age gap is too big, the friendship is no longer a brotherly one.

Democracy is seen in households where there's no clear leader, and everyone is treated equally. It's also found in households where the head of the family is weak, and everyone does as they please.

Each of these types of government involves friendship, just like they involve justice. The friendship between a king and his subjects depends on the king's ability to do good things for them. A good king takes care of his people like a shepherd cares for his sheep. This is why Homer called Agamemnon the "shepherd of the people." The friendship between a father and his children is even stronger because the father gives the greatest gifts: life, care, and upbringing.

Ancestors are respected for the same reasons. By nature, a father rules over his children, ancestors rule over their descendants, and a king rules over his people. These friendships are based on the superiority of one person over the other, which is why ancestors are honored. Justice in these relationships isn't the same for both sides. It's based on what each person deserves, just like the friendship is. The friendship between a man and his wife is like an aristocracy because the better person gets more of the good things, and each person gets what suits them. The same is true for justice in these relationships. The friendship between brothers is like the friendship between comrades because they are equal in age and similar in feelings and character. This is also similar to the friendship in timocratic governments, where the goal is for all citizens to be equal and fair. The leadership is shared equally, and the friendship fits this kind of equality.

In the corrupted forms of government, there is little friendship, just as there is little justice. The worst form of government, tyranny, has almost no friendship. Where there's nothing shared between the ruler and the ruled, there's no friendship because there's no justice. For example, there's no friendship between a craftsman and his tool, between the soul and the body, or between a master and a slave. The tool benefits its user, but there's no friendship or justice toward lifeless things. The same is true for horses or oxen, and even for slaves as slaves. There's nothing shared between a master and a slave. The slave is a living tool, and the tool is a lifeless slave. As a slave, a person can't be a friend, but as a human, they can be. There can be some justice between any two people who are part of a system of law or agreement, and so there can also be friendship between them as humans.

In tyrannies, there's almost no friendship or justice. But in democracies, there's more of both because the citizens are equal and have more in common.

Every type of friendship involves some kind of partnership, as we've said. But we can separate the friendships of family members and comrades from the rest. Friendships between fellow citizens, members of the same tribe, or people traveling together seem more like partnerships because they are based on agreements. We can also include the friendships between hosts and guests in this group. Family friendships seem to come in many forms, but they all depend on the parent-child relationship. Parents love their children because they are a part of themselves, and children love their parents because they come from them.

Parents know their children better than children know their parents, and the parent feels a stronger connection to the child than the child feels to the parent. The child comes from the parent, not the other way around. Also, parents start loving their children as soon as they are born, but children only start loving their parents later when they gain understanding. This explains why mothers love their children more than fathers do.

Parents love their children as they love themselves because children are like another version of them. Children love their parents because they were born from them, and brothers love each other because they share the same parents. This is why people talk about "the same blood" or "the same family." In a way, brothers are the same person in different bodies. Two things that help build friendship are being raised together and being close in age. "People of the same age stick together," and people who grow up together tend to be comrades. This is why the friendship between brothers is similar to that of comrades. Cousins and other relatives are connected because they come from brothers or the same ancestors. They are closer or more distant based on how close the original ancestor is to them.

The friendship between children and parents, and between humans and gods, is based on viewing them as something good and superior. Parents and gods give the greatest gifts—they are the reason for their existence, nourishment, and education from birth. This kind of friendship is more pleasant and useful than friendship with strangers because they live more closely together. The friendship between brothers is similar to that of comrades, especially when they are good people. In general, people who are alike become friends more easily because they share more with each other, and brothers naturally love each other from birth. Since they are born to the same parents, grow up together, and receive the same education, they tend to be more similar in character. The test of time strengthens and confirms their bond.

Friendship among other relatives is proportional to the closeness of the relationship. The friendship between a husband and wife seems to be natural because humans are naturally inclined to form couples, even more than to form cities. The household comes before the city, and reproduction is a common drive in both humans and animals.

While animals unite only for reproduction, humans live together not just for this purpose but also for the various needs of life. From the start, their roles are divided, with men and women contributing different skills to the household. This cooperation makes their friendship both useful and pleasant. If the husband and wife are good people, their friendship can also be based on virtue, as each has their own virtues, and they take pleasure in them. Children seem to strengthen the bond between them, which is why childless couples tend to separate more easily. Children are a shared good, and what is shared tends to keep people together.

The way a husband and wife, or any friends, should treat each other is similar to how justice requires them to act. A person doesn't owe the same duties to a friend as they do to a stranger, a comrade, or a classmate.

There are three types of friendship, as we mentioned earlier: some friendships are between equals, while others are between those who are superior or inferior. Not only can equally good people become friends, but also a better person can be friends with someone worse off. In friendships based on pleasure or usefulness, the friends can be equal or unequal in the benefits they provide. When friends are equals, they should balance things equally in love and all other matters. When they are unequal, they should give and receive in proportion to their differences. Complaints and resentments arise mostly in friendships based on usefulness, which makes sense. Friends who care about virtue try to help each other, as this is a sign of both virtue and friendship. When people are competing to help each other, there are no complaints or quarrels. No one is upset with someone who loves them and treats them well. If a person is kind, they will repay kindness with kindness. A friend who excels at helping won't complain because they are achieving what they aim for, which is to do good. In friendships of pleasure, there aren't many complaints because both friends get what they want by enjoying each other's company. Even if one friend didn't bring enough pleasure, it would be silly to complain since they can simply stop spending time together.

Friendships of utility are full of complaints because each person uses the other for their own gain. They always want to get more than they give and feel like they are receiving less than they deserve. They often blame their partners for not meeting their expectations. Those who do favors for others can't always help as much as the other person wants.

It seems that, just as there are two kinds of justice—one unwritten and one legal—there are two kinds of friendship based on utility: moral and legal. Complaints arise when people don't end the friendship in the same way they started it. The legal kind is based on fixed terms. In purely business relationships, repayment happens immediately, while more generous relationships allow for delayed payment but still expect something in return. In these relationships, the debt is clear and not confusing, but the delay adds a friendly element. Some societies don't allow lawsuits over such agreements, believing that those who lend on credit should accept the risks. The moral kind of friendship isn't based on set terms. In this case, a person gives something to a friend without expecting immediate repayment, but they still expect to receive as much or more eventually. If they end up worse off after the friendship ends, they will complain. This happens because people often want to be noble but choose what benefits them. It's noble to help someone without expecting repayment, but receiving help is more beneficial. Therefore, if we can, we should repay what we received. We shouldn't force someone to be our friend against their will. We must acknowledge that we made a mistake by accepting a benefit from someone we shouldn't have and should settle the debt as if it were a business transaction.

There is some debate about whether we should measure a favor by how useful it was to the person who received it or by the kindness of the giver. The receivers often say they didn't get much because it was something small for the giver, or they could have gotten it from someone else, downplaying the favor. On the other hand, the givers say they gave the best they had and something that couldn't be easily obtained elsewhere, especially if it was given in a time of need. In friendships based on utility, it seems that the benefit to the receiver should be the measure. After all, the receiver asks for the favor, and the giver expects an equivalent return. The help given is equal to the advantage received, so the receiver should repay what they got or even more, as that would be nobler. In friendships based on virtue, complaints don't arise because the intention of the giver is the true measure. Intention is central to virtue and character.

Friendships between people of different status can also lead to disagreements because each expects to get more out of it. When this happens, the friendship falls apart. The superior friend thinks they should get more because they are better, while the more useful friend expects more because they believe a lesser person shouldn't receive the same benefits. They argue that, just like in business partnerships, those who invest more should receive more in return. But the friend in need argues the opposite, thinking that a good friend should help those in need. They ask, "What's the point of being friends with someone powerful or virtuous if it brings no benefits?"

Both sides seem justified in their expectations. Each should receive more from the friendship but in different ways. The superior friend should receive more honor, while the lesser friend should gain more material benefits. Honor is the reward for virtue and generosity, while material gain helps those in need.

This is also true in political arrangements. A person who doesn't contribute to the common good isn't honored. Public resources are given to those who benefit the public, and honor is one of these resources. It's impossible to receive both wealth and honor from the public at the same time because no one is willing to take the smaller share of everything. Therefore, the person who sacrifices wealth is given honor, while the person who wants to be paid receives wealth. This balance keeps the friendship intact, as we mentioned earlier. This is also how we should treat unequal friendships. The person who receives wealth or virtue should give honor in return, repaying what they can. Friendship asks a person to do what they are capable of, not necessarily what matches the merits of the situation. For example, no one can fully repay their debt to the gods or their parents. But a person who serves them to the best of their ability is considered good. This is why a person can't disown their father, although a father can disown his son. Since the son is always in debt, he should always try to repay it. However, just like creditors can forgive a debt, a father can forgive his son. At the same time, people think that a father wouldn't reject his son unless the son was extremely wicked. Besides the natural bond between father and son, it's human nature not to reject help from a child. But if the son is wicked, he will likely avoid helping his father or won't do so with much enthusiasm. Most people like to receive help but avoid giving it, seeing it as unprofitable. That covers these issues.

Book 9

In all friendships between people who are different, as we have said, it is balance that keeps things equal and preserves the friendship. For example, in political friendships, the shoemaker gets something back for his shoes that equals their value, and the weaver and all other workers do the same. Here, a common way to measure value is money, so everything is judged by this and compared to it. But in the friendship of lovers, sometimes the lover complains that their great love isn't returned (maybe because they aren't lovable), while the beloved might complain that the lover, who used to promise everything, now delivers nothing.

These problems happen when the lover loves the beloved for pleasure, while the beloved loves the lover for usefulness. They don't both have the qualities the other person expects. If these are the reasons for their friendship, it falls apart when they no longer get what they originally wanted. Each person didn't love the other for who they are but for certain qualities, and these qualities weren't lasting. That's why these friendships don't last. But the love between two good people, as we've said, lasts because it's based on their character.

Problems arise when what each person receives is different from what they wanted. It feels like you're getting nothing if you don't get what you were aiming for. There's a story of someone who promised rewards to a lyre-player, saying they would give more the better he played. But in the morning, when the player asked for his rewards, the person said they had given him pleasure for pleasure. Now, if both wanted the same thing, that would have been fine. But if one wanted enjoyment and the other wanted money, and only one person got what they wanted, then the friendship wasn't balanced. Each person focuses on what they want, and they give what they have in order to get that.

But who gets to decide the value of the service—the person making the sacrifice or the person who benefits from it? It seems like the second person leaves it up to the first. This is what Protagoras supposedly used to do; whenever he taught anything, he let the learner decide how much the teaching was worth and accepted whatever amount they set. But in situations like this, some people prefer the saying "let a man have his fixed reward." Those who get paid first and then don't do what they promised are naturally complained about, especially if their promises were exaggerated. This happens a lot with sophists because no one would pay for what they actually know. So, if these people don't do what they were paid to do, it's no surprise that others complain about them.

But where there is no official contract, people who give something up for the sake of someone else can't be complained about (as we said earlier). This is the nature of virtuous friendships. The return should be based on the intention behind the act because intention is what matters most in friendships and in virtue. This also applies to people who study philosophy together. The value of what they offer can't be measured in money, and no honor is enough to repay what they've done. Still, like with the gods or our parents, it may be enough to repay them by doing what we can.

If the gift wasn't like that but was given expecting something in return, then it's best to make sure the return is fair to both parties. If this can't be achieved, it seems fair and necessary that the person who got the service should set the value. If the person who gave the service gets back something equal to the benefit the other person received or what they would have paid for the pleasure, then they've gotten what's fair.

We see this happening with things that are sold. In some places, there are even laws that say no one can take legal action over voluntary agreements. This is because the law assumes that if you gave someone credit, you should settle with them based on the terms you originally agreed to. The law believes it's more fair for the person who received credit to set the terms than the one who gave it. Most people don't value things the same way when they have them as they did before they got them. They tend to think what they own is worth more than what others have. Still, the return is made based on what the receiver thinks it's worth. The receiver, though, should value the gift based on what they thought it was worth before they received it, not afterward.

There's another question: Should we always put our father first and obey him, or should we trust a doctor when we're sick? When choosing a general, should we pick someone with military skills? And, similarly, should we help a friend or a good person, or should we repay a benefactor or help a friend if we can't do both?

These kinds of questions are hard to answer clearly, aren't they? There are many variations depending on how important the help is and how noble it is. But it's clear that we shouldn't always put the same person first. Most of the time, we should repay benefits rather than do favors for friends, just like we should repay a loan before lending to someone else. But even this isn't always true. For example, if someone has been rescued from kidnappers, should they rescue the person who saved them, or should they save their father? It seems like they should save their father, even before saving themselves.

As we've said, the general rule is to repay what you owe, but if the gift is exceptionally noble or necessary, we should consider that first. Sometimes, it's not even fair to return an equal favor, like when one person does something good for someone they know is virtuous, but the other person repays someone they believe is bad. In such cases, it wouldn't be fair to repay the favor. Even if the person lent to you, expecting to be repaid, they might not expect the same if you believe they are bad. So, if the situation really is that way, the demand for repayment isn't fair. And if it only seems that way, people might still refuse to repay, thinking they aren't doing anything wrong.

As we've often said, discussions about emotions and actions can only be as precise as the topic allows.

It's clear that we shouldn't repay everyone in the same way, and we shouldn't always put our father first in everything, just like we don't sacrifice everything to Zeus. But we should give different things to our parents, brothers, friends, and benefactors. We should give each group what's appropriate and fitting. This seems to be what people actually do. They invite relatives to weddings because relatives are part of the family, and family events affect them. At funerals, relatives gather for the same reason. In matters of food, we should help our parents first because we owe our own nourishment to them. It's more honorable to provide for the people who gave us life, even before providing for ourselves. We should honor our parents like we honor the gods, but not with just any honor. We shouldn't give our parents the same honor we give a philosopher or a general. We should honor them as parents. We should also show respect to older people by standing when they enter and offering them seats. For friends and brothers, we should allow more freedom and sharing of everything. For other relatives, fellow citizens, and people from the same community, we should try to give each group what's appropriate, considering how close we are to them, their virtue, and their usefulness.

It's easier to compare people when they belong to the same group, but it's harder when they're from different groups. Still, we shouldn't avoid the task, but we should do our best to make a fair decision.

Another question is whether or not friendships should be ended when the other person changes. It seems natural to end a friendship based on usefulness or pleasure when the person no longer has those qualities. After all, we were only friends because of those qualities, and when they're gone, it's reasonable to stop loving them. But someone could complain if, while they loved us for our usefulness or pleasantness, we pretended to love them for their character. As we said earlier, most disagreements between friends come when they don't really understand the basis of their friendship. So, if someone believed they were being loved for their character when that wasn't the case, they should blame themselves. But if they were tricked by the other person pretending to love them for their character, then they have a right to complain. They could even argue that the deception was worse than counterfeiting money because the wrong was done to something more valuable.

If someone thought another person was good and that person turns out to be bad, should they still love them? It doesn't seem possible because not everything can be loved—only what is good. We can't and shouldn't love what is evil. It's not right to be a lover of bad things or to become like what's bad. We've said that people love what is similar to them. So, should we immediately end the friendship? Not always. This should only happen if the person's badness can't be fixed. If they can be reformed, it's better to help them improve their character or their situation. This is more in line with what friendship is about. But if someone breaks off a friendship with someone who can't be saved, they aren't doing anything wrong. After all, they didn't become friends with this bad person, and since their friend has changed and they can't help them, they give up on the friendship.

But what if one friend stays the same while the other gets better and becomes far more virtuous? Should the more virtuous person still treat the other as a friend? It seems they can't. When the gap between them becomes too large, it's obvious that the friendship can't continue. For example, in childhood friendships, if one friend remains childlike in their thinking while the other matures into an adult, how could they still be friends? They wouldn't enjoy or value the same things, and without that, they can't be friends because they can't share their lives together. We've already discussed these ideas.

Should the person who's changed treat their former friend as a complete stranger? Not exactly. They should still remember the old friendship, and just like we treat old friends better than strangers, we should also give some credit to people we used to be friends with, as long as the reason for ending the friendship wasn't too severe.

The way people treat their neighbors and the signs of friendship seem to come from how people relate to themselves. For example, we call someone a friend if they want and do what is good for their friend, or at least what seems good, for their friend's sake. Or we call someone a friend if they wish their friend to live and thrive, which is what mothers do for their children, and what friends do for each other even if they've fought. Others define a friend as someone who lives with you and has the same interests. Or they define a friend as someone who shares your joys and sorrows, which mothers do more than anyone. Friendship is defined by one or more of these traits.

Each of these traits applies to how a good person relates to themselves (and to everyone else in so far as they see themselves as good). Virtue and the good person, as we've said, seem to be the standard for everything. A good person's desires are consistent, and they want the same things with all their heart. So, they wish what's good for themselves and do what's good. It's part of being good to put good into action. They do this for their own sake because they do it for the part of them that thinks, which is considered to be the true self.

A good person wishes to live and be preserved, especially the part of them that thinks. Existence is good for a virtuous person, and everyone wishes good for themselves. No one would choose to possess everything if it meant becoming someone else. Even now, we believe God possesses the good. People only want good things if they can remain who they are while getting them. The part of us that thinks seems to be the real person, or at least more so than any other part.

A good person enjoys spending time with themselves. They find pleasure in remembering their past actions, and they have good hopes for the future, which makes them happy. Their mind is full of things to think about. They feel grief and joy with themselves more than anyone else because the same things are always painful or pleasant to them. Their feelings don't change from one moment to the next. It's like they never have anything to regret.

Since all these traits apply to how a good person relates to themselves, and they treat their friends the same way they treat themselves (because a friend is like another self), friendship is thought to be based on these traits. People who have these traits are friends.

Whether or not someone can be friends with themselves is a question we can put aside for now. But there does seem to be friendship within a person in so far as they are like two or more people. This can be seen from the traits of friendship we've mentioned and from the fact that the highest form of friendship is compared to a person's love for themselves.

Even though most people have these traits, even if they aren't great, should we say that when they are happy with themselves and think they are good, they share in these traits? Definitely, no one who is completely bad or irreligious has these traits or even seems to have them. These traits barely apply to less-than-great people either, because they are in conflict with themselves. They want one thing but logically know they should want something else. This happens to people who lack self-control; they choose things that feel good but are harmful instead of the things they know are better. Others, because they are afraid or lazy, avoid doing what they know is best for them. Those who have done many terrible things and are hated for their wickedness even avoid life and might hurt themselves. Wicked people often look for others to spend time with and avoid being alone with themselves. When they are by themselves, they remember all the awful things they've done and imagine doing more bad things, but when they're with others, they forget. Because they don't have anything lovable about them, they don't love themselves. This is also why they don't feel happy or sad with themselves. Their soul is split apart because of their wickedness. One part of them feels sad when they stop themselves from doing certain things, while the other part feels pleased. They feel pulled in different directions, almost like they are being torn apart. Even if a person can't feel happy and sad at the same time, they might soon feel sad because they were once happy, and they wish those things hadn't made them feel happy at all. Bad people are weighed down by regret.

Because of this, a bad person doesn't seem to even like themselves since there's nothing in them to love. If this is the height of misery, we should do everything we can to avoid wickedness and try to be good. Only then can someone be a friend to themselves or someone else.

Goodwill is a friendly feeling but is not the same as friendship. You can have goodwill toward someone you don't know and without them knowing it, but that's not true of friendship. This has been mentioned before. Goodwill isn't even the same as feeling friendly because it doesn't involve strong feelings or desire. Those feelings come with real friendship. Friendship means being close, but goodwill can happen suddenly, like when we feel it for competitors in a contest. We feel goodwill toward them and hope for the best for them, but we wouldn't necessarily do anything with them. As mentioned before, goodwill happens suddenly and is only a surface-level feeling of love.

So, goodwill seems to be the start of friendship, like how admiring someone's looks is the start of love. No one loves someone if they aren't first pleased by their appearance. But just liking someone's appearance doesn't mean you love them. Love only happens when you long for the person when they're not around and crave their presence. In the same way, people can't be friends unless they first feel goodwill for each other. But just because people feel goodwill doesn't mean they're friends. They only wish good things for each other, but they wouldn't go out of their way for each other or put in the effort. So you could say that goodwill is like friendship that hasn't been acted on yet. But when it grows stronger and leads to closeness, it can become friendship—not the kind based on usefulness or pleasure since goodwill doesn't start that way either. If someone has goodwill toward someone because they received help from them, that's just being fair. If someone wishes success for another person because they hope to get something from them in return, that's not really goodwill toward the other person but more like goodwill toward themselves. It's like how someone isn't truly a friend if they only care for someone because they can get something out of it. In general, goodwill comes from admiring something good in another person, like their beauty or bravery, as we pointed out earlier with competitors in contests.

Unanimity also seems to be a kind of friendly relationship. That's why it isn't just agreeing on the same opinion, because that could happen between people who don't even know each other. We don't say that people who agree about everything are unanimous, like people who agree on facts about the stars. Unanimity about things like that doesn't create a friendly bond. But we do say that a city is unified when everyone agrees on what's best for them and chooses to take the same actions together. Unanimity, then, is about actions, especially those that are important and where both or all parties can get what they want. For example, a city is unified when everyone agrees that government officials should be elected or that they should form an alliance with Sparta. Or, when they agree that Pittacus should be their ruler and he is willing to lead them. But when two people both want the same thing only for themselves, like the captains in the Phoenissae, they aren't unified; they are in conflict. Unanimity only happens when everyone agrees that the same person should have something. For example, both the common people and the upper class want the best people to lead. Only in this way can everyone get what they want. Unanimity, then, seems to be political friendship, and it is often said to be so. It deals with things that benefit everyone and that affect our lives.

True unanimity is only found among good people. They are unified with themselves and with others because they have one purpose. They want justice and what is beneficial, and these are the things they work toward together. But bad people can only be unified a little, just like they can't truly be friends. They try to take more than their fair share of benefits while avoiding their share of work and public service. Each person tries to get what they want for themselves and criticizes others for doing the same. They get in each other's way, and when people don't watch out for each other, things quickly fall apart. As a result, they end up in conflict, forcing others to do what's right while they refuse to do the same.

People often think that those who help others love the people they've helped more than the people who received the help love the person who helped them. This idea is often seen as strange. Most people think it's because the person who was helped feels like they owe something, while the person who helped is like a creditor. Just like in financial debts, the person who owes money wishes their creditor didn't exist, while the creditor wants the debtor to be safe so they can be repaid. So, people think that benefactors want those they've helped to be around so they can get gratitude, while the people who received help don't care much about returning the favor. Epicharmus might say that this way of thinking is negative, but it's natural for people to act this way. Most people are forgetful and would rather receive kindness than give it.

But the reason for this goes deeper. The comparison to financial debts doesn't even fit. Creditors don't necessarily feel friendship toward their debtors; they just want them to be safe so they can get their money back. But people who help others feel love and friendship toward the people they've helped, even if they never expect anything in return. This is similar to how a craftsman loves his work more than the work could ever love him if it came alive. Poets feel this way about their poems, loving them like their children. This is the same for benefactors. The people they help are like their creations, and that's why they love them more than the recipients of the help love them. The reason for this is that life itself is something everyone values and loves. We exist by living and doing things. When a person helps another, they are acting, and that action makes them feel alive. So, the person who helps loves the person they've helped because it is through their actions that they experience life.

At the same time, the benefactor sees something noble in their actions, so they feel pleasure in the person they helped. But the person who was helped doesn't necessarily see anything noble in the benefactor. At most, they see something useful, and that's less pleasant or lovable. What is pleasant is the act of doing something in the present, the hope of the future, and the memory of the past. But the most pleasant thing is the act itself, and that's also the most lovable. For the person who did the act, the memory of the good thing they did stays with them because what is noble lasts. But for the person who was helped, the benefit fades away. Memories of noble things bring joy, but memories of useful things are not as pleasant, though the opposite is true when we think about the future.

Also, loving is like doing something, while being loved is like being on the receiving end. Loving someone is more active, while being loved is more passive.

Everyone loves what they've worked hard for more than what they've gotten without effort. For example, people who earned their money love it more than those who inherited it. Being treated well doesn't require effort, but treating others well does. This is why mothers often love their children more than fathers do. They went through more pain to bring their children into the world, and they know for sure that the children are theirs. The same applies to benefactors.

There's also the question of whether people should love themselves the most or someone else. People criticize those who love themselves most, calling them selfish, and they use the term in a negative way. A bad person seems to do everything for themselves, and the worse they are, the more they do it. People criticize them for not acting on their own accord. But a good person acts for the sake of honor, and the better they are, the more they act for the sake of their friends, even sacrificing their own interests.

But this idea doesn't quite match the facts, which isn't surprising. People say that we should love our best friend the most. And our best friend is someone who wishes well for us for our own sake, even if no one else knows about it. These traits are found most of all in how a person relates to themselves. The other traits that define a friend are also true of how a person treats themselves. As we said, the way we treat ourselves is the model for how we treat our friends. The old sayings agree with this, like "a single soul," "what friends have is shared," "friendship is equality," and "charity begins at home." All these sayings apply most to how a person relates to themselves. We are our own best friend, so it makes sense to love ourselves the most. This makes it a reasonable question: which of the two views should we follow? Both seem reasonable.

We need to separate these arguments and figure out where and in what way each view is correct. If we understand how each group uses the term "self-love," the truth becomes clear. People use the term "self-love" as an insult when they talk about people who give themselves more wealth, honors, and physical pleasures than anyone else. These are the things most people want and compete for because they think they are the best things. So, people who are selfish in this way satisfy their desires and emotions, especially the irrational part of their soul. Most people act like this, which is why the term "self-love" has a negative meaning—it reflects this common but bad form of self-love. It's only fair, then, that people who are selfish in this way are criticized. It's clear that most people call someone selfish when they give themselves more of these things.

However, if someone was always concerned with acting justly, with self-control, or with other virtues, and always tried to do what is right, no one would call that person selfish or criticize them.

But that kind of person is actually more of a "self-lover" than the others because they are giving themselves the best and noblest things. They satisfy the most important part of themselves and always listen to it. Just like a city or any organized system is identified with its leading part, a person is most identified with their reasoning mind. So, the person who loves and follows this part of themselves is the true "self-lover." Besides, people are said to have self-control if their reason is in control because that part is considered to be the true self. The things we do based on rational thought are considered our most real and voluntary actions. It's clear that this is the true self, or at least more so than any other part. It's also clear that the good person loves this part of themselves the most. So, it follows that they are the truest "self-lover," but in a very different way from those who are criticized for being selfish. The difference is like the difference between living according to reason and living according to emotion, or between wanting what is noble and wanting what seems useful. People admire and praise those who focus on noble actions. If everyone aimed for what is noble and worked hard to do the best deeds, everything would be better for everyone. Each person would also get the greatest good for themselves, which is virtue, the highest good.

Therefore, a good person should love themselves because they will benefit from doing good deeds, and they will help others too. But a bad person shouldn't love themselves because they will harm themselves and those around them by following their bad desires. A bad person does things that go against what they should do, but a good person does what they ought to do. Reason always chooses what is best for itself, and a good person follows their reason. It's also true that a good person does many things for their friends and country, even giving up their life if necessary. They will give up wealth, honors, and other things people usually compete for in order to gain something greater—nobility. They prefer a short time of intense pleasure over a long period of mild enjoyment, a year of noble life over many years of dull living, and one great and noble action over many small ones. People who die for others achieve this kind of greatness. So, they are really choosing something wonderful for themselves.

They will also give up wealth if it means their friends will gain more because while their friend gains money, they achieve nobility. They are actually giving themselves the better good. The same goes for honor and power. They will give these things up for their friend because doing so is noble and praiseworthy. This is why they are rightly considered good because they always choose what is noble over everything else. Sometimes, they will even let their friend take action instead of them because it might be nobler to help their friend act than to act themselves. In all the ways people are praised for their actions, a good person takes the larger share of what is noble for themselves. In this way, as we said before, a person should love themselves, but not in the way most people do.

There is also a debate about whether a happy person needs friends. Some say that those who are perfectly happy and self-sufficient don't need friends because they already have everything good. If they are self-sufficient, they don't need anything else. A friend, who is like another self, provides something a person can't give themselves, which is why people say, "When fortune is kind, what need is there for friends?" But it seems strange to say that a happy person has everything good but not friends, who are considered the greatest of external goods. Also, if it's more characteristic of a friend to do good for someone else than to be helped themselves, and if doing good is the mark of a virtuous person, and it's nobler to help friends than strangers, then a good person needs people to help.

This is why people ask whether we need friends more in good times or bad. It's assumed that people need friends in bad times to help them, but those who are doing well also need friends to do good for. It would be strange to think of the happiest person as being all alone. No one would choose to have the whole world if it meant being alone. Humans are social beings who naturally live with others. Therefore, even a happy person needs to live with others because they have all the good things in life. It's clearly better to spend your time with friends and good people rather than with strangers or random people. So, the happy person needs friends.

What exactly is the first group saying, and in what way are they right? Do they mean that most people think of friends as useful? If so, then a truly happy person wouldn't need these kinds of friends because they already have everything they need. They also wouldn't need friends just for enjoyment, or they'd need them very little because their life is already pleasant without outside pleasures. And since they don't need these types of friends, people think they don't need friends at all.

But this isn't true. We said before that happiness is about activity, and activity happens over time, not all at once like owning something. If (1) happiness comes from living and being active, and a good person's actions are virtuous and naturally pleasant, as we mentioned earlier, and (2) doing something yourself makes it more enjoyable, and (3) we can observe other people's actions more easily than our own, and (4) the actions of virtuous friends are pleasant to good people— then, if this is all true, a truly happy person will need friends like these. Their goal is to think about worthy actions, especially their own, and a good friend's actions are both good and pleasant.

Moreover, people believe that a happy person should live a pleasant life. If they were alone, life would be difficult because it's not easy to stay active all the time by yourself. But with others, it's easier to stay active. With friends, their activity will be more constant, and it's naturally pleasant, as it should be for a truly happy person. A good person enjoys virtuous actions and is bothered by bad ones, much like a musician enjoys good music and dislikes bad music. Spending time with good people also helps train us in virtue, as Theognis said before.

If we think more deeply about it, it seems that a virtuous friend is naturally something a good person would want. That which is naturally good is good and pleasant for a virtuous person. Life for animals is defined by their ability to sense things, and for humans, it's defined by their ability to sense or think. Abilities are defined by the activities they lead to, and life is essentially about perceiving or thinking. Life itself is one of the things that are good and pleasant because it is definite, and definite things are naturally good. That which is naturally good is also good for a virtuous person. This is why life seems pleasant to everyone. But we shouldn't apply this to a wicked or painful life, since such a life is undefined, as are its qualities. The nature of pain will become clearer later. But if life is good and pleasant—and it seems to be, since everyone desires it, especially those who are good and truly happy—and if someone who sees knows they are seeing, and someone who hears knows they are hearing, and someone who walks knows they are walking, and this applies to all other activities too—if we know that we are being active, and if knowing we are active is also knowing we are alive (since being alive is defined as perceiving or thinking), and if knowing we are alive is itself pleasant (since life is naturally good, and it's pleasant to be aware of good things in ourselves), and if life is desirable, especially for good people because for them existence is good and pleasant (since they are happy to be aware of the good within them)—and if a good person feels about their friend the same way they feel about themselves (because their friend is like another self)—then, if all this is true, just as each person's own existence is desirable, so is the existence of their friend. A person's existence is desirable because they are aware of their own goodness, and this awareness is pleasant in itself. Therefore, a person needs to be aware of their friend's existence, which happens through living together and sharing thoughts and conversations. This is what "living together" means for humans, unlike animals who just share a space for feeding.

If being alive is naturally good and pleasant for a truly happy person, and their friend's life is much the same, then a friend is something they will desire. Since they desire this, they must have it, or they will be missing something important. Therefore, a truly happy person will need virtuous friends.

Should we then try to have as many friends as possible? Or, like with hosting guests, should we aim for something in between—not too many but not none at all? Should this apply to friendship as well?

When it comes to friendships based on usefulness, this idea makes sense. Doing favors for many people can be exhausting, and life isn't long enough to help everyone. So, having more friends than necessary is pointless and can get in the way of living a good life. We don't need too many of these friends. The same goes for friendships based on pleasure. Just a few are enough, like a little seasoning is enough in food.

But when it comes to good friends, should we have as many as possible, or is there a limit, like there is with the size of a city? You can't have a city with only ten people, but if there are 100,000, it's not really a city anymore. So, there's probably no single perfect number of friends, but there is a range. The largest number of friends we can have is probably the most we can live with, since living together is a key part of friendship. And it's clear that we can't live closely with too many people or divide ourselves among them. Also, these friends should all be friends with each other if they're going to spend time together. It's hard for this to happen with a large group. It's also difficult to share happiness and sadness deeply with many people because you might have to rejoice with one friend while mourning with another. So, it's best not to aim for as many friends as possible, but just enough to live well with. It's actually impossible to be a great friend to many people. This is why we can't truly love many people at once. Love is an intense form of friendship, and that can only be felt for one person. Great friendships, too, are only possible with a few people. We see this in real life—famous deep friendships are always between two people. Those who have many friends and are close with all of them are often thought to not really be close to anyone. These people are more like fellow citizens than true friends, and they may be seen as overly eager to please.

In the case of fellow citizens, you can be friends with many without being seen as insincere, but you can't have deep, virtuous friendships with many people. We should be satisfied if we find even a few true friends.

Do we need friends more in good times or bad? We need them in both. In bad times, people need help, and in good times, they need people to share their lives with and to be generous toward. People want to do good for others. Friendship is more necessary in bad times because useful friends are needed, but it's more noble in good times because we seek good friends to help and share our lives with. The very presence of friends is comforting in both good and bad times because sorrow is lessened when friends share in it. Some might ask if they help carry the burden of our grief, or if their presence alone, and knowing they feel sad for us, makes our pain lighter. Whether it's this or something else that lightens grief doesn't matter. What we've said seems to be true.

Their presence seems to have a mix of effects. Simply seeing our friends is comforting, especially in tough times. They help us cope with grief, both by being there and by offering comforting words if they know us well. A friend knows what pleases and pains us, and seeing them upset by our problems can also be painful because no one wants to make their friends sad. That's why strong-willed people try not to burden their friends with their troubles. They avoid sharing grief because they don't want to cause their friends pain. They also don't like to grieve themselves, so they avoid having others mourn with them. On the other hand, people who are more sensitive enjoy sharing their sorrow with friends and see them as companions in their grief. But in all things, we should aim to imitate the better type of person.

In contrast, having friends around in good times makes life more enjoyable. It's pleasant to see friends happy for our success. This is why we should eagerly invite our friends to share in our good fortune. A generous spirit is a noble one. But we should hesitate to bring them into our bad times because we want to burden them as little as possible with our troubles. Hence the saying, "Enough with my misfortune." We should only ask for help when our friends can do something important for us with little effort.

On the other hand, it's right to go to a friend's aid without being asked and to do so quickly, especially when they're in need. This is a key part of friendship, and it's nobler to help without being asked. It's also more pleasant for both people. But when friends are doing well, we should join them in their activities, but we shouldn't be quick to take advantage of their kindness. It's not noble to be eager to receive help. Still, we should avoid seeming ungrateful or rude by turning down their kindness, as that can sometimes happen.

So, it seems that having friends around is desirable in all circumstances.

Doesn't it follow, then, that just like lovers want to see their beloved most of all, friends most desire to live together? Friendship is a partnership, and as a person feels about themselves, they feel about their friend. Just as we enjoy being aware of our own existence, we also enjoy being aware of our friend's existence. This happens when we live together, so it's natural that friends aim for this. Whatever life means to each person, whatever they value most, they want to share that with their friends. Some people drink together, others play games or sports, go hunting, or study philosophy. Each person spends time with their friends doing what they love most in life. This is how they experience living together. The friendship of bad people leads to bad things because they unite in harmful activities and become worse by being like each other. On the other hand, the friendship of good people is good because they improve each other through their companionship. They become better through their activities together and by influencing each other's virtues. That's why it's said that "noble deeds come from noble people." So much for friendship. Our next topic will be pleasure.

Book 10

Next, we should probably talk about pleasure. It seems to be deeply connected to human nature, which is why when we teach children, we guide them with pleasure and pain. It is also believed that knowing how to enjoy the right things and hate the wrong things is very important for developing good character. These feelings affect our whole lives and play a significant role in both virtue and happiness because people tend to choose what feels good and avoid what feels bad. For this reason, we shouldn't skip over discussing pleasure, especially since it's a topic of much debate. Some people say pleasure is the ultimate good, while others say it's entirely bad. Some believe this because they think it's true, while others say it's better to claim pleasure is bad, even if it's not, to help people avoid it. They think that since most people are naturally drawn to pleasure, they should push them in the opposite direction to reach a balanced middle ground. But this way of thinking isn't right.

Arguments about feelings and actions are less trustworthy than facts. When they go against what people actually experience, they are often dismissed, which hurts the truth. For example, if someone argues against pleasure but is then seen seeking it, people might assume that all pleasure is worth pursuing because they aren't good at making distinctions. So, truthful arguments are the most useful, not just for gaining knowledge, but for living well. Since truthful arguments match the facts, they are more believable and motivate people to live by them. That's enough on that topic; let's move on to reviewing the opinions people have had about pleasure.

Eudoxus believed pleasure was the ultimate good because he saw that both rational and irrational beings aim for it. In everything, what is most sought after is considered the best, and the fact that all living things seek pleasure suggests it is the greatest good for all. He argued that just as every being finds its own good, like how each species finds the right food, the good is what all living things aim for. His argument was taken seriously, not just because of what he said, but because of his reputation for self-control. People believed he wasn't just defending pleasure because he liked it, but because it really was the truth. He also believed that this was obvious when you consider the opposite of pleasure: pain. Since all living things avoid pain, its opposite, pleasure, must be something they choose. He also argued that the things we choose for their own sake are the most desirable, and pleasure fits this description because no one asks why they are pleased—they just are. Finally, he said that when pleasure is added to any good, such as a just or temperate action, it makes it even more desirable. This shows that pleasure is one of the goods and that it can increase the value of other good things.

This argument suggests that pleasure is a good but not necessarily the highest good, because every good thing is more desirable when paired with another good. This is how Plato argued that pleasure is not the highest good. He said that a life with both pleasure and wisdom is more desirable than one with only pleasure. If the combination of pleasure and wisdom is better than just pleasure, then pleasure can't be the highest good because the highest good wouldn't become better by adding something else. This idea shows that if any good thing becomes more desirable when combined with another good, then it's not the ultimate good. So, what exactly meets this standard and is something we can experience? That's what we're trying to figure out.

Some people argue that just because all living things aim for something doesn't mean it's good. But that idea seems wrong. We believe that what everyone seeks must be good, and anyone who challenges this belief probably doesn't have a better argument. If only unintelligent creatures sought after pleasure, maybe there would be something to this objection. But since intelligent beings also seek pleasure, this argument doesn't make sense. Even among lower animals, there seems to be a natural drive toward their own good.

The argument about pleasure's opposite also doesn't seem right. Some say that just because pain is bad doesn't mean pleasure is good because good and bad are opposites, and both are also opposed to neutral things. While this is true in some cases, it doesn't apply here. If both pleasure and pain were bad, we should avoid both. If they were both neutral, we shouldn't avoid or seek either one. But clearly, people avoid pain as something bad and seek pleasure as something good. This shows that they are opposed in nature, not both bad or both neutral.

They also argue that because pleasure isn't a quality, it can't be a good. But activities connected with virtue aren't qualities either, nor is happiness. Some say that the good is fixed and unchanging, while pleasure is changeable because it comes in different degrees. But if they're judging pleasure based on how it feels, then the same could be said about justice and other virtues. We often say people are more or less just or brave and that their actions can also be more or less virtuous. Just like people can act more or less justly, they can experience different degrees of pleasure. If they're judging based on the variety of pleasures, they aren't identifying the real cause, especially since some pleasures are pure and others are mixed. Just like health can come in degrees without being uncertain, why couldn't the same be true for pleasure? The same amount of health isn't always present, and its intensity can vary. The same could be true for pleasure.

They also say that the good is complete, while movement and change are incomplete. They try to show that pleasure is a type of movement or change. But this doesn't seem right either. Movements, like walking, are described as having speed or slowness, and if a movement doesn't have its own speed, it still has it in relation to something else. But pleasure doesn't work like that. While you can quickly become pleased or angry, you can't be pleased quickly in the same way you can walk or grow quickly. You can shift into a state of pleasure quickly, but you can't experience pleasure as a fast process. So, pleasure isn't a type of movement.

How can pleasure be something that comes into being? We don't think just anything can come from anything else. Something can only come from what it's made of, so if pain is the destruction of something, pleasure must be the creation of the same thing. They say that pain comes from lacking what's natural, and pleasure comes from being restored. But these are bodily experiences. If pleasure is the restoration of what's natural, then the body would be the one feeling pleasure. But that's not what people think. Therefore, restoration itself isn't pleasure, although being restored can cause pleasure, just like an operation can cause pain.

This idea seems to come from the pain and pleasure connected with hunger. When people are hungry, they feel pain, and when they eat, they feel pleasure from being filled. But this doesn't apply to all pleasures. Learning, and even some physical pleasures like smells, sounds, sights, memories, and hopes, don't come from a lack of something. So, what are these pleasures restoring?

To answer those who bring up shameful pleasures, we can say that these pleasures aren't truly pleasant. If things are pleasant to people with bad character, that doesn't mean they are pleasant for everyone else. Just like we don't trust the tastes of sick people when it comes to food, we shouldn't trust the judgments of people with poor character. Or we could say that while pleasure is desirable, not all sources of pleasure are. For example, wealth is desirable, but not if it comes from betrayal, and health is desirable, but not if it comes from eating anything and everything. It's also possible that pleasures differ in kind. The pleasure that comes from good things is different from the pleasure that comes from bad things. You can't experience the pleasure of a just person without being just, or the pleasure of a musician without being musical, and so on.

The fact that a true friend is different from a flatterer also shows that pleasure isn't the highest good or that pleasures differ in kind. A friend is thought to be with us for our good, while a flatterer is there for our pleasure. The friend is praised, and the flatterer is criticized because their intentions are different. No one would choose to have the mind of a child for their whole life, even if they could enjoy the things children enjoy. Nor would they want to gain pleasure from doing something disgraceful, even if they never had to feel pain afterward. There are many things we would pursue even if they brought no pleasure, like seeing, remembering, knowing, and having virtues. If pleasure does come with these things, that's fine, but we would still choose them even if they didn't bring pleasure. So, it seems clear that pleasure isn't the highest good, nor is all pleasure desirable. Some pleasures are good in themselves and differ from others in kind or in their sources.

What exactly pleasure is, or what kind of thing it is, will become clearer if we start again from the beginning. Seeing, for example, seems complete at any moment because it doesn't need anything else to finish it. Pleasure also seems to be like this. It's complete in itself, and you can't find a pleasure that needs to last longer to be complete. This is also why pleasure isn't a movement. All movements, like building, take time and are aimed at a goal. They are only complete when the goal is reached. During the process, each step is incomplete and different from the whole movement. For example, placing stones is different from shaping the columns, and both are different from finishing the temple. The temple is complete because it reaches its goal, but the parts are incomplete. Each part of the process is different, and the complete movement only happens when the entire project is finished. The same is true for walking and other types of movement. Moving from one place to another has many forms—walking, flying, jumping, and so on. Even within walking, there are differences depending on where you are going. But pleasure doesn't work this way. Pleasure is complete at every moment. So, clearly, pleasure is not a movement. It is whole and complete, unlike movement.

This shows that the thinkers who say pleasure is a movement or a process of becoming are wrong. These concepts only apply to things that are divisible and not complete. Seeing, a point, or a unit don't "come into being," and neither does pleasure, because it's already whole.

Since each sense is active in relation to its object, and a sense that's in good condition works perfectly when it encounters the best possible object, the best activity of any sense is when it's at its best and focused on the best object. This activity is the most complete and pleasant. While pleasure can come from any sense, as well as from thinking and contemplating, the most complete pleasure comes from the best-conditioned sense interacting with the best object. The pleasure completes the activity, not in the same way as the sense or object itself, but as something that adds to it, like the bloom of youth adds to a person's appearance. As long as the sense and the object are as they should be, pleasure will be part of the activity because the sense and the object naturally produce this result when they work together.

Why, then, can't anyone feel pleasure all the time? Is it because we get tired? That's likely, because no human can stay active all the time. Therefore, pleasure isn't continuous because it comes with activity. Some things delight us when they're new, but less so over time for the same reason. At first, our mind is highly engaged, but eventually, our activity slows down, and so does the pleasure.

One might think that everyone desires pleasure because they all seek life. Life is an activity, and each person is active in the things and with the abilities they love most. For example, the musician uses his hearing to listen to music, the student uses his mind to think about theories, and so on. Pleasure completes these activities and therefore completes life, which people desire. So, it makes sense that they also desire pleasure, since it completes life. But whether we choose life for the sake of pleasure or pleasure for the sake of life is a question we can set aside for now. It seems they are connected and can't be separated, because without activity, there's no pleasure, and every activity is completed by the pleasure that comes with it.

Because of this, pleasures seem to be different depending on the activity. For different things are completed by different things, as we see in nature and in man-made objects. For example, animals, trees, paintings, sculptures, houses, and tools are all completed by different processes. In the same way, activities are completed by different pleasures. The activities of thinking are different from those of the senses, and both are different from each other. So, the pleasures that complete these activities are also different.

This is clear because each pleasure is connected to the activity it completes. An activity is improved by its proper pleasure because when people enjoy an activity, they do it better. For example, those who enjoy geometry become better at it and understand its principles more easily. Similarly, people who enjoy music or building improve in those activities by finding pleasure in them. So, pleasure enhances activities, and what improves an activity is unique to it. But things that are different in kind have different pleasures.

This is even clearer when we see how activities are disrupted by pleasures from other sources. For example, people who love playing the flute can't focus on a conversation if they hear someone playing the flute because they enjoy flute-playing more than the conversation. So, the pleasure from flute-playing disrupts their ability to pay attention to the conversation. This happens in all cases where a person is doing two things at once; the more enjoyable activity takes over, and if it's much more enjoyable, it will cause them to stop the other activity. This is why when we enjoy something a lot, we don't do anything else, and when we don't enjoy something, we tend to do something else instead, like eating sweets during a boring play.

Since activities are made better by their proper pleasures and hindered by unrelated pleasures, it's clear that different kinds of pleasure are very distinct. Unrelated pleasures act similarly to pain because activities are harmed by their proper pains. For example, if someone finds writing or doing math unpleasant, they won't write or do math because the activity causes them pain. So, activities are affected in opposite ways by their own pleasures and pains. Unrelated pleasures can have the same effect as pain, but usually to a lesser degree.

Since activities differ in how good or bad they are—some are worth choosing, some are worth avoiding, and some are neutral—the same is true of pleasures. Each activity has its own proper pleasure. The pleasure that comes from a good activity is good, and the pleasure that comes from a bad activity is bad, just like desires for good things are praised, and desires for bad things are criticized. But the pleasures that come with activities are more closely tied to them than desires because desires are separate in time and nature, while pleasures are closely connected to the activities themselves. In fact, it can be hard to tell the difference between the activity and the pleasure, which leads some people to think they are the same thing. (Though it would be strange to think that pleasure is the same as thinking or perception, it can seem that way because they always happen together.) As activities differ, so do their corresponding pleasures. For example, sight is more refined than touch, and hearing and smell are superior to taste. The pleasures that come with these activities are also superior, and the pleasures of thinking are even greater. Within each category, some pleasures are also better than others.

Each type of animal seems to have its own specific pleasure, just as it has its own specific function. This corresponds to its unique activity. If we look at different species, this becomes clear. For example, horses, dogs, and humans enjoy different things. As Heraclitus said, "Donkeys would prefer trash to gold," because donkeys find food more enjoyable than gold. So, animals of different kinds experience different pleasures. It's reasonable to think that the pleasures of one species don't differ too much, but in humans, they vary quite a lot. The same things delight some people but cause pain to others, and what one person finds pleasant, another may find unpleasant. The same thing happens with food; what tastes sweet to a healthy person may not taste sweet to someone who is sick. The same is true for other experiences. But in all these cases, we trust what the good person finds pleasant. If this is correct—and it seems to be—then virtue and the good person are the standard by which we measure pleasure. The things that seem pleasant to a good person are truly pleasant. If someone enjoys things that a good person finds boring, it's no surprise, because people can be damaged and corrupted in many ways. In these cases, the things aren't truly pleasant but are only pleasant to those who are in this specific condition.

Clearly, shameful pleasures shouldn't be called true pleasures, except to those with a distorted sense of enjoyment. But of the pleasures that are considered good, what kind should be seen as the proper pleasure for humans? This can be understood by looking at the activities involved. Pleasures come from these activities. Whether a truly happy person has one or several activities, the pleasures that complete these activities will be considered the true pleasures for humans. The other pleasures will be secondary, just as the activities that bring them are secondary.

Now that we have discussed virtues, friendships, and the types of pleasures, we can outline the nature of happiness, which we say is the ultimate goal of human life. Our discussion will be shorter if we first summarize what we've already said. We've said that happiness is not a state of being because if it were, a person who slept through their life or someone who suffered terrible misfortunes could be considered happy. Since these implications are unacceptable, we must see happiness as an activity, as we've said before. If some activities are necessary and are chosen for the sake of something else, while others are desirable for their own sake, it's clear that happiness must be among those that are desirable for their own sake, not for the sake of something else. Happiness is self-sufficient and lacks nothing. The activities that are desirable for their own sake are those that don't aim for anything beyond the activity itself.

Virtuous actions are considered desirable for their own sake because doing good and noble deeds is valuable on its own. Fun activities are also thought to be like this because we don't choose them for the sake of something else. In fact, we might neglect our bodies and possessions for the sake of fun, which can actually harm us. But many people who are thought to be happy focus on these kinds of activities, which is why quick-witted entertainers are highly valued at the courts of tyrants. They make themselves enjoyable companions in the tyrants' favorite activities, which makes them desirable. But just because people in power enjoy these activities doesn't mean they represent true happiness. People in power don't prove anything about what true happiness is because virtue and wisdom, which lead to good activities, don't depend on having power. Just because these powerful people, who have never experienced pure and meaningful pleasure, choose physical pleasures doesn't mean those pleasures are more valuable. Even children think the things they value most are the best things. It's natural that just as different things seem valuable to children and adults, different things seem valuable to bad people and good people. As we've often said, the things that are valuable and pleasant are those that seem so to a good person. To each person, the activity that matches their character is most desirable, and for a good person, the activity that matches virtue is most desirable.

Therefore, happiness is not found in amusement. It would be strange if the goal of life were amusement and we went through all the struggles of life just to have fun. Almost everything we choose, we choose for the sake of something else—except happiness, which is the ultimate goal. Working hard just to have fun would seem childish. But having fun so that we can work hard, as Anacharsis said, seems right. Fun is a kind of relaxation, and we need relaxation because we can't work all the time. But relaxation isn't the goal of life; it's something we do so we can get back to activity.

A happy life is thought to be a life of virtue. A virtuous life requires effort and isn't focused on fun. Serious things are better than trivial, amusing things. The activity of the better part of ourselves—or the better person—is the more serious activity. And the activity of what's better is automatically superior and more like happiness. Even a slave can enjoy physical pleasures just as much as the best person, but no one would say a slave shares in happiness unless they also think the slave shares in human life. Happiness isn't found in these kinds of activities but, as we've said before, in virtuous activities.

If happiness is activity according to virtue, it makes sense that it would come from the highest virtue, which is the best part of us. Whether this is reason or something else that is our natural guide and helps us think about noble and divine things, the activity that comes from this part of us will be perfect happiness. We've already said that this activity is contemplation.

This seems to fit with what we said before and with the truth. First, this activity is the best because reason is the best part of us, and the things reason thinks about are the best things to know. Second, it's the most continuous because we can think about the truth for longer periods than we can do anything else. Happiness is thought to include pleasure, and the activity of philosophical wisdom is considered the most pleasant of all virtuous activities. The pursuit of wisdom offers pleasures that are pure and lasting, and those who know the truth are expected to enjoy life more than those who are still searching for it. The self-sufficiency that we talk about must also belong most to the contemplative life. While a philosopher needs the necessities of life just like a just person or someone with any other virtue, once they have those things, the just person needs other people to act justly toward. The temperate person, the brave person, and everyone else needs other people to live out their virtues. But the philosopher, even when alone, can contemplate the truth, and the wiser they are, the better they can do this. They may do it better with companions, but they are the most self-sufficient. This activity is loved for its own sake because nothing comes from it except the act of contemplation itself. In contrast, practical actions give us something beyond the action itself. Happiness is thought to depend on leisure because we work so that we can have leisure, and we make war so that we can live in peace. The practical virtues are shown in political and military actions, but these activities seem to be the opposite of leisure. Warlike actions are completely unleisurely because no one chooses to go to war for the sake of being at war. A person who starts fights just to fight would be considered murderous. Political actions are also unleisurely because they aim at something beyond themselves, like power, honor, or happiness for oneself and others.

So, even though political and military actions are considered noble and important, they are not leisurely and aim at something beyond themselves. But the activity of reason, which is contemplation, seems to be superior in value and doesn't aim for anything beyond itself. It also brings its own pleasure, which enhances the activity. The self-sufficiency, leisure, lack of exhaustion (as much as possible for a human), and all the other attributes of the truly happy person are connected to this activity. Therefore, this is the complete happiness of a person, if they are allowed to live a full life, because none of the qualities of happiness are incomplete.

However, such a life might seem too lofty for a human. A person doesn't live this way because they are human, but because there is something divine within them. The activity of this divine part is far greater than the activity of the other kind of virtue, just as this part of us is greater than our human nature. If reason is divine compared to a human being, then living according to reason is divine compared to living a human life. We shouldn't listen to those who say that since we are humans, we should focus only on human things, or that since we are mortal, we should think about mortal things. Instead, we should do our best to live according to the highest part of ourselves. Even if this part is small in size, it far surpasses everything else in power and worth. This part of ourselves seems to be our true self because it is the most authoritative and valuable part of us. It would be strange to choose to live according to something else instead of this.

What we said earlier applies here as well: what is natural to each thing is the best and most enjoyable for that thing. So, for humans, the life according to reason is the best and most pleasant, because reason is the most human part of us. Therefore, this life is also the happiest.

But in a secondary sense, a life lived according to the other kind of virtue is also happy. The activities that come from this virtue are suited to our human nature. Acts of justice, bravery, and other virtues are things we do in relation to each other. We fulfill our duties when it comes to contracts, services, and various actions, and we deal with emotions. All of these things seem to be distinctly human. Some of them seem to come from the body, and the virtues of character are closely tied to emotions. Practical wisdom is also connected to virtue of character, and virtue of character is linked to practical wisdom, since the principles of practical wisdom align with moral virtue, and moral virtue is guided by practical wisdom. Since moral virtues are connected to emotions, they belong to our human nature. Therefore, the life and happiness that come from these virtues are also human. The excellence of reason is something separate from this. We don't need to go into too much detail here because that would go beyond the scope of our discussion. However, it seems that this kind of life needs fewer external things than a life of moral virtue. Both need the basics, of course, but the work of a statesman is more concerned with the body and material things. For this reason, there is little difference between the two. But there is a big difference in what each life needs to carry out its activities. A generous person will need money to do generous things, and a just person will need money to repay others because intentions are hard to see, and even people who are unjust can pretend to act justly. A brave person will need power to carry out acts of bravery, and a temperate person will need the right circumstances to show their temperance. Otherwise, how can anyone recognize them?

People also debate whether virtue is more about intention or action, and virtue is assumed to involve both. It's clear that virtue is complete when both are present. But to carry out virtuous actions, many things are needed, and the greater and nobler the action, the more things are required. But someone who is focused on contemplating the truth doesn't need any of these things, at least not for the sake of their activity. In fact, these things can even be obstacles to contemplation.

However, since they are human and live in society, they will choose to do virtuous acts, so they will need these aids to live a human life.

We can see that perfect happiness is a contemplative activity from this thought: we believe the gods are the most blessed and happy of all beings. But what kind of actions can we attribute to them? Do they perform acts of justice, like making contracts or returning deposits? Wouldn't it seem silly for gods to do such things? How about brave acts, where they face dangers because it's noble? Or generous acts? Who would they give to? It would be strange if gods had money or needed anything like that. What about self-control? Praising them for not having bad desires seems pointless. If we consider all kinds of human action, none of them seem to fit gods—they seem trivial and unworthy of divine beings. But everyone assumes gods are alive and active; we don't think they just sleep like the myth of Endymion. If we take away action and productivity from a living being, what is left except contemplation? So, the activity of God, which is superior in blessedness, must be contemplative. And of all human activities, the one most like this is contemplation, which makes it closest to true happiness.

We see this in the fact that other animals don't share in happiness because they are completely deprived of this kind of activity. The whole life of the gods is blessed, and humans can share in this blessedness when they engage in similar activity. But animals aren't happy because they can't contemplate. So, happiness extends as far as contemplation does, and those who contemplate more deeply are more truly happy—not as a side effect, but because contemplation itself is valuable. Therefore, happiness must be some form of contemplation.

However, being human means we also need external things for happiness. We aren't self-sufficient for contemplation—we need a healthy body, food, and other necessities. Still, we shouldn't think that a happy person needs a lot of material things. Just because we need some external goods doesn't mean we need an excess of them. We don't need to rule the earth and sea to do noble deeds. Even with modest means, people can live virtuously. This is clear enough because private individuals are seen to do virtuous acts as much as rulers—perhaps even more. So, having enough of the basics is sufficient for a happy life lived according to virtue. Solon may have been right when he described a happy person as having modest possessions but having performed noble acts and lived a temperate life. Anaxagoras also seemed to think the happy person didn't need wealth or power, saying that to most people, the happy person would seem strange because they judge happiness by external things. The opinions of wise people seem to support these ideas.

But even though such ideas are convincing, we must look at the facts of life because they are the final test. If what we've said matches the facts, we should accept it. If not, we should see it as just a theory. A person who uses reason and develops it is likely to be in the best state of mind and closest to the gods. If the gods care about human affairs, it makes sense that they would value what is best and closest to them—reason—and reward those who value and honor it most. Those who care for what the gods care about and act rightly and nobly will be most dear to the gods. It's clear that this best describes the philosopher, so the philosopher must be most dear to the gods. And because of this, the philosopher will also be the happiest.

If we've covered the topics of virtue, friendship, and pleasure well enough, are we done? Not quite. As the saying goes, when there are things to be done, the goal isn't just to recognize them but to do them. So, with virtue, it's not enough to know about it—we must try to have it and use it. We must find any way we can to become good. If arguments alone were enough to make people good, they would deserve great rewards, as Theognis said. Such rewards should be given, but in reality, while arguments can inspire and encourage young people with noble hearts, they can't make most people good. Most people don't naturally respond to shame but only to fear. They don't avoid bad actions because they are bad, but because they fear punishment. They live by their desires, chasing after their pleasures and avoiding pain, without understanding what is truly noble and pleasant because they've never experienced it. What argument could change such people? It's hard, if not impossible, to remove bad traits through argument alone, especially when those traits have become deeply rooted. We should be satisfied if, with all the available methods for developing virtue, we can get people to develop even a little bit of it.

Some think we are made good by nature, others by habit, and others by teaching. The role of nature is clearly beyond our control and comes from divine causes in the truly fortunate. Argument and teaching, on the other hand, don't work for everyone. A person's soul must already have been shaped by good habits to enjoy noble things and hate what is bad, like soil prepared to nourish seeds. Someone who follows their desires won't listen to arguments against their behavior, and even if they do, they won't understand them. How can we convince someone like that to change? Passion doesn't usually yield to reason but to force. So, people's character must already have a natural tendency toward virtue, where they love what is noble and hate what is base.

It's hard to train people in virtue from a young age if they aren't raised under good laws. Living a temperate and disciplined life isn't pleasant for most people, especially when they're young. That's why their upbringing and activities should be regulated by law. When something becomes a habit, it stops feeling painful. But it's not enough to raise children well—they must continue practicing good habits as adults. We'll need laws for this too, covering the whole of life, because most people obey necessity rather than reason, and punishments rather than what is noble.

This is why some believe that lawmakers should encourage people toward virtue by appealing to what is noble, assuming that those who are well-raised will respond to such influences. They think punishments and penalties should be used for those who disobey or have worse natures, while those who are incurably bad should be banished completely. Good people, who live with their minds focused on what is noble, will follow reason, while bad people, who seek pleasure, can be corrected by pain, like a beast of burden. This is why punishments should be opposite to the pleasures that bad people love.

If a person is to become good, they must be well trained and continue to practice good habits. They must spend their time on worthy activities and avoid doing bad things, either by choice or by necessity. This can only happen if people live according to reason and order, enforced by laws. The command of one person, even a parent, doesn't have the same power as the law, unless that person is a king or something similar. The law has force because it's based on reason and practical wisdom. While people often dislike those who oppose their desires, they don't find the law as burdensome when it directs them toward what is good.

In Sparta, the lawmaker seems to have focused on upbringing and activities, but in most states, these things are neglected, and people live as they please, like the Cyclops, making their own laws for their family. It's best when the state takes care of these matters publicly, but if the state neglects this, individuals should help their children and friends toward virtue. They should at least have the will to do this if not the power.

From what we've said, it seems a person can do this better if they become capable of making laws. Public life is governed by laws, and good governance requires good laws. It doesn't matter whether these laws are written or unwritten, or whether they guide individuals or groups—just as in music or athletics. In cities, laws and the character of the people hold power. In households, it's the father's guidance and habits that hold power, and these are even stronger because of the natural bond between parent and child. Children are naturally affectionate and obedient. Private education has an advantage over public education, just like private medical treatment. While rest and fasting are generally good for someone with a fever, they might not be good for a specific person. A boxing coach doesn't train all his students the same way. So, personal education can be more precise because it's tailored to the individual.

However, it's best if a doctor, coach, or teacher has general knowledge of what's good for everyone or people of a certain type. After all, sciences are concerned with what is universal. But an experienced, non-expert person can sometimes take good care of themselves because they've studied their own case carefully. Some people seem to be their own best doctors, even though they couldn't help anyone else. Still, if someone wants to master an art or science, they should study what is universal and understand it as well as possible. Sciences deal with general principles.

So, anyone who wants to make people better—whether a few or many—must learn how to make laws if we become good through laws. It's not just anyone who can guide people toward the right condition. If anyone can do it, it's the person with knowledge, just like in medicine or any other skill that requires care and wisdom.

We must now ask where or how someone can learn to make laws. Is it, like in other fields, from experts? It used to be considered part of being a statesman. Or is there a difference between statesmanship and other sciences and arts? In other fields, the same people who practice the art also teach it, like doctors or painters. But while sophists claim to teach politics, they don't actually practice it. Politicians seem to do their work through skill and experience, not theory. Politicians don't write or talk much about politics, even though it would be more valuable than writing speeches for courts or assemblies. They also don't train their own children or friends to become statesmen. If they could, it's reasonable to think they would have done so, because there's no greater skill they could have passed on to their cities or kept for themselves and their loved ones. Experience clearly plays a role. Otherwise, how could they have become politicians by practicing politics? So, those who want to understand the art of politics need both knowledge and experience.

But the sophists who claim to teach politics seem far from actually teaching it. They don't even know what kind of thing it is or what subjects it deals with. If they did, they wouldn't confuse it with rhetoric or think it's less important. They wouldn't believe that you can legislate well just by collecting laws that seem good. They think it's possible to choose the best laws as if doing so didn't require intelligence. But good judgment is the most important thing, as it is in music. People who are experienced in a field can judge whether something is well-made and understand how it was achieved and what works well together. But those without experience can only see whether a work is good or bad, like people judging a painting. Laws are like the 'works' of politics. How can someone learn to be a lawmaker from them or judge which laws are best? Even doctors aren't trained just by reading books. Some medical books include not only treatments but also how to treat specific types of people and their conditions. These books are helpful to experienced people but useless to beginners. So, while collections of laws and constitutions might be helpful to people who can study and judge them, those without experience won't be able to make good judgments unless they have some natural gift. Still, they might become more knowledgeable.

Our predecessors didn't fully study the subject of lawmaking, so we should take it up ourselves. We should study the constitution to complete our understanding of human nature. First, let's review what earlier thinkers said on the topic. Then, using the constitutions we've collected, we should study what helps or harms states and what influences preserve or destroy different types of constitutions. We should also consider why some states are well-governed while others are poorly run. Once we've studied these things, we'll be in a better position to understand which constitution is best, how it should be organized, and what laws and customs it should use to be at its best. Let's begin our discussion.

On Sense and The Sensible

Aristotle

Section 1

Now that we have fully considered the soul and its different abilities, the next step is to look at animals and all living things to understand which abilities are unique to them and which are shared. What we've already determined about the soul on its own will apply here too. Now, we need to address the remaining aspects that involve both the soul and the body, starting with the most basic ones.

The most important traits of animals, whether shared by all or unique to some, are clearly those of both the soul and body together, like sensation, memory, emotions, desires, and pleasure and pain. These traits can be said to belong to all animals. However, beyond these, there are some traits shared by all living things, while others are unique to certain types of animals. The most important of these traits can be grouped into four pairs: being awake and asleep, youth and old age, breathing in and out, and life and death. We must try to understand these scientifically, figuring out what they are and why they happen.

The philosopher who studies nature must also understand the basics of health and disease because neither of these can exist in things that aren't alive. In fact, we can say that most physical researchers and doctors who study medicine philosophically complete their work with discussions on health, while doctors often base their medical ideas on principles learned from nature.

It's obvious that all the traits listed above belong to both the soul and body working together because they all involve sensation in some way or depend on it. Some are feelings or states related to sensation, others protect and preserve it, and some cause its loss or absence. It's clear from both reasoning and observation that sensation occurs in the soul through the body.

In our work on the soul, we already explained the nature of sensation, how we perceive through it, and why this ability belongs to animals. Sensation must indeed be attributed to all animals because its presence or absence is what separates animals from non-animals.

Now, looking at each sense individually, we can say that touch and taste are necessary for all animals. Touch is essential for the reasons we explained in the work on the soul, and taste is needed for nutrition. It's through taste that animals distinguish between pleasant and unpleasant foods, so they can avoid the bad and go after the good. In general, flavor is a quality of nourishing substances.

The senses that work through external media—smell, hearing, and sight—are found in all animals that can move. For all animals that have these senses, they serve as tools for survival, allowing them to seek food and avoid harmful or dangerous things based on prior sensations. But for animals that also possess intelligence, these senses help them reach higher levels of understanding. They provide information about many different qualities of things, leading to knowledge of truth, both theoretical and practical, in the soul.

Of the last two senses mentioned, sight is more important for basic survival needs, but hearing is more important for developing intelligence. Sight, because all bodies have color, provides information about many different characteristics of things, allowing us to perceive common qualities like shape, size, movement, and number. Hearing, on the other hand, only tells us about the unique qualities of sound and, for a few animals, voice. However, indirectly, hearing contributes more to the growth of intelligence. This is because speech, which teaches us things, is heard. Speech is made up of words, and each word represents a thought. Therefore, among people who are born without either sense, those who are blind are generally more intelligent than those who are deaf and mute.

We've already discussed the unique abilities of each of the senses.

Now, let's consider the nature of the sense organs, or the parts of the body where each sense is naturally found. Many researchers base their ideas on the basic elements that make up everything. But they struggle to match five senses with just four elements, which confuses them about the fifth sense. For example, they believe that the organ of sight is made of fire because when the eye is pressed or moved, it seems like fire flashes from it. This happens most clearly in the dark or when the eyelids are closed, because darkness is produced then too.

But this idea only solves one problem while creating another. Unless we assume that someone can see an object without realizing it, this theory would mean that the eye sees itself. But why doesn't this "flash" happen when the eye is still? The true explanation for this can be found in understanding how smooth things naturally shine in the dark, without giving off light. The black part of the eye, its center, is smooth. The flash only happens when the eye moves quickly because this movement makes one object appear to be two. The speed of the motion makes what is seen and what is seeing seem like two different things. This doesn't happen unless the motion is fast and in the dark. It's in the dark that smooth things, like the heads of certain fish, naturally shine. If the eye moves slowly, the same object can't appear to be two at once. In reality, the eye sees itself in this flash the same way it does when reflected in a mirror.

If the organ for sight really was made of fire, as Empedocles believed, and as it's suggested in the Timaeus, and if sight was caused by light coming from the eye like from a lantern, why can't the eye see in the dark? It's pointless to say, like in the Timaeus, that the visual ray is "quenched" in the dark. What does it mean for light to be "quenched"? Something hot and dry, like burning coals or fire, can be quenched by something cold or wet. But light doesn't seem to have heat or dryness. Or if it does, and it's just so slight we can't notice, we should expect the sun's light to be quenched during rain or in freezing weather. Flames and burning objects can be put out this way, but sunlight is not.

Empedocles sometimes explains vision by light coming from the eye, like in this passage:

"Like someone preparing a lantern
To shine in the stormy night,
Setting clear sides around the fire
To protect it from the wind,
While the fire leaps out and shines
Its constant beams over the threshold."

Here, he explains vision by fire within the eye, but at other times, he says vision comes from things outside the eye.

Democritus, on the other hand, correctly says the eye is made of water. However, he is wrong when he explains sight as just reflecting images like a mirror. The reflection happens because the eye is smooth, and the reflection occurs not in the eye that is seen, but in the one that sees. It's just a case of reflection. But even in his time, there wasn't enough knowledge about how images and reflections form. It's strange that he didn't ask why, if his theory is true, the eye is the only thing that sees, while other reflective surfaces do not.

It's true that the eye is made of water, but it sees not because of that, but because it is translucent, which is a quality shared by both water and air. However, water is easier to contain and condense than air, which is why the eye is made of water. This is proven by actual experience. When eyes decompose, the liquid that comes out is water, and in embryos, this liquid is cold and shiny. In animals with blood, the white part of the eye is oily and fatty to prevent the moisture from freezing. This is why the eye doesn't feel cold; no one feels cold in the area protected by the eyelids. Bloodless animals have eyes protected by a hard scale, which serves the same purpose.

Overall, it doesn't make sense to say the eye sees because something comes out of it. The idea that light from the eye stretches all the way to the stars, or only to a certain point before joining rays from the object, is unreasonable. If this were true, the merging of rays would happen inside the eye itself. But even this is just speculation. What does it mean for light to "merge" with other light? How could the light inside the eye merge with the light outside it, when the membrane around the eye is in between?

We've said before that sight is impossible without light, but whether the medium is air or light, vision happens through that medium.

Therefore, it's easy to understand that the inner part of the eye is made of water, because water is translucent.

Just as vision is impossible without light outside the eye, it's also impossible without light inside the eye. There must be something translucent inside the eye, and since it's not air, it must be water. The soul, or the part of it that perceives, isn't on the surface of the eye but somewhere inside. That's why the inside of the eye must be capable of letting in light. We know this is true from real experiences. When soldiers are wounded in battle by a sword that cuts through the eye's passages, they suddenly feel darkness, as if a lamp went out. This is because the pupil, the translucent part that acts like an inner lamp, is cut off from the soul.

So, if all these facts are correct, it's clear that if we explain the sense organs by matching them with the four elements, we should say the part of the eye involved in vision is made of water, the part involved in hearing is made of air, and the sense of smell is related to fire. (I'm talking about the sense of smell, not the organ itself.) The organ of smell is only potentially what the sense of smell becomes when it is activated by its object. Smell is like a smoky vapor, and smoke comes from fire. This helps explain why the olfactory organ is near the brain, as cold matter has the potential to become hot. The same reasoning applies to the development of the eye. Its structure comes from the brain, which is the wettest and coldest part of the body.

The organ of touch is made of earth, and taste is a specific kind of touch. This explains why both touch and taste are closely connected to the heart, since the heart, being the hottest part of the body, balances the coldness of the brain.

This is how we should understand the characteristics of the sense organs.

We have already discussed the qualities connected to each of the senses, like color, sound, smell, taste, and touch, in On the Soul. There, we talked about their purpose and how they become actual through their respective sense organs. Now, we must explain each of them in more detail—what we mean by color, sound, smell, taste, and touch. Let's start with color.

Each of these can be thought of in two ways: as potential or as actual. In On the Soul, we explained how the actualized version of color or sound is similar to and different from the act of seeing or hearing. The goal of this discussion is to figure out what each sensory quality must be in itself in order for it to be perceived.

We already said in On the Soul that light is the color of the translucent, and this happens when a fiery element is present in a clear medium. When the fiery element is not present, the result is darkness. However, translucence itself isn't something unique to air, water, or any other clear substances; it's a quality that can be found in all bodies to some degree. Translucence doesn't exist by itself but is present within these substances. Since every body with translucence has an outer boundary, translucence must also have one. So, we can say that light is the nature of the translucent when it is not limited by any boundaries. However, when translucence exists within a bounded body, its boundary must be something real. This is where color comes in— color is found at the outer limit of the body, either as part of the body's surface or as the surface itself. This is why the Pythagoreans called the surface of a body its "hue," because hue lies at the boundary of a body. But the boundary isn't a separate thing; we can imagine that the same substance that carries color on the outside also exists inside the body.

Even air and water seem to have color because they are bright, which is similar to having color. But the color of air or the sea is different depending on how far away you are from it. When you get closer, the color changes. In solid objects, the color is fixed unless the surrounding atmosphere changes it. This shows that the thing that allows color to exist is the same in both cases. So, it's the translucence in bodies that causes them to take on color, depending on how much translucence they have. Since color exists at the boundary of the body, it must also exist at the boundary of the translucent part within the body. Therefore, we can define color as the limit of translucence in a solid body. Whether we are talking about translucent things like water or solid things with fixed colors, they all show their colors at their outer surfaces.

The same thing that produces light in air can also be present in the translucence inside solid bodies, or it might not be present, resulting in the absence of light. Just like how air can have light or darkness, solid objects can have the colors white or black.

Now, let's talk about the other colors and go over the different ideas people have come up with to explain how they are created.

1. It's possible that white and black are mixed together in such tiny amounts that neither one is visible on its own, but the combination of both creates a new color. This new color wouldn't be white or black but something different. This could explain how we get a variety of colors besides white and black. These colors could also be produced by different ratios of black to white. For example, the ratio could be 3 to 2 or 3 to 4, creating different colors, while other colors might not follow any specific ratio. Some of these colors might be like the notes in music, where certain ratios are more pleasing, such as purple, crimson, and a few others. These colors are rare for the same reason that musical harmonies are few in number. Other colors might come from irregular combinations of black and white. Some colors could be based on precise ratios, while others might be irregular, leading to impure colors due to the way the ratio is arranged. This is one possible explanation for how we get different colors.

2. Another idea is that black and white appear through each other, creating an effect like what happens when painters layer one color on top of another to make an object look like it's underwater or in a fog. The same thing happens when the sun, which is naturally white, looks red when seen through a fog or smoke. According to this idea, different colors could also arise from this mixing, depending on the ratio of the top color to the bottom color. But it doesn't make sense to say, like some ancient thinkers did, that colors come from objects emitting something. They would still have to explain how sense perception happens through touch, so it's better to say that perception happens because the object affects the medium between it and the sense organ.

If we accept the idea of colors being side by side, we also have to assume that both the size of the colors and the time they take to appear are so small that we don't notice them. This way, the combination of colors appears as one. But if we follow the idea of one color being on top of another, we don't need to make this assumption. The effect that the top color has on the medium will change depending on whether it is affected by the color underneath it. So, the result will be a color that is neither white nor black. If we can't assume that any size can be invisible, and we have to believe that everything is visible from some distance, then this second idea of colors being layered can also be seen as a valid theory of color mixing.

3. There is also a third idea, which says that bodies don't just mix by putting their smallest parts side by side, but that their material is fully combined together. We discussed this in the treatise on Mixture. This kind of mixing, where the material is blended together, is the most complete form of mixture. When bodies mix this way, their colors are mixed too, and this is what causes there to be many colors. When bodies mix, the color looks the same from any distance, unlike when colors are just layered or placed side by side, where the color changes depending on how close you are.

Colors will still be many in number because the materials can combine in many different ratios. Some colors will come from specific ratios of materials, while others will result from irregular amounts. Everything we said about colors being side by side or layered also applies to this kind of mixing.

We will discuss later why colors, tastes, and sounds exist in specific types instead of being infinite in number.

We have now explained what color is and why there are many colors. Before this, in our work On the Soul, we explained the nature of sound and voice. Now, we need to discuss smell and taste. These two are almost the same in how they affect us physically, though they come from different sources. Tastes are easier for us to understand than smells because the sense of smell in humans is weaker than in animals. Among our senses, smell is the least perfect, while our sense of touch is the finest, and taste is a part of touch.

Water, by itself, doesn't have much taste. But since we can't taste without water, we have to think about how water works with taste. Either (a) we can say that water already has tiny, invisible amounts of all different tastes mixed in it, as Empedocles believed; or (b) water is like a base that can develop different tastes from different parts of itself; or (c) water doesn't have any taste on its own, but something else, like heat or the sun, causes it to have taste.

(a) It's easy to see that Empedocles' idea is wrong. When fruits are picked and left in the sun or put near fire, their juices change because of the heat. This shows that the change doesn't come from the water they got from the ground, but from something happening inside the fruit. We also see that juices, when left out, change from sweet to bitter or other tastes over time. Boiling or fermenting these juices can also give them new tastes.

(b) It's also impossible that water is made in a way that different parts of it can produce different tastes, because we see different tastes come from the same water, which is used to nourish them.

(c) The only option left is to think that water changes by receiving some effect from something else. It's clear that water doesn't get its taste just from heat. Water is thinner than any other liquid, even oil. Although oil is thicker and stickier, it's easier to handle than water because water doesn't hold together. Since pure water doesn't become thick when heated, we have to think that something besides heat causes taste. All things with taste have some level of thickness. Heat helps in this process, but it isn't the only cause.

The juices in fruits come from the earth. That's why some of the older philosophers said that water takes on the qualities of the earth it flows through. This is especially clear with salty water from springs, because salt is a type of earth. Also, when liquids are filtered through ashes, they become bitter. Some wells have bitter water, some are acidic, and others have different kinds of tastes.

As we might expect, the plant world has the most variety of tastes. In nature, moist things are affected by their opposite, which is dryness. That's why moist things are affected by fire, which is naturally dry. Heat is the main property of fire, just as dryness is the main property of earth. So fire and earth, by themselves, can't affect each other directly. In fact, no two natural things can affect each other unless there is some kind of opposite quality between them.

Just like people can wash colors or tastes into water, nature does the same thing. It washes the dry and earthy things in moisture and filters it. This happens when heat moves through the dry and earthy parts, giving the water a certain quality. This change, caused by the dry part acting on the moist, makes it possible for us to taste. Taste takes what was just a potential ability to sense and makes it an actual experience. This is similar to how our other senses work, not by learning something new, but by using what we already know.

Tastes belong to food that can nourish us, and this becomes clearer when we realize that neither dry things without moisture nor moist things without dryness can nourish. Only things made from a mix of both can feed animals. The tangible parts of food, like whether it is hot or cold, are what cause animals to grow or decay. Heat or coldness directly causes growth or decay. But it's the taste of food that gives nourishment. All living things are nourished by sweetness, either by itself or mixed with other tastes. We will discuss this more in our work on Generation, but for now, we only need to mention what is necessary for this discussion. Heat causes growth and helps the food become digestible. It pulls in the light things, like sweetness, and rejects the heavy things, like salt and bitterness. The heat inside living things works the same way the heat outside of them does. This is how nourishment comes from sweetness. Other tastes are added to food in the same way we season food with salt or acid to balance out the sweetness. These tastes stop the sweet food from being too rich and light for the stomach.

Just like mixing white and black gives us in-between colors, mixing sweet and bitter gives us in-between tastes. These mixed tastes either have a specific balance or an undefined mixture of the two. Some tastes are mixed in exact amounts, which affects how they stimulate us, while others are mixed in ways that can't be exactly measured. Tastes that are pleasing come from a balance in their mixture.

The sweet taste is rich, and rich can be seen as a kind of sweet. On the other hand, salty is very similar to bitter, since both lack sweetness. Between sweet and bitter are harsh, pungent, astringent, and sour tastes. There are about as many different kinds of tastes as there are colors. We can say there are seven main kinds of each. For example, we could consider gray as a kind of black, or we could group yellow with white, just as rich goes with sweet. The basic colors like crimson, violet, leek-green, and deep blue are between white and black, and all other colors come from mixing these.

Just as black is the absence of white in something transparent, bitter or salty is the absence of sweetness in food. This is why ashes of burned things are bitter, because the sweet moisture has been burned away.

Democritus and other natural philosophers who study sense-perception are wrong because they treat everything we sense as a kind of touch. If that were true, it would mean all of our senses are really just touch, but that doesn't make sense.

They also treat things that all senses can perceive as if only one sense can perceive them. Qualities like size, shape, roughness, and smoothness are things that can be sensed by sight and touch, and this is why we can sometimes make mistakes about them. But when it comes to things that only one sense can perceive, like color or sound, there is no confusion.

They also confuse things that are specific to one sense with things that all senses can perceive, like when Democritus says white and black are just different kinds of rough and smooth. He also says taste comes from atomic shapes. But it's clear that no one sense, or if any, it would be sight, is better at perceiving common qualities. If taste were better at this, it would mean taste could sense shapes better than anything else.

All the things we sense have opposites. For example, white is the opposite of black, and sweet is the opposite of bitter. But no shape is the opposite of another shape. So, which polygon shape that Democritus says is bitter is the opposite of the spherical shape he says is sweet?

Since there are an infinite number of shapes, there should also be an infinite number of tastes. But if that were true, why would we be able to sense some tastes and not others?

This finishes our discussion of taste. The other effects of taste will be talked about more in our study of plants.

Section 2

Our understanding of smells must be similar to how we understand tastes. Just like how dry things with taste affect both air and water but in different ways, the dry things that cause smell affect air and water too, but through different senses. We usually say that both air and water are transparent, but they don't carry smells because they are transparent. Instead, they carry smells because they can wash and absorb the dry substances that create smells.

Smell exists not just in the air but also in water. We know this because fish and shellfish can smell, even though water doesn't have air in it (because any air in water rises to the surface), and these animals don't breathe. So, if we assume that both air and water are moist, then smell is a natural substance made of dry things that have taste, spread out in the moisture, and anything like that would be something we can smell.

We can see that the ability to smell is based on something having taste by comparing things that have smell to things that don't. The basic elements, like fire, air, earth, and water, don't have smells because the dry and moist parts of them don't have taste unless something is added to give them taste. This explains why seawater has a smell—because, unlike pure water, it has both taste and dryness. Salt also has more smell than natron, as we can see from the oil that comes from salt. Natron is more similar to pure earth than salt is. A stone doesn't have a smell because it has no taste, but wood has a smell because it does have taste. Different types of wood that have more water in them smell less than others. If we look at metals, gold has no smell because it has no taste, but bronze and iron do have smells. When the moisture with taste burns out of these metals, the leftover slag has less smell than the metals themselves. Silver and tin smell more than some metals, but less than others, because they contain more water than some but less than others.

Some people think that smell comes from fumid exhalation, which is a mix of earth and air. Heraclitus seemed to believe this when he said that if everything turned into smoke, we would use our noses to sense them. Many people believe that smell comes from some kind of exhalation. Some think it comes from water, others think it comes from smoke, and others believe it comes from either one. Aqueous exhalation is just a form of moisture, but fumid exhalation is a mix of air and earth. When the first type condenses, it turns into water. The second type turns into a specific kind of earth. But it's unlikely that smell comes from either of these. Vaporous exhalation is just water, and since water has no taste, it has no smell. And fumid exhalation can't happen in water, but, as we've already said, creatures in water also have the ability to smell.

Also, the idea that smell comes from exhalation is similar to the idea that it comes from emanations. If the emanation theory isn't correct, then the exhalation theory probably isn't either.

It makes sense that moist things, whether in air or water (since air is also naturally moist), can absorb the effects of dry things that have taste. If the dry things in moist places like air and water create an effect as if they have been washed, then smells must be something like tastes. In fact, this is true in some cases, because we use the same words to describe both smells and tastes. For example, we say that smells and tastes can be pungent, sweet, harsh, astringent, or rich. We can even think of bad smells like we think of bitter tastes. This is why bad smells are unpleasant to breathe in, just like bitter tastes are unpleasant to swallow. So, it's clear that smell in both water and air works in a similar way to taste, which only happens in water. This also explains why cold and freezing make tastes dull and completely get rid of smells, because cold stops the heat that helps create taste.

There are two types of smells. Some writers say that smells can't be divided into types, but this isn't true. We need to explain how these two types can be recognized.

One kind of smell is like tastes. Whether these smells are pleasant or unpleasant depends on other factors. Since tastes are qualities of food, the smells related to them are nice when animals are hungry for the food, but not nice when they are full and don't want the food anymore. These smells aren't pleasant to animals that don't like the food the smell comes from. So, as we said, these smells are pleasant or unpleasant based on the situation, and this is why all animals can sense these smells.

The other kind of smell is the kind that is pleasant by its very nature, like the smell of flowers. These smells don't make animals want food and don't create appetite; in fact, they might even have the opposite effect. As the poet Strattis joked about Euripides: "Don't use perfume to flavor soup." This shows a truth—perfume doesn't belong in food.

People who add perfumes to drinks these days are teaching us to mix different sensations of pleasure, so we start to enjoy a mix of things that should feel separate.

Humans are the only ones who can sense this second type of smell. The first kind, the one connected to taste, can be sensed by all animals. Since the pleasantness of these smells depends on taste, they can be divided into as many types as there are tastes. But we can't say the same for the other type of smell, the one that is pleasant or unpleasant on its own. The reason humans are the only ones who can sense this type of smell is connected to the way our brains are. The human brain is naturally cold, and the blood in it is thin and pure but cools easily (this is why food smells, when cooled by the brain's coldness, can cause unhealthy effects like runny noses). So, these kinds of smells are made for human health. That is their only purpose, and it's clear that they do this job. Food, whether dry or moist, might taste sweet but still be unhealthy, while a pleasant smell is almost always good for our health.

For this reason, the sense of smell works through breathing in, but this only happens in humans and some other animals with blood, like four-legged animals and those that breathe air. When smells, which have heat in them, rise to the brain, they help the health of this part of the body. Smells naturally give warmth. This is why nature uses breathing for two things: first, to help the chest, and second, to let in smells. When an animal breathes in, the smell comes in through the nose, almost like sneaking in through a side entrance.

The second type of smell we talked about is only sensed by humans, and not by all animals. This is because humans have larger, moister brains than any other animals compared to their body size. This is also why humans are the only animals who seem to enjoy the smell of flowers and similar things. The warmth and stimulation caused by these smells match the coldness and moisture in the human brain. For other animals with lungs, nature gave them the ability to sense one of the two types of smell (the one related to food) when they breathe, so they don't need two different organs to sense smell. For these animals, breathing gives them the ability to sense the type of smell they need, just like humans can sense both kinds of smell through breathing.

It's clear that animals that don't breathe can still smell. Fish and insects, for example, have a strong sense of smell for finding their food, even from far away. Bees and small ants, like those called knipes, can smell their food from a distance. Marine animals like the murex and other similar creatures can also smell their food clearly.

It's not always clear which organ they use to smell. This question of how they smell can be tricky if we think that smelling only happens when animals breathe. It's clear that animals that breathe only smell while breathing, but the animals we just talked about don't breathe and still smell things—unless they have some unknown sense. But that's impossible. Any sense that detects smell is a sense of smell, and these animals clearly do smell, though they probably don't do it in the same way as animals that breathe. For animals that breathe, the act of breathing removes something that covers the organ of smell (this explains why they can't smell when they're not breathing). For animals that don't breathe, this covering is never there, just like how some animals have eyelids that block their vision when closed, while animals without eyelids can see all the time.

Based on what we've said, no lower animals avoid things that smell bad unless the bad smell is actually harmful. They can still be harmed by these smells, just like humans can. Humans can get headaches or even die from strong fumes like those from charcoal. Similarly, lower animals are killed by the strong smells of things like sulfur or bitumen. This is why they avoid these smells, not because they dislike them but because they have learned from experience that the smells are dangerous. They don't care about unpleasant smells unless those smells change the taste of their food.

Since we have an odd number of senses, and an odd number always has a middle point, smell is in the middle between touch (which includes taste) and the senses that work through a medium (like sight and hearing). This means that the things we smell are connected to both food (which is a tangible thing) and to things that can be heard or seen. This is why creatures can smell both in air and in water. So, smell belongs to both these worlds, connected to both things we touch and things that are heard or seen. This is why we describe smell as something dry that gets washed in something moist and fluid. That's how we should understand when it makes sense to say that smells have different types.

The idea some Pythagoreans had, that some animals live off smells alone, is incorrect. First, we see that food has to be a mix of things because the bodies it feeds are not simple. This is why waste is produced from food, either inside the body or, like in plants, outside of it. Even water on its own can't be food because something that can nourish must have a solid form. It's even harder to imagine that air could become solid enough to be food. Also, all animals have a place in their bodies to store food, from which the body absorbs it. The organ for smelling is in the head, and smells enter with the breath, going to the lungs. So it's clear that smell, by itself, doesn't give nutrition. But it's also clear that smell is good for health, as we can sense directly and as we've already discussed. Smell is to general health what taste is to nutrition and the body.

This concludes our discussion of the senses and how we perceive them.

One might ask: if every physical object can be divided into smaller and smaller parts forever, can the things we sense, like color, taste, smell, sound, weight, cold, heat, heaviness, lightness, hardness, or softness, also be divided forever? Or is this impossible?

This is a good question because each of these qualities is something we can sense, and they all get their name because they can affect our senses. So, if this is true, our ability to sense them should also be able to divide forever, and every tiny part of a body, no matter how small, should still be something we can sense. For example, it's impossible to see something that is white without it being a certain size.

If the qualities of a body couldn't be divided just like the body itself, we could imagine a body that exists without color, weight, or any other quality like that. This would mean that the body wouldn't be something we can sense at all because those qualities are what we sense. If that were true, then every object we can sense would be made of parts that we can't actually sense. But that can't be the case because objects aren't made of abstract or mathematical parts that don't exist in reality. Also, how would we be able to recognize these hypothetical real things without any qualities? Would we use reason? But reason doesn't deal with physical objects unless it works with our senses.

If this idea were true, it would support the idea of atoms. This could solve the question we started with, but the atom theory is impossible. We've already explained our views on atoms in our work on Movement.

Solving these questions will also explain why the kinds of color, taste, sound, and other qualities are limited. For everything that lies between two extremes has to be limited. Opposites are extremes, and everything we sense has an opposite. For example, in color, white and black are opposites. In taste, sweet and bitter are opposites, and all other senses have opposites as well. Something that is continuous can be divided into an infinite number of unequal parts but only into a limited number of equal parts. Things that are not continuous can only be divided into a certain number of species. Since the things we sense are divided into species, and they are continuous, we have to understand the difference between potential and actual.

This difference explains why we don't see every tiny part of a grain of millet, even though we can see the whole grain. It also explains why we don't notice the sound within a small musical interval, like a quarter-tone, even though we hear the whole song. The extremely small parts of things we sense go unnoticed because they are only potentially, but not actually, visible unless they are separated from the whole. Just like how a foot-length exists potentially within two feet, it only becomes real when it is separated from the whole. But if these tiny parts are separated from the whole, they could disappear into their surroundings, like a drop of flavored liquid dissolving in the sea. Even if that doesn't happen, since the sense-perception itself isn't something that can be sensed by itself or exist separately, we can't sense its tiny objects when they are separated from the whole. But even though these tiny parts are hard to perceive, they are still considered potentially perceptible and will become actually perceptible when they are part of a larger whole.

So, we have shown that some magnitudes and their qualities escape our notice and explained why this happens and how they are still sensed or not sensed. When these tiny parts of things we sense come together in a whole in a way that we can sense them again, not just because they are part of the whole but even when they are separate from it, their qualities, like color, taste, or sound, are limited in number.

One might also ask: do the things we sense, or the movements that come from them (whether we sense them by something being emitted or through some kind of motion), always first reach a middle point between the sense organ and the object, like smells and sounds do? For example, someone who is closer to the source of a smell will notice it before someone farther away, and we hear the sound of a hit after it has already happened. Is this also true for things we see and for light? Empedocles, for instance, says that the light from the sun first reaches the space between us before it reaches the earth or our eyes. This could seem reasonable because anything that moves through space has to travel from one place to another, and that would take time. But since any amount of time can be divided into parts, we would have to assume there is a time when the sun's rays hadn't yet reached us and were still traveling through the space in between.

Now, even if it's true that the act of hearing or seeing happens all at once and doesn't involve a process of becoming, just like how the sound from a hit has already happened before it reaches our ears, we still know that the sound takes time to travel through space. We can prove this because we sometimes hear words from a distance in a distorted way, which shows that sound is moving through space. So, the question is: does the same thing happen with color and light? We don't see something just because there is a general relationship between us and the object, like two things being equal to each other. If that were true, it wouldn't matter how close or far the object is.

It makes sense that this happens with sound and smell because they, like air and water, are continuous, but their movement can be divided into parts. This is why the person closest to the sound or smell perceives the same thing as the person farther away, but the farther person perceives it later.

Some people question this and say it's impossible for two people in different places to hear, see, or smell the same thing. They argue that the same thing can't be divided between them. But the answer is that everyone senses the same original object, like a bell, some incense, or fire. But each person's perception of the object is numerically different, even though it is the same type of thing. This is how many people can see, smell, or hear the same object at the same time. These things, like smells and sounds, are not bodies but are processes or effects of something. If they were bodies, then it wouldn't be possible for multiple people to sense them at once. But they do depend on a body to exist.

However, light is different. Light exists because something is there, not because of movement. In fact, qualitative change, like color, is different from movement in space. When something moves from one place to another, it has to pass through a middle point first (and sound is thought to be the movement of something through space), but we can't say the same about changes in qualities. These kinds of changes can happen all at once. For example, it's possible that water could freeze everywhere at the same time. But even in these cases, if the body being heated or cooled is large, each part of it changes in sequence, with the part next to it changing first. The part that changes first is changed by the source of the change, but the change throughout the whole body doesn't happen all at once. Tasting would be like smelling if we lived in a liquid environment and could sense flavors from a distance before touching the food.

Naturally, the parts of the space between a sense organ and its object don't all get affected at the same time, except in the case of light and sight, for the reasons we just discussed. Light causes us to see.

Another question about sense-perception is this: if it is natural that when two sensory inputs happen at the same time, the stronger one always pushes out the weaker one from our awareness, can we still perceive two things at the same time? This idea explains why people don't notice things in front of them when they are deep in thought, scared, or listening to a loud noise. We should accept this idea and also another one: it is easier to sense something in its pure form than when it is mixed with something else. For example, it is easier to taste wine by itself than when it is mixed with something, or to taste honey in its pure form. The same goes for color or hearing a musical note by itself rather than together with other notes. The reason is that when things are mixed, they tend to cancel out some of each other's characteristics. This happens whenever different things are mixed to form something new.

If the stronger input tends to push out the weaker one, it also means that when they happen together, the stronger one will be less noticeable than it would be by itself. This is because the weaker one blends with it and takes away some of its uniqueness, based on the idea that simple things are always easier to sense clearly.

Now, if two inputs are equally strong but different from each other, you won't be able to sense either one clearly. They will cancel each other out. If this happens, you won't be able to sense either one in its pure form. So, either you won't sense anything at all, or you will sense a mixture of both, which will be different from either one alone. This is what seems to happen when things are mixed, no matter what kind of mixture it is.

Since a mixture is created from some things that happen together, but not from others, and since things that belong to different senses don't mix (for example, you can't mix white and sharp, except in an indirect way, like how harmony is made from high and low notes), it follows that it's impossible to sense two different things at the same time. We have to assume that when two inputs are equal, they cancel each other out because they don't combine into one thing. But if one is stronger, only that one will be sensed clearly.

It's also more likely that the soul would sense two things at the same time when they are from the same sense, like low and high sounds. It's easier for inputs from the same sense to happen at the same time than inputs from two different senses, like sight and hearing. But it's impossible to sense two things at the same time with the same sense unless they are mixed together because once they mix, they become one. And when the object is one, the act of sensing it is also one, and the act of sensing something one is naturally happening all at once. So, when things are mixed, we have to sense them at the same time because we sense them as one. When something is one thing, we sense it with one perception. But when things haven't been mixed, we have two separate perceptions, which means we sense them one after the other, not at the same time. This is because the sense faculty can only have one act of perception at any moment, and since the sense organ is one, it can only focus on one thing at a time. This means that it's not possible to sense two different things at the same time with the same sense.

If it's impossible to sense two different things at the same time with the same sense, it's even less possible to sense things from two different senses, like white and sweet, at the same time. It seems that when the soul perceives something as one, it's because it senses it at the same time with one act of perception. But when it perceives two different things, it recognizes them as two because they are sensed in different ways. For example, the same sense can perceive white and black because they are part of the same type of perception, even though they are different from each other. Another sense, like taste, can perceive sweet and bitter. Both of these senses perceive things in their own ways, but the way they work is similar. For example, taste perceives sweet in the same way sight perceives white. And just like sight perceives black, taste perceives bitter.

If inputs from opposites are themselves opposites, and opposites can't exist together in the same subject, and if opposites like sweet and bitter are perceived by the same sense, then it's impossible to sense them at the same time. It's also impossible to sense things from the same sense that are not opposites but still different from each other. For example, in colors, some are grouped with white, and others with black. The same goes for tastes; some are grouped with sweet, and others with bitter. You can't sense the parts of mixtures at the same time (for example, the octave or the fifth in music, which are ratios of opposites), unless you sense them as one. Only by perceiving them as one can we sense the ratio between the high and low notes as one whole thing.

If things from different senses, like sweet and white, are even more different from each other than things from the same sense, like black and white, it is even less possible to sense them at the same time. Therefore, if it's impossible to sense things from the same sense at the same time, it's even more impossible to sense things from different senses at the same time.

Some writers on musical harmony say that the sounds we hear together don't actually reach us at the same time but just seem to because the time between them is too small to notice. Is this true or not? Some might take this idea further and say that even when we think we see and hear things at the same time, it's just because the time difference is too small to notice. But this doesn't seem right. It's hard to believe that there could be a moment of time that is too small to notice because it's possible to sense every moment of time. This must be true because it's impossible for a person to be aware of themselves or anything else during continuous time without noticing each moment. If there were a moment of time that couldn't be noticed, then during that time, a person wouldn't be aware of themselves or what they were sensing, and that doesn't make sense.

If there were some amount of time or some object that was too small to sense, then you wouldn't actually be sensing anything during that time or sensing that object. You would only be sensing part of the object during part of the time. For example, if you imagine a line divided into two parts, and that line represents an object and a corresponding amount of time, if you are seeing the whole line, you are seeing it during the whole time. But if part of the time is cut off, you wouldn't be seeing anything during that time. So, you would only be seeing part of the object during part of the time, just like you only see part of the earth when you look at a specific area. But if you weren't seeing anything during one part of the time, then it doesn't make sense to say you saw the whole object during the whole time. This idea leads to the conclusion that you would never see the whole object during the whole time, which is absurd because it would mean you can never fully perceive anything.

Therefore, we have to conclude that all things can be sensed, but their exact size doesn't always appear right away when we sense them. For example, you can see the sun or a rod that is four cubits long from a distance, but you don't immediately know their exact size just by looking at them. Sometimes, something you see might seem like it has no size at all, but nothing you see is actually without size. We've already explained the reason for this. So, it's clear that no part of time is too small to be sensed.

Now, let's return to the original question: is it possible to sense multiple things at the same time? By "at the same time," I mean sensing several things in a single moment, where that moment is continuous and not divided.

First, is it possible to sense different things at the same time but with different parts of the soul? Or should we reject this idea? For example, if we assume the soul perceives one color with one part and another color with a different part, that would mean the soul has multiple parts that are the same in kind because the things it perceives are all colors.

If someone argues that just like we have two eyes, the soul could have something similar, the answer is that our two eyes work together as one organ, and that's why they perceive as one. If the soul is like this, then whatever part of the soul is formed by both would be the true perceiving subject. But if the two parts of the soul remain separate, the comparison with the eyes wouldn't work because the eyes function as one unit.

Furthermore, if the soul needed different parts to sense different things at the same time, each sense would be both one and many, like having different kinds of knowledge. But you can't have perception without the right kind of ability, and you can't have perception without an actual act of sensing.

If the soul doesn't sense multiple things at the same time with different parts, then it's even less likely that it senses things from different senses at the same time. As we've already said, it's more likely that the soul could sense multiple things from the same sense than from different senses.

If the soul uses one part to sense sweet and another part to sense white, then either these two parts form one whole or they don't. But there must be one whole because the general ability to sense is one. What single object does the soul sense when it perceives something that is both white and sweet? There isn't one because no single object is created from combining white and sweet. So, we have to conclude that the soul has one general ability to sense all things, but it uses different organs to sense different kinds of things.

Can we then say that the part of the soul that senses white and sweet is one when it acts as one and different when it acts as separate parts?

Or is the soul's way of perceiving things similar to how things themselves exist? The same thing can be both white and sweet and have many other qualities, while still being one thing. The qualities aren't actually separated in the object, but each quality exists in its own way. In the same way, the soul's ability to sense is one in number but different in kind. It is different in kind for some things and different in species for others. So, we can conclude that the soul can sense multiple things at the same time with one ability, but this ability changes depending on what it is sensing.

We can show that every object of sense has size and that nothing we sense is without size. For example, the distance from which you can't see something isn't a specific point, but the distance from which you can see it is. The same goes for smells, sounds, and all other things we sense without touching. There is a point in the distance where you can't see the object, and a point where you can see it. This point, where the object becomes visible, must be a specific spot. So, if any object were without size, it would have to be both visible and invisible at this point, but that's impossible.

This finishes our discussion of the characteristics of the organs of sense-perception and their objects. Next, we will consider the topics of memory and remembering.

Thank You for Reading

Dear Reader,

We hope this timeless classic has sparked your imagination and enriched your literary journey. Now that you've turned the final page, we want to share a vision for the future of reading—one where every classic you've ever wanted to explore is at your fingertips, in a format that best suits your life.

We'd like to invite you to gain immediate, unlimited digital & audiobook access to hundreds of the most treasured literary classics ever written—along with the option to secure deluxe paperback, hardcover & box set editions at printing cost. Together, we can spark a new global literary renaissance alongside our small, independent publishing house called "The Library of Alexandria."

Thousands of years ago, the Library of Alexandria stood as a beacon of knowledge—until it was lost to history. We aim to reignite that spirit of preservation and discovery right now, in the modern age—only this time, it's accessible to all, in every language and every format.

Picture a world where every timeless classic, novel, poem, or philosophical treatise is not only available to read but also updated for today's readers—modernized, translated into any language or dialect, and ready to enjoy in any format you choose, whether that is in an eBook, audiobook, paperback, or deluxe hardcover & box set version a printing cost.

By joining our movement to rebuild the modern Library of Alexandria, you become part of an unprecedented mission to offer:

- **Unlimited Audiobook & eBook Access to the Greatest Classics of All Time**

  Instantly explore thousands of legendary works, from Plato and Shakespeare to Jane Austen and Leo Tolstoy. All are instantly ready to read or listen to, giving you a complete literary universe at your fingertips.

- **Paperback & Deluxe Editions at Printing Costs:**

  Purchase any title in a paperback, deluxe hardbound, or deluxe boxset edition at printing costs, shipped right to your doorstep. Curate your personal library of Alexandria with editions worthy of display—crafted to last, designed to captivate, and delivered straight to your door.

- **Modern translations for Contemporary Readers in all languages and dialects**

  Discover a vast selection of classics reimagined in clear, current language—no more struggling with outdated phrases or obscure references. Next to the original versions, we aim to offer translations in as many languages and dialects as possible.

  As we continue our translation efforts and add new languages, readers everywhere can connect with these works as if they were written today. By bridging linguistic divides, you're contributing to ensuring that these timeless stories become more meaningful, accessible, and inspiring for people across the globe.

- **Your Personal Library of Alexandria:**

  Over the months and years, you'll curate a unique physical archive of classics—each volume a testament to your taste, curiosity, and love of knowledge. It's not just about owning books—it's about curating a cultural legacy you'll cherish and pass down for generations to come.

- **Join a Global Literary Renaissance:**

  Your support fuels an ongoing mission: allowing us to reinvest in offering deluxe print editions (including special boxsets) at their true cost, broaden the range of available formats and translations, and extend the reach of these works to new audiences worldwide. By joining today, you're not just preserving a legacy of masterpieces; you set in motion a powerful wave of literary accessibility.

  We are more than a publisher—we're a movement, and we can't do it alone. Your support lets us scale our mission, preserving and reimagining history's greatest works for tomorrow's readers.

Become a Torchbearer of knowledge.

Thank you for picking up this book and allowing us into your literary journey. As you turn the pages, know that you're part of something larger: a global effort to keep these stories alive, share their wisdom across borders and generations, and spark a true cultural revival for the modern era.

If this resonates with you—please consider taking the next step by visiting:

www.libraryofalexandria.com

With gratitude and a shared love of knowledge,

The Modern Library of Alexandria Team

Visit:

www.libraryofalexandria.com

Or scan the code below: